The Fire Slayers

Liminal Books is an imprint of Between the Lines Publishing. The Liminal books name and logo are trademarks of Between the Lines Publishing.

Between the Lines Publishing
1769 Lexington Ave N, Ste 286
Roseville MN 55108
btwnthelines.com

First Published: October 2020

ISBN: (Paperback) 978-1-950502-32-5

Second Edition: July 2024

ISBN: (Ebook) 978-1-958901-94-6

The Fire Slayers

PJ Braley

For Mom and Dad

Jim and James

I will love you forever

Ghosts

The desert wind careening through the abandoned compound is not silent. It carries the thunder of horse hooves and, in the evenings, a woman's soft laughter weaves among the deserted buildings like wind chimes.

Pillars from the back porch stand as sentinels between the blackened skeleton of what were once horse stables and the stone wall separating an overgrown garden from the limitless sand. Some mornings, when a silica haze shrouds the dawn, the shadow of a servant can be seen holding a lantern as he peers beyond the paddock gate, watching for two dark riders on a single grey horse.

The illusion lasts only a moment. The advancing rays of the rising sun pierce the apparition, and he dissolves as day breaks across the desert. The light continues relentlessly over the ripples and eddies of sand until it reaches the southeast corner of the garden, striking the crystals lying scattered upon the remnants of an unmarked grave. Soot-stained and fractured, they cast jagged rainbows onto the burned-out house, the scorched earth.

Neither footfall nor word disturbs the solitude of the day as the shade from the few remaining trees tracks the journey of the sun from horizon to horizon until the dusty golden light melts below the earth's edge.

Darkness settles over the land, and cool breezes enter the garden from the direction of the oasis. Like phantoms of memory, they drift through open windows and stir the ashes concealing a charred cradle lying splintered and broken in the corner bedroom.

People from the village refuse to come here. It is haunted, they say, by them—the tall man and the beautiful one with eyes like the sea. Riding across the sand forever together, her laughter floats on the desert air; Alazar's hooves echo like thunder in the distance.

Venzel

Restitution

Venzel's caravan traditionally left at sunset following the new moon. The camels, caravanners, and guards stood next to the wagons as silent as silhouettes in the half-light. Packing away the small chest of gold in the lead wagon, Venzel glanced westward as he waited for his horse and the final list of items to purchase for the colony.

"Venzi!"

Venzel smiled as his younger brother, Zsiga, stepped onto the porch waving a clipboard. Hating delays and eager to get the caravan underway, he walked quickly toward the porch. Before reaching the first step, the serenity of the compound was shattered by the high-pitched cry of a horse in pain. The brothers' eyes met for an instant.

Already running toward the back of the house, Venzel turned his head and shouted, "Get the rifle, Zsiga!"

Shaking her head back and forth, Sadet fought the reins that the groom held tightly in his fist. Face red with anger, Deniz slapped the brass-tipped ends of the reins against her neck. Ignoring the ruby drops staining the pale beauty of her coat, he pulled back his arm to strike her again.

In a flying tackle, Venzel knocked Deniz off his feet. Freed from restraint, Sadet reared above the men on the ground. Her hooves, polished and razor sharp, pawed the air dangerously above their heads. With his right hand pressing Deniz's face into the sand, Venzel lowered his left hand, palm down, and the horse's two front legs landed gracefully next to him.

Settled but trembling, there was a glint of wildness in Sadet's eyes that Venzel did not like. Standing quickly, he seized her bridle to prevent her from bolting or rearing again.

Still angry, Deniz attempted to rise to his hands and knees but froze at the sound of a rifle's lever action. Venzel forced him down with his riding boot and removed a knife from his belt. Cutting the shirt from Deniz's back, he smiled grimly when he saw the bite mark.

Venzel knew exactly how much that hurt, but the critical thing at that moment was assessing the damage to his favorite mare. Pressing the cloth gently against Sadet's wounds, the only sound in the courtyard was Venzel's steady voice trying to calm the quivering thoroughbred.

"Yes, my beautiful Sadet. I know it hurts, yes, I know."

In the same tone, he added, "My brother would like nothing better than to shoot you, Deniz, and if you move one finger or say one word, I will let him."

Sadet's trembling gradually subsided as she responded to Venzel's gentle voice and felt the long smooth strokes of his hands over her body. Pressing his ear against her shoulder, Venzel listened to her heart and nodded to himself.

"Deniz, what is the first rule in my stables?"

Trying to spit the sand out of his mouth, Deniz answered, "Nothing is more important than the safety of your horses."

"And the second?"

"Hold the bit in one hand and the reins in the other."

"Yes."

Satisfied that the cuts were not serious, Venzel bent down and firmly grasped Deniz by the back of his neck. Catching Sadet's reins, he led them both back to the stables. It was not long before the groom's screams echoed throughout the compound as a horsewhip came down again and again on his bare back and shoulders; his apologies, promises, and entreaties gained him no reprieve.

The men standing by the wagons pretended not to hear, but Ezri, working in the kitchen, winced with every crack of the whip as he gathered bandages, herbs, and ointments. Waiting in the shadows for the screams to stop, he saw Zsiga come in from the porch and pocket one of the small bags of silver coins that were set aside for such incidents. Zsiga paused at the door on his way out and shook his head in Ezri's direction. Walking toward the stables to join Venzel, Zsiga's rifle gleamed with the last rays of the setting sun.

Ezri sighed and returned the medical supplies to the cabinet with trembling hands. Retribution was not a good way to begin a caravan, he thought.

Edging back into the shadows, he covered his ears and prayed.

Kizi

Beads of sweat trickled down the back of Venzel's neck as he walked with the headman through a maze of tents located behind the village's only bazaar. He would have preferred to wait until early evening, but there were two more villages to visit before the caravan could return to the compound, and time was growing short.

The few villagers who looked in their direction quickly averted their eyes. The headman did not acknowledge them or Venzel. As their leader, it was well known that no one walked *beside* him. If the tall stranger had any manners at all, he would be walking behind the headman.

They did not know that Venzel followed no one.

Stopping in front of a dusty brown tent, the headman pulled back the loosely woven flap that covered the tent's entrance. Welcoming any relief from the unrelenting midday heat, Venzel gratefully entered the first interior room.

No one was there to greet them.

Venzel's eyes narrowed suspiciously at the headman. It would not be the first time he had walked into an ambush. His hand moved slowly to the knife at his waist. Undaunted, the headman cleared his throat. Less than a moment later, they heard footsteps, and the curtains separated for an older man leading a veiled woman by the arm. Stepping aside, he left her standing in the center of the room.

The headman, who Venzel paid quite well to have knowledge of the women he sought, spoke first.

"I thought there were two."

"There is just this one. The other we will keep."

The headman nodded. Putting his hand in front of his mouth, he leaned toward Venzel and whispered that there were rumors in the village that the man's older daughter, Kenalari, was unofficially betrothed. Venzel understood more than the headman was telling him. With the colony's gold for the services of this daughter, her father could provide Kenalari's dowry, collect the bride price, and secure the future of his grandchildren.

Knowing she must love her sister very much to spend her youth in servitude, Venzel felt inexplicably drawn to the woman quietly standing in front of him. Walking around her, he felt her father's eyes following him from the corner of the tent. After one complete turn, Venzel made a slight hand gesture, and the headman removed the longer of her two veils. She did not tremble or cry out but stood like a living statue, graceful and still. Her serenity was not lost on Venzel. Even if she had not been so perfectly formed, he would have chosen her for that attribute alone.

When the small square of silk covering her face drifted to the floor, Venzel admired her fine profile and the slight blush on her cheek. Although her eyes were fixed firmly on the carpet in front of her, he did not need to see them to know she was lovely. Venzel turned and looked directly at her father.

"Yes," he said.

Her father nodded silently.

Unlike many marketplace transactions, no bargaining was allowed. Venzel did not purchase the women he procured for the colony but merely compensated the families for the loss of their daughters' household services and companionship. Although Venzel would shrewdly negotiate the price of a horse all day, he would not, for one moment, discuss the price of a woman.

They did not belong to him.

Hearing the headman count under his breath as each piece of gold was pressed into the father's hand, Venzel tried not to sneer. It was a contemptible business, he thought, receiving a fee for both finding the women *and* arranging their employment, but it was necessary. Guardians could not be trusted; only the headman knew the exact age of everyone in the village.

Expressionless, the man watched his daughter follow the cloaked stranger out of the tent. Touching his forehead, he bowed to the headman. "Her mother wants to know when he will send her home."

The headman held out his hand. "It's hard to say," he said. "None of the others have returned."

Her father quickly scanned the crowded bazaar as he handed the headman his fee. When he could not find her, the look of indifference returned to his face, and if he had any questions about the arrangement, he kept them to himself. Shoving the remaining gold into his pocket, he bowed slightly as the headman departed.

Alone in a room that only a few moments earlier had held the light of his life, he picked her small silk veil from the floor and allowed himself a sigh of regret. Draping the soft netting over his heart, he walked into the deeper recesses of the tent seeking the smiles of his remaining daughter.

Carrying only a small bag and veiled once again from head to foot, the young woman silently followed Venzel to a wagon waiting on the edge of the village. Her serenity piqued his curiosity, and instead of settling her under the canopy, he made her comfortable on the driver's bench next to him. Traveling toward the caravan's encampment, he noticed she did not look back.

"You do not miss your family, your sister?" he asked.

"No, Master."

"Why? Were they unkind?"

She bit her lip and shook her head.

Not accepting gestures as answers, Venzel continued to look at her expectantly.

"I belong to you now," she said simply. Separating the lace edges of her veil, she slowly raised her eyes to his face.

A hammer hit Venzel's chest. Although he had seen that shade of blue only once, he recognized it immediately. Beneath long dark lashes, her eyes were the color of the cool depths of the Aegean Sea. Caught without any defenses at all, he breathlessly drowned in them.

The eight years Venzel had traveled for the colony were filled with beautiful women. His brothers, unable to travel with him, appreciated the finer aspects of human women and responded to their beauty, fragrant skin, and gentleness, and relied on Venzel to find them. To facilitate his search, Venzel cultivated contacts in several of the larger villages who knew his preferences, thereby allowing his annual procurement caravan to proceed smoothly and, more importantly, on time.

It had not always been that way. Venzel distrusted human men and never ventured out unarmed. Although he tried to keep his caravans inconspicuous, word spread among the villages that he carried gold—and women. He was not surprised or unprepared when thieves attacked his second caravan. The colony, however, did not have to rely on restored or surplus World War II weaponry but possessed the finest artillery in the region. As a result, he and his men killed most of their attackers outright. Staking the wounded to the ground, Venzel carved deep slits into their flesh for the ants and scorpions to feast upon, but he was careful to leave one mostly alive, intact, and loosely tied. The horrific stories told by the few survivors made even the fiercest desert raider think twice, and the wisest of them moved on to easier, though less lucrative, targets.

Discovering that women liked to talk, Venzel sat motionless in the dark near their tent and listened. Soon realizing that women lie, he learned to distrust them as well. Never forgetting for one moment that the continued existence of the colony depended upon his success, he paid close attention to their conversations. Occasionally, as the caravan journeyed across the desert, one or two met with an accident or were left sleeping at an oasis. It was a regrettable waste of gold, but they could not afford any mistakes.

Staring wordlessly into her eyes, the images of all the women he had brought to the compound flashed through Venzel's memory. No one compared with her. During his brief inspection in the dimness of her father's tent, her lightly golden skin reminded him briefly of Delara, but, unlike Delara, her hair was dark, rippling and falling down her back like a shadow. Well brought up, she had modestly kept her eyes on the ground, but he had seen her high cheekbones and delicately shaped lips, and, as her downcast eyes indicated submission, he had accepted her without feeling the need to look further.

Now, however, he could not make himself look away.

Misunderstanding his unblinking stare, an expression of panic came over her face. Quickly lowering her eyes, she dropped the edges of her veil and pressed her palms together.

"I'm sorry, Master, please forgive my insolence."

Released from her spell, Venzel began to breathe again.

When he could trust his voice, he asked sharply, "Why do you say you belong to me? Is it because *I* hired you? I may be acting for someone else."

"No, Master. I've been waiting for you."

"For me?"

"Yes, well, no…," she stammered, "my grandmother told me before she died that a stranger would come for me…. It was like a promise. Forgive me, Master. I cannot explain it very well, but it's almost like I've been waiting for you."

"What else did she tell you?"

"That this person would change my life."

Venzel nodded. If he could forget his reaction to her loveliness, he would simply accept it as a fanciful explanation, but Venzel believed in fate.

"What is your name?" he asked.

"Kizi."

"*Daughter* is not a name."

"It is who I am, Master."

"Not anymore."

As he drove through the desert, she sat quietly beside him as though it had always been her place. When he offered her an intricately embroidered scarf to protect her face from the dust, she accepted it, lowering her head in gratitude. She did not look at him again, but he knew she was only a fingertip away, and his heart quickened at the thought of touching her. For the others he could wait, but this one, this one he wanted now.

Although his annual caravans had always been a procurement mission for the colony, perhaps, if he requested it, they would let him keep her for himself. It was time. He was nearly twenty-five and wanted a wife and a family of his own.

With that single hope in mind, he pressed his fists to his eyes and, in words she did not understand, prayed, "Blessed Anya, beloved mother of us all, *please.*"

Each time the caravan stopped to add more young women from the remaining villages, Kizi watched as they were taken to the tapestry-draped wagons and wondered why she was the only one who rode in the lead wagon with the master. He rarely spoke to her as they traveled, silently brought her food at mealtimes, and although she slept in the corner of his darkened tent during the day, he did not disturb her. Gradually, she relaxed and paid careful attention to his likes and dislikes so she would be a good servant when they arrived at his home. Sometimes memories of her family swept over her, but believing her grandmother's promise, Kizi knew she would never return to them and put that part of her life behind her like a dream from which she had finally awakened.

Venzel halted the caravan at an oasis a day's ride from the compound. It was important that the women were refreshed and beautifully arrayed when meeting his brothers. He ordered the men to raise the tents and erect tall curtains around a secluded bathing area. The shields were more for the women's sense of modesty than any real protection. The caravanners had buried two men this trip, and there was not one man working for Venzel who would risk paying *any* attention to the women.

Situating the wagons in the shade of the trees, Venzel escorted the women to the edge of the staked curtains. He was surprised to see Kizi hurrying to join them.

He caught her arm.

Bending his face close to her ear, he said, "No. You will bathe later. Look to the arrangement of my tent." Turning his back to her, he left her no chance to reply.

Kizi entered the shaded interior of Venzel's purple and blue striped tent. As instructed, she unrolled the rugs and organized his sleeping cushions and eating area around the small brazier that glowed in the center of the largest carpet. When everything was set the way he liked it, she staked open the tent flap and waited for him. The women returning from the lagoon saw her sitting on a small rug beneath the awning. Hurrying to their larger, brighter tent, they ignored her tentative smile and giggled among themselves.

They did not see Venzel standing motionless in the dark. Gazing through a disguised mesh opening in the canvas, he watched as the women entered the tent. Once inside, the women gasped. In one corner, two trunks overflowed with exquisite caftans, scarves, and shawls. In the opposite corner, beaded headdresses and a variety of fine powders, tinted face creams, and brushes were set out in front of a large mirror. Seeing their delight, Venzel smiled to himself and walked around to the entrance.

Tapping a small gong to announce his presence, Venzel counted to ten before entering while the women scurried to adjust their bathing sheets to make sure they were modestly covered.

Addressing them all, he said, "Tomorrow we will arrive at my home, and you will meet the other members of my family. I expect you to look as radiantly beautiful as you can make each other. There is much here. Be patient, help each other, and do not argue. The first woman to utter a cross word will be drowned. The second will have her tongue removed. It is my way to be generous, but I expect you to be grateful to me and respectful to each other. I will not tolerate anything less."

The women sat in stunned silence and did not, for one moment, doubt he would do exactly as he said.

"Food will be brought to you soon. In the meantime, enjoy the garments and adornments you see before you. They are yours. Choose the most pleasing for yourself and for each other. Tomorrow, at sunrise, you will be awakened and given time to apply whatever cosmetics you desire and help each other dress. I want all of you to look your loveliest. If the woman next to you is not beautiful, it will be your responsibility to tell me why. We will not stop once we begin, so get as much rest as you can tonight."

Snapping the camel whip against his left hand, he looked at each woman individually and added, "It is my sincerest wish that I will not have to return to this tent for *any* reason."

The candles shuddered in the breeze as Venzel disappeared into the night. The women stared at each other and did not move for several minutes until, one by one, they crept toward the trunks and graciously shared the beautiful clothes.

Kizi heard every word Venzel said. Bringing her knees up under her chin, she wondered what he expected of her and whether he would drown her if she displeased him. Lost in her thoughts, she did not hear him approach and was startled when she heard his voice.

"May I help you up, my latif? You need to bathe before dinner."

Kizi blushed at the endearment. No one had called her *beautiful* before, and although she had never bathed in the presence of a man, he had been so kind that she was not afraid. Taking his hand, she let him pull her up and followed him to the edge of the pool. As he started to wade in, she dropped to her knees and touched her forehead to the damp sand.

"Please, Master, do not drown me. I will do anything you ask; I will not argue. I will be a good servant to you. Please do not drown me."

Laughing, he lifted her from the sand.

"My dear girl, I have no plans to drown you or any of the women, but I will not tolerate disrespect. They may be together for a long time, and it is important that they see each other as sisters. The warning was just my way of beginning that process. Hear how courteous they are being to each other?"

As she listened, she heard only small exclamations of joy and pleasure as the women pulled one lovely garment after another from the trunks.

He took her hand. "Because my men have taken down the curtains, I must bathe you under the water where no one can see you."

Fully dressed, she followed Venzel into the lagoon. He loosened her headscarf. Released from their colorful prison, the dark tresses of her hair tumbled over her shoulders. Taking a small cloth from his sleeve, he dipped it in the water and, with long cooling strokes, lightly caressed her face, neck, and shoulders. Moving behind her, he dipped the cloth again, letting the water soak into her hair as it fell in ringlets and cascaded into the water.

Relaxing against him, Kizi felt transported in time. In the darkness, she could not distinguish the dots of glowing campfires on the distant shore from the stars in the sky. His hands moved from under her hair to under her clothes as the soft cloth dissolved the dust and sweat from the last few days.

"Has another man ever touched you like this," he whispered.

"No, Master," she said quietly, "no one has ever touched me like this."

"My name is Venzel, latif. Say, *Venzel.*"

"No, Venzel."

"Would you like me to stop?"

"Would it please you to stop?"

"No."

"Then," she said, looking around nervously, "you needn't stop."

Venzel watched her eyes travel over the water and smiled at her. "Are you afraid that if you say yes, I will drown you?"

"That is part of it."

"And the rest?"

"It makes me feel close to you and—"

"Yes."

"That feels so nice."

Venzel didn't want to frighten her, but he ached to hold her and feel her skin next to his. He wrapped his arms around her shoulders and brought her closer to him.

"Would you like it to feel nicer, my darling? Much, much nicer?"

Relaxing in his arms and almost floating in the warm water, she looked up at him with disbelief. "Better than this, Venzel?"

"Yes," he whispered hoarsely.

At the sound of his voice, the look of incredulity faded from her expression, and her smile became tender. Reaching up, she touched his face.

"Then, yes, Venzel," she said softly.

Venzel pressed her small palm against his cheek with a gratitude he knew he had no right to feel. His eyes swept the edge of the lake to make sure they were alone, and he swam with her to the opposite shore, where an outcropping of rocks and boulders created a sheltered hollow. Sitting on one of the partially submerged rocks, he took off his cloak and draped it on the boulders to dry.

More concerned about interruptions than danger, he pulled himself up onto the tallest boulder and surveyed the moon-washed hills along the horizon. Scanning the landscape, he inhaled deeply and listened to the wind but could not detect any movement, flicker, scent, or sound that threatened the night.

Although she heard him climbing above her, Kizi had lost sight of Venzel in the shadows of the rocks, but when he stood on the highest boulder, she found him again.

Moonlight glistened on his wet skin, outlining his body against the sky, and when he shook his head, water droplets flew like sparks in every direction. Believing she was invisible in the darkness, Kizi looked up at Venzel without shyness. His profile scrutinizing the distance, her gaze moved across the broad shoulders, strong back, and long muscular legs. In that moment, he appeared unconquerable and infinite. She did not know what he was searching for, but she felt an inexplicable longing to stand there with him and see the world through his eyes.

As though her thoughts were whispers on the wind, Venzel turned and read the secrets in her face. With the casual grace of a tiger, he dropped silently to the rocks near the lagoon.

It wasn't the cool desert air that caused Kizi to tremble slightly as Venzel moved deliberately toward her, but a mounting sense of vulnerability. She felt it when she watched him in the moonlight, and she felt it now as the space between them grew less and less.

She slowly backed away.

Venzel saw fear in her eyes and reached for her hand. "Do not be frightened, I promise I will not hurt you."

He pressed the palm of her hand against his lips. Pulling her toward him, he added, "And remember, you asked."

Kizi smiled. It was the same voice, the same underlying tenderness she was learning to trust. Pushing away her fear, she allowed him to embrace her.

"I remember, Venzel," she said.

Sliding back into the water, Venzel began to loosen her wet clothes and laughed softly at her attempts to help him. Brushing her hands away, he deftly unwrapped the yards of silk encasing her and tossed the wet fabric onto the rocks.

Her skin was soft beneath his lips, and the perfume from her hair was intoxicating. Holding her against him, the soft cloth in his hand moved over the more delicate areas of her body. He felt her heartbeat quicken and heard her catch her breath. Turning in his arms, her lips found his. The cloth disappeared in the water. His kisses were warm and unhurried as his hands glided over the wetness of her body.

Caught in the sensations of her first arousal, Kizi pressed herself against him and murmured his name. He knew she did not understand what was happening to her, but despite all his best intentions, he could not stop. Her desire electrified his body. He had never wanted a woman more. Lifting her out of the water, he carried her to the cavern between the boulders.

Dropping to his knees, he carefully set her down.

"Are you sure? I promised I wouldn't hurt you."

Kizi's heels dug into the sand as she arched her back. "How could you hurt me? Please, Venzel… you must come back to me."

Her hands reached for him in the darkness.

Venzel took her in his arms. Her passionate response to his touch could not be denied, and for the first time in his life, Venzel made love to a woman without his brothers' permission.

Unable to keep his hands or mouth from her body, Venzel stifled her gasp of pain—then her pleasure—with his kisses. With a freedom he had never known, he loved her like a man possessed. Reveling in his adoration, she could not resist drawing him into her, time and again, on the wet sand or in the shimmering ebony of the water.

Happily exhausted, he wrapped her in her silks and, throwing on his cloak, carried her to his tent. Placing her on the softest cushions, he smothered the embers of the fire and secured the door. Singing softly, he pressed his forehead against the back of her neck and closed his eyes.

Please, sweet Anya, mother of us all, let me keep her. I will do anything, if I can keep her.

The Compound

Venzel fired flares into the sky at sundown. Mounting his horse, he raced ahead of the caravan and stopped at the walled garden surrounding the main house. He threw the reins over the gatepost and stood back as Zsiga opened the gate.

"Venzi, I do not know why you insist on taking camels and wagons when we have automobiles… you would have been back days earlier. You are too old-fashioned for this modern world," he said, laughing.

"It's not me! You know I would prefer to ride in an air-conditioned Mercedes than depend on camels or horses any day, but the villagers won't entrust their daughters to strangers in automobiles. Besides, the full moon isn't for another four days. So, despite the slow pace, we are ahead of schedule. And at any pace, my brother, it is good to see you."

"And you, Venzel."

Venzel smiled as Zsiga peered over his shoulder in the direction of the oasis.

"Speaking of daughters, how many did you bring this time?" Lowering his voice, he added, "You will not believe the honor we have been given, but more on that later. So, how many?"

"Nineteen."

"Nineteen? There is no balance in nineteen women. Eighteen, yes. Twenty, yes. However, I do not believe you have brought us nineteen. Unless…."

"Unless?"

"Some misfortune occurred along the way," he said, watching Venzel's expression closely.

"No woman died, Zsiga, if that is what you mean. And you are right; there is no balance in nineteen. I have returned with twenty women, but I have chosen one for myself."

Zsiga laughed, "But Venzi, they are all for you."

"To keep, Zsiga. I found one I wish to marry." Venzel's smile disappeared, and his voice became serious. "I hope it can be arranged."

Zsiga regarded his older brother affectionately. Venzel's father died during a cholera epidemic shortly after the Second World War, leaving his wife and only child destitute. Starving and near death, they were found by one of the Lyostian colony's foraging patrols and brought back to the compound. Grateful to have a home for herself and her son, Damla unquestioningly did as she was told. When she successfully gave birth to Zsiga, she nursed him and several other offspring whose mothers were not as fortunate. In the following years, she became a loving mother to all the colony's children. Dying when Venzel was fourteen and Zsiga ten, Damla was mourned by the entire colony.

Despite being fully human and possessing physical characteristics that marked him as different, Zsiga's Lyostian culture did not recognize half-brothers, and both of Damla's sons received the same training and education. As they grew to manhood, Venzel was strong, intelligent, and fearless; Zsiga was just as strong and intelligent but had the innate dread of outsiders that all Lyostians possessed.

Using that small human distinction to his—and their—advantage, Venzel was integral to the colony's structure. There was, however, one crucial divergence: Lyostians were connected telepathically to each other and their governing elders. As he was human, Venzel was neither part of their collective consciousness nor was he controlled by it. Believing he owed the Lyostians his full allegiance for saving his mother, Venzel's commitment to the colony's success was equal to that of any Lyostian residing there, and, as part of that commitment, he allowed himself to be governed by their needs.

As the colony's first line of defense, Venzel negotiated with the village leaders for additional land, hired and fired servants, and procured whatever they needed through several postal and delivery services and, when necessary, by caravan. Learning to navigate in the dark nearly as well as the Lyostians, he was the only brother not confined to their underground labyrinth of tunnels and chambers. Able to travel during the day, he represented the colony among humans as a human, allaying any distrust or suspicion.

Zsiga knew his brother well, and those were not his only abilities. There was another reason their colony flourished. Venzel did not tolerate dissension, and his impatience with disobedience had come into play many times when their human servants needed to be disciplined. Quick to discern the pain threshold of nearly everyone on the compound, Venzel never hesitated to test those limits when necessary.

Through the reports from colony leaders, the collective was very much aware of Venzel and considered him the most valuable asset of Breeding Colony SCM Sector 1/51 and wished they had more. They did not consciously seek voluntary human assistance, but when such loyalty demonstrated itself, arrangements and accommodations were always made. Concerned that their hold on Venzel was tenuous because he was not physically or mentally dependent on their support, Zsiga knew the collective would do nearly anything to strengthen his ties to the colony.

Weighing Venzel's worth to the collective and the worth of one woman out of twenty, Zsiga tilted his head and confidently forwarded Venzel's request to the colony leadership.

"Nineteen is an excellent number! And three more than we anticipated, so there is no loss to our plans. I am quite sure it will be as you wish. Anything else?" he asked, gesturing toward the colony's compound.

"Yes. As it is unoccupied, the southeast room on the topmost floor."

Zsiga was stunned. Pressing his palms together in prayerful reverence, he said, "But that is our mother's room."

"And it will be again," Venzel promised.

"Yes?"

"Yes. I request one son of my own and then as many for the colony as Anya, mother of us all, will provide."

"Your wife… she will be a blessing to us."

"It is what I wish, but it will be as Anya decides."

Zsiga's hopes soared. The possibility of a human mother who would willingly stay and nurture their offspring was something the colony had been searching for in the decade since Damla's death.

"Of course, Venzi, it would be wonderful if—"

"Speaking of wonderful," Venzel interrupted teasingly, "when would you like to see the young women I have brought for you?"

"Will they be ready for viewing this evening?'

"That is my plan."

"And the one you have chosen; will we be meeting her as well?"

"Only after we are married."

"She must be very beautiful if you wish to keep her to yourself."

"She is pretty enough, but there is a sympathy between us that I would like to preserve as long as possible. Throwing her into the midst of nineteen truly beautiful women and my devilishly handsome brothers could damage that connection. She will be sent, along with my baggage, to my room."

"She is not to stay in the harem with the other women?"

"No. They know she has slept in my tent. It would be better if they think she is a servant."

Zsiga nodded in agreement; it would be best for everyone if she wasn't asked any questions. He tilted his head for a moment and grinned at Venzel.

"It will be as you desire, my brother. You have been too good to us to be denied this request. The marriage date?"

"When are the others arranged?"

"In eighteen days. The next new moon."

"Good enough. She will stay with me, and after the ceremony, we will move into the second room on the balcony floor. Our mother's bedroom will remain undisturbed."

Zsiga brought his hands together again. "She will be a blessing to us."

Venzel did the same. "Yes."

The tinkling of the bells attached to the camels' reins drifted in the evening air, bringing smiles to the brothers' faces. Walking to the gate, Venzel couldn't resist teasing Zsiga again.

"So, my brother, is everything prepared? The food, candlelight, and music for the dancing?"

"That is my plan," Zsiga said, mimicking Venzel. They laughed together, and Zsiga turned toward the house. "But just in case...."

"Go on, I'll wait here. Please send Ezri out if you don't need him."

"I will do that," said Zsiga. Grinning in anticipation, he bounded the porch steps two at a time.

Venzel was relieved to be waiting for the wagons alone. He lit several lanterns and placed them throughout the garden. Opening the other half of the gate, he halted the lead wagon with a wave of his hand and shielded Kizi from view as he helped her down.

He reached under the wagon seat and pulled out a full-length burka.

"Put this on now," he said.

Peeking around him, Kizi's eyes widened at the sight of the large house and outbuildings. Without a word, she pulled the fabric over her head. Covering her entirely, only a thin strip of mesh in the hood of the rough garment allowed her to see.

Kizi followed the lead wagon into the yard. As the other wagons moved forward, she watched Venzel assist the young women through the gate. Not even in the largest marketplaces had she seen such beautiful women. With their fine silken scarves flowing in the desert breeze, kohl-accented eyes, and elaborate henna designs decorating their hands and forearms, they entered the garden as colorful butterflies wearing gossamer wings.

Venzel led the women into the full light of the lanterns for inspection. Seeing the stern look on his face, they became quiet and lowered their eyes. Removing a handkerchief from his sleeve, he looked at each woman carefully. He wiped away a smudge from one face, rearranged the fall of another's hair, and turned his back for a moment while two of the women exchanged scarves and shawls.

Rewarding them with a sweeping glance of approval, he said, "Thank you for your cooperation. You are all very beautiful tonight. In a few moments, you will meet my brothers. It is up to them—and you—whether you will be their servants… or their wives."

Venzel paused as the women looked at each other in surprise. "I realize this is not what you anticipated upon your arrival, but I ask for your patience. My brothers will have two weeks to choose among you. This is not a competition; they can afford as many of you as pleases them. If you wish to become wives, you must be pleasant, dress like this every day, and treat everyone with respect. In return, they will treat you with generosity, kindness, and respect. However, should my brothers find you unattractive or disrespectful, we will assume you prefer to be a servant, and you will dress like this." He turned his head in Kizi's direction.

Nineteen pairs of eyes narrowed as they regarded her small, shrouded figure.

He saw the burka tremble slightly under their disapproving gaze and was grateful for the distraction of Ezri's padded footsteps on the porch.

The manservant entered the garden and bowed.

"I am glad your journey has brought you safely home, Master."

"As am I, Ezri. Take my baggage from the wagon and this," he said, gesturing toward Kizi, "to my room."

Addressing Kizi directly, he added, "I will expect food and tea when I get there. Ezri will show you how I prefer it."

Ezri walked toward the wagon, but Venzel's voice stopped him. "Watch her. She is careless and stupid. Do not let her get lost."

Kizi picked up the bundle Ezri set next to her. With her free hand, she lifted the grey fabric so she would not trip and followed him into the house.

Watching her go, Venzel felt a twinge of conscience and wished he had told her what to expect when they arrived, but she was so deliciously warm and loving that morning that he forgot to warn her.

Knowing he wasn't the only one watching Kizi walk away, Venzel turned his head in time to read the disdainful expressions on the faces of the women standing in the garden and silently congratulated himself.

Nineteen new mothers for the colony.

Hearing music and smelling food she knew was not intended for her, Kizi trailed Ezri into the house and through a web of hallways and stairs. She lost direction many times and was thankful he glanced back often to make sure she was still behind him.

Stopping at the end of a long corridor, Ezri opened the door and set down his bundles. Lighting a candle, he looked down at her.

"Unpack and put these things away," he said. "I will be back with the rest, then I will bring food and tea." Adding, not unkindly, "I will bring enough for two."

Kizi tried to keep her voice steady. "But I cannot see to put anything away."

Ezri lit a second candle. "Get used to the dark. It is how they like it."

Left alone, Kizi pushed the hood from her face and looked around Venzel's room. In the dimness, she could only see that it was large and plain, with a map that covered half the wall. Still unable to see well enough to do her assigned tasks, Kizi lit four more candles and placed them throughout the room. In the brighter candlelight, she saw she was mistaken. The room was not plain. Relief work of beautifully intricate and interlocking circles filled with animals and birds decorated the curved ceiling. In the flickering light, the animals seemed to move, the birds to fly.

She hurried to unpack the bundles and boxes before Venzel's arrival but could not untie the stiff knots. Defeated, she sat on the bed and put her face in her hands. Venzel's harsh words echoed in her ears and now she was afraid he would think her lazy as well as careless and stupid.

Where was his kindness?

Fighting tears of misery that crowded her eyes, the events of the last two days came back to her as she tried to understand Venzel's sudden indifference. Recalling what she'd overheard her mother and sister say about men, it wasn't long before she realized what had happened the night before. The most precious gift that was hers and hers alone—the single attribute men valued most highly in a woman—she had willingly given away *for nothing*.

Struck by the obvious difference between herself and the radiantly dressed women who did not go into the water with Venzel, she pulled the hood over her face and began to weep.

He would never love her now.

It Must be Done

Kizi intended to wait for Ezri's return so he could help her with the knots, but the bed was so soft that she tumbled over onto the cushions and slept.

Thinking she had been asleep for only a few minutes, she awoke instantly to the sound of the door closing and dishes rattling.

"Wait, Ezri, I will help."

"No. You will not move."

A thrill of fear touched her spine. Venzel had arrived, and she had not unpacked anything or tended to the food. Afraid he would punish her, she edged to the floor to beg his forgiveness for falling asleep.

"Did I not just say to stay where you were?"

"Yes, Master."

"Did you move?"

"Yes. But Master—"

"Are you arguing with me?"

"No, Master."

"Venzel."

"No, Venzel."

He pulled her to her feet. By the light of the one candle still burning, she saw the bundles and boxes open and emptied. Food was set out on the table with two plates and cups. A large bathing tub was placed in the corner of the room.

Venzel slid the hood of the burka away from her face and, with one sweep of his hand, lifted it from her body. Her eyes grew huge when he pulled the knife from his belt.

"Close your eyes."

"But—"

"Are you still arguing with me, latif?"

She bit her bottom lip and shook her head, scattering the tears that fell beneath her closed eyes.

Venzel did not want to treat her like this, but even if she never loved him, she had to obey him if he was to keep his promise to Zsiga. His intention was to break her gently like one of his treasured Arabian mares, letting her keep enough of her spirit to believe she could defy him but ingraining obedience so deeply that it would never occur to her to do so.

"This is for your disobedience."

Hating every movement, he lifted one lock of hair after another and cut a few centimeters from the ends until she stood in a dark circle that glinted copper in the candlelight.

"This is for arguing with me."

Still using his knife, he slowly cut her clothes from her body. Piece by piece, the silk fell around her as she stood trembling in her chemise.

"Open your eyes."

She did as he asked. Looking for some defiance in their turquoise depths, he saw nothing but a silent plea for mercy. He waved the knife at the shreds on the floor.

"Clean this mess up. Then bathe," he said, pointing to the tub of water. "I expect you to be standing exactly like this when I return. I will be back before the candle burns out."

Without another word, he sheathed the knife and left the room.

He hesitated outside the door and listened. There was no sound of the hysteria he expected, nor was she throwing anything around the room in anger. All he heard was the swish of a broom on the carpeted floor. Smiling as he walked toward the music, he wondered how long she would stand there, waiting for him to return.

"Do not let her leave, Ezri."

The eunuch nodded. Crossing his muscular arms, he stood guard in front of the door.

Venzel was not surprised to see Zsiga waiting for him at the tunnel entrance.

"Mamet did not return?"

"No. I contrived to have him caught sneaking around the women's tent. Regrettably, he was unable to keep up with the wagon we tied him to and stumbled. Before anyone could stop them, the horses trampled him almost beyond recognition. I sent his brother ahead of the caravan to their village, but we found his body the next day. He, um, had been set upon by bandits."

"Both of them dead? Venzi, was that wise?"

Venzel looked meaningfully into Zsiga's eyes.

"They were *brothers*, Zsiga. We could not take the risk that Mamet kept his suspicions about the colony to himself. Receiving two extra shares of the caravan's wages will soothe their family's grief."

"Thank you for taking care of that matter for us."

"Do not thank me, Zsiga. It must be done. Our colony is our mother, and no one is allowed to endanger her. No one. Guarding her sanctity and sanctuary is why we live. It is who we are."

"And we—" began Zsiga.

"—are one," answered Venzel.

After nearly three hours spent listening to his brothers discuss the attributes of the new women and regaling them with stories of his recent travels, Venzel returned to his room. Knowing the candle had burned out at least an hour earlier, he was a little surprised to find Ezri calm and unmoved.

"Tell me every sound you've heard since I've been gone."

"I heard water splashing."

"Yes."

"That is all, Master. Just water splashing."

"When was that?"

"Right after you left."

"And nothing since? No movement, no sound?"

"No, Master."

To hide his sudden anxiety from Ezri, Venzel curtly dismissed him and waited until he turned down the corridor to his own quarters in the house before slowly opening the door.

The room was completely dark. Pulling a small flashlight from his pocket, he pressed the button and stepped into the room. Without stopping to light a candle, he went immediately to the bathing tub and felt relieved to find it empty. He directed the light to the center of the room, but she wasn't standing where he left her, nor was she on the carpet if she had fallen asleep. He flashed the light on the bed, but it, too, was empty.

"I'm over here, Venzel." There was a deadness in her voice that made him reluctant to turn the light in her direction. "I thought it best to get it over with at once."

Sitting at the table with his hunting knife in her hand, Kizi was cutting off the rest of her hair. With unfeigned horror, Venzel looked at the cap of short dark curls and realized with a jolt that had he not returned in time to stop her; she would have cut her hair down to her scalp and possibly beyond that.

He set the flashlight upright on the table and cautiously walked toward her.

"May I have the knife?" he asked, watching her eyes.

She nodded and did not resist as he gently removed the knife from her hand and placed it on top of the mantel. Her hands free, she wrapped them around her chest and shivered. It was only then that he understood she was cold because he had destroyed her clothes. Cursing himself for an arrogant fool, he immediately wrapped a blanket around her and carried her to the bed. Sitting down, he tried to embrace her to warm her, but she would not rest against him.

After a few moments, she said, "Venzel, I'm very tired. May I sleep now?"

At a loss for a way to reach her, he was afraid that if he said no, she would sit like a doll in his lap with her eyes open, staring into the dark.

"My latif—"

"No, Venzel. Kizi. My name is Kizi. I am no one's *latif.*"

"Yes," he sighed, "you may rest now."

Her eyes closed, and within moments, she was asleep in his arms.

What had he done?

His conscience recounted the litany of his wrongs against her. He had taken her away from her home and family, isolated her, seduced her, and, thinking she would fight him if he did not take the fight out of her first, punished her cruelly. Holding her close to him, Venzel realized he had made a dreadful miscalculation. She did not share the temperament of his thoroughbreds, possessing certain traits that he could reinforce or winnow out. Regardless of the method he used to train them, his horses never lost the spark of their indomitable spirit.

But this woman…. No, he thought, this was no woman in his arms but a girl. Like her name, Kizi, he was only holding someone's daughter. Regardless of how old the headman said she was, tonight she was just a child with no spirit at all.

Although there was intelligence in her eyes, enthusiasm in her smiles, and kindness in her touch, there was no resistance in her. Realizing he was mercilessly trying to force her into becoming someone she already was, Venzel worried he may have destroyed the very woman he desired. Singing softly, he spent the night considering and discarding ways of bringing her back to him. Devising a plan he believed would work, he waited until dawn and rang for Ezri.

"She suffered from a fever all night and has been ill. Stay with her while I find Rauf. Do not disturb her or leave this room until I return."

When he first entered the room, Ezri thought it was a boy in Venzel's bed, but Venzel's words and the thin coverlet left little doubt as to the sex of the dark-haired waif who slept so quietly that he checked often to make sure she was breathing.

Settling on a cushion near the door where he could watch her and listen for footsteps, Ezri awaited Venzel's return. At the sound of her sigh, he started to stand because he thought she was going to awaken and sat back down when she turned away from him, brushing her hand over her face as though to wipe away tears.

As soon as he heard footsteps in the hall, Ezri opened the door and stood aside as Venzel hurried in with a small box in his hand.

"Has she opened her eyes? Or said anything at all?" he asked quietly.

"No, Master, just a sigh. I have not seen her face, but I don't think she's opened her eyes."

"You can go. No. Better stay in the hall. I'll call if I need you. *Do not* disturb me. No matter what you hear, do not enter unless I call you. Do you understand?"

Ezri thought he understood perfectly. In his five years at the colony as Venzel's personal manservant, Ezri had seen enough to know not to ask any questions if he wanted to live.

Without meeting Venzel's eyes, he said, "Yes, Master. I understand."

Ezri glanced toward the bed.

Poor little thing, he thought.

Closing the door as quietly as possible, Ezri took his usual stance in the hallway.

Venzel removed a honey-scented candle from the box and lit it. Although he'd grown up with the fragrance of these candles in the house and tunnels of his home, he never liked it, and they were never burned in the corridor where he slept. Next, he reached into the box for a small jar. Aware of its addictive properties, he had not intended to offer her any of the bitter honey served to the other women, but he knew from personal experience how much the women liked it and preferred it above all other food. Unsure of what to expect when she woke up, Venzel wanted every advantage the colony's doctor could offer.

Within moments, the candle's scent began to permeate the room. Carrying the open jar to the bed, he gathered Kizi in his arms, touched his finger into the honey, and lightly stroked her lips. Holding her as he had all night, Venzel sang Anya's song of protection and waited.

He awoke to a gentle caress along his jaw.

"Venzel, Venzel...." she whispered.

He opened his eyes slowly and looked into her face.

"Latif?" he whispered.

"Have I been ill?"

The eyes looking into his were clear. The deadness from last night had disappeared from her voice.

"Yes," he lied. "You have been ill. I thought I was going to lose you and did everything I could to take the fever away."

A moment later, she licked her lips. "Oh, Venzel. This is the most delicious honey I have ever tasted."

"Our flowers are very fragrant, and our honey is..."—he gritted his teeth—"...unique."

"Is there more?"

Venzel cringed inwardly. It wasn't the way he hoped it would be, but almost too late he had discovered that she was too fragile to bind to the colony, and to him, by his will alone.

"Yes, but you can only have a little at a time."

He walked over to the table, broke off a piece of bread, and dipped it into the honey.

Trying to make it last as long as possible, she ate it slowly. When she finished eating, she looked around in the semi-darkness and saw the open boxes.

"I am so sorry; I have to finish unpacking for you." Attempting to jump out of bed, she noticed she was only wearing her chemise and dived back under the coverlet.

Venzel laughed from pure relief that she was herself again.

Ezri heard the joy in Venzel's voice and smiled.

The girl made him laugh. For that reason alone, he promised to pray for her every day for the rest of his life.

Venzel rapped softly on the door. "Ezri, you may go. Come back in two hours and bring fresh food and tea. And thank you for your help this morning."

Ezri was baffled. Venzel had not thanked him for anything, ever. After five years of orders and expectations, Venzel now said, "Thank you" because of this slip of a girl. It was now obvious that she was more than a servant, but who was she? She was not one of the usual women Venzel brought to the compound to live. They always stayed in the harem rooms unless they died or moved into the nursery to care for the children.

As long as he had known Venzel, no woman had ever woken up in his room.

Still smiling with relief, Venzel looked at the tangle of curls and big eyes hovering above the edge of the coverlet. Smiling back, she lifted her hand and raked her hair with her fingers, and almost immediately, her fingers were empty. Modesty aside, the coverlet fell to her lap as she sat up and ran both hands through her hair repeatedly, trying to understand. She looked up at him with tears in her eyes.

"I've lost everything," she cried piteously. "Venzel, you have left me nothing, nothing."

"You were ill with a fever; it is a remedy we use. Perhaps it is primitive, but it takes a lot of heat from your body and, my sweet, I said I tried everything to save you. It will grow back, I promise."

Gathering her into his arm, he felt her shaking. He prayed it was the chill of the room and not shock. Opening his cloak, he pressed her against his bare skin to warm her and pulled up the coverlet.

"Shh, latif, it will grow back."

He sang to her until her trembling stopped. After a few moments of silence, he asked, "When you said, 'I have left you nothing,' what did you mean?"

She took a hiccupping breath. "If your brothers are pleased, the other women who came with us, they still have their virtue to give to their new husbands, and their... their beauty is also untouched. I have nothing left to offer a husband, Venzel." Although she tried to smile bravely, he saw heartbreak in her eyes. "But if you will be patient with me, if, if I cannot be anyone's wife, I will try to be a good servant to you."

"Yes," he said slowly, "if my brothers are pleased, the women who came with us will find husbands here."

"And will, will one of the women you brought, will she become your wife?"

"Yes, if she is willing."

"She will stay in the harem?"

"No. She will be here with me. Always with me."

"When will you marry?"

"In seventeen days."

"So, I have that time, then, to care for you alone. Have you chosen?"

"Yes. I knew the moment I saw her that I wanted her for my own."

"Does she know?"

He smiled slightly.

"Evidently not."

With a quick rush of concern on her face, she said, "Venzel, you should tell her, soon. Every moment she does not know she is yours would be like a year to someone who cares for you. Think of the joy you are depriving her of, of the joy you are keeping from both of you. You should go and tell her now how fortunate she is." Avoiding his eyes, she looked around the room. "I will be very busy...."

Her suggestion confused him. *Did she want him to leave? To love someone else? Had his selfishness frightened her so much that she would prefer to be his servant than his wife?*

Venzel considered taking her to the harem to stay with the other women, but he had come so near to losing her that he could not bear the thought of being apart from her for a single night. Trusting that she still believed she belonged with him and deciding to accept her response, whatever it was, he put his hand under her chin and brought her face to his.

Looking into the eyes he knew he would love even after he died, he said, "My beautiful one, in seventeen days, will you wear the white and gold bridal veil and marry me? I ask you this now so as not to deprive you of any happiness that thought may bring you." He did not release her face but stared into her eyes as she processed everything he had said.

Believing she had nothing to offer any husband, Kizi did not fully understand Venzel's question. She had to repeat it to herself twice before she realized what he was asking her.

"Me, Venzel? Me? You want me to always be with you? But I have nothing to give you—"

"Because, as you said, you have already given it all to me. Say you will promise to marry me, and when our children come, you will love them and stay with me."

Venzel saw understanding in her eyes and happiness, but before she could answer him, he added seriously, "Know that if you accept my proposal, I will hold you to your promise and never let you leave me."

Her arms went around his neck, and her lips barely touched his ear as she whispered, "I promise, Venzel, to marry you, to love our children, and never leave you."

It was all he needed to hear.

"Karisi."

She would be his wife, his beloved karisi, forever. With grateful joy, Venzel made love to her as a proper husband, leaving no area untouched, unkissed, or any pleasure unexplored. He found her curiosity about his body endearing. Except for the soft rap at the door when Ezri brought their lunch, the only sounds heard in the corridor that afternoon were the murmurs, soft laughter, and sighs of love.

Venzel

Early that afternoon, while Kizi slept, Venzel left Ezri to guard the door and went to tell Zsiga of her promise.

"How much is she to know regarding your responsibilities here?"

"As little as possible. Although she will live with me, she need not know the details of my occasional absences. I will show her the stables so she understands I am responsible for the horses and certain acquisitions. Which I am, of course, but no one, Zsiga, will speak of my more delicate duties to the colony. She is emotionally fragile, and I will not have her hurt."

"I completely understand, Venzi. It will be as you wish."

"Thank you."

"So, when do I get to meet her?"

"In two weeks. Until then, she will be with me or in my room."

"Swaddled, no doubt, from head to toe."

"No doubt," he said laughing, and turned to leave.

"Venzel, one other thing. Rauf mentioned you have started giving her honey. That must be slightly revolting for you. I thought you would wait until after your son was born."

"That was my original intent, but it is important to me that she feels like she belongs here. The smell of honey permeates the colony, and it will be one more inducement for her to stay if she becomes homesick. Once we are married, I will ease it from her for a while."

He put his hand on Zsiga's shoulder. "It is my wish, my brother, that she becomes a part of everything I love."

"It is our wish as well, Venzel."

"Thank you, Zsiga."

Venzel was almost fifteen when Damla died. After a decade of living as one of them, he understood that the Lyostians were unable to endure sunlight or travel far from the compound and voluntarily undertook several errands on their behalf. Content merely to be useful, he was unaware these errands were tests by the elders to determine his loyalty—and therefore his value—to their colony.

His success in fulfilling these responsibilities was the reason the elders decided to give him the options they did. They suspected he had no desire to leave either his brother or the only home he had ever known. Remembering no other life, Venzel spoke Lyostian and worshipped Anya, the mother of all Lyostians, and to compensate for not sharing the collective consciousness, he devised a sign language so he could silently communicate with Zsiga like his other brothers.

Two years prior to his mother's death, Venzel had taken over the physical management of the compound and garage. When he expressed an interest in raising Arabian horses, Kadri, the colony leader, made the case to the collective that it would provide a motive for increasing the size of the compound and would present a visible human presence to any outsiders. After several years of training horses and constructing outbuildings and corrals, Venzel grew confident, tall, and strong. Kadri consulted the elders of the colony and they agreed. It was time.

He was seventeen when Kadri proposed the first procurement caravan and hired an experienced caravanner from the village to lead the expedition. Venzel, hoping the colony might assign him this responsibility in the future, watched the man carefully. Buying women was illegal, but hiring women servants and compensating their guardians for the loss of their companionship was not. That all of these "servants" were young, beautiful, seemingly docile, and unspoiled was not lost on the villagers, and once the women were sequestered in the wagons, their names were never spoken again.

Venzel's first caravan was a revelation. Far from the shelter and supervision of the colony, he was free to enjoy the changing sights, sounds, and people. His only assignment from Kadri was the management of the wagons and livestock. When his duties were finished, he could do as he pleased.

Astride one of his own horses, Venzel explored the land and villages. The colorful bazaars, unfamiliar buildings, and different kinds of food fascinated him. He found he had an affinity for languages—and for bargaining. With only a few coins in his pocket, he was able to buy gifts for Zsiga and all his younger brothers.

If those experiences weren't enough to make the journey memorable, being near women his age made it unforgettable.

When he could drag his eyes from their beauty, he watched the faces of the people who took Kadri's gold. Many mothers cried into their shawls as the caravan leader carefully assisted their daughters into the wagons. Some fathers looked off into the distance or down at the sand, while others counted the money in their hands over and over, never glancing up.

Although inexperienced, Venzel did not care for the caravan leader's attitude toward the young women. After a show of treating them kindly in front of their parents, he ignored their requests for water and rest, and gave them less respect than Venzel accorded his horses. Seeing himself as the colony's representative, he worried about the women's welfare and sat near their tent, listening to their conversations and muffled tears. Occasionally, kind words and friendly laughter drifted from the tent, and Venzel wished he could see through the canvas.

One evening, he heard a young woman refer to him as handsome, and he swelled with desire at the sweet sound of her voice, but when another laughed and said he was "only" a boy, his confidence fell, and he hid his burning face in the hood of his cloak. It was not long before Venzel learned that women did not keep their secrets well, and the evenings spent in the shadow of the women's tent were not wasted. By the time they arrived at the compound, he knew some of them were not as chaste as their fathers had claimed. Upon Kadri's acceptance of the servants and other cargo, he paid the caravan leader the agreed price for his services, but he demanded more. Admiring Venzel's horse, he insisted on one of the compound's Arabians in addition to his payment. With much reluctance, Kadri agreed and, after a brief discussion with Venzel, told him to take the caravanner to the stables. Venzel did not utter one word when the man chose the colony's handsomest stallion. Swinging up onto the horse's back, he sent Venzel to instruct his family to meet him by the paddock gate. Venzel waited there, too. Bursting through the stable doors like a starting gate, the caravan leader was showing off his newly acquired prize when the horse reared suddenly, throwing him to the ground.

Venzel ran quickly and caught the horse. Bending over the fallen rider, he pulled a rock from under his cloak and, with a single strike, crushed the small bones near the man's temple and set the bloodied rock next to his head. By the time his family reached him, the caravan leader was dead. Venzel apologized many times, promising to pay twice what the horse was worth so that he might have the pleasure of destroying such an ungrateful beast. Taking up the horse's reins, he walked toward the stables.

As Kadri was paying the grieving widow for the horse, a gunshot reverberated throughout the compound. Shaking his head at the sad turn of the day's events, Kadri ordered their finest wagon to return the body of their former caravan leader and his now wealthy family to the village. Satisfied that justice had been done and crying copious tears, they thanked him and counted their money.

Venzel replaced the rifle in the gun rack and led the very much alive horse back into his stall. As he brushed the stallion's rippling coat, Venzel praised his beauty and skill with soft words.

While traveling with the caravan, Venzel had missed his horses so much that he planned to spend that night in the stables, but music drew him to the house. Curious, he stood outside the door and watched the women dance for his elder brothers' enjoyment.

"Come in," they said. "Join us for the dancing."

When they invited him to stay for the banquet, he quickly agreed and found he could identify the women by their voices. He smiled at some, but his eyes narrowed at others. After the women were escorted to their rooms, the elders turned to him and asked about the caravan. He told them nearly everything he saw and learned, including the names of the women he suspected of being impure.

Kadri nodded.

"We will wait until the next new moon, to be sure, and hold the weddings in four weeks."

"And the beddings in six!" laughed Karamat.

Venzel blushed as they teased him. Noting his obvious discomfort, Kadri asked to walk with him to the stables to see the horse that would obey the slightest movement of Venzel's hand. Eager to escape the good-natured jests of his older brothers, he accepted the opportunity to show off Alazar's training.

Approaching the stables, Kadri listened as Venzel explained his technique, but what Kadri really wanted to know was how the horses felt about Venzel. Someone who held so much power would be either feared or respected. Kadri stopped behind the door and allowed Venzel to walk in alone. The horses, immediately aware of Venzel's presence, welcomed him. It was obvious, even to Kadri's untrained eyes, that they did not fear him.

Transmitting his findings to the collective, Kadri received permission to approach Venzel about the one remaining duty the Lyostians required of him that would determine his future within the colony.

"So, Venzi, now that we are outside the colony circle, tell me truthfully, is leading these caravans something you would be interested in taking over for us, as our former employee is now deceased?"

"Yes, Kadri."

"You are young. Do you think you could do as well as he? Ten healthy, beautiful young women, good prices, no accidents, and returned on time without any interference?"

"I think I can do better."

"In what way?"

"He was disrespectful to the women. Many cried all the way here. That I would never do. Their health is too valuable to risk. And...."

"And?"

"Some of the parents misled our former employee as to the status of their daughters. He paid full price without warning them of the consequences of deceit. I would not be so generous."

At Kadri's request, Venzel led the beautiful grey stallion out of his stall to the center of the practice ring.

"Good, Alazar," he whispered. Dropping the reins, he rejoined Kadri by the door.

"What would you like him to do?"

"Rear, like he did earlier today."

Venzel's left hand, palm up, rose about three centimeters. Alazar immediately reared up on his back legs, shaking his head menacingly until Venzel turned his hand over and lowered it. Cupping his fingers slightly, he pulled them toward his body, and Alazar walked toward them until Venzel halted him with the flat of his hand facing outward.

He smiled at Kadri. "More?"

"Yes, please," he answered, watching Venzel's face.

Without speaking or changing his expression, Venzel instructed the horse to lie down, back up, sprint toward them, and come to a dead stop. Thinking the exhibition over, Kadri was surprised to see Venzel kneel. Without giving the horse any outward signs, Alazar walked to Venzel and knelt beside him. In a single motion, Venzel rolled over Alazar's broad back, and the horse stood up with Venzel sitting upright.

"Impressive."

Dismounting, Venzel pulled Alazar's head to his chest and pressed his face between the horse's ears for a moment, then returned him to his stall.

"No reward?" asked Kadri. "I would think there must be an apple or pear for such perfect obedience."

Venzel shook his head. "Loving him is his reward."

Sitting on the tack bench outside the paddock, Kadri regarded Venzel with new respect.

"How do you know how to make such a horse—one this intelligent—willing and obedient? Is it a matter of chance or relentless training?"

"Some of it is luck and technique, but a lot of it is from observation, intuition, and selective breeding for intelligence and even temper. If a horse doesn't possess those qualities, it will never understand the subtleties of the training, and I would have to rely on the carrot or the whip. Those are the horses we sell. Beautiful and fast, but stupid."

"This one is rare; anyone can see that, and when you have such a one, why train another? How many rearing horses do we need?"

Venzel smiled slyly. "Well, Kadri, you never know...."

Kadri nodded approvingly. After a moment, he said, "Speaking of beautiful, Venzel, what did you think of the dancing tonight?"

Caught off guard, Venzel blushed. "What?"

"The women. Surely, you noticed them. Lovely shoulders, flowing hair, flashing eyes? A rainbow of swirling silk? Have you forgotten them already?"

Venzel had not forgotten. In his mind, he still saw them, especially Delara, with the golden tint to her skin. The one, he knew now by her voice, who said he was handsome. Remembering her loveliness, he became uncomfortable and looked at the floor in embarrassment.

Kadri saw immediately that Venzel was ready, able, and, with a little encouragement, would be willing. He had taken a gamble on this untested human male, requesting funds to bring women to the colony on the promise that he had the means to turn his dwindling outpost into a flourishing breeding compound. The collective approved his plan and allowed him enough money to purchase ten "servants" with the expectation of at least two offspring. Three would be magnificent. Any more than that would be all the success they would need to justify strengthening their connections to other colonies in the area by increasing their tunnel system toward the village.

With the understanding of a father, Kadri looked into Venzel's tortured face. "It doesn't have to be that way, Venzel," he said softly.

"Really, Kadri? Then please explain to me what my options are because right now, well, right now, I'd really like to hear them."

Kadri did not answer right away.

Seeing the seriousness in the older man's face, Venzel's eyes turned flat and cold. "No. I will leave, or you will have to kill me. I will not live as half a man."

Closing his eyes and shaking his head, Kadri laughed softly. "No, Venzi, not that. Never, unless it was your own choice."

"Then what? I have no money. I cannot purchase my own female servant or wife."

"Why would you purchase your own when you already have ten?"

"Ten what?"

"Ten female servants—or wives—if that is their choice. They can all be yours. They belong to the colony, and you are becoming an important member of our colony. As such, you should expect to share in the beauty of our women as we share in the cleverness of your horses."

"Kadri, my elder brother, I apologize for my confusion, but what do the women have to do with the horses?"

"As you said, to produce the qualities you want in your horses, you choose their mates carefully. And we, with the approbation of the collective, have, with your acceptance, chosen you."

Still not understanding, Venzel knelt at the older man's feet. "What are you asking me to do, Kadri? I owe the colony my life, and I will do anything to help sustain it. Forgive me if I seem especially dense this evening."

Kadri watched Venzel's face carefully.

"We, your elder brothers, would like to take the lovely women you brought us as true wives, but Venzi, among our evolutionary limitations is our inability to make love to our wives as we would wish. Therefore, we have no hope of children. Because we love you, trust you, and want you to always be one of us, we were wondering if, with Anya's grace, you would help us with that husbandly duty."

"You mean you can't—"

"No, not for hundreds of years. If it were not for the way humans consistently fail to value and protect the females of their species, we would have ceased to exist long ago. Regardless of their cost in gold or human lives, these women," he said, pointing in the direction of the house, "are priceless to us. They are our only means of survival, but regrettably, their beauty and softness do not arouse us. There is hope, a glimmer of a promise, that at some point in the next millennial, we may be able to produce our own daughters again, but until that glorious day, we must depend on the daughters of our enemies who live upon the earth to secure our future generations."

Stunned, Venzel sat back on his heels. He would have all of them? The slender one with the golden skin, too? Embarrassed again at his immediate response, he stood and walked toward Alazar's stall. There had to be more. There was something Kadri was not telling him, but to touch *her*, he would have agreed to nearly anything.

Kadri was aware of Venzel's unspoken suspicions.

"Yes, Venzel, there is more. We have traditions and permissions, and there are certain medical protocols, and naturally, we are not sure how successful this endeavor might be. But what I want to know tonight, so that we can begin the preparations, is if you are willing to try."

He waited a moment, but Venzel still did not answer. "It is a man's duty we are asking of you. We would appreciate a man's response."

When Venzel turned around, Kadri saw that his words had not been lost on the younger man and was momentarily taken aback. There was nothing of the boy, Venzi, remaining in his face, and he did not smile when he said, "Yes."

Kadri tilted his head and transmitted Venzel's response. He felt a rush of approval and smiled at their slim hope of success, but his smile dimmed a little at the memory of Venzel's expression and his words, *"The consequences of deceit...."*

Kadri had a sudden premonition that the colony, and possibly the entire collective, would someday regret this arrangement.

Returning to the house, Venzel asked, "Why me, Kadri? There are other men who work here."

"Yes, Venzel, but when you consider the offspring of your horses, whom do you choose?"

"Alazar, of course."

"Because he is here?"

"No. I choose him because I want his traits reproduced in the colts of my mares."

"Because he is the finest horse you have?"

"No, Kadri. Because he is the finest horse there is."

"Exactly, Venzel."

After a few minutes, Venzel continued, "The women, will they know who?"

"No, they will be given something to help them sleep. You will be a shadow to them."

Kadri paused for a moment. "It can be as you wish. However, we would prefer them to have a pleasant experience.... It is important they maintain close relationships with their husbands. Do you, um, need a book, or could we arrange a movie, perhaps?"

Venzel laughed for the first time that evening. "No, Kadri, I breed horses, remember? I think I have a fairly good idea of how it is done."

"Women are not horses, my brother. My limited experience is that they require a certain amount of coaxing."

Venzel stopped for a moment and looked at the older man. "I can make a horse leap into the air with all four feet tucked beneath his body. Now that, Kadri, takes a certain amount of coaxing. And patience. I will honor your wives with no less."

"Thank you. Rauf, a doctor specializing in these matters, arrives in a few days. He will determine the timing of who and when, but the 'how' Venzel? We will leave the how up to you."

Not remembering how he got there, Venzel found himself in the room he'd lived in since his mother died. Sometimes, Zsiga slept there, but he usually stayed in the tunnel dormitory with the other boys his age. Venzel had been alone too long. The mythical birds and animals he had carved into the ceiling had lost their power as companions, and it was only with his horses that he felt alive, pushing the limits of his patience with their training, and allowing himself the slender comforts of their patience with him.

It was hard to believe how much everything had changed in just a few short weeks. Stable master and horse trainer were all Venzel thought he would be to the colony. He was different, and because they could not read his thoughts, he knew it was difficult for them to trust him completely. He never expected to have any real standing among his brothers, but a leader of caravans was an important position. He would go out into the world with prestige and the authority to acquire all that the colony needed in goods and, apparently, women.

Ah, he thought, *the women*. The golden one's voice echoed back to him, and he wondered how long it would be before he could touch her and breathe in the fragrance of her perfume. His heart started beating rapidly when he realized he wouldn't have to stop with merely touching her. He would have her, embrace her beauty, and feel her skin moving against him.

His entire body burned at the thought of her.

Unable to stay in his room a moment longer, Venzel ran to the stables. Not bothering to saddle Alazar, he headed out across the desert, courting the coolness of the evening air.

Karamat smiled as he and Kadri stood on the porch and watched him leave. "Like his mother, the son will be a blessing to us."

"Yes. But I fear when he is older, he will understand what we have taken from him, and there will be a reckoning," answered Kadri.

"Perhaps, Kadri, but that reckoning could tilt to our side, and he will kneel and thank us."

"Let us pray for that. Regardless of the future, brother, I am fond of him and glad he did not die tonight."

"As am I."

Almost exactly eight weeks later, Kadri instructed Venzel as to the time and room he should visit that evening. It was the longest two months of his life. For the first six weeks, he and his brothers watched the women dance and joined them for dinner every night. Swept off their feet by the kindness and generosity of his older brothers, it didn't take long for the women to accept their shy proposals, and the colony's wedding plans commenced immediately.

Every night for two weeks after the ceremonies, Venzel watched the moon wax, and its increasing light matched his anticipation. Working himself to exhaustion during the day was the only way he could close his eyes at night, and even then, Delara would drift into his dreams, and he cried out in his sleep from the ache of her.

On the fifteenth morning after the weddings, Rauf met him as he was leaving for the stables. The waiting was over.

At the appointed time, Venzel approached one of the small rooms next to the harem and was surprised to see Rauf closing the door.

"Rauf, is something wrong?"

"No. Just a precaution. The children must be boys or the embryos will die. There are certain chemicals that assist with that gender preference. The capsule takes about five minutes to melt, and the effectiveness lasts about twenty minutes." He glanced at his watch and looked at Venzel. "It's time," he said.

The honey-scented candle assailed his senses as soon as he walked into the room. He immediately extinguished it. Removing a small flashlight from his pocket, he set it upright on the table, and a circle of light softly illuminated the room. Women's bodies were new to him, and he wanted to see what he was doing.

Murmuring softly as he did when approaching a young horse, he walked around her, touching her skin, smoothing her hair, and pulling the coverlet back a little at a time. Although this one was too tall, Venzel wanted to pretend it was the golden girl as he slowly removed her clothes, saving the veil for last.

The sight of her lying there, waiting for him, was all the inducement Venzel needed to respond to her. But, he reasoned, if they had given him twenty minutes, why not make it last twenty minutes?

Resting next to her, he brushed his hands over the curves of her body. Inhaling her perfume, he kissed her neck and her shoulders and became lost in the smooth softness of her skin until she began breathing faster. He drew back.

Was she waking up?

Her eyes were still closed, but he pulled back the veil to see her face more clearly. Recognizing the woman who laughed and called him a boy, Venzel's expression changed. For the first time, a smile crossed his face that would eventually strike fear into the heart of every woman and most men who were unfortunate enough to witness it.

He found the warm, moist opening he sought, and when he heard her gasp, he did not care. Feeling her trying to back away, he tried to control himself but realized he could not. The sensations coursing through his body overwhelmed him until, with one final thrust, one small cry, it was over.

Breathing hard from exertion and passion, he rolled over and away from her. When he finished dressing, he turned to take one last look. He did not expect to see tears seeping from beneath her eyelids. More confused than remorseful, he relit the candle and slid the flashlight into his pocket.

When Venzel opened the door, Rauf hurried past him, followed by Kadri.

Looking from the woman on the bed to Venzel, Kadri took him by the arm and said, "Apparently, we need to discuss the definition of a pleasant experience."

Venzel, slightly embarrassed but not ashamed, was quiet as Kadri pulled him into the corridor and explained.

"You must understand why treating our wives well is important. If we misjudge their most fertile time, you will need to revisit them. If they are hurt, that may not be possible within our time constraints. Venzel, these women are, within certain parameters, your wives, too. Is this how you intend to treat all of them?"

Unable to confess his real reason, Venzel told the first lie of his life.

"No, Kadri, I don't know what happened. I think it was the twenty-minute time limit. Why not let me have the capsule? That way, there will be less anxiety about the time. Making it a more 'pleasant experience' for everyone involved."

Kadri was charting new territory, and Venzel's response made sense to him. If Venzel felt he was running out of time, then that would explain his hurried and heartless performance. However, if he had more control over the timing… well, then it would be a matter of practice and discipline, two areas in which Venzel was highly skilled.

Standing near the stairs, Kadri tilted his head. A few moments later, Rauf came down the hall.

"How is she?"

"Not dead."

Venzel's head whipped around. "What do you mean 'not dead'? I could have killed her?"

Hurting her was one thing—she had hurt him—but he did not mean to make her cry and definitely didn't want her dead. He knew exactly how much she cost. If he hurt their wives, what would they do to his horses? Kadri and Rauf watched his face grow pale in the darkness, and although they did not know exactly why, they knew he finally understood the seriousness of what he had done.

Rauf answered, "Yes, Venzel. Young women are mentally and physically fragile. They require a gentle touch, especially with any new physical experiences. Bahari will recover, but whether this particular interaction will be successful remains to be determined. I will have to keep her sedated while she recovers."

He paused for a moment.

"However, you have a point when you say that the time element may have made it difficult for you, resulting in a level of anxiety we did not anticipate."

He handed Venzel a small box. "Use only one capsule, and don't remove it from the box until our wives are able to accept it comfortably. It may start to melt if you hold it too long." He looked at Venzel steadily. "Do you have any questions for me? I have been a doctor at several breeding colonies and have an extensive level of understanding in these matters."

"No, Rauf, thank you for your patience, and thank you for helping Bahari." He put his hands over his face, "I just didn't know."

Venzel dropped to his knees and prayed for forgiveness.

Rauf put his hand on Venzel's head. "It will get easier, and better, with experience."

He looked at Kadri. "Perhaps you should have had a woman from the village to practice with, but it is too late for that. Find it in your heart to care for them, Venzel, and treat them gently. Their response might surprise you."

When Rauf had gone, Kadri put his hand on Venzel's shoulder. "I love you, Venzel. You are my brother, but you know these women are necessary to us. Please do not put me in the unhappy position of having to choose their well-being over yours."

Venzel then understood it wasn't only his horses' lives at stake. Although he was willing to die to protect them, he realized it wouldn't be him *or* the horses; it would be him *and* the horses.

He nodded. "I understand, Kadri, and I did before you threatened me. I love my brothers, too, and I will not betray your faith and trust in me or endanger another one of your wives with my clumsiness again."

They gave him the following day to think about his abrupt initiation into manhood and asked him to visit two women that evening. Before going to them, Venzel went to the stables and walked among the horses he treasured. He stroked their backs, necks, and long legs, noticing how they responded to his touch. He whispered to them, watching their ears twitch, and heard them answer with their own soft sounds.

As he bathed, he reviewed everything he had learned in the last twenty-four hours and accepted that if he wanted to stay here—and stay a man—loving the colony's women was something he needed to do well. If his brothers wanted children, then, Anya willing, he would give them children. Praying to Anya for guidance, Venzel began to regard the women in the harem not as women, or even wives; to him, they all became possible mothers. Smiling softly, he remembered his own beloved mother and, more than anything Rauf or Kadri had said, was instantly humiliated. Closing his eyes in shame, Venzel cried silently at the thought of anyone treating her as he had Bahari and vowed to his mother's memory he would never deliberately hurt another one.

Although he was a little subdued that evening, he recalled how his horses responded to his whispers and touch. He gently stroked his wives of the evening, brushed his hands along their breasts and thighs, nuzzled their necks, and told them they were beautiful. When their breathing came in soft gasps, he inserted the capsule and, checking his watch to be sure, slowly and gently made love to them. He knew he hurt them a little, but it was as little as he could manage. He was careful not to let his passion overwhelm him and thrust a little deeper each time so that, at the end, he was where he needed to be.

He was on his way back to his room when Rauf stopped him.

"Venzel."

"Rauf."

"Excellently done this evening. Both women. No tears, no bad dreams. I didn't expect you to learn so quickly."

He ignored Rauf's critique. "How is Bahari?"

"Recovering. We will be bringing her out of sedation tomorrow evening. I suspect that other than a little discomfort, she will be fine."

"Thank you… Rauf?"

"Yes?"

"How long before we know if they are pregnant?"

"With the technology we have available to us, three days."

"Thank you for all of your help."

Rauf tilted his head as Venzel walked away and transmitted the conversation to Kadri. Moments later, Rauf met him in the tunnels beneath the house.

"And?"

"Flawlessly executed, both times. He was gentle, arousing them so they were ready for him, causing little discomfort to your wives. I think you will find them very loving toward you tomorrow." Smiling at Kadri, he added, "So consider yourself forewarned."

"Thank you, Rauf. Are you sure he did not know you were in the room?"

"Yes. And I hope this means I never have to watch him again."

"No, you are released from that particular duty. However, at least for this first week, it would be appreciated if you could be around afterward in case something happens that he's not ready for."

"Thank you, I will." He turned to leave, then stopped.

"Kadri, have you given any thought to what might happen to him if none of them becomes pregnant? Not all young human males are... virile. No matter how willing they are."

"Yes, I considered all possibilities, and that one occurred to me. However, I care too much for him to entertain a solution. There being only one."

"No, two."

Remembering Venzel's face and the words, *you will have to kill me first*, Kadri said sadly, "No. Only one."

"Humans," Rauf sighed. "Well, we will know more in a few days."

"Yes."

There was only one visit scheduled the following night. Venzel was slightly surprised to find no one waiting in the hall. He blew out the candle and turned on the flashlight when he entered the room. Looking at the delicate figure on the bed, he did not have to see her skin to know immediately who she was.

Delara.

Singing Anya's song of thanksgiving, he circled her bed, pulling the coverlet back a little more with each orbit. He had not removed the clothes of the women the night before; it was not necessary to him, but he wanted to see and touch all of her. She had haunted his dreams every night for two months, and now, if for only a short while, she was exclusively his.

Venzel left no region of her unexplored. He memorized her curves and textures, and where his hands went, his lips followed. Slowly, he became aware of how her body responded to his touch, his lips, and his voice. Her breathing became short, quick gasps, and her back arched. When he touched her to insert the capsule, she pressed against him, and he thought he held her beating heart in his hand. He looked at her face, saw her smile, and heard her sigh.

Desire for her rang in his ears, but despite her arousal, he knew he could still hurt her. He eased gently into her, and when she gasped, he kissed her to take her mind away from the pain. Her arms came up as she kissed him back and moved with him, just as she had in his dreams. When it was over, he did not leave her but stayed, kissing her neck, and breathing in the fragrance of her as he ran his hands along her sides, still whispering his longing in her ears.

A few minutes later, her hands traveled along his back to his hips. Thinking he had nothing left to give her, Venzel started to pull away, but when she clutched him to her and began moving against him, he realized he was wrong. Unsure of who was making love to whom, he abandoned his earlier careful pace. Not knowing exactly where it was going to take him, he let her passion control their momentum. When he thought he could no longer restrain himself, she began to make little noises in her throat, and at the same moment he felt the sweet ripple of her against him, the world exploded into a kaleidoscope of pleasure.

For the first time, he had everything he desired. He lingered, not wanting to leave her, but the evening that she could be his was over. He kissed the palm of her hand and whispered, "I love you, Delara."

Her answering smile went straight to his heart. As he left her room, Venzel picked up her iridescent green scarf and hid it in his cloak.

Caught up in the memories of the evening, he was blissfully walking on air toward his room and did not see Rauf standing in the shadows by the stairs.

"So, is it like I promised, getting easier, better?"

Venzel, lost in the memory of Delara's body, could not suppress his smile.

"Well, yes," he said, looking down at his feet. A moment later, he looked back at Rauf. "Rauf, did you know that, um, women can respond like men? Well, not like men, exactly, but they have, um, tremors, like men?"

"Yes. I told you their response would surprise you. I just wasn't sure how to describe it."

"Well, she has been the only one."

"The only one so far. This means that you are learning what women like and are anticipating their desires. When you do this, you should not be too surprised to find that they will respond to you—even subconsciously. Anything else?"

Venzel stopped smiling. "Yes. Small confession. We did it twice. It wasn't just me; she seemed to want me to."

"Good."

"That's all right?"

"There was only one visit scheduled for tonight, and you're young. These are *our* wives, Venzel; you are allowed to enjoy them, and, Anya willing, they will enjoy you as well."

Venzel began to smile again. Rauf turned to leave but paused and looked back.

"Venzel, just one more thing."

"Yes."

"They are not all the same. What one woman responds to, another will not. You must not take it personally if what you do on a particular evening fails to produce the results you expect. Remember why you are there; a woman's pleasure should be your intention, but her pregnancy is the goal."

"Yes, Rauf. Still, it's quite wonderful when it happens."

"Yes, yes, it is."

Saying goodnight to Venzel on the stairs, Rauf went into Delara's room. He carried her to a secluded underground bathing area and washed Venzel's human smell from her body. Returning with her to his room, Rauf wrapped her in silk and waited patiently until she grew warm and fragrant. Pushed almost past his endurance, Rauf removed the silk from her body and mimicked everything he watched Venzel do the night before. When

Delara responded to his touch as well, he called her his darling, kissed her hands, and placed them above her head. Starting at the base of her throat, Rauf began to sip the honey-infused nectar that emanated from every pore in her skin. When she awoke, she kissed him and called him husband.

By the end of the following week, Rauf reported to the colony and the collective that all the women Venzel visited were pregnant, and they were all pregnant with boys. The technology they had was working. Twenty-six weeks later, when blessed with six healthy infants, Venzel became, quite literally overnight, the most valuable asset the colony ever possessed.

After doing everything he could to save her following the birth of her son, Delara died in Rauf's arms. It was not unexpected; childbirth was difficult in the desert colonies, and Rauf knew they could lose some of their mothers. Expressionless and silent, he kissed her one last time, wrapped her in white gauze, and carried her to the catacombs.

He never requested another wife.

It did not take long for Venzel to understand that such a gift of beauty and pleasure did not come without cost or sacrifice. When he asked about the women, the elders made it clear to him that one tender evening was all he would have with the colony's wives, and when he left their embrace, he would not see or touch or hold them again. As generous as his brothers were in sharing their wives with him physically, any affection the women bore in their hearts was reserved for their Lyostian husbands. Knowing there were women outside the compound, Venzel made plans to visit the village, but Rauf took him aside and gave him a graphic lesson in disease. Thoroughly committed to devoting his life to the colony's needs, he knew that any infection would decrease his usefulness and thanked Rauf for warning him. There were many things Venzel could live without, but his brothers' trust was not one of them.

Although he was unaware of it then, eventually, all the faceless women in the dark harem rooms became Delara, and he called them by her name. During the next seven years, when he was afraid she was becoming only a dream, he would take her scarf from beneath his pillow and breathe in its fading fragrance. In those moments with the iridescent silk pressed against his face, Venzel promised himself that someday he would meet a woman like Delara and marry her.

And never leave her.

Loving Her

Returning to his room, Venzel found Kizi dressed in the burka, the hood tossed behind her. Empty boxes were stacked against the wall, and the largest trunk, still unopened, was at the foot of the bed. The remnants of her hair and clothes from last night were nowhere to be seen. Inhaling her perfume, he smiled and closed the door. Quickly walking over to her, Venzel picked her up, and they fell onto the cushions of the newly made bed.

"Do you like wearing this, latif?"

"Well, it's better than wearing nothing. You never know who's going to walk through the door."

Venzel was suddenly still. "Who else has been here?"

"Ezri came for the trash and ashes."

"Anyone else?"

"No. Were you expecting someone?"

"No. Did Ezri see your face?"

"No, Venzel. I had just pulled this on, and the hood still covered my head."

Venzel's eyes narrowed. Ezri had always been loyal to him, but it was an untested loyalty. Leaving Kizi on the bed, he tugged on the bell pull and opened the door.

Ezri walked calmly down the corridor, but seeing the look on Venzel's face, he inwardly quaked. What had he done to provoke his master's anger? More than anyone else, he knew what that look on Venzel's face meant. Stopping in front of him, Ezri knelt and touched his forehead to the floor.

"Ezri, did you enter my chamber earlier today without knocking?"

"Yes, Master. I saw you leave and came in to clean… as I do every day."

"When you saw me leave, did you see anyone with me?"

"No, Master."

"Then why would you enter a bedchamber where there was a woman alone without asking permission? Tell me," Venzel said slowly, "is it your wish to die? And when I say die, Ezri, I mean die in the desert… staked and screaming."

Terrified, he suddenly knew Kizi wasn't just *a woman alone*—she was *his* woman alone. That was why Venzel had been so grateful earlier that morning. Ezri sighed, from that level of gratitude to threats of torture and death for something so irrelevant. Focusing his thoughts that day—as every day—on Venzel, he had completely forgotten she was there.

Knowing the truth might not save his life, but could save him a lot of pain, Ezri confessed.

"Master, please forgive me. I watched you leave as I do every morning, and then I came in to clean as I usually do. When I saw her dressed as a servant today as yesterday and already neatening your room, I took no notice of her but removed the ashes and trash she had set aside."

Venzel looked at Kizi.

Nodding, she did not take her eyes from Venzel's face. When Venzel reached for the camel whip, she rushed up to him, touched his wrist, and said softly, "No, Venzel, please. He did not know."

A dangerous smile crossed Venzel's face. Leaving the whip, he straightened up and addressed the man on the floor.

"Ezri, the woman in this room is mine. She is dressed like this because I will suffer no other man's eyes to look upon her until we are married. Her safety, protection, and well-being when I am not with her are now your responsibility. Always. If anything happens to her, and you are not already dead, you will wish a thousand times that I killed you today."

"Thank you, Master, it will be as you say."

"Yes," said Venzel, closing the door.

Left alone in the hallway, Ezri felt as though a voice as sweet as cool water had pulled him back from a pit of endless torment. He was not dead. He wasn't going to be dead unless something happened to her. An edge of Venzel's resolve seeped into him, and he vowed, even more than Venzel commanded, to guard her with his life.

Pushing the hood from her face, Kizi smiled at Venzel, and he took her in his arms.

"Thank you, Venzel," she whispered.

That evening, she fulfilled every promise Venzel had made to himself. Each kiss that fell upon him made her more precious. Every touch brought her closer and blurred the lines between them until they existed in a timeless circle of space and motion. He loved her. The heartbreak of all the women of his memory that he could not love because they were not his disappeared, and his heart was whole again. He had never experienced such happiness, holding her, and knowing she would be there tomorrow and the next day. He would not have to leave her side at night, and she would not disappear forever from him in the morning. She loved him completely and found joy in him. He could not pull her close enough, and she became the sun, the moon, and the stars because, like them, she would always be with him.

It was hours before he allowed her to steal away from his embrace, and he counted the moments until she returned. Drawing her in beside him, Venzel used his body as a shield between her and the rest of the world. Someday, he thought, he wanted to die like that, loving her and keeping her safe.

Riding Lessons

Venzel left early the next morning to see to the stables after promising to take her riding in the afternoon. Reluctantly, she let him go, and when Ezri came in to clean, she asked if there were any apples.

"Yes, a few. Shall I bring them to you?"

"Perhaps. Venzel is taking me to the stables later, and I think that a couple of apples will make the horses like me."

"Do you like horses?"

"I don't know. But they are important to Venzel, and so I think it would be best if they liked me... I can learn to like them."

"Like you *learned* to like Venzel?"

It was clear he still did not understand. Afraid she may not be able to save him next time, Kizi pushed the hood of the burka away from her face. Dazzled by the love sparkling in the depths of her sea-green eyes, Ezri realized immediately not only who she was to Venzel, but also what he was to her. He immediately fell to his knees.

"Forgive me, Mistress. Please forgive my insolence. Once again, I can only say that I did not know."

"Yes, Ezri," she said, pulling the hood back over her head. "But now that you do, I know he would like you to keep it to yourself. I am sure he would prefer others to believe as you did. For some reason, it seems to suit his purpose."

"Yes, Mistress. Now I understand both of you. Please forgive my ignorance."

"That's all right, Ezri."

"What's 'all right, Ezri'?" They had not heard Venzel's footsteps in the hall.

Relieved that the hood of the burka covered her face, she looked up. "It's all right that there are only a few apples to take to the horses."

"Yes," he said, patting his pocket, "and I've got them all right here."

A delicate hand appeared from the long sleeve of the burka, and Venzel helped her up from the cushions. Before they stepped onto the back porch, every human on the compound knew who she was to Venzel, and no man looked at the small, shrouded figure whose hand was captured so firmly in his. Arriving at the stables, Venzel called out to one of the stable hands, and the most beautiful animal she had ever seen was led into the paddock. At a word from Venzel, the man dropped the reins and walked away.

Kizi watched in awe as the horse performed a series of movements in time to the music of Venzel's hands. Pirouetting on his hind legs, Alazar leaped into the air and landed on all four feet like a cat. A moment later, the horse reared, hooves pawing the air and, at the end, bowed to her with his forelegs bent beneath him, his nose on the ground. Kizi could not restrain herself. Running up to the horse, she wrapped her arms around his neck and kissed him.

Venzel followed slowly. Settling her on the horse's back, he said, "Hold the reins with one hand and his mane with the other."

Venzel curled his fingers a bit. The horse stood up so gracefully that she was barely jostled.

"Latif, I would like to introduce you to Alazar, the only thing that was truly mine before I met you. I love you more, but I do not love him less." He took her hand, and she slid into his arms.

"Then I would say that we are both very lucky."

Venzel set her down. "Come," he said. "I want you to meet the family."

Alazar followed Venzel into the stables like a puppy and walked into the first stall on the right. Removing the blanket and bridle, Venzel gave Alazar one of the apples, touching his forehead between the stallion's large grey eyes. Without meaning to, Kizi had found Venzel's only weakness and witnessed a side to him that his brothers rarely saw. They only appreciated that the horses obeyed him without hesitation and the amount of money they brought into the colony. Only Zsiga understood, as Kizi instinctively did, how much Venzel needed them.

Taking her hand, they visited each stall as Venzel told her the name and lineage of every horse in the building. At the back were four mares, each with a foal. The mares backed up when they saw her, but the foals were curious and stumbled forward on stiff legs.

Venzel walked into the mares' stalls, looked into each foal's eyes, and felt the length and sturdiness of their legs. Glancing up at her, she could not miss the pride in his face.

"They are like your children."

"Yes."

Walking toward the paddock doors, she pointed to an empty stall. "Whose is this?"

"Aljerhra," he said wistfully. "I sold him before we left on the caravan. Fast, like his father, but not as smart. He will be a great racehorse... for a while."

Venzel did not like to speculate on the brilliant but short futures of the horses he sold for the racetracks of the world, but he could not keep them all. The horses that were bought by equestrians were cherished and petted, and if they did not break a leg—and sometimes even if they did—they were assured pleasant lives. However, some colts did not have the temperament to learn even the rudimentary basics of dressage, and although racehorses brought more money, Venzel only sold his horses to the tracks if he could not make anything else out of them.

Wanting to take the sadness from his face, she gently reminded him, "I thought you were going to take me riding."

Venzel looked from her to the empty stall. "I was. But perhaps today, we will just be content with introductions."

He took two strides toward her and lifted her off her feet. She looked around quickly to make sure no one saw them. Laughing at her shyness, he set her down.

"Hasad!" he called.

They heard his hurried footsteps before they saw him.

"Yes, Venzel."

"I'm thinking of moving some of the horses around. Bring fresh hay and straw for this stall while I decide exactly what I am going to do."

In about as much time as it took her to make a bed, Hasad had filled the stall with a bedding of straw and covered it with a layer of sweet-smelling hay.

"Anything else, Venzel? Can I help you move the horses?"

"No, in fact," For a moment, Venzel's face looked so stern that Hasad swallowed nervously. "In fact, I need some time to think without any distractions, so, no, you cannot help me. The wisest thing you can do for both of us right now is to take yourself, and everyone else in or near the stables, and leave for about an hour."

"An hour, Venzel? What would you like us to do for that hour?"

Venzel didn't even blink. "Not be here."

Hasad was quick with horses but slow with people, and it wasn't until he saw the slight tremble of her burka that he understood what Venzel was telling him to do. Fighting the urge to look at her because he really did want to *walk* out of the stables, Hasad answered, "Yes, Venzel."

Turning abruptly, Hasad closed the stable doors behind him, called to the men, and began running toward the porch. It would not be worth his life to tell them of his suspicions; he only said that Venzel had given them an hour off, and he, for one, was going to spend it taking a nap in the shade on the other side of the barn.

One of the men started to smile and said, "Wait a minute, is she—"

Hasad trapped him with such a stare that the man did not dare speak the rest of his thought.

"Why don't you go in there and ask him?"

The man paled at the suggestion, and they all decided it was an excellent time for a nap and put the barn between them and the stables.

Just as Venzel knew they would.

Placing a bar across the doors, he smiled.

Throwing the burka's hood behind her, Kizi's trembling released into soft laughter. "Really, Venzel, you didn't have to scare him."

"Perhaps next time."

"Well, perhaps... but I don't think he'll ever ask again."

"Yes."

Taking a clean blanket from the rack, Venzel placed it on the straw and gently removed the burka. Dressed only in her chemise, he brushed his hand from her legs to her neck. Looking into her eyes, he saw the same expression that dazzled Ezri earlier.

"That much, my darling?"

"Yes, Venzel."

"Even here?"

"Even anywhere."

He pulled the chemise over her head and put it behind her for a pillow. Covering her body with his, Venzel brought the two things he loved best as close together in his heart and mind as he could. Then, because it was not in his nature to hurry, he smiled and asked, "Have you ever ridden a horse?"

Caught up in Venzel's lovemaking, Kizi was a little disconcerted at the interruption.

"Um, no, Venzel, but I will learn."

Smiling at her confusion, he said, "Well, my dear, consider this lesson number one."

Turning over so his back was against the blanketed straw, she was, at first, unsure what she was supposed to do. Starting gently, he taught her to match her posting rhythm to his, letting her passion set the pace until she began gasping for breath, and he felt her fluttering response. Only then did he allow himself the same pleasure.

"Oh, Venzel, I think," she said, catching her breath, "I'm going to like riding."

Venzel laughed, and Kizi, exhausted and fulfilled, fell into his arms and laughed with him. The horses, hearing the pure joy in the echoes of their happiness, answered with gentle sounds of their own.

While waiting for the new moon, Venzel taught Kizi how to ride the gentler horses, and every time they returned to the stables, they found the empty stall filled with fresh hay and straw and a clean blanket draped over the stall door. Never looking at Kizi directly, Hasad helped Venzel unsaddle the horses, and then he and every other stable hand on the premises disappeared to the shady side of the barn for an hour.

Venzel never had to ask again.

Courtship

Catching Ezri alone, Zsiga grilled him for details about the woman in Venzel's room, but all Ezri would say was that she was young, had dark brown hair, and a voice that he had only heard muffled through the door or under the burka she always wore. Curiosity was not a Lyostian trait, but it was a human one, and it was the little bit of humanity Zsiga possessed that made him as interested in Venzel's bride as his own as he counted the nights to the colony's upcoming wedding.

Zsiga wasn't the only one. All the brothers agreed that Venzel brought them a beautiful selection of wives this year, and they were impatient to get to know them better. However, despite their eagerness, the colony had certain pre-nuptial protocols that were always followed.

It began with greeting the women when they first arrived. Fresh from village life and intimidated by their luxurious surroundings, most, when asked certain questions, were too unguarded to lie. This year, as occasionally happened, one of the women who had a little too much wine the first evening confessed to being already pregnant.

"No one knew," she whispered to another woman behind her veil. "It was a secret...."

It was also a secret that due to their limited vision, Lyostians had evolved an acute sense of hearing.

The next morning, she woke up tied beside the desiccated and decayed body of another false wife in a candlelit catacomb. No one heard her screams then, and no one heard her screams that night when they came for her. Despite her delicate condition, she took a long time to die.

Nothing in the colony was wasted.

During the second phase, the brothers spared no expense to ensure the remaining eighteen prospective wives were as comfortable as possible. Each evening the women joined the men after dinner to dance, tell stories, and play games. To the women, the brothers looked very much alike in their tinted glasses, with only slight differences in their physical appearance and personalities to distinguish one from the other. The brothers were careful not to show any partiality, but it was rumored that nine of them would each choose two wives, and, in the harem and the dormitory, preferences were discussed, and decisions were made.

The third phase—the most important to the prospective wives—was the evening the brothers chose the women they wished to marry. It was also equally important to the brothers. The essence of the honey the women had consumed for nearly three weeks was beginning to perfume their skin, and the Lyostians were finding it harder each night to let them return to the harem.

Venzel, absent for all of the preceding evening parties, never missed the announcement party. Not directly involved with either the women's or his brothers' desires, he was the perfect person to conduct this phase of the courtship by reminding everyone of the colony's proprieties.

At sunset, the women entered the room as lively and bright as butterflies. Seeing Venzel sitting next to Zsiga, their smiles faded, and they immediately quieted down. Lowering their eyes, they knelt gracefully on the carpet placed in front of their husbands-to-be.

"Quite an effect you have on women, Venzi," Zsiga whispered to his brother.

As he stood, Venzel gave Zsiga a quick smile. His expression became stern again when he faced the women.

"Because you have been kind, respectful, and well-behaved, each of my brothers has chosen two of you for his wives. Once again, I stress that this was not a competition, and I will not tolerate any extreme outbursts. You are sisters here. Be happy for each other that you have found favor in the eyes and hearts of my brothers.

"The adjoining room has been arranged with food and partitions separated by curtains. This is not your wedding night. Nothing is expected of you except courtesy and polite conversation. You may show your pleasure and gratitude quietly. If you are disappointed, my brother will return you to me." He unfolded a faded burka. "I have several of these, and I've been told the kitchen is in need of help."

Venzel did not return to his seat next to Zsiga. He stood in the entryway between the two rooms to watch each woman's face as she was chosen. It was essential to know the women who were secretly unhappy. They would receive special attention because each attempted escape meant one less prospective mother.

In order of hierarchy, then seniority, each brother stood and took his intended wives into the next room. Because they took turns listening in the corridors, the brothers knew how the women divided them up, and they chose accordingly. Their highest priority was making sure the women were happy, and since the Lyostians desired the women equally from the first night they stepped into the banquet room, it was immaterial to them which of the women they "married." The women belonged to the colony—not to any specific individual.

Watching each face carefully, the only one that concerned Venzel was the delicate beauty Zsiga had chosen. She seemed pale and a little shaken as Zsiga led her and his other choice, a lovely girl whose eyes flashed adoringly at him, out of the room.

As arranged, the women received the husbands they wanted, and no one was brought back to him. Venzel, making a mental note to speak to Zsiga, left early to return to his room, where his chosen wife waited for him.

A Wedding

It was vital to Venzel that his was a real wedding and not the charade the Lyostians staged for the women's sense of propriety. His brothers considered it binding, in their way, as it bound the women to the colony, but it did not bind the men to the women they pretended to marry. Venzel wanted a human wedding that would remove all doubt that she belonged to him first and forever—not to the colony.

Without mentioning it to anyone, Venzel had arranged to be married in the village the day before his brothers' weddings. With the main house in an uproar over the evening's pre-wedding festivities and the next day's nuptials, Venzel and Kizi walked unnoticed to the stables. If anyone other than Ezri had paid attention, they would have seen Venzel turn Alazar toward the village instead of their usual ride circling the compound.

"Why are we here, Venzel? Do we need something for the wedding?"

"No, latif, we are here to get married."

"But we are getting married tomorrow, Venzel. In the house, with your brothers…." her voice trailed off when she saw the look on his face.

"Are you arguing with me, latif?" he asked quietly.

"No, Venzel. I'm just confused."

He smiled as he helped her down from the horse. "Then, my love, you must trust me."

"I do, Venzel. Venzel?"

"Yes?"

"Am I going to be married in this?" she asked, tugging at the fabric of the burka.

"Yes, today you are. You may pull back the hood if the priest asks to see your face, but only if he asks."

"Tomorrow?"

"We will see what tomorrow brings." Looking steadily into her eyes, Venzel asked, "Are you ready to marry me and be my wife forever?"

The sound of confusion in Kizi's voice became one of absolute confidence. "Yes, Venzel," she said softly. "I am ready to marry you and promise to stay with you as long as you wish."

Holding her hand and leading Alazar, they approached the small building with the sphere and sword on the door and knocked. The young man in black robes who opened the door nodded at Venzel. Wrapping Alazar's reins around a post, Kizi and Venzel walked inside the cavernous cathedral.

Kizi could see that the church had once been beautiful, but the paint had faded, and some of the windows were boarded over instead of repaired. She moved closer to Venzel when a slightly older man and woman dressed in black entered from a side door and met them beneath the altar bearing a two-headed eagle. The ceremony was brief, but Venzel didn't mind. This wedding was real. It wasn't at the compound but in the village, with an ordained priest and human witnesses. Looking around at the empty church, he regretted his brother was not there but felt his mother would understand why he chose to be married without Zsiga standing next to him.

Kizi was lost in the words but followed Venzel as he led her through the ceremony and the steps. At the end, the priest closed the book and smiled at her.

"May you live in peace, always."

Seeing her new husband put out his hand for hers, Kizi pulled the long sleeve of the burka above her hand. Removing a gold bracelet from his pocket, Venzel slipped it on her wrist. She glanced at it for only a moment before pulling her hand back into the shelter of her clothes. After the ceremony, the priest signed the registry and prepared two certificates for Venzel.

Kizi followed Venzel like a proper wife as he walked into the town magistrate's office. They waited as the clerk signed the documents and kept one for the official record.

At a table by the door, the calligrapher took Venzel's copy and joined their names with sweeping swirls. When Venzel handed the artist a few coins, he continued to embellish the certificate with drawings representing luck, prosperity, and fertility. When the ink was dry, he folded the paper and placed it in a red envelope. Sealing it with a final flourish, he handed it to Kizi, who immediately turned and gave it to Venzel.

Walking into the sunlight, Venzel took his first solid breath in several weeks. In the eyes of the church—and the law—they were married.

His eyes sought the cloudless sky. *Thank you, Anya, mother of us all.*

He slipped the red envelope into his wallet. Anya, the blessed mother of all Lyostians, had granted his prayer; no one could take her away from him now.

Kizi followed Venzel as they reclaimed Alazar from the street children who stood in a semi-circle staring at the horse in awe. Smiling, Venzel gave them small coins, and the children whooped as they ran down the street. Kizi re-mounted Alazar but, instead of sitting in front of Venzel, now rode behind, her arms clasped around his waist. Riding through the village, Kizi's eyes looked longingly at the small marketplace and the few colorful caftans, skirts, and scarves hanging there. Feeling the gold surrounding her wrist and remembering the money he gave to the calligrapher and the children, Kizi knew Venzel could afford to buy her something pretty to wear at their wedding tomorrow. When he did not slow down or even glance in the direction of the market stalls, she sighed and thought of the one silk scarf folded in the closet.

Her thoughts unknown to him, Venzel felt happier and more relaxed than he had in a long time. Taking both of her hands in one of his, he pressed them to his heart and smiled. It was only when they were back in his room that he realized she had not spoken a single word since the ceremony.

"What is the matter, karisi? Are you unwell?"

"No, Venzel, my husband, I am well," she said, pushing the burka's hood from her face.

"I thought women were happy on their wedding day, but you are not happy, my love. Why?" Taking her in his arms, he looked into her eyes. "Please tell me, whatever it is."

"No, Venzel. You will think me foolish, proud, and ungrateful," she said, moving out of his embrace. "I would prefer you thought me unhappy. It's not true, but I would rather you think that than worse things."

Venzel did not understand. More than anything, he wanted to please her, to bring her close to him, but she seemed so far away. Reaching for her again, he said in his softest voice, "But I do not wish to think you are unhappy, latif. I want you to feel as I do. Please tell me what has taken the light from your day. You do not like the bracelet?"

She would not look at him. "Oh, Venzel, it's the most beautiful thing I've ever worn. No, it's not that...." Tears fell from her eyes, and she grew quiet again.

Her tears confused him. He had spent quite a bit of time and not a little money to arrange the wedding, and now, when she was his to love and protect forever, she was trying to appease him without telling him the truth. He turned toward the door.

"It isn't going to be like this, karisi. I am not going to spend our life together trying to read your mind. So, for the last time—"

He looked back in time to see her pull at the burka's rough fabric. Realization took only a moment, and Venzel laughed.

"All of these tears because of that?" he asked, pointing to the ugly grey tent she was wearing. He walked over, and before she knew what happened, he stripped it from her and tossed it in the fireplace.

Circling her, Venzel looked her up and down much as he did when he met her.

"Well, you are right. I do remember saying that you would wear a white and gold veil when we marry with my brothers tomorrow, and you shall, my love, if that is your choice."

"But Venzel, I have no white and gold veil. I just have this," she said, taking the silk scarf he had given her from the closet. "And it is lovely, but—"

"My wife, are you arguing with me again?"

She sat on the floor in a heap and bit her lip.

"No, Venzel."

He could not resist her. Walking over, he picked her up and swung her around.

"My darling wife, you have much more than this," he said, setting her down and tossing her only scarf in the air.

"I do?"

Without answering, he went to the trunk he had not opened since their arrival. Taking a key from the top of the mantel, Venzel opened the three locks. His eyes teased her as he lifted the lid slowly. When she started to run over to him, he raised his hand, and she stopped, but she could not keep from hopping from one foot to the other in anticipation.

"Venzel…," she pleaded.

"Well, let's see if we can find a white and gold veil somewhere in here."

He stepped back as she dropped to her knees in front of the trunk. Exotic scents that spoke of the countless bazaars where Venzel had traveled on business for the colony floated up and enveloped her with their mystery. Mesmerized by the splendor in front of her, she didn't rummage through it all at once as a child might but removed one lovely fabric at a time, smoothing the soft folds of the silk with her hands and pressing colors against her skin.

Although temporarily forgotten while she was entranced by the gossamer rainbow surrounding her, Venzel didn't mind. Contenting himself with thoughts of her gratefulness, he waited patiently as she brought out, caressed, and set aside each item. When the last swirl of silk joined the others, she turned her luminous eyes on him, and he was not disappointed.

"I never understood," he told her afterward, "why I bought those clothes or for whom I'd purchased them until I saw your face and felt your touch. You were the hope I dared not speak of to anyone and the wife I believed I would never possess."

Her hand moved from resting on his chest to the back of his head, and she pulled his lips to hers, giving herself once more to her husband and the only man she would ever love.

They received an invitation to the evening's festivities in the colony, but as he told Zsiga, his brothers would have a much better time without him. Remembering the women's reaction at their last sighting of Venzel, Zsiga grinned and reluctantly agreed. Unknown to Zsiga, however, by keeping to their room they had the best of the party. The music drifted in through the open door, and Ezri brought them delicacies from the banquet tables. Banishing him from the corridor for the remainder of the evening, they entertained each other as Venzel told her stories of his travels, and she, wide-eyed and enraptured, drank in every word, and believed her husband to be the bravest man who ever lived. When his stories wound down, she drew him into her, whispering to him of his courage and her admiration.

It was a night Venzel carried in his memory for the rest of his life.

Arrangements

The colony's occupants spent the next day anticipating the wedding ceremonies. Scheduled to begin at sunset and more solemn than the previous evening's events, the honored guest at a Lyostian wedding was Anya, their guide, goddess, and mother. Although not legally binding in any country on the planet, it was still, within the framework of the colony's social structure, taken seriously by the brothers who were fortunate enough to play the part of the grooms. Regardless of traditional accuracy, the Lyostians deemed the ceremony a necessary formality. The information in the archives was quite clear that a woman who believed she was married was considerably less difficult than a woman who felt she could leave at any time.

The day's preparations began at dawn with the formal delivery of wedding clothes to the participants. To symbolize Anya's pure light, each groom received a new white tunic. For the first time, Ezri brought Venzel a tunic and hung it in the narrow closet.

Feeling the garment's fine linen, Venzel smiled at him. "Are the wagons on their way, Ezri?"

"Yes, Master, they left an hour ago."

"The horses?"

"Will be where you wish them to be."

"Do not be late, Ezri."

"No, Master," he said. It was going to be a busy day for him, too, but Ezri would have agreed to anything that made Venzel this happy.

Closing the door behind Ezri, Venzel glanced at the bed and watched Kizi wake up. Deciding to help her with that in the most provocative manner possible, he reached under her embroidered cotton gown and uncovered one of her feet. Stroking the graceful arch, he began kissing her small dainty toes. Shrieks of laughter echoing throughout the room were soon followed by sighs of pleasure as Venzel continued his adoration from the curves of her delicate feet to the curves of her smile that promised a lifetime of such mornings.

An hour before sunset, Ezri brought fresh water for Kizi, and Venzel joined his brothers in the underground cistern. Zsiga noticed small welts on Venzel's body, but when questioned, his brother laughed and said something about getting flea bites from the horses.

"I'm not sure I believe you, Venzi, but I am far more curious to know if we are finally seeing your wife this evening. I must confess I am quite anxious to meet her. Ezri won't tell me a thing. All I know is she has brown hair, and since half the colony's women have brown hair, he hasn't been any help at all. I must tell you, though, I'm expecting a beauty."

Venzel smiled at his younger brother. "I told you, Zsiga, she is pretty enough, but there is something about her that I am sure you will find almost as lovely as I do."

"Well, I hope so after all this mystery. Are you going to stay and get dressed with us? Then we will all be together when they come in. There's safety in numbers, I'm told."

"No, I'm going back to my room. She has no one to help her dress. Ezri could help her, but—"

"Yes, I know. You would have to kill him." Zsiga laughed at his own joke, and the other grooms joined in. Only Rauf noticed that Venzel wasn't laughing.

Smiling indulgently at Zsiga, Venzel slid into his cloak.

"See you there, my brothers."

Knowing she was waiting for him, Venzel climbed the stairs two at a time. He was already hurrying down the corridor, but seeing Ezri pacing nervously back and forth in front of the door, he broke into a dead run.

"Thank goodness you are here, Master."

"What happened?"

"I don't know. She's crying, and when I ask how I can help, she tells me to go away."

Venzel smiled and took a deep breath. "Go on, Ezri, you have things to do. We'll be ready in a few minutes."

"Do you know what is wrong?"

"Not exactly, but I have a fairly good idea of how to fix it. Thank you, Ezri. Don't worry."

Opening the door, it was as he suspected. His wife was sitting on the carpet in a white chemise surrounded by a rainbow of silk, satin, and gauze. Looking from one lovely ensemble to the other and unable to choose among them, she broke into fresh tears.

Trying hard to keep the smile on his face, Venzel slammed the door.

"What is this?"

"Venzel!" she said, jumping up.

"Who were you expecting?"

"Truthfully, my husband, I wasn't expecting anyone."

"Is that why you were sitting on the floor crying?"

"No, but look, Venzel," she said, as her eyes started to fill with tears again, "they are all so beautiful, and there is no one to help me choose."

"Here," he said. "I'll help you choose."

With those words, he swept the garments from the carpet and placed them on the bed. Reaching to the top of the closet, pulled out a dust-colored burka and tossed it at her feet.

Horrorstruck, she stared at him.

"You have ten minutes," he said, sitting down at the table to watch her.

Kizi looked from the grey pile of fabric on the floor to the exquisite colors on the coverlet. Stepping over the burka, she tiptoed to the bed and began setting some things aside.

"Venzel, do you have a favorite color?"

"Have you looked in the mirror lately?"

Smiling to herself, she pulled out a few more items. "Husband," she asked sweetly, "can you help me dress? It seems I am short on time."

Venzel stood up so quickly that his chair fell back on the floor. He lifted her in his arms and swung her around. Laughing, he said, "One day when we're old, remind me to tell you how adorable you were on our wedding day, wailing in the middle of the floor."

He kissed her, and she turned toward him, putting her arms around his neck. "Oh, Venzel," she said. "You are so mean. I thought you were really going to make me wear the burka."

"Well, I might yet if you don't hurry. I have to get dressed, too, you know."

"We'll help each other."

"Yes, my love, we will."

He did not want to let her go, but there were things to do. Zsiga and his brothers were expecting him. Besides, he thought, they had later—years and years of later. He set her down and, with a couple of minor changes, approved the clothes she had chosen to wear.

He fastened the silk around her body and arranged the tasseled ends of the shawl at her back. Setting the sheer aquamarine scarf on her shoulders, he placed the white and gold veil over her head. Asking her to hold the veil for a moment, he went back to the trunk and removed a large flat box. Lifting a gold filigree headdress from the tissue, he placed it on her head. In addition to keeping her veil in place, the dangling crystals and blue beads masked her eyes.

"You may take this off after the ceremony, but not before."

Backing away from him, she twirled in the center of the room.

"How do I look, Venzel?"

Although he had spent the last seven years of his life seeking out beautiful women for his brothers, Venzel knew she was the loveliest woman he had ever seen.

Somewhat hoarsely, he observed, "You will be the most enchanting bride there, my love." Taking her hand, he noticed something was missing. "Where is your wedding bracelet?"

"Here, but Venzel, as beautiful as it is, it is too big and keeps falling off my wrist."

"That is because you wear it here," he said, pushing it above her left elbow. "Not on your wrist."

"Then it is perfect."

"Yes."

Wearing new black trousers and slipping into his white tunic, Venzel brushed his wet hair back away from his face and turned around.

"How do I look?"

"There are no words good enough, Venzel."

He smiled at her and pulled her hand into the crook of his arm. Checking his watch, he kissed her lightly and said, "Time to go. Nervous?"

She looked up at him. "You'll be there, right?"

"Every minute."

"Then I'm fine," she said, smiling mischievously into his eyes. "Everyone else will be nervous."

Ezri, standing in the shadows, watched them leave. Gaping in awe at how beautiful they were together, he listened as their whispers and laughter died away as they left the underground corridor.

Anya's Ceremony

Having already experienced one marriage ceremony, Kizi thought the second one would be boring. She could not have been more wrong. Lost in a sea of unknown faces, she was immediately aware that Venzel had done her a disservice by keeping her sequestered from the other women and his brothers. She remembered being overwhelmed on the day of their arrival by the size of the compound, but that memory did not prepare her for the scope and magnificence of the interior of the main house.

Not realizing how uneasy she was in the confusion and opulence surrounding her, Venzel handed Kizi over to Militos, one of his younger brothers who was not participating that evening, and went to join the other grooms. Without touching her, Militos guided her to where the other women waited for the ceremony to begin.

Kizi, dazzled by all the beautiful brides in their colorful clothes, was so busy looking at them that she failed to notice how surprised they were to see her. They all knew immediately who she was. She belonged to Venzel. Given their experience with him, especially when she did not appear in the harem, they had never expected to see her again. When she turned her head to look for Venzel, she did not hear their quick intake of horror at the sight of her short hair. Only one person would have been cruel enough to cut off all her beautiful hair, and feeling very sorry for her, each bride came up, introduced herself, and complimented her clothes, jewelry, or veil. Overcome by their kindness, Kizi quietly murmured her thanks.

As Lalei backed away, Kizi noticed tears in her eyes.

"What is wrong, Lalei? Are you ill?"

"No," she said, turning her head and dabbing gently at her eyes. "Just homesick. I miss my little sisters, and sometimes I think I am never going to see my mother again. They are better off with the money than with me, but I cannot help missing them."

"I'm sorry. Lalei," she said, taking the girl's hand. "Perhaps you will let me be your sister."

"You are very kind. Senkali said the same thing. I'm sure I will be fine. Zsiga seems like a nice man."

"I haven't met him yet, but I'm sure he is."

Militos walked in, and a hush fell over the women. Still not touching them, he put the brides in hierarchical, then alphabetical, order corresponding to their groom's status in the colony. Kizi was slightly surprised to find herself at the end of the line. Surely Venzel was somewhere in the middle; he couldn't be the lowest—ranking brother who was getting married.

Some of the women at the head of the line looked back at her. She saw by their expressions that they felt that perhaps they had been too nice to Venzel's wife; he wasn't as important as he pretended to be. Kizi felt her face burn. Then she remembered his soft caresses and his teasing. Touching her gold bracelet and the delicate fabric of her bridal clothes, she thought of his generosity and knew she was the luckiest woman in the room.

Lost in memories of Venzel, Kizi smiled behind her veil. She just wanted to be in his arms again, in their room, in the stables, or sharing his cloak on the sand. It didn't matter where he ranked in the colony; he was her husband, and, in her eyes, he was the most important person on earth.

Militos began explaining the ceremony, and since she didn't want to be in the wrong place or standing next to the wrong brother, she shook herself out of her thoughts of Venzel and listened.

"Just a few words as to protocol, and then I will answer any questions as long as they are brief. There are nineteen chairs on the left side of the altar room and there are ten corresponding chairs on the right side." Pointing to the brides at the beginning of the line, he said, "You will walk to the end of the aisle and sit in pairs, and you,"—he smiled in Kizi's direction—"will occupy the single chair at the front of the aisle."

He heard a short gasp from one of the women at the front of the line.

"Anyone unwell?" he asked.

No one answered him.

"Fine. The ceremony begins when each groom takes the hand of his wife, or wives, and walks in front of the altar and kneels. We will sing a short prayer, and then you and your new husband will respond together, 'Blessed Anya, mother of us all, we thank you.' As you return to your seats, you will find an additional chair moved next to yours. In most cases, the husband will sit on the inside with a new wife on either side of him. There will be some singing by those brothers, such as myself, who are not grooms, wishing you happiness. I cannot emphasize enough that this is a sacred occasion for us and remind you that although it may be different from the wedding you imagined, it is a binding contract in our culture. Any questions?"

"What happens after the ceremony?"

A chorus of giggles interrupted him.

Smiling, he said, "Well, that's up to you, isn't it?"

Pausing as more nervous laughter ensued, he continued, "Following the ceremony, there will be a small reception, after which you will accompany your new husband to his room. There will be wine and food for your pleasure, but, as men of our culture take the long view concerning our wives, we expect nothing of you beyond kindness and gentle conversation. We prefer not to force our physical needs upon our wives until we expect children from them. During the day, you will reside in the harem; after supper, you will join your husbands for the evening. Any more questions?"

Militos's request was met with silence.

Standing alone at the back, Kizi was the calmest person in the room. Despite what Militos had said, she already knew what was expected of her as Venzel's wife. Her eyes grew luminous as she thought of the children she would give him: tall, handsome boys to help him in the stables and beautiful daughters who would tease him and make him smile. She smoothed her skirt in front of her and wondered if one was beginning in there now.

As the music from the baglama began, the brides moved forward into the altar room. White floors blended into a pale golden yellow on the walls that melted back into white at the ceiling. Although the room was square, every artistic effort had been made to give the impression that she was standing in the middle of a glass globe. Slightly intimidated by the display of reverence and devotion of the artisans, Kizi felt that she was part of something that was much bigger than she ever expected. Full of flowers, the room was as fragrant as the garden. White alabaster vases suspended from the ceiling held the loveliest blossoms while the petals of those less perfect were tossed upon the white floor like confetti. The last in line, Kizi felt Venzel's stare before she saw him. Looking at him with loving eyes, she sat down next to him, crossed her palms on her lap, and bent her head. Venzel noticed that every woman sitting behind her mimicked her deferential pose.

The tempo of the music slowed. Every eye in the room watched as Venzel stood, took her hand, and led her to the altar. Kneeling gracefully in her long skirt beside Venzel, the seriousness of the ceremony washed over her, and she knew how much it meant to him.

Reciting the words together at the end of the prayer, Kizi's voice was clear and strong, and there was a commitment in her words that Venzel had not heard the day before. Pressing his fists against his eyes, he silently repeated his prayer of gratitude, adding, *I promise to protect her and her children with my life.*

Getting to his feet, Venzel helped his wife to stand. Keeping her close to him, he guided her back to their chairs. Not once during the following nine weddings did he release her hand.

When the last two brides were married, and the words of the final prayer faded, they all stood as Venzel and his bride led the procession into the next room for the reception.

Passing through the doorway, Venzel whispered, "Do not leave my side. Not for one moment, not for anything. Now and forever, my love, your place is standing right next to me. Never, and I cannot stress this enough, make me look for you."

The look in his eyes and the intensity of his voice could not be misunderstood.

"Yes, Venzel. I promise you will never have to look further than your elbow to find me."

When she playfully pinched his elbow, Venzel felt the tension ease out of him.

His curiosity finally rewarded, Zsiga headed straight for Venzel's new bride. "Hi! I'm Zsiga, Venzel's brother, and—"

"And he is dying to meet you."

Smiling over her head at Zsiga, Venzel turned Kizi to face him.

"I promised you could take this off after the wedding, my dear, so let me help you."

Looking into her eyes, Venzel removed the headdress and adjusted the silk gauze so it fell back on her shoulders like a soft mist around her face. Kissing her forehead gently, he turned her toward Zsiga.

"Zsiga, I would like to introduce you to my wife. Destani, this is my younger brother, Zsiga."

Upon hearing her new name, Destani leaned softly into Venzel's embrace and her face filled with light as she looked up at him. For a moment, Zsiga could only stare.

"Destani. *Eyes like the sea.* Your name suits you but doesn't do you justice." He looked at Venzel. "You are right, Venzi; she is 'pretty enough.'"

Laughing for a moment, he added, "I suspect that if there is a shortage of burkas in the house, we should check your room."

Smiling down at Destani, he said, "Wonderful to meet you, my… sister. I hope you will be very happy here."

"Thank you, Zsiga. It is my hope as well."

During the reception, each of Venzel's brothers came up to meet her, and all walked away dazed by her beauty and grace.

When Militos offered her a glass of tea, she moved to accept it, but Venzel shook his head. She did not contradict him and saw Militos flash him a small, apologetic smile. After Militos moved away, she said, "Venzel, I really am thirsty."

"We will be leaving soon. Until then, my love," he said, bringing her hand to his lips and kissing her palm, "be patient."

With her heart in her eyes, she answered, "Yes, Venzel."

Every woman there envied Venzel's gallant gesture, and the love that was evident on Destani's face was not lost on any of his brothers.

Zsiga murmured under his breath, "Thank you, blessed Anya, mother of us all."

Rauf, standing behind Zsiga, heard but did not share his prayer. In Rauf's mind, their most valuable resource had just become the most dangerous man in the colony—all in the space of one hour. Venzel was not one of the docile human males they hoped to rule someday. He was, as he had always been, a volcano sleeping in their midst. Looking at Destani, Rauf feared he saw the seismic event that could awaken its fury and irreversibly change all their lives.

As Venzel promised, they left shortly after Militos walked away. Their departure seemed to signal the beginning of the end of the reception, but sometime during the remainder of the evening, as his brothers talked and laughed with their brides, each kissed their new wife's hand as Venzel had done and, in return, every wife attempted Destani's look of complete devotion. Most of them failed, but a few succeeded. Senkali, one of Zsiga's new wives, didn't have to try. She had fallen in love with Zsiga the first evening she met him.

Militos had not lied. In the days following the wedding, the Lyostians introduced the new wives to their style of husbandly affection. During the day, the women were treated like queens, living in luxury and comfort on the second floor of the house. They were fed copious amounts of fruit and honey and took turns playing music, singing, or reading aloud for each other's pleasure. In the evenings, they shyly descended the staircase to join their husbands for dessert in their rooms on the first floor.

Beautiful fabrics lined the walls of these rooms, creating candlelit havens of intimacy. Reclining on soft divans, the brides were served a specially blended tea and salted almond cakes. Waiting for the tea to take effect, the grooms helped their wives find comfortable positions on the cushions as they slowly succumbed to the restful effects of the tea. Allowed to eat as much honey as they desired and trapped in the heat of their silk skirts, scarves, and shawls, the women became as fragrant as the colorful flowers they resembled. As soon as they were asleep, their new husbands got up and opened the door to another brother who was waiting in the hall. The brothers shared everything, even the sweetness that lay on the tender flesh of their new brides.

Sheltered in women's quarters all their lives, the wives believed themselves to be quite lucky and thrived under the attention of husbands who found their beauty, softness, and compliance almost as delectable as their bodies. However, the Lyostians knew that the deliciousness of their brides was faint compared to what it would be once they were pregnant, and they counted the days until Venzel's return.

It was the only part of the wedding ritual Militos failed to explain. Despite the courtship and engagement banquet, the women didn't marry the men they desired. He was only Anya's representative and their guide through the ceremony—not their husband. In a language they did not understand from a culture they could not fathom, the women were married to every man in the room, including Venzel.

Flight

Venzel was wrong thinking they could slip away unnoticed. Their exit was observed by nearly everyone in the room, and Zsiga was requested to follow them. However, instead of taking the stairs to his room in the tunnels, Venzel led Destani to the porch at the back of the house, where Ezri stood holding the reins of Alazar and a pack pony.

"Everything ready?"

"Yes, Master."

He handed her jewelry to Ezri. "Put these things in my trunk and lock it. You know where the key is."

Ezri took the headdress and bracelet, exchanging them for Alazar's reins.

"When they ask, and they will ask, Ezri, tell them three days."

"Yes, Master. Will it be three days?"

"No. You can tell Zsiga we will be back before the full moon... but do not tell him until the fourth day."

"It will be as you wish."

Something in Ezri's voice caught Venzel unaware. Looking into Ezri's face, he saw a small piece of his own happiness reflected there and grasped the man's upper arm.

"Thank you, Ezri, for everything you've done. You have always been a good servant to me."

Venzel mounted Alazar, and when Destani moved to sit behind him, he took her hand and set her in front.

"But Venzel—"

"Shh, latif karisi, I cannot hold you back there."

Looking down at Ezri, he asked, "And the other matter?"

"It, too, will be as you wish."

"Thank you, Ezri."

From the shelter of Venzel's arms, Destani waved at him and echoed, "Thank you for everything, Ezri."

They were on the far side of the wall when Zsiga found Ezri locking the gate.

"Where did they go?"

"I am not sure, my master's brother. He did not tell me and packed the pony himself this afternoon. All I was asked to do was bring it and Alazar to the porch at this time."

"Did he say how long he will be gone?"

"Yes. He said to tell you he would be gone three days."

"Oh, then he must not be traveling too far."

Zsiga silently watched them ride into the darkness with some concern. Most of the talk among the women at the reception was the shortness of Destani's hair. Discussing the matter with Senkali, she confirmed it was long when they arrived.

"How does he treat her, Ezri?" he asked seriously.

"The same way he treats everyone… except sometimes—"

"Yes, sometimes?" asked Zsiga, expecting the worst.

"Sometimes she makes him laugh, and he is like a boy again."

Zsiga knew exactly how long it had been since Venzel was a boy.

Sweet, blessed Anya, mother of us all, thank you, he prayed gratefully. Then, bowing slightly in his brother's direction, returned to the house.

Staring after them, Ezri said his own prayer for their protection and joy. He didn't tell Zsiga everything he suspected, but it seemed to him that the woman filled a hole in Venzel's heart that he did not know was there, but now finding himself so wonderfully complete, his happiness spilled over. His love for her had changed him and opened his eyes.

Ezri was unsure how Venzel would treat him in the future, but tonight, Venzel saw him as a man, a real man. It only lasted for a few moments, and even if it never happened again, for Ezri, it was validation enough.

He watched until Venzel's white tunic became one with the darkness of the night. He felt the desert wind on his face and looked up at the cloudless sky. Nodding to himself, he smiled as he walked through the tunnels to Venzel's room to return the wedding jewelry to the trunk. Locking it, he set the key back on the mantel.

He went upstairs to the balcony and searched the horizon for a man he knew he could not see. He rubbed the scars on his wrists. Even after all these years, he could still feel the ropes binding his hands, the pain of the crop of the whip upon his back—but that was still better than the lash. He knew the sting of that as well.

Despite those painful memories, he smiled.

It had been nearly six years since he had been found tied to a tent pole and cowering under the skin-splitting blows of the slaver's riding crop. Cut, bruised, and sobbing, his lack of understanding of what he had done to cause his owner's outrage only added to his confusion and pain.

Suddenly, the beating stopped, and, raising his eyes from the shelter of his arm, he saw a tall man wearing a dusty cloak wrestle the wooden handle away from the slaver and throw it into the road. During the struggle, the stranger's cloak fell open, and Ezri could see that although his face was young, he had the body—and bearing—of a man.

"If you want to kill him, do it in private," he said, "not in the middle of the bazaar."

"Why do you care what happens to him?"

"I do not. But what I do care about," he said, advancing on the slaver, "is having my morning disrupted by murder." Recognizing the yellow and red band on the servant's arm, a knowing expression passed over his face, and he said in a softer voice, "Or is it suicide?"

"It is forbidden," Ezri said in a horrified whisper, and even though he shook his head in denial, the idea came to him as a possibility. Although it passed swiftly, Ezri was unable to conceal the thought from his eyes.

Not moving his gaze from Ezri's face, the young man knew the moment the eunuch decided to die.

He looked at the slaver. "Did he steal from you?"

"No. For that, he would already be dead. He is insolent and lazy."

"He is weak and underfed."

"Again, why do you care?"

"Again, I do not."

At those words, the man turned and left him tied to the tent pole. Ezri felt his life already ebbing away as he watched the slaver walk into the yard to retrieve his whip. Just as he was bending down to pick it up, the stranger's boot held it fast to the ground. The slaver looked up.

"Now what?"

"I just remembered that I cannot take dinars out of the country, and I am leaving tomorrow for my home. Now, there are many ways I could spend them—most much more pleasurable than this—but I need a servant, and this one," he said, pointing in Ezri's direction, "needs a better master."

To Ezri's amazement, the man thrust a handful of dinars at the slaver, but it wasn't the silver coins that made his owner change the markings on the paper; Ezri had seen the glint of gold as well.

His new master tucked the transfer paper into his sleeve and led Ezri away. Behind them, the slaver yelled at the two men.

"You might need this!" he said, throwing the whip at Ezri's head.

Turning quickly, the man caught the handle in his fist and, before the slaver could move, threw it back at him, knocking the slaver from his feet. They could not miss the snap of his leg as he fell to the ground, and the slaver's howls and curses followed them as they disappeared into the crowd.

Losing themselves among the vendors and patrons, his new master leaned close to Ezri and said, "At least we won't have to worry about him following us."

Too stunned to speak, Ezri could only nod.

After a few minutes, Ezri was roughly pushed between two tents. Out of sight of the crowds, the man pulled his knife from his belt. Ezri, still reeling and weak, saw only a merciful death and fell to his knees. Holding up his hands in supplication, he could not find the words to beg for his life.

Ezri felt the ropes being cut from his hands and the armband torn from the sleeve of his tattered tunic. Abruptly lifted to his feet, Ezri watched as the man shrugged off his cloak and wrapped it around his emaciated body.

Pulling the hood close around Ezri's ears, he said, "There is money and your release paper in the pockets. Now go. Leave this place. Learn a trade and make a life for yourself."

Ezri did not move. "I cannot, Master," he said.

"Cannot what?"

"Learn. Letters, numbers, are nothing to me, so I was apprenticed to an artisan, but there is no grace in my hands." He looked down at the torn armband at his feet. "That's... that's why my parents allowed this. Because I could not earn a living doing anything else. I can cook, and I can serve, and I can obey, but I cannot learn."

"How old were you?"

"Fifteen."

No one, not even his mother, had looked at him with such an expression of understanding and pity. It was several moments before the man spoke again.

"Can you count money?"

"Small amounts."

Standing motionless and gazing at him with eyes so dark they seemed to penetrate Ezri's soul, he took a deep breath and asked, "Do you know where the fountain is located?"

"Yes, Master."

"Go to the food stalls and buy enough to last us the rest of the day. I will meet you at the fountain. I will wait 30 minutes. If you are not there with food in 30 minutes, I will leave. I will not look for you."

Bowing slightly, Ezri hurried. He had to be there as promised. He had no doubt the man would leave him behind. He wasn't a fool, but he was easily distracted and clumsy. He slipped his hand into the pocket. He could tell by the weight of it that there was enough money to get him home, but what then? To be sold again, and yet again?

Fear gripped his heart. He bought the food and ran to the fountain.

The man wasn't there.

But he would be. Ezri knew he would be because he said he would. There was plenty of time left. As the minutes wound past the appointed time, Ezri imagined several things that would delay him; good things like meeting friends or perhaps the sight of a fine horse had caught his eye. But as the minutes eased closer to an hour, Ezri began imagining bad things. Perhaps his new master had been hurt—or worse—and he wondered at the sorrow he felt.

It was as though he had lost his last chance.

Unclaimed and alone, he sunk slowly to the ground. His back pressed against the coolness of the stone did not ease the pain of the beating, and although he was starving, he would not open the bags. He did not know what to do. Remembering his earlier resolve, he slipped his hand into the sleeve that held the man's money and wondered how much opium he would need to sleep forever.

Someone stepped in front of him.

"What is your name?"

Recognizing the voice, Ezri quickly looked up, but the man was wearing a new cloak that hid his face, and it took him a moment before he was sure. Relief spread through his heart and shone in his eyes.

"Ezri, if it pleases you."

"Let's find some shade, Ezri."

The man took his arm and helped him stand but did not loosen his grip until Ezri looked up into his face.

"I am Venzel," he said.

Sitting under the awning of an empty feed shed, Ezri ate as Venzel explained that he had never let him out of his sight, but he had to make sure that he could trust him—that he was not bait in a trap.

"It has only happened once, Ezri," he said, placing his hand on his knife, "but that was enough for a lifetime."

Ezri held up two fingers. "Trust is two ways, Master."

"Yes, and that is why I didn't leave you sitting on the ground." He took a deep breath. "I cannot take you to my home, Ezri, for if I do, you can never leave. If you try, my brothers will either kill you or you will die in the desert. Those would be good deaths because if I find you, you will pray a thousand times we had never met, and it still will not save you. Do you understand?"

Ezri did not speak or take his eyes off Venzel's face but only nodded.

"That will not do, Ezri."

"Yes, Master, I understand I will never leave. May I ask a question?"

"This would be the time for questions."

"What such a place is your home?"

"It is in the desert a few days ride from here where I raise horses. There is a large main house, a barn, horse stables, a garage, and some smaller outbuildings. We have cars in the garage and a generator for the house, but few other modern conveniences. Should you decide to accompany me, you will be the only servant who lives there. We have a few day servants from the village that you would supervise, and I hire grooms and stable hands from the village as I need them. There is an underground spring that allows us to have a garden by the house and a small orchard behind the barn. Once a year, I command a caravan that procures what is needed that we cannot raise, shoot, or purchase locally."

"The horses?"

"I train them in the basics of dressage for equestrians. Once every two years, I take four to a show in Cairo and interview prospective buyers."

"Interview?"

"They are the beauty of my life. I do not let them go easily."

"Who is 'we?'"

It was the first time Ezri saw Venzel smile.

"My brothers and I live there."

"Will I cook and serve them as well?"

Venzel stood up and, to Ezri's dismay, handed the remainder of the food to a passing child in rags who, as soon as he opened the bag, bowed, and quickly ran off into the crowd.

"Let us walk, Ezri," he said, heading away from the noise and dust of the bazaar.

Ezri scrambled to follow him. He thought Venzel was going to stop several times, but he turned this way and that until, finding two large rocks under a solitary olive tree, he sat down on one rock and motioned to Ezri to sit on the other one.

"Ezri, I believe I can trust you, but if I am wrong, tell me now. If this morning's beating was a farce, then say so. I have met people who do worse things to survive and will not hold it against you. You can keep the money and return to him because you cannot unhear what I am about to say. If I find you have breathed a word to anyone, I will—"

"Yes, kill me."

"No. I will cut out your tongue and sell you for a catamite."

Ezri slipped to the ground and looked at Venzel with tears in his eyes.

"Why these threats, Master? You saved my life. I am your servant forever. Your distrust hurts more than these marks." His voice dropped to a whisper, "You needn't... needn't be so cruel."

"If my horses are the beauty of my life, Ezri, then cruelty is its culture. But so is love, friendship, and joy, but I must introduce you to the cruelty first because without it, the others cannot exist. I will tell you as much as I know, and I will share the rules under which we all must live. So, knowing what you risk, what do you say?"

No one had ever asked Ezri what he wanted to do with his life. So much had happened in such a short period of time that it was hard to know what to do, but he was simple, not stupid. Venzel's clothes were clean, he was well-spoken, and although Ezri was sure he was older than his new master, Venzel had more command of the world than many men twice his age, and there was a fairness to him that Ezri admired. There had been so little fairness in his life that, when he thought it over, he realized there was nothing to decide. Wherever this man went, Ezri wanted to go.

"If I obey you, will you ever sell me?"

"No. You will, as you said, be my servant forever."

Ezri pushed himself from the ground and regained his seat. "Then, Master, I promise I will be your servant. I will never leave your house. I will keep your secrets. Now, if it pleases you, tell me the words that are worth a man's tongue."

Venzel stared at him for a full minute, took a deep breath, and said, "Although there are bedrooms in the main house, my brothers do not sleep there, nor will you see them often—"

"Where—"

"Do not interrupt me, Ezri. The time for questions is over, although I will allow you one question when I am finished, only one."

He looked beyond Ezri into the crowd, nodded to himself, and continued, "Preferring the constant temperature and the darkness, my brothers live and sleep in underground rooms that were excavated hundreds of years ago. Because they have lived like this for such a long time, bright lights hurt their eyes. They rarely leave their rooms or the house in the daytime without dark glasses and hats. My rooms are on the first level directly under the house, but their rooms are much deeper and are connected by an extensive tunnel system. Under no circumstances—and I say this for your protection—are you to go beyond my rooms by yourself. When they get to know you and come to trust you,

you may be permitted to visit the lower levels for additional duties. It is up to you, Ezri, how helpful you want to be, but understand that these men saved my life and my mother's life after my father died. I owe them everything and will protect them—even to my death."

Standing, Venzel took a deep breath and surveyed the horizon in each direction. Instead of returning to his rock, he sat next to Ezri. Ezri started to move, but Venzel clutched his arm and held him still. Pulling the hood of the cloak across his mouth, he lowered his voice. "There are other reasons they live underground, Ezri, and I share this with you only because I must. My brothers look like men, but they are not like you and me. They are members of a society who call themselves Lyostians and live in subterranean colonies throughout the Levant, Northern Africa, and into Europe… possibly even farther. Although they prefer to live underground, do not think that they are dirty or primitive. Their rooms and catacombs are as beautifully furnished and decorated as you'd see anywhere. As we share everything—good and bad—your own rooms will be as opulent and comfortable as you wish. Usually, visiting brothers sleep in the dormitory on one of the lower levels, but the ones who stay longer or live there prefer their own rooms. They understand our language but also have one of their own, which I speak; however, it is forbidden for outsiders to learn.

"I have never pried into their origins, but I think one of the reasons we look so much alike is that we started the same way, but their desire to live underground made them evolve differently from us. Despite our similar outward appearance, they are different in three or four specific ways you may notice. I tell you this now so that you will not be frightened or run to me with tales of monsters. I encourage you to understand that we are not the only people to inhabit this earth and accept them as they accepted me.

"As I said, they look like men, but one of the differences is their eyes. Although they can align them as one pair, their eyes have splintered into quarters that move independently on the surface of the eye. I know that sounds strange, but that way, they can see in as many directions as possible in the dark. It can be disconcerting at first when you look at them, but since most wear dark glasses in any light, you may never notice it. It is one way they have acclimated to their preferred environment, and since I grew up living and playing underground, I find that I, too, prefer the coolness of sandstone rooms and can see quite well in the dimmest light. You may use a candle, but if you are asked to shade or extinguish it, do so at once. I will give you a small flashlight as you learn the way, but you must shine it only on the ground to see where you are walking, never straight ahead. Bright lights are like daggers in their eyes.

"Since you will only need to come into the tunnels once a day to clean my rooms and change the linen, it may be weeks or months before you meet any of them underground. Your duties will be continuous but not complicated; the house must be clean, the food well prepared, and the staff organized and efficient. Remember, no one enters the tunnels but you, Ezri."

He stopped speaking for a moment, and although Ezri could not see his mouth, a smile shone from Venzel's eyes. "Did you know that Americans have a saying, 'Curiosity killed the cat?' In the Lyostian language, we have something similar, but we do not say cat. So, Ezri, as you hope to live, treat them with respect, but do not impose on them. They have little regard for outsiders and will not hesitate to isolate you if they think you are dangerous. I will not stop them."

"Isolate?"

Venzel did not answer right away. "There will be nothing left but your bones," he said.

Ezri looked at Venzel, turned his face toward the bazaar, then back at Venzel, and nodded.

Venzel continued, "The second characteristic which you probably will never see, but I do not want you to be alarmed if you should, is the haustellum. It's a kind of feeding tube in their throats. Usually, they are shy about eating around strangers, but you might see someone drinking with it. My brother, Zsiga, showed me how it works, but even he does not know why they evolved that way. The third consideration is they can send each other messages with their minds. If you see them tilting their heads, they are either talking or listening to each other. You must be polite and wait until their heads are straight and they are looking at you before you talk to them.

"Lastly, they are very protective of their locations. The colonies are kept small and far apart, so if one is found, we lose as few brothers as possible. We have well-stocked armories, and even as a child, I was taught how to use military-grade weaponry to protect the colony from thieves or intruders, but such preparation will not save us against an outside army who sees us as a threat or believes we are an aberration of God."

"Why do you say, 'save us' and 'we'? You are not one of them."

"Is that your only question?"

"Yes, Master."

"I am one of them. Zsiga is my mother's son. The fact that he is Lyostian, and I am human does not change our relationship as brothers—and because I am his brother, I am a brother to all the Lyostians—we are one."

Ezri nodded. "When do we leave?"

A sense of relief showed plainly on Venzel's face as he regarded the Ezri's acceptance. Standing up, he dropped the edge of the hood and held out his hand.

"It will be unlike any existence you have ever known, Ezri," he promised.

Venzel had been right about that. There were things, however, that Venzel did not foresee. Every year, the responsibility he carried in the colony grew heavier, taking the boyish softness from his face. As Zsiga took over the administrative duties, he relied on Venzel's knowledge of the outside world and his ability to get things done. The fair-minded and easy-going young man matured into one who shouldered much of the responsibility for the colony's provisions and its revenue. He became short-tempered, demanding perfection in all things and, because Ezri watched him carefully, neither slept nor ate much. Only with the girl had he relaxed, laughed, and his innate kindness returned. But regardless of what the future held, Ezri knew he would never regret saying yes that afternoon on the rocks. The admiration he felt then had turned to loyalty and loyalty to love, and nothing on earth—above or below it—was ever going to change the promises he had made to Venzel.

A Thousand Kisses Deep

In the darkness of the new moon, only the stars lit their path as Alazar trekked through the desert sand. His slow pace and gentle rocking soon had Destani dozing in Venzel's arms.

"Tired, my dear?" he asked softly.

"A little tired, Venzel, but a little curious, too."

"Do you want to know where we are going?"

"No. I don't care where we are going as long as we are together."

"Then what are you curious about, latif? I will try to answer all your questions."

"Destani, Venzel? My name is Kizi."

"No, karisi, you ceased being a daughter the moment I took you from your father's tent. That Kizi no longer exists. There is only my wife, who has eyes like the sea, and her name is Destani. She is my beloved." Pulling her close, he bent and kissed her cheek. "Next question."

"Only a little one. Why wouldn't you let me drink the tea Militos offered us?"

"That tea was especially made for the brides who might be worried about their wedding night. It was a calming tea so that they would not be anxious about their, um… physical obligations to their new husbands."

"But Militos told them they didn't have to worry about that until children were expected of them."

"And do you think they all believed him?"

Remembering Lalei's pallor and tears, she said, "No."

"So, for some, it might have been a welcome precaution. Once they are used to being with their husbands, they will begin to trust them."

"And you, Venzel, are you expecting children from me?"

"As Anya provides, my beautiful wife. As Anya provides."

A cool breeze swept over them, and she shivered slightly. Bringing the pack pony alongside Alazar, Venzel reached over and removed his cloak from one of the bags. Wrapping it around both of them, he said, "You will be warm now, my love. Rest, it will be several hours before we stop."

Safe in the arms of her husband, Destani slept.

Of all the things she expected when she opened her eyes again, the top of Venzel's blue and purple striped tent was not one of them. Sitting straight up, she looked around. The cushions and brazier were set on the central carpet, and parcels, boxes, and trunks were lined up against the canvas walls. Chilled in the morning air, she realized she was only wearing her chemise and quickly reclaimed the warm space next to Venzel.

Gazing at him in the semi-darkness, she knew he was the man she always expected to love. It would be enough in this life, she thought, to be the light in his eyes and the reason for his smile. Tall, strong, handsome as a sultan, Venzel's eyes were so darkly blue that sometimes she could not tell the pupil from the iris. His hair, bleached by the sun, was dark brown underneath and curled around the back of his ears.

Completely at ease, she placed her head gently on his chest and, in time to his heartbeat, began walking her fingers up his thigh. She heard his heartbeat quicken, and his much larger hand closed over hers. Pressing it slightly into his flesh, he brought her hand slowly and deliberately up the length of his body until it reached his lips. Only after kissing her palm, did he open his eyes.

Seeing his smile reflected in her eyes, a sensuality that Venzel had rarely permitted himself to feel possessed him. Yes, he wanted her to have his children, but that was not why he had brought her here, alone and away from everything he knew and loved. He wanted time to discover her without the constant interruptions and expectations that accompanied his contributions to the rhythm of colony life. They had fourteen days and fourteen nights. The full moon would come soon enough, and as his hands moved up her body, he did not plan to waste a single moment they had together. Pushing all thoughts of the duties awaiting him at the compound to the back of his mind, he turned his full attention to the woman he loved.

His fingers traced the contours of her neck until they reached the silk of her chemise. Unhurriedly, he ripped it a little at a time. After every small tear, he kissed the newly exposed flesh, then another centimeter and another until she was fairly humming with desire. As his mouth traveled slowly from her neck to her breasts, he reached for her, and at his touch, it felt as though a small bird shivered slightly against his hand.

Feeling the exultation building in her throat, Destani clenched her teeth to keep from crying out as his body covered hers.

"There is no one to hear you, latif," he whispered.

Moments later, her joy in him resounded throughout the tent; as it died away, another, deeper sound followed. Caught between a sob and a sigh, Venzel closed his eyes against his grateful tears. He knew Anya would never allow an irredeemable man this much happiness. For the first time in eight years, Venzel felt forgiven for his selfish cruelty to Bahari.

Gently holding Destani, he sang Anya's prayer of thanksgiving for letting them begin their lives together with such a revelation and her blessing.

They had not spent a night apart since the day he found her waiting for him, but it was still a miracle to Venzel when he opened his eyes in the morning to find her lying next to him. He made it a game to wake up before she did so that he could see her face when she awoke. It was magical the way her eyes transformed from distant dreams to recognition, and as he watched, love touched her eyes like sunlight on water. He never saw a sunrise afterward that did not remind him of the warmth and welcome that shone from Destani's face every morning.

Not having to be anything to anyone except a cherishing husband to her, the years fell from Venzel's shoulders. Like a boy, he chased her along the water's edge and, catching her, tumbled laughing into the cool spring-fed water. When she asked him to tell her more about his travels, he stood in the shade of the palms and acted out all the parts of his escapades. If the stories were mysterious, she was completely enthralled, and if they were comical, she rolled in the sand and her peals of laughter, lifted by the desert wind, traveled for miles and echoed among the dunes.

At sunset, they feasted on whatever Venzel caught in the net or trap, adding it to the provisions he'd brought from the house, and as the evening breezes blew over the water, he thought of new ways of loving her. One unforgettable evening, he opened a trunk and removed a handful of crimson and gold scarves. Setting up a screen, he asked her to dress however she wished for dinner.

Tying the scarves by the opposite corners to make one long ribbon, she wrapped it around her body from neck to hips. When she walked around the screen, he smiled at the challenge. After dinner, she stood in the middle of the tent, and instead of unwrapping her all at once, he patiently untied one silken knot at a time, pressing his lips against each slight indentation where the knot had pressed against her skin. When the final scarf lay across her bare shoulders, he pulled it slowly from her neck. Tying one end of it to her wrist and the other to his, Venzel led her out of the tent.

The lagoon stretched out in front of them gleaming like molten silver. Unable to swim, Destani clung to Venzel as he waded into the deeper water, the silken leash billowing on the water's surface. Knowing she could not touch the bottom or swim away, Venzel floated her in front of him and licked the drops of water from her skin. Every time she reached for him, she started to sink, and he would let her.

Bringing her back up sputtering, he whispered, "You must trust me and not move."

She knew he would do this all night until she did as he asked—or drowned. Taking a deep breath, Destani relaxed and let his hands support her. Staring at the crescent moon, she gradually lost her place in time. In delightfully slow motion, she felt the movement of Venzel's lips against her skin. His hands brushed over her and below her as she drifted, at his mercy and pleasure, in the endlessness of space.

Destani did not know how long she floated there. As Venzel sang, his caresses became more insistent, and a cresting wave of desire lifted her into the air. Carried beyond the fire of countless stars, she touched the sky with outstretched hands and cried his name to the heavens. Connected to the earth by a single strand of golden silk, she began her descent as graceful as moonlight and fell a thousand kisses deep into the limitless sea of Venzel's passion.

Suspended within two loving hearts, Destani forgot to breathe and slowly began to sink beneath the inky darkness of the lagoon. Knowing she trusted him to save her, Venzel raised her from the water and embraced her. No longer separate spirits, he realized that if he did not hold her, she would drown, and all that he was would die, too.

The day Venzel dreaded dawned early. Each night, he watched the moon wax a little more until it signaled their last day at the oasis. Tomorrow morning, the wagons would arrive to take down the tent and pack the trunks and boxes. Tomorrow night, they would sleep on a real bed under a hard roof. He wondered when they would have this chance again. If she were, as he hoped, pregnant soon, he would not let her venture so far from the compound. Although he could not bear the thought of being without her, he knew a caravan was not a safe place for children and did not think she would leave them behind to travel with him.

Listening to the small creatures stirring in the grass outside his tent, Venzel gradually understood that if everything he hoped for happened, these few weeks at the oasis, filled with wonder and the enchantment of unforgettable days when the lagoon shimmered like gold and star-splashed nights when it gleamed like silver, was the only time they would have. Never again would they be this young, this free, and this much in love.

Pulling her to him, he pressed his lips against the warmth at the nape of her neck, and the slight twinges of guilt he'd felt about leaving the colony for so long evaporated in the coolness of the early morning air.

He wanted to make the day last as long as possible and tried to wait patiently for her to awaken but gave up after a few moments. Kissing her slowly, he teased her a little so that when her eyes opened, they were already full of desire. His mouth came down hard on hers, and she welcomed him with a love that matched his own.

After breakfasting and bathing in the tent, Venzel wrapped her in his cloak and ran to the rocks above the deepest part of the lagoon. Standing on a boulder, he dropped her playfully into the water. When he dove in after her, she splashed him in revenge. They laughed like children until her eyes grew soft, and he could not resist their tender promise.

Spreading his cloak in the shade of the palms, Venzel carried her out of the water and knelt beside her. His slow glance took in every aspect of her body, from her small feet and delicate ankles to her rounded hips, curved waist, soft breasts, and graceful neck. His glance lingered on her lips, and meeting her eyes, he realized she was doing the same to him, both of them trying to capture this moment forever in memory.

Reverently, in total silence and commitment, they stared into each other's eyes and made love as though for the first and last time. Being possessed and possessing each other completely, they moved together as dancers slowly dancing to ancient music that only they could hear. For an infinitesimal moment in the scope of all eternity, an invisible veil dropped over the world, and as two heartbeats became three, they existed beyond the eye of God.

When the moment passed and the veil lifted, they looked at each other in wonderment. Standing, he reached for both of her hands, gently pulled her up against him, and kissed her mouth. As his hands followed the curves of her body, he knelt and wrapped his arms around her hips, pressing his face to her abdomen.

"We have created a new life," he said, looking up at her. "I can feel him as though he was already grown and standing beside me."

He saw a similar light in her eyes as she turned her head, suddenly aware of another presence, and nodded. "Yes, I feel him, too, Venzel. Strong and…"—suddenly her breath caught—"powerful."

He stood up and wrapped her in his cloak. Taking her hand, he admonished, "You must be very careful, my love. Take no chances with our son."

Where two hours earlier he ran with her through the brush and rocks to the water, he now led her and carefully pointed out each branch, root, or stone that might cause her to trip. He did not let go of her hand until she was safely back in the tent and resting on the cushions he gathered for her. Settling next to her with his head in her lap, he spun wonderful stories about the son he imagined so clearly standing in the dappled sunlight.

"He's going to be tall, like me, though," he said teasingly, "maybe not as handsome."

"But almost…." she urged him on.

"Almost, but he will have your eyes, my love. I simply insist on that. Of course, he'll be a natural horseman and perhaps one of the finest equestrians on the Mediterranean coast. We'll take him to Spain; you won't believe how wonderfully they ride. And he'll be smart, too. He'll go to the university in Cairo." Seeing her eyes begin to close, he whispered, "And he will be… he will be… ours, Destani. Our son."

"Our son, Venzel," she repeated softly, a small smile on her lips.

He took her in his arms and gazed down at her face. In just a few short weeks, she had become almost a miracle to him. Closing his eyes, he counted every breath until she slept.

At first, Destani thought she heard firecrackers and dreamily wondered who was setting off fireworks in the middle of the day. A moment later, Venzel was shaking her and urgently calling her name.

"Destani, wake up. Now. You must get dressed."

"Why are there firecrackers, Venzel?"

"Those are not firecrackers, Destani, they are gunshots, and you must get dressed. Now. I will help you."

Instead of helping her dress in a caftan, skirt, and shawl, Venzel handed her the long silk pants she would normally wear under her clothes and one of his shirts. Momentarily grateful her hair was short, he thought she might pass for a boy… but knew that he could not risk even that. A boy with her eyes would be as vulnerable as a woman.

In a few short moments, she watched his expression change from confidence to despair.

"What is it, Venzel? You are scaring me."

"I am scared for you, too, latif. I do not know who they are, but most caravans or honest travelers do not announce themselves with gunfire. It could be a hunting party, or it could be slavers or bandits."

"Can't we escape?"

"No, not now. There is not enough time. They are still on their horses. Alazar is fast and can outrun them, but they will see us leave and surround us before we can get clear. Perhaps they are just here to water their horses. Or if they plan to stay, we will leave quietly once they've settled down." Trying to sound calm, he added, "It is not unexpected. We've been uncommonly lucky, you know, to have the oasis to ourselves these few weeks."

Despite his reassuring words, he opened the trunk nearest the door and removed a scimitar, a knife, and a pistol. Slipping the first two under his sash, he tied the third to his ankle with a slipknot.

"What are you doing?"

"I must go out to meet them, latif. It is a matter of manners and custom. If I do not, then they will try to come in here, and I will not allow that."

"Then I will go with you," she said, getting up.

He turned on her fiercely. Putting his hand on the knife, he hissed, "No! You will not venture out of this tent, Destani, no matter what you hear. You will hide beneath the cushions and blankets and wait for my return. If you do not do as I ask, I promise I will cut your throat myself before I will let one of them touch you. If anything happens to me, slip out the back of the tent. Alazar is tied on the other side. Whisper 'ishkari' and hold on to his mane. No one will be able to catch you, and he will take you home."

Tears fell on her cheeks, and she silently shook her head.

Sharing his worst fears with her, he said, "If you do not do as I ask, my dear, they will rape and kill you, and when they find him, they will kill and eat Alazar."

Destani's eyes grew wide with horror. "They would hurt Alazar? No, that cannot be...." Swallowing her tears, she nodded. "I will do whatever you say, Venzel."

Venzel stared at her steadily and turned back to the trunk that held his clothes. Finding what he was searching for, he handed her an embroidered silk sheath.

"I thought to give this to you on a happier occasion, my love."

Unwrapping the silk, she removed the dagger from the leather-lined scabbard. Twenty-five centimeters of pure gold with a jewel-encrusted handle, the weapon was a work of art.

Destani looked from the long slender blade to Venzel's worried face. It was the most beautiful thing she had ever held in her hands, but its beauty could not disguise the dagger's lethal purpose—or why Venzel gave it to her now.

There was no trace of tears in her eyes when she bowed slightly and said, "Thank you, my husband."

Knowing she fully understood his reasons for giving her the dagger, Venzel embraced and kissed her. Reluctantly releasing her, he quickly pushed the cushions and blankets to the back wall of the tent. After making sure she was undetectable, he scanned the tent's interior, threw the few things that were obviously hers into a trunk, and closed it. Standing in the center of his tent, he said, just loud enough for her to hear, "I love you, Destani, my wife."

Muffled under layers of cloth and batting, she answered, "I love you, Venzel, my husband."

He hoped he was not hearing it for the last time.

Venzel pressed his fists against his eyes for a moment of prayer. Walking out of the tent, he stood under the striped awning, crossed his arms, and waited.

Ezri

On the morning of the fourth day after the weddings, Ezri was not surprised to see Zsiga in the tunnel corridor by Venzel's room.

"Have you received any message from Venzel?"

"No, brother of my master."

"But it is the fourth day, and he has not returned."

"He said to tell you on the fourth day that he would be back before the full moon."

Zsiga grew very still. "You told me he would be back in three days. Are you aware of the penalty for lying to me, Ezri?"

Attempting to diffuse the anger he knew he deserved, Ezri knelt at Zsiga's feet.

"Yes, I know the penalty, but I did not lie. I said he told me to tell you he would be back in three days, and I did as he instructed."

"It is deceit, Ezri, and you will be punished for it."

"As you wish, brother of my master, but I would rather be punished by you for deceit than my master for disobedience."

Zsiga sighed in defeat.

"Yes, Ezri, I know you would… and, I suppose, if I went to the stables and asked the men where he has gone, they would tell me what he told them to say, just as you did?"

Ezri was silent.

Zsiga stared at the door to Venzel's room. "If he does not wish to be found for ten days, so be it. But Ezri, if he is not back by the end of next week, you will not have to worry about being punished for disobedience. So, if there is anything else he told you to tell me… on the eve of the full moon, for example… I suggest you tell me now and try to save your head."

It was clear that Zsiga did not understand. Having his head cut off would still be more merciful than what Venzel would do to him if he was found and made to return one second before he desired. However, Venzel had not left him any further instructions.

"There are no other messages, brother of my master."

"Is there anything else…?"

"It is my most humble regret if the delay in giving you this information has caused you any worry of the heart."

"My only 'worry of the heart,' Ezri, is that I do not believe any of my servants are as loyal as you. I just hope it doesn't cost you your head one day."

"That will be as the Creator wishes.

"You are wrong, Ezri. It will be as I wish. Crows will be plucking the seeing eyes from your head the morning of the full moon if Venzel has not returned."

Ezri knew Venzel had not lied to him about his plans, but accidents happened in the desert. He watched the moon grow brighter each night, and every morning before dawn, he stood beside the paddock gate and, holding the lantern high, searched the horizon for two dark riders on a single grey horse.

Halil

Expecting the worst, Venzel waited as a group of five young men halted their horses in front of his tent. Gazing beyond them, he did not see any wagons with women or servants. All looking enough alike to be from the same clan, each man on horseback carried only a rifle, a bedroll, and two saddle bags, one he knew was full of ammunition and the other, food. It had to be a hunting party.

Waving to them, Venzel stepped from the shelter of the awning.

"Welcome," he said.

"Thank you," said the man sitting on the horse nearest to him. He was not the oldest, but neither was he the youngest rider. Darkly tanned with black hair, his sharply intelligent brown eyes took in Venzel and his weapons and narrowed when he looked at the tent.

Venzel did not miss the expression on the rider's face. "I have coffee here," he said, pointing to the pot on the fire, "and a rabbit to spit for supper. You are welcome to join me."

"No, thank you."

"Halil, yes or no?" asked one of the older men behind him.

At first, Halil did not answer but looked around and saw nothing except this man and the tent.

He turned back and, in a tribal dialect he did not believe Venzel understood, said, "Maybe, but there is something wrong here. Where are

114

his horses, wagons, companions? No one travels in the desert alone, and no one carries a tent this size on his back. Especially this tent."

"I still have some flares left, do you want me to fire it?" the older man asked, pulling a lighter from his pocket and reaching toward his saddlebag.

"Not yet. He is well armed and may not be alone. If it comes to a fight, we will have to kill him, and I don't want him dead. I want her, and there is much this man can tell us—if he is the right man. A dead man will tell us nothing."

In a single fluid motion, Halil slipped from his horse and landed on his feet, his rifle pointing downward. He bowed slightly in Venzel's direction.

"I am looking for a woman."

"Aren't we all?" replied Venzel to the general amusement of the other men in the party.

Halil ignored them. "I am looking for a very specific woman who, I was told, was hired as a servant by a man who owned a tent with blue and purple stripes. What I want to know, and we will kill you if you lie, are you that man?"

"How will you know if I lie? There are many blue and purple striped tents."

"Not as many as there were three weeks ago."

Rapidly putting together a plan, Venzel took the scimitar and knife out of his sash, laid them on the ground in front of him, and fell to his knees.

"If you intend to destroy his tent, please kill me now before my master returns, for he will kill me a hundred times before I will be allowed to die."

"Where is he?"

"He is hawking with the rest of his company."

"When will he return?"

"Tomorrow evening."

"Do you know which way he went?"

"They headed east, but they go where the birds take them."

Halil nodded. "How long have you been with him?"

"Five years."

"Were you with his last caravan?"

"I am with all of his caravans."

"Did you see any of the women?"

"It is death to go near the women, but we see them sometimes. Most are very beautiful."

"Do you remember one with soft golden hair?"

"Two or three."

"With eyes the color of the morning sky?"

"Lalei," he said quietly.

Without warning, Halil backhanded Venzel across the face. "Do not say her name, dog! Servant of a dog master! Do not even breathe her name. Never!"

Halil put his hands to his head in anger and turned his back. Venzel's face burned as he stared at the sand in front of him. He slowly moved his hand and heard the simultaneous lever action of four rifles—all aimed in his direction. His hand was only a few centimeters from his pistol, but though he might shoot Halil and one or two others, it was impossible from his position to fight them all.

For a few moments, no one moved.

"Stop."

Venzel turned and saw Destani at the tent's opening. No longer dressed in harem pants and his shirt, she looked almost ethereal wrapped in ivory gauze and silk. Held in her left hand, the dagger's point hovered above her heart. Standing behind Venzel, she put out her right hand.

"Please do not kill Ezri. It is not his fault."

The men on horseback and the one on the ground lowered their rifles. They had been searching for three weeks. Twice, they believed they had found the man who hired Lalei. Eventually, Halil was convinced that the traders were guiltless, but not before he and his clan burned the suspects' blue and purple striped tents—and all their possessions—to the ground.

It had been a long three weeks; the horses were thin, and everyone was tired, but Halil would not give up. Searching for her had become his life's work, but they would not let him go alone. Now, at an oasis in the middle of the desert, a servant and the loveliest woman they could imagine would finally answer Halil's questions.

Stunned that she knew their dialect, Halil turned around and stepped forward.

"Who are you?"

"I am Kizi. I was also hired as a servant on the last caravan."

"You may lower the dagger, Kizi. We will not harm you."

"So you say, but I have been lied to before, and as you have already struck one innocent person, the dagger will stay where it is. Even if you speak the truth, it would not be worth my life for my husband to return and find Ezri dead and the tent burned. He…," she paused and partially lowered the ivory and gold scarf so that they could see her hair, "can be cruel."

At the sight of her short hair, Halil fell to his knees and screamed, "Lalei!"

"Halil," she said softly, "La… she is not harmed. When I last saw her, she was not happy, but she was well. No one has hurt her, nor will they. Not anymore."

Looking up at her, he said, "You, you can say her name. I, I don't mind."

Destani smiled gently at him. "Lalei is fine. Not one hair on her head has been harmed."

Halil stood up and took a step toward her.

"Stop," she said, pressing the dagger into the fabric. "Please do not come any closer. If you touch me, he will kill me himself."

Halil stopped. When Destani relaxed, none of them doubted her determination. They could all see the blood staining the ivory silk above her heart.

"Why do you say that no one will hurt her *anymore*?" Halil asked. "What has happened? Where is she? I have money," he said, patting his saddlebag, "to bring her back, I just need to know where she is."

Destani's sad smile broke Halil's heart. He knew, even before she spoke the words, that Lalei was lost to him.

"We were all hired as servants, Halil, and were given the choice to remain servants or become wives. Each of us, including Lalei, willingly chose to become wives. We were not forced, and we were given three chances to change our minds. No one did. Our husbands," she said, smoothing the fine fabric with her hand, "are very generous."

Swallowing hard, Halil managed to choke out, "When?"

"How long has it been since the wedding, Ezri?"

"Fourteen days, Mistress," said Venzel.

"Hmmm," she said, stroking the jeweled handle of the dagger. "Seems longer, somehow."

Halil could not hide the hopeless anguish he felt.

Destani smiled gently at him. "I am so sorry if I have caused you pain, Halil. If you let me live and I see her again, is there a message I can give her?"

Words burned in Halil's throat. Words of undying love and devotion that he could not speak because she had three chances to stay true to him and willingly chose a different path. Looking into the second most beautiful pair of eyes he had ever seen, he said, "I will let you live, Kizi, though I am uncertain as to what kind of life you will have. For La—" he bit down hard and clenched his teeth, "her, no. I have no message for such as she."

"Thank you, Halil," she said, bringing her hands together in gratitude over the glittering hilt of the dagger. Bowing slightly, she smiled kindly at him and then at the rest of the men.

"It shall be as you wish."

Keeping the dagger poised above her heart, she put her other hand on Venzel's shoulder as Halil and his kin rode away. The youngest kept looking back at her to see if she was real or an apparition that would vanish into the air.

As the riders disappeared behind the dunes to the southwest, Venzel took the dagger from her hand, swept Destani into his arms, and carried her inside. Going back out, he picked up the weapons from the ground and closed the tent opening. Untying the revolver from his leg, he put it in his waistband. He set his rifle next to the door and returned the rest of the weapons to the ammunition box. Only then did he turn around to stare at Destani.

Venzel had decided at a very young age not to let fear rule his life and faced every challenge with intelligence and cunning. His success had, perhaps, made him over-confident, but it was a confidence earned through courage, hard work, and experience. Yet this girl, who he'd determined only a few short weeks earlier had no courage at all, stood between him and certain—and Venzel knew it was certain—death. Resolutely holding a dagger to her heart with a hand that did not shake, she saved him with a voice that was soft, clear, and unafraid.

Picking up a clean cloth and the basin of water, Venzel walked toward her.

With her eyes downcast and hands folded in her lap, Destani waited for the storm she knew was coming. She had disobeyed him again. She knew instinctively he would not harm her, but his disapproval hurt most of all. She couldn't even apologize. Where would she start? She'd done everything he told her not to do. Hearing his footsteps coming nearer, she trembled. Standing in front of five men with guns was easier than being with Venzel when he was displeased. Vowing never to disobey him again, her eyes filled with tears as she stared at the carpet.

"Please, Venzel," she whispered. "Please don't be angry, I'm so sorry."

Kneeling beside her, he moved the bloodied fabric away from her skin and pressed the dampened cloth lightly on the small cut. Satisfied it would heal in a day or two, he leaned over and kissed the wound. Taking her hands from her lap, Venzel kissed both of her palms and placed them on his heart. He lifted her face to his and said, "Thank you, latif Destani, for saving us all."

"But Venzel...."

"My darling wife, are you going to argue with me our entire lives?"

She bit her lip. "No, Venzel."

Laughing softly, he said, "Now, why don't I believe you?"

Hearing the laughter in his voice, she asked, "You forgive me?"

"Yes, love, this time, but only because your disobedience saved our lives and Alazar. It could have so easily gone the other way."

She gently touched the fading red mark on his cheek. "I know how hard it was for you to protect us. I heard what he said, and I was afraid that if it came to a fight, you might die. I cannot live without you, Venzel, and I will not raise your son without you."

"You won't have to, my love. We will pack up the weapons and a few other things to take with us and leave after sunset. The pony and everything else will be brought back with the wagons. We will intercept our men on their way here, warn them, and supply them with extra weapons in case Halil decides to return."

"He won't be back, Venzel," she murmured.

"Why do you say that?"

"I saw it in his eyes. She broke his heart. He hates *her* now, not you."

"Perhaps, but I will not endanger your life again." Venzel looked down at the small hands against his heart. "Tell me, latif, how did you do that? Regardless of what you called yourself, 'Kizi' could never have faced those men today, and despite what you say about being unable to live without me, that still does not explain where you found the courage to leave the tent."

"I told you, Venzel. Your son is very powerful." With those words, she took his hand and placed it under her skirt. Sliding into his arms, she said, "He is much like his father that way."

Brushing his hand lightly over her body, Venzel knew he owed her his life, and he held her until the sun was low in the sky and then, because she was sleeping, held her a little longer.

At dusk, Venzel eased away to feed Alazar, promising the horse that he would sleep in his own stall the next day. Adding all the weapons to one of the larger saddlebags, he put water and food in the other. He cleaned her dagger, returned it to the sheath, and hid it beneath his tunic. When she awakened, he helped her dress as he had that morning, his shirt hanging long over her arms, her legs wrapped in silk to keep her warm. He would take no chances that a chill carried on the night air might harm her.

Raising himself into Alazar's saddle, Venzel reached down and pulled Destani in front of him. Remembering her vow, she did not argue but settled into his embrace as he took the reins and turned Alazar toward the compound. When they met the men and wagons from the compound, she did not speak as Venzel warned them and handed them his weapons but pulled her veil over her head and blended into the shadows near his heart.

As the men continued to the oasis, he brushed her veil aside and could not look away from her face in the moonlight. He thought her beautiful before, but nothing compared to the serene beauty of his wife safe in his arms with the gift of his son in her eyes. All the way back, they talked, whispered, and laughed. Affectionately punctuating the pauses in their conversation, her hand caressed his chest or thighs, and when she leaned her head against his shoulder, he kissed her cheek, his free hand resting protectively in her lap.

Homecoming

On what very well could have been his last day on earth, Ezri's loyalty was rewarded. Lifting the lantern twice to signal he was there, he opened the gate and then ran to the porch to await their arrival. Venzel, stopping long enough to wrap Destani in his cloak, carefully set her down next to Ezri before turning Alazar toward the stables.

Destani's eyes followed Venzel until he reached the paddock. Looking up at Ezri, she smiled.

"I suspect I should get comfortable; he hasn't seen them for two weeks."

"Would you like to go inside and wait for him, Mistress?"

"No, Ezri," she said, "he will expect to find me here."

He brought her a small divan to rest upon, as well as fruit, warm bread, and honey. When she reached for the tray, the cloak fell away, and he stared at her clothes. Seeing the look of consternation on his face, she laughed.

"Yes, I know, but the night air was cold, so he covered me from head to fingers to toes."

Ezri smiled at the change in her. In the short time they had been away, she had transformed from a bewildered girl into a gentle wife. He wondered what changes the last several days had made in Venzel and hoped they were as good. When Venzel sprinted from the stables to the porch less than fifteen minutes later, the expression on his face when he saw Destani waiting for him left no doubt in Ezri's mind that these two weeks had transformed Venzel as well.

After joining her for a few minutes, Venzel picked her up and looked at him.

"Is everything ready?"

"It is as you wished, Master."

"Thank you. When you see Zsiga, tell him I will meet with him at noon."

Pleased to be able to give Zsiga such welcome news himself, Ezri smiled.

"Yes, Master," he said.

Trying to keep the grin off his face, Venzel began climbing up the stairs instead of down.

"Where are we going, Venzel?"

"You'll see," he said with a mysterious glint in his eyes.

The door to the upstairs corner room was ajar, and he nudged it open with his foot.

Thin golden rays cutting through the shuttered windows illuminated the room. Twice as large as Venzel's underground chamber, it was complete with English-style furnishings, including a small table and chairs in front of a broad fireplace. Venzel's chest was at the foot of the bed, and in the shaded corner, a rocking chair and cradle waited.

Destani's eyes sparkled with happy tears. "Oh, how did you know?"

"I didn't know, karisi, but I hoped."

Looking from his face to the room, she put her arms around his neck and whispered, "Thank you, Venzel, I've never been happier."

Setting her down gently, he took her hand.

"Well," he said, "there is a little more to show you."

With a small flourish, Venzel opened a door that Destani thought was a closet, and she was right, but the room also contained a sink, a bathing tub with faucets, and a mirror.

She clapped her hands. "Ezri will be so happy he doesn't have to bring me water all the time."

Exploring the room with Venzel was another adventure. He showed her the drawers where her clothes were kept, the armoire that held his clothes, and a small dresser that not only held her wedding jewelry but silver bracelets for her wrists and cascading silver and gold earrings. Opening one small hand-carved box, she found a silver and turquoise anklet.

Handing it to him, she looked up through her lashes and said shyly, "Can you put this on me? I'm not sure I can fasten the clasp."

"I'm not sure I can put it on over all this fabric."

"Um, hum."

Laughing and setting her on the bed, it took nearly all morning before he was able to fasten the clasp on her anklet. Drowsing among the cushions, she smiled at him as he started to dress.

"I am going to wash up and see Zsiga as I promised. Stay here and rest until I get back. If you need anything, ask Ezri."

"Where is he?"

"Where he will be for the rest of your life, Destani—outside the door protecting you when I cannot."

Recalling the events of the day before, she grasped the edge of his pillow and pulled it toward her. Just soft enough for him to hear, she murmured, "I love you, Venzel."

Zsiga was not alone when Venzel met him in the underground dining hall at noon. Rauf was with him, and neither was smiling.

Venzel, on the other hand, was smiling enough for all three of them. Walking up to Zsiga, he gave him a quick embrace, and when he shook Rauf's hand, they looked at him as if expecting him to sprout wings and fly.

Quickly recovering his composure, Rauf began, "We've missed you, Venzel. The little game you played with your servant was not appreciated and nearly got him killed for his insolence."

"I've missed you, too, my brothers, and grateful, more than I can say, that Ezri is not harmed." Deciding to change the subject, he asked, "How are your wives?"

Rauf's expression did not change, but Zsiga smiled softly. "They are well. Some of their temperatures are beginning to peak, which is why," his smile suddenly disappearing, "we were so concerned about your absence."

"I knew you would not need me before the full moon, and I wished to take Destani away for a while and have her to myself. I felt it was necessary so that she would come to rely on me and obey me in all things."

"And…?" asked Rauf.

"And it worked so well she saved my life yesterday."

Zsiga gasped. "What?"

Telling the story almost as it really happened, Venzel's point was that instead of taking Alazar and leaving him to die alone, Destani held a dagger to her heart until the men rode away.

"She has courage," said Rauf.

"Yes," answered Venzel, "and she is precious to me." Thinking of her sleeping so many floors above them, he wanted to finish this conversation quickly and return to her.

He looked at the two men sitting at the table.

"I am sorry for leaving without telling you where I was going or, truthfully, how long I would be gone. I wanted to be alone with her without any distractions. However, my commitment to our continued success has not diminished, so please, my brothers, tell me you forgive my prolonged absence and let me know how I can best serve our colony."

Rauf smiled indulgently at Venzel. "No harm done, Venzel, but you were alone, and that is always dangerous. Next time, take a few men with you."

"No, Rauf, I do not foresee there will ever be a 'next time.' We are here, and here is where we will stay as long as our presence benefits the colony."

Zsiga impulsively reached across the table and grabbed Venzel's arm. "Do you mean that, Venzel? Really? I'm not going to wake some morning and find you gone where I cannot reach you?"

Venzel wondered at the pain in his arm. He looked at Zsiga and saw a glimmer of panic in his eyes. Smiling gently, he said, "Yes, Zsiga, my brother, I mean it. It has never been my desire to leave the colony, and I hope to stay here all my life."

Zsiga released Venzel's arm. "Thank you, my brother."

He smiled reassuringly at Zsiga. Taking a deep breath, he turned to Rauf.

"Will I be visiting anyone this evening?"

"No, but Tatiana tomorrow night, and then we expect it to escalate from there."

Hoping to hide his reluctance, he thought of his sweet wife and smiled at them.

"Thank you, my brothers, for your kind patience with me."

He stood to leave, but Rauf stopped him.

"Venzel, I realize you are married now, and that entails certain marital responsibilities, but I—"

"You need not finish that sentence, Rauf. Please be assured that the honor and comfort of the colony's wives will always be my first concern of the day—and night."

Zsiga followed Venzel upstairs. When they came to the landing that would take him aboveground, Zsiga stopped and signed to him.

Who were the men looking for?

Venzel had decided not to burden Zsiga with the truth, but there was something in his expression that made him believe Zsiga already knew.

"Lalei."

"Someone called 'Halil,' I suppose."

Venzel felt the blood rush to his face at the sound of the name but kept his expression neutral.

"Yes, Zsiga, I did not know. She, like the others, came willingly. How did you find out?"

"She talks in her sleep and sometimes cries. She told Senkali she was homesick, and I believed that, but she said his name the other night when I was… well… anyway, now it makes sense."

Zsiga looked in the direction of the harem and shook his head. "I cannot bear to think how close I came to losing you for the sake of a faithless woman. Please tell your wife that I am her brother, too."

"Thank you, Zsiga. I appreciate that more than you know."

Tatiana

At the time he reviewed Rauf's schedule, Venzel did not realize the difficulty of visiting his brothers' wives. In the past, he had found traits in each woman that he appreciated and, if he could not love each of them fully, loved the qualities he admired. Since they were powerless to resist him, he pretended that they, too, found things about him they could love. This method worked well because, since he did not love any one of them, he was free to love them all.

It was different now.

The only woman he wanted was Destani. Entering each chamber that week, he placed one of her scarves next to his brother's wife as he made love to her. Breathing in Destani's scent made him feel more willing and less guilty for taking this intimacy away from her. At the end of each visitation, he went to the bathing room and scrubbed his entire body before returning to her.

He had to.

After leaving Tatiana's chamber that night, Venzel, eager to join his own wife, went straight to their room, unknowingly carrying traces of Tatiana's perfume. Although Destani did not say anything, her eyes filled with tears when he made love to her. As soon as she could, she got out of bed and began opening the windows.

When he asked her what was wrong, she refused to look at him and whispered, "Tatiana."

Cursing himself for being an insensitive oaf, he left that moment to wash and vowed never to do that to her again. When he came back to their room, he noticed her hair was wet and realized that she had bathed as well. The bed had been remade with fresh linens, and the used sheets and cushion covers were outside on the balcony.

He would not make that mistake twice.

He tried to pull her close to him, promising, "Never again, latif. Never again."

Resisting his embrace, she asked, "Were you... were you...?" Dreading his response, her voice broke, and she could not say the words.

"It isn't what you think, Destani. My responsibilities to my brothers' wives do not end with their marriage. Because I am familiar with village life, sometimes I am asked to, um, mediate certain differences. It is our hope that Tatiana will eventually enjoy being married to Rasim, as Aylala is but, in the meantime, she needed to learn some patience."

Destani sat up and looked at him. "Did you... did you hurt her?"

"Have I ever hurt you?"

"Not until tonight, but that isn't what I meant."

"I treat all my brothers' wives with the same consideration as I treat you. So, no, I did not raise my hand to her, Destani, if that is what you are asking. A wife has, as you know, inescapable duties to her husband. We just interacted for a few minutes, and if she was hurt, it was as little as possible. When I left, both she and Rasim were smiling."

It was the truth, no matter how obliquely put.

Destani shivered and moved closer to Venzel. Looking up at him with all the trust in the world shining from her eyes, she said, "I believe you, Venzel."

"I am truly sorry for hurting your feelings, love," he whispered. "I have many responsibilities here, and it will take a while to acquaint you with all of them. But my first responsibility is to you, and I beg you to forgive me. Say you forgive me, Destani."

"I will forgive you anything, Venzel, as long as you never stop loving me."

"Latif Destani, it is impossible to stop loving you. You are my wife, my heart—"

She kissed him before he could finish, and his hands moved slowly from her shoulders to the curves below her waist. He knew she did not completely understand why she was forgiving him, but it was what he needed to hear. His lips never left her skin until, sighing and exhausted, they fell asleep in each other's arms.

Nineteen

There was something in Rauf's eyes as he scanned and rescanned the physicians' report that Zsiga did not like. Pale like all Lyostians, Rauf was ashen. The hand reaching toward the chair for support trembled.

"Rauf, what is it? What's wrong? Are colony's wives not pregnant?"

Pulling the chair out and sitting down, the paper fluttered from Rauf's hands onto the conference table as he covered his eyes.

"Yes. They are pregnant. All of them."

"Was something wrong with the DNA serum?"

"No."

"Then what is it?"

Taking one hand away from his face, Rauf pushed the report in Zsiga's direction.

"The medical technicians saw all of the colony's wives, Zsiga," he repeated. "All *nineteen* of them."

"Nineteen?"

"Yes."

"Oh, no." Zsiga became as pale as Rauf. "Destani."

"Yes."

"How, why?"

"She must have been visiting the harem, drank the tea, and was taken with the rest."

Zsiga's eyes grew wide with fear. "He will hate us. He will hate us!" Dropping to his knees, Zsiga prayed for guidance. How was he going to tell Venzel that they had taken his son and killed his dreams? It was nearly a full minute before Zsiga realized the full impact of what had happened. Raising his head, he sought Rauf's eyes.

"Yes," the older man said sadly. "Statistically, he has lost her as well."

Thinking of Venzel's pain at losing both Destani and their son, a sob caught in Zsiga's throat. Lyostians rarely cried. They were not human enough to sympathize and, because they moved together as one, did not understand the concept of personal regret. Death, they accepted as inevitable. Banishment was their only real fear—the unrelenting pain of being alone—and that was the fear Zsiga felt for Venzel.

Rauf saw the torment in Zsiga's eyes and shared it, but not for the same reason. Zsiga's litany of "he will hate us" echoed in Rauf's ears as "he will leave us." Venzel's loss to the collective would be immeasurable. He pressed his still trembling hands to his eyes.

"Zsiga, have you given any thought to what would happen to the colony if Venzel left? Besides your own sorrow and loss, Venzel is, on many levels, irreplaceable. I have always known it was a mistake, and this is precisely why our mandate forbids dependence on humans."

Hearing Venzel referred to as human momentarily shook Zsiga from his grief.

"Venzel is our brother and has been, Rauf, since long before you arrived, and we are not separate from him. He has always cared for, provided for, and protected the brothers of our colony; we are his family. Yes, he exists outside the collective, but he is like the pearl in our oyster, covered with so many layers of Lyostian culture that the only difference is his speck of individual consciousness. Regardless of what happens, I do not believe he will leave us. Even—" Zsiga's voice stopped, and he covered his eyes.

"Even what?"

"Even if he does not love us anymore."

"We will wait a couple of weeks before we say anything," advised the doctor. "She may naturally miscarry; it happens even with fully human embryos."

Zsiga looked up. "And if she doesn't?"

"We will have no choice, Zsiga. We must tell him the truth. Anya, have mercy."

Rauf knelt on the floor next to Zsiga. Together, they prayed for guidance and divine intervention that never appeared.

Two weeks later, Rauf met Zsiga in the tunnels. "We must tell him. If we do not and something happens that such knowledge could prevent, it will be worse, for he will blame us."

"He will already blame us."

"No. This was not our fault. It is who we are, and, as you said, he accepts that. It's just horrible, tragic timing. The medical technicians did not know who she was, and we were not there to stop them." Rauf waited a moment. "Do you want me to tell him?"

"No, I will tell him."

"Do you want anyone with you? In case, well, you know… he becomes violent."

"No. I do not want anyone with me, and you are mistaken. Venzel would never hurt me."

"As you wish, but call if you sense any danger. There are several of us in the tunnels today. We could help you."

Zsiga had just about enough "help" from his brothers lately. He needed to talk to Venzel alone. His relationship with Venzel was more than Rauf understood. They were real brothers, a link shared between very few Lyostians. Zsiga loved his Lyostian brothers, but none of them suspected he would trade all of their lives not to break Venzel's heart. He knew he was the only one who could control Venzel, and even he couldn't guarantee Rauf's safety. If Venzel became violent, he didn't want any witnesses. An attack on one was an attack on all, and they would kill him. Zsiga was quite sure there was nothing Venzel could do to him that would be worse than helplessly watching his beloved brother being torn to pieces.

"Thank you, Rauf, I will be fine. Venzel won't be fine… ever again."

"Maybe she will recover. Some women do, you know."

"Perhaps, but her children are lost to him forever."

A moment later, they heard his hurried footsteps in the hall.

"Did you expect him?"

"No, but since he's here, I'll tell him now. Close the door behind you when you leave, Rauf."

Venzel rushed past Rauf into the underground conference room. Almost running, he came around the table and embraced Zsiga like he had the day he returned from the oasis.

"Guess what, Zsiga?"

"What, Venzi?"

"You are going to be an uncle."

Zsiga smiled. "You have made me an uncle many times, Venzi."

"No, no, a real uncle! Destani's pregnant. I knew it; I just knew it! I tell you, Zsiga, I've already seen him. Tall, he looks like me, but he has her eyes." Suddenly, Venzel had the feeling he was talking to himself. Zsiga's smile had disappeared, and Venzel sensed something was wrong, very wrong.

"Don't worry, Zsiga, we aren't planning to go anywhere. I think this would be a great place to raise him. He can help me with the horses. Unless, of course, the colony doesn't want us to stay." He looked at his brother closely. "Is that it, Zsiga, our brothers want us to leave?"

"No, never, Venzel," Zsiga smiled weakly, "never that."

"Then what is the matter?"

"I already knew, Venzel."

"Knew what?"

"That Destani is pregnant."

"But how could you know? She's only a couple of days…."

Venzel's words died away in the silence of the room. There was only one way Zsiga could know of Destani's pregnancy, and that was if someone else told him. The only one who could possibly know would be Rauf, and he would only know if…. Feeling the full impact of his brothers' betrayal, the volcano Rauf had feared since the wedding exploded.

"No!" he roared. "How could you do this?"

The chairs nearest to Venzel flew against the walls as he paced in front of Zsiga. "I don't understand. It was a promise! I have done everything you—and everyone here—has asked of me. *Everything*. You could not allow me this happiness? Why? I have given you my life, and she is all I've ever asked for in return. You have no idea what you have done, do you? You've taken the most precious thing in my life from me, Zsiga. You've taken *my wife*."

Venzel did not want to hurt Zsiga, but his anger was slipping out of control. He wanted to give his brother a chance to explain before committing an act that would end in both their deaths. Venzel grabbed the last chair and, instead of crashing it against the wall, pressed it into the ground with all his strength.

Zsiga had never experienced the full force of Venzel's anger, and although the unpredictability of where it might lead frightened him, he refused to back down or call anyone.

"We did not know, Venzel, the procedure is not performed by us. The team of specialists arrives when we confirm the pregnancies. The women in the harem are sedated, a sonogram locates the embryo, and the serum is injected into the developing cells. It sounds simple, but at such an early stage, the embryo is infinitesimal, so the technique is very precise. They won't even allow Rauf to assist. No one who knew Destani was there to stop them."

"Then stop it now," he demanded. "Take it out of her."

Zsiga struggled to keep the horror from his face. "Who does that benefit? Even this early, taking it from her is risky. We lose a brother—you lose a son and could lose your wife. No, Venzel, we will not do that."

"Then I'll take her to a hospital. They can help her… abort…."

Unable to keep his face neutral any longer, Zsiga's expression of total panic subdued even Venzel's anger.

"Please stop. You mustn't ever say that out loud. No, Venzel. If they thought you would actually do such a thing, they would kill you both. And I, I don't think I would do that well without you." Zsiga continued in their sign language: *Please, brother, don't make such plans or ever say such words. We have ears everywhere, and you will be stopped. You will never be allowed to expose us. I… I won't be able to stop them, and if I try, they will banish me… so I will be dead, too, either way.*

Venzel knew Zsiga was right. He had participated in some defensive tactics to protect the colony's identity, and most of them resulted in either human or Lyostian deaths. He knew they wouldn't want to kill him, but they would. Venzel did not want to die, but more than that, he did not want to be the certain cause of Destani's death or Zsiga's. He loved them too much.

Zsiga watched the look of surrender come over Venzel's face and wanted to give him some good news—at least Zsiga thought it was good news.

"Venzel, there are no words to express how much I regret that this happened. If it gives you any comfort at all, I want to tell you that this is a very special generation. The collective only hinted at it before, but the report confirms our hopes. Venzi, your son will be of the Tuzurias hierarchy! You know what that means? He will be a leader within his generation."

He put his hand on Venzel's shoulder.

"He will change the world."

In a voice from the grave, Venzel asked, "And my world, Zsiga? What becomes of that?"

"Keep as much of it as you can. Take every care with her. Don't let her walk around too much or risk stumbling or falling. An injury could tear the membrane surrounding the baby; if that does not kill her outright, any leakage could affect her memory."

"Her memory?"

"Yes, it doesn't happen often," he sighed, "but it happens." With the shared pain of loss in his eyes, Zsiga signed to him. *After the baby, take her far away from here. Find another world.*

Remembering his promise to Anya, goddess mother of all Lyostians, that he would do anything if he could have her, Venzel nodded.

Surrendering his son was Anya's price.

There was something unnaturally quiet about Venzel as he entered their balcony rooms. He knew Zsiga would not lie to him, but perhaps he was mistaken. Perhaps it did not happen as he said, or perhaps it had not happened at all.

Destani looked up at him with a smile that quickly faded when she saw his expression.

"Destani, did you go to the harem about three weeks ago without Ezri?"

When he saw the blush on her cheeks, he knew everything Zsiga said was true.

"Yes, Venzel. Senkali came up and said Lalei was ill and asked for me. I had just asked Ezri to take some apples to the stables, so I went to the harem with Senkali to see her."

"Was she ill?"

"Not so much ill as distraught. Apparently, um, Zsiga expects children. Senkali said she had been crying for three days and refused to eat anything, and she thought I could help."

Venzel's face was a mask. It all came back to him. It was because of who he was and his responsibilities to the colony that the guilt of this tragedy lay at his feet. Powerless, he regarded her with a half-smile.

"And my dear, did you help?"

Destani did not understand what was wrong. Venzel didn't seem angry, but she could not know that he was past anger. He was standing on the narrow edge of hope between resignation and despair.

She answered him quickly, "Yes, I think so. The servants brought food and drink, and although I didn't get her to eat much, she did eat something and drank some tea."

"And you, my wife, after everything I've asked you not to do, did you eat the food and drink the tea as well?"

She swallowed hard. "Yes, Venzel, I was trying to… to set an example." Her eyes filled with tears. "My love, tell me what I have done. Truly, my husband, you are frightening me."

When he didn't answer, she said in a calm voice, "Punish me if you must, Venzel, but please don't hurt the baby."

He looked into her unclouded turquoise eyes and wondered how long he would be allowed that pleasure before she, too, was taken from him forever.

Turning toward the door, he laughed a little as he said, "I would ask you not to leave the room, Destani, but I am quite sure you will do whatever pleases you, regardless of anything I say."

"Venzel?" The word caught in her throat, and if he heard it, he didn't look back.

A few minutes later, the thunder of horse hooves echoed across the courtyard, and she ran to the balcony in time to see Venzel on Alazar racing across the desert. Shadowed by the burning sun setting behind them, they appeared as a centaur in silhouette.

At a loss to understand, she walked back into the room and opened the door to find Ezri standing there, staring straight ahead with tears running down his face.

"Ezri?"

Using his sleeve, Ezri quickly brushed the tears away. "Yes, Mistress?"

"Is someone hurt or dead?"

"No, Mistress."

"Then why are you crying?"

"I am not crying, Mistress. Some sand blew into my eyes."

"I would like to speak to Zsiga. If not in here, then somewhere appropriate, please. As soon as possible."

"Yes, Mistress," he answered without moving.

"Ezri, aren't you going to get him?"

"No, Mistress, someone will be along the hall in a few minutes, and I will send him."

"Thank you, Ezri," she said, quietly closing the door.

When she heard a small tap at the door, she found Rauf standing in the hall next to Ezri.

Glancing over his shoulder, he said, "You may go Ezri."

Ezri did not move.

"Apparently, Rauf, I am destined never to be alone again."

"That is not always a bad thing. I'm sorry Zsiga could not join you; perhaps I can help."

"Do you know why Venzel is acting so strangely this evening?"

"I think he is worried about your health, my sister. Having babies in the desert is dangerous."

"But you are a doctor, Rauf, and you are here. How dangerous can it be?"

"Dangerous enough to concern a caring husband."

"What can I do?"

"You must not give him any reason to worry about you. Stay in here, stay calm, and take no, and I mean *no*, chances with your health. That means no stairs, no riding, and as little walking as possible. Let Venzel and Ezri take care of you for a while."

"If I do all those things, Rauf," she said, twisting her hands and staring at the desert, "do you think he will forgive me for disobeying him and maybe, one day, love me again?"

"He already loves you more than his own life, Destani. I do not think he could love you any more than that. But, as I am sure you already know,

Venzel is a man who does not tolerate disobedience in anyone, especially someone he trusts. You must be patient. Be kind to him, and never disobey him again."

Rauf motioned her toward the chair, and when she was settled, he lifted a light blanket from the bed and covered her.

He turned slowly in the doorway.

"One more thing, Destani. When your child is born...."

"Yes, Rauf."

"Love him."

"Of course, I'll love him, Rauf," she said, smiling at him as if she couldn't believe she would feel any other way.

"Yes, well, have Ezri send someone for me if you begin to feel unwell. The first two to three months can be, um, uncomfortable."

"Thank you, Rauf."

"Thank you, Destani, wife of my brother."

Venzel wished he could ride Alazar to the ends of the earth. Perhaps if they kept running, he could escape the pain, recrimination, and guilt that were eating him alive. The pain of losing the son he imagined so clearly only a few weeks earlier cut him to the heart, but the pain of losing her was more than he could bear thinking of. How would he endure it if it truly happened?

It was his fault. He should never have left her alone, not even for those few hours. He would have killed Ezri outright, but he saw in Ezri's face that death would be a mercy and decided to let him live in torment with his shame.

As the distance between Venzel and the compound grew, he worked through the endless self-reproach for leaving her alone. Then Lalei's face rose up before him, and he felt a stab of raw guilt such as he had not known since Bahari.

Lalei was his own brother's wife, and he remembered how she whimpered in her sleep when he first came into the room. He intended to treat her as he treated all the women of the colony: with respect, gentleness, and affection, but he could not do it. Looking at Lalei, Venzel once again felt the sting of Halil's hand on his face, the helplessness of kneeling in the sand while everything he loved was minutes from being destroyed, and, finally, the silent terror of watching Destani die by her own hand before his eyes.

He had known the encounter with Lalei was not going to end well and that he should leave her. Zsiga would have understood… he would try again during the next full moon when, maybe, he didn't hate her so much. But he had never failed to accomplish the objective on time. Needing to clear his head of resentment, Venzel walked around Lalei's bed, pulling the coverlet down a little more, trying to tease himself into wanting her, but for the first time in eight years, all he wanted to do was walk away.

It was not possible. Even if he left, Venzel knew he would eventually have to return to her. Trying to set aside his loathing, he circled her one more time, removing the coverlet altogether. Her clothes were still loosely draped about her because Zsiga, reluctant to leave her, had misjudged the time. Thinking about his brother enjoying what he could from her body, Venzel began to believe that he might be able to enjoy the rest.

Focusing on Zsiga's pleasure more than his own, Venzel brushed the back of his fingers over her breasts and the concave of her stomach. Barely touching her, he started again, beginning a little higher, at the base of her neck, and finishing a little lower; again, higher, brushing her ear, his hand adding a gentle pressure as it traveled the length of her body. Her body began moving with his hand, and, reclining next to her, Venzel inserted the capsule. Closing his eyes and calling her Delara, he caressed her until her breathing came in short gasps, and she began to move against him. His eyes still closed, he began to make love to her as he did all the young wives, gently, tenderly, carefully.

Over the years, the colony's wives had murmured many things in Venzel's ear. Some had whispered instructions—to move faster or slower—and occasionally, they murmured the name of one of his brothers, as Senkali had two nights before. Usually, their words made him smile, but Lalei did not know what she did when she turned her head toward him and whispered, "I love you, Halil."

His illusion destroyed, all the tenderness he felt for her was replaced by a sudden rush of revulsion that completely took over his mind and body. Only years of practicing restraint kept him from killing her. He watched as she bit her lip, and when she gasped in pain, he imitated Halil's dialect and whispered in her ear, "Oh Lalei, I love you, too."

Never wanting to see her again, Venzel quickly finished.

Hesitating only long enough for his convulsions to cease, he left her and slipped on his cloak. She pulled her knees to her chest and turned away from him, hiccupping softly as she cried in her sleep. Venzel tried to pity her, but he could not. His hatred was still too fresh. The only satisfaction he felt when he left her that night was the knowledge that the love Halil had tried to take from him, he had taken from Halil.

When Zsiga met him on the stairs the next day, he signed to him one word. *Why?*

I am sorry, my brother, he answered, *she called me Halil*. Zsiga watched Venzel's expression when he signed the name, as well as the signs he made afterward.

Zsiga nodded. He knew then that they were lucky she was still alive. He cared for both of his wives. However, despite Senkali's obvious affection, Lalei was sweeter, but since Venzel's visit, each time he touched her, she trembled and would not stop crying.

Now, alone with Alazar, it seemed to Venzel that Halil had reached his hand across the desert and taken it all back. His son was lost to him—the collective would take him and make what they would of him—and his wife…. Venzel suddenly realized that Halil had not taken Destani. His beautiful karisi still belonged to him and loved him with her soft, gentle ways, and was waiting for him to return to her, to hold her, to love her back. Halil would go to his grave wanting that from Lalei.

He turned Alazar around. Whispering *ishkari* in his ear, the horse began loping toward home.

Taking the stairs two at a time, Ezri thought he saw a glimmer of hope in Venzel's eyes and stood aside as he walked into the room. Before the door slammed shut, Ezri watched Venzel gather Destani into his arms and kiss her.

All Venzel had to do was keep her alive.

When Venzel wasn't managing the compound for the colony, he was by her side every moment. He would barely let her walk two steps on the level floor of their room, and she thrived under his watchful attention. He had stopped making love to her for fear of jostling the embryo, but he held her, sang to her, bathed her, and did all that he could to keep her safe.

Destani found joy in her pregnancy, and her beautiful eyes fairly danced when she talked of the baby, but when Venzel gently changed the subject, she wondered why his enthusiasm did not match hers. Voicing her concern, he held her close and said that it was just her imagination, but Destani knew she was not imagining his increasing silence and anxiety as her pregnancy moved into its final and most dangerous phase.

Daybreak

No one else would have noticed it so quickly, but as he paid attention to little else, Venzel immediately became concerned the morning Destani began arranging her breakfast according to color.

"Are you going to eat it or play with it?" he asked gently.

"Eat what?"

"Eat your breakfast," Venzel said, pointing to the groups of grapes, flatbread with honey, and olives piled in different areas of her plate.

"This is food?" she asked, picking up a grape. Regarding it like she had never eaten one before, she put it into her mouth.

"Hmm, sweet," she said and picked up another.

As he stared, she broke off a small piece of the bread and looked up at him expectantly. "Venzel, is this food, too?"

"Yes, my love," he said, backing toward the door. Turning quickly, he opened it and whispered urgently to Ezri.

"Go get Rauf and Zsiga. Now. Tell them they must come at once. Tell them,"—his voice broke—"the worst has happened."

Venzel walked back to the bed and removed her breakfast tray. Knowing it could be for the last time, he gathered her up in his arms.

"I love you, Destani, latif karisi."

Sensing the seriousness of the moment, Destani placed her hands on either side of his face and gazed into his eyes.

"I love you, Venzel, my husband." She kissed him and rested her head on his shoulder. "It's the baby, isn't it?"

Unable to speak, he nodded his head.

"It will be all right, Venzel… and… in a little while, you will have both of us to love."

His only response was to clasp her tightly to him. Even when Rauf came in and slipped a thin needle into the top of her hand, and she was unaware of Venzel's embrace, it took all Zsiga's persuasion and two additional brothers to pry her from his arms.

Surrendering his wife to Rauf's care, Venzel stood aside as his brothers carried Destani downstairs on a stretcher. Dragging his eyes from the doorway, he looked at Zsiga.

"What now?"

Even with his hands cupped around the edges of his glasses to block out as much of the morning light as possible, Zsiga was clearly in pain. He wished he could follow Rauf, but he would not leave Venzel.

"We have summoned the two closest obstetricians… They are on their way."

"How long?"

"Only a couple of hours."

"Why are you waiting that long? Can't Rauf operate?"

"Rauf does not have the training for this kind of surgery. This is early, Venzel. They were not scheduled to attend our wives for two more weeks."

"But every minute… Zsiga, you know what every minute means."

"It means that maybe she won't die, Venzel. Something I cannot promise you if we have to depend on Rauf's limited surgical experience and training. Obstetric surgery is its own area of expertise. So much can go wrong."

"Can I see her?"

"She will not know you."

"Zsiga." His voice was hard. "Again, my brother, can I see her?"

"Yes, of course." Thinking it could not be any more painful for Venzel, and a lot less painful for him, Zsiga took Venzel down to the spotless white room on the third underground level.

Venzel was impressed at the advanced technology evident in the operating room compared to the rest of the buildings in the compound, but then he realized that this room was the main reason for their colony's existence. Unlike the other tunnel chambers of decorated sandstone and clay, this room was fully tiled with large, marbled slabs, and the ceiling was paneled so no speck of errant dust or falling grain of sand would distract the surgeons or infect the mothers. The hard surfaces and whiteness of the room allowed a single candle to illuminate every corner.

On the table, looking slight and pale, Destani's hands were crossed above the white sheet folded below her breasts. If not for the steady rise and fall of those small hands, he would have thought her already dead. He found a stool under the stainless-steel counter that encircled the room and pulled it next to the bed. Picking up one of her hands, he pressed it to his forehead and prayed.

Zsiga sat on the floor by the door and prayed, too. Unknown to both of them, Ezri had followed them downstairs and knelt in the corridor, offering up his own prayers. Zsiga began singing Anya's song of protection, and Venzel slowly became aware of the multitude of voices joining Zsiga's echoing throughout the tunnels. Pressing her hand to his lips, he whispered the words.

He had never felt so powerless. Like sand running through his fingers, minutes became hours as pieces of Destani's memory slowly slipped away.

The specialists arrived sooner than Zsiga expected. Rushing over to her, they telepathically told everyone to leave the operating room. Venzel moved away from the bed but, unable to hear their thoughts, stood at the doorway. Assuming everyone had left the room, one of the doctors pulled back the sheet and cut away the fabric of her gown. Taking a scalpel, the other drew a small vertical line that, as Venzel watched, quickly became red.

Then Destani screamed.

Venzel lunged toward the operating table.

"Stop! Stop! You are hurting her!"

Pushing the doctor with the scalpel against the wall, Venzel started to pick her up, but before he could touch her, he felt a sudden jab in his shoulder and fell into Rauf and Zsiga's arms.

He awoke on the front porch of the main house. Zsiga, wearing a hat and tinted goggles, sat next to him on the divan, tapping his arm. Pushing Zsiga's hand away, Venzel tried to stand but fell back against the cushions.

"How long have I been out here?"

"About forty-five minutes."

"And Destani?"

"She lives."

"The b—"

"He lives as well."

Her screams filled his head, and he tried to stand again. This time, he held onto the porch post and was able to stay on his feet.

"I must see her. She was in such pain, Zsiga. I must see her for myself."

Grasping the porch posts one by one, he walked unsteadily toward the door, pausing often to let the dizziness clear from his head.

"Venzel, she did not scream from the pain. She could not feel any physical pain. Whatever made her scream was in her mind."

Venzel let go of the post and pressed his hands to his eyes. Turning away from the house, he staggered through the walled garden and opened the gate to the limitless desert. Dropping to his knees, he brought his fists down from his face, and a single strangled syllable echoed in the vast emptiness before him.

"Why?"

When the sounds of Venzel's grief subsided, Zsiga left the shelter of the porch and walked to the edge of the garden. One hand completely covering his eyes, he took Venzel's arm.

"Come, my brother. She will be waking up soon, and you should be there. She will need you. Please Venzel, I… I cannot stay out here much longer."

Hearing the pain in his voice, Venzel allowed Zsiga to help him walk back to the house and down into the dark tunnels where his wife and newborn son slept.

Venzel found her alone.

Although it was the doctors' primary goal that Destani care for and feed her son, they took the baby to the nursery until they could assess her mental damage. They would not risk her harming one of the Tuzurias offspring.

Grateful she was still alive, he carefully carried Destani to their room and held her hand as she came out of the anesthesia.

When Destani slowly opened her eyes and smiled at him, Venzel was elated. If she knew him, no matter how bad everything else was, he would be able to bear it. Suddenly, she squeezed her eyes shut.

"Too much light, too much light," she cried.

He immediately shuttered every window and sat on the bed next to her.

"There, my darling, the light is gone, you can open your eyes. Please open your eyes, latif."

One eye slowly opened, and then the next. She looked up at him through her lashes and whispered, "Venzel?"

"Yes, love?"

Her eyes filled with tears. "What did I do wrong? Why did you kill my baby? You took him from me, and he died."

He took her in his arms as she cried piteously against his shoulder.

"Why, oh why?"

It broke his heart to hear her echoing his own words of the afternoon, and he tried to reassure her.

"No, no, love. He is in the nursery. We were worried about you. I wanted to be sure you were well before bringing him to you. Do you want to see him?"

Suddenly smiling, she pulled back from him. "Of course, I want to see him. Oh Venzel, where is he?" She looked at the door as if she expected him to appear at any moment.

Venzel went to the door and told Ezri to ask Rauf to bring the baby.

A few minutes later, Rauf appeared holding a small bundle in his arms. Venzel's eyes narrowed when he noticed Rauf also carrying a syringe.

Standing above Destani, Rauf asked, "Do you remember what you promised me, wife of my brother?"

She stretched out her arms for the baby. "Yes, Rauf, I promised to love my son. But I cannot do that until you give him to me."

Destani took the baby. Nestling against her, she glanced up happily at the two men watching her. That radiant smile was all either of them was ever going to see. Lowering her eyes to the bundle in her arms, she pushed the blanket away. Less than a moment later, she quickly covered him back up again and shoved him at Rauf.

"That is not my son," she said. "I am not even sure what kind of animal that is, but it is not my son." Her eyes locked onto Venzel's face. "Where is *my* son? Did you bury him in the garden?"

Before Rauf could stop her, Destani stood and threw herself at Venzel. Hysterically pounding his chest, she accused him repeatedly of murdering his own son.

Rauf handed the baby to Ezri and quickly inserted the needle into Destani's hip. Venzel caught her as she fell and laid her on the bed. When he backed away from her, Rauf noticed the front of Venzel's tunic was covered in blood. He ran over to Destani.

"Dear sweet Anya, she's pulled out the stitches. We must get her back onto the operating table. Venzel, you will have to carry her. There is no time for a stretcher. Ezri, wash your hands five times and boil the cleanest water you can find. Dip your finger into the cooled water and let it fall one drop at a time into his mouth. Do not unwrap him, and whatever you do, do not uncover his face, just his mouth. His eyes are incredibly light sensitive at this stage—you could blind him."

At Rauf's last words, Venzel looked at Ezri, and he knew that the baby would not be the only one blinded.

Looking in Venzel's direction, Ezri said, "I understand, Master."

Setting the baby down in the cradle, Ezri walked into the little bathroom to wash his hands. Five times.

It took twenty minutes to stop the bleeding. Had she been anyone else, the surgeons would have given it up as impossible, but as the minutes ticked away her life, they were able to get the bleeding under control and re-suture the incisions. Calling Venzel to watch over her, they met with Rauf in the corridor.

"That is the best we can do, Rauf. We cannot suture her again. When she tore the first set of stitches, she shredded her flesh such that there was very little left this time."

"How long before she is healed?"

"If she stays quiet, and no infection sets in, about ten days."

"When are you coming back for the other mothers?"

"We have decided to stay here unless we are called elsewhere. We believe we may be of some help in the event any of your other wives experience difficulties."

Rauf smiled inwardly. Although they had lost three almost immediately, a luxurious harem occupied by the colony's remaining pregnant wives was a powerful incentive to brothers who rarely saw them at that stage.

Telepathically broadcasting his response to the entire colony, Rauf said, "My brothers, we are honored to have you stay with us. Do you think it would be advantageous to, perhaps, examine two of the colony's wives each evening while you are here? I am sure we would be happy to offer you the opportunity to, um, anticipate any difficulties."

"That is generous of you."

"On the contrary, it is our honor and our pleasure as well."

A few moments later, Kasim, who had drawn that evening's short straw, walked into the corridor. Smiling broadly, he led the two doctors to his room. Later that evening, Kasim closed the door softly as he and Militos withdrew to sleep in the dormitory. Circular, like most of the tunnel chambers, the central room of the dormitory resembled a military officers' club with topographical maps of the Levant and northern Africa lining the walls. A table laden with honey-sweetened tea, overripe fruit, and olives mashed in oil was placed in the center of the room, surrounded by upholstered chairs. Newspapers and books were stacked on low tables along the perimeter, where clusters of cushions sat on a sandstone floor polished by the thousands of Lyostian feet that had walked these rooms.

Although not as comfortable as their chambers upstairs—and lacking the delicious warmth of their wives—Kasim and Militos found beds waiting for them in one of the small alcoves encircling the central room, and the constant hum of their brothers' thoughts as they rested in alcoves of their own lulled them to sleep quickly enough.

Priorities

Venzel stood by the door of their apartment the next morning and watched as the orderlies carefully placed Destani on the bed.

When Rauf came in to reattach the IV to her hand, he said, "She cannot move for at least ten days, Venzel. Keeping her alive and sedated at the same time is problem number one. Problem two is that her son needs to be fed, and until one of the other mothers gives birth, she is the only one capable of nursing him."

Venzel did not care whether the boy was fed or not, but he knew the only way to bring Destani back to him was to prove he had not killed her son. He looked into her sleeping face and thought of a way to keep both of them alive.

"Come with me," he said to Rauf. Fixing Ezri with a stare, he said, "Do not move from this spot."

Venzel did not tell Rauf where they were going, and at first, Rauf believed they were looking for Zsiga, but he soon realized they were walking in the direction of the harem. Not bothering to hit the gong to let them know a man was entering, Venzel walked in. Assailed by the scent of fifteen pregnant women together in an enclosed space, Raul was tested almost beyond his endurance. Unable to enter the room, he stood in the hall with his jaw clamped shut to keep the haustellum in his mouth.

Instead of the surprised screams that would have greeted any other man walking into the harem, Venzel's entrance was met with hushed silence.

"My wife, Destani, gave birth yesterday to a boy. However, due to complications surrounding the child's prematurity, she had an operation that has left her weak and bedridden for the next two weeks. The doctors had to sedate her to give the incision time to heal, but she also needs to feed her son and be encouraged to keep up her own strength. I am here to ask for your help."

Senkali was the first to stand. "I will, Venzel. Just tell me what to do, and I'll help for as long as I'm needed." She looked down shyly. "I'm pregnant, too," she added.

"I am happy for you and Zsiga, Senkali, and thank you, more than you know, for your assistance."

Aylala volunteered next, then Tatiana, who could not bear to be parted from her. Venzel's eyes found Lalei, and she paled under his stare but looked at her feet and shook her head.

"Thank you, ladies, for your kind concern for my wife."

The three women followed Venzel out of the room, and with Rauf joining them, they walked up to the balcony floor.

Venzel opened the door to their darkened room. The women rushed in only to stop in mid-flight when they saw the wan creature lying on the bed. Only Senkali went to Destani's side, climbing into bed with her and brushing her hair away from her face.

"Oh, Destani," she said, tears in her eyes. At the sound of her voice, the spell was broken. Tatiana and Aylala went to her. Tatiana held the hand not attached to the IV, and Aylala took a cloth, dipped it in the water bowl, and gently sponged Destani's face, neck, and arms.

Rauf, grateful to be in a room with windows, was finally able to open his mouth to speak. "Ladies, thank you for your help. I think the best way to do this is to divide your care to ensure your own rest. Ezri will be here to help with anything you need."

Rauf looked in Venzel's direction. "If she needs to be moved, you must ask Venzel, who will not be where Ezri cannot find him.

"I will bring the baby every four hours and request that you help her nurse him. I will keep her sedated as lightly as possible, but if she tears the stitches out again, she will die. This means she needs help with everything. Please accept my gratitude and know your kindness has not gone unnoticed."

Senkali listened to Rauf, but she watched Venzel's face. He was expressionless until Rauf said she would die, and Senkali saw the torment that he kept carefully hidden. At that moment, and ever after, a little of the love she felt for Zsiga spilled over onto Venzel.

"Any questions?"

"Will the baby stay in the room?" asked Aylala, pointing to the cradle in the corner.

Answering Aylala's question but looking at Rauf, Venzel said, "No. He will stay in the nursery. Rauf or Ezri will bring him to you when he needs to be fed."

"Why?"

Rauf spoke up. "Because of his eyes. Being premature, his eyes are very sensitive to light and must not be uncovered. In fact, I will be folding the blanket over his face so that only his mouth is showing. Understand this: you may not remove the covering from his head or his eyes or unwrap the blanket from around his body. First, excess light can blind him, and second, his body must remain at a constant temperature. We only bring him to you to be fed, not to be played with."

He smiled kindly at them. "That will come later."

They smiled shyly back. Senkali said, "I'll take the first shift, then Aylala, and then Tatiana. We can manage this. I know she would do it for us. Rauf, would you please escort them back to the harem and bring me that boy? He's probably starving."

She waved at Aylala and Tatiana on their way out and then looked at Venzel. "Is there anything else, Venzel? Anything Rauf didn't say?" The gentle concern in her voice broke past his defenses, and the mask completely fell from his face. Sliding down the wall to the floor, he put his head in his hands.

After a moment, he lifted his head. "The doctors think her mind has been affected."

Senkali nodded. "How bad?"

"They don't know and won't know until she comes out of this phase of her recovery, and they clear her mind of the sedation drugs."

"So, for two weeks, we will hope for the best and then deal with whatever comes afterward."

"Yes. Thank you, Senkali. Zsiga has not told me how fortunate he is to have you."

She looked down at her hand resting on her abdomen and smiled. "Oh no, Venzel, I am the fortunate one to have him."

Looking at his wife, he could only answer, "Perhaps."

There was a short knock on the door, and Rauf walked in with the baby.

"Venzel, could you help me here for a moment?" asked Senkali.

Venzel lifted Destani into her arms and went back to stand by the door.

Senkali looked at Venzel. "Are you sure you want to stay for this?" she asked.

Venzel didn't answer or move.

Rauf handed her the baby.

"Oh, goodness, he is so small," she said, smiling at the baby who could not see her.

Carefully pulling the edge of Destani's robe away from her body, Senkali created a tent of fabric draping from Destani's shoulder to her waist and fed the baby without compromising Destani's dignity.

Five or six minutes later, she noticed the baby was finished and handed him back to Rauf.

"We'll be back in four hours, Senkali. Thank you for your help."

After he left, Senkali looked at Venzel and said, "That was all? What else can I do?"

A knock prevented Venzel from answering Senkali's questions, but before he could open the door, Zsiga walked into the room. Immediately rushing to Senkali's side, he took her hand.

"Are you all right?"

When she smiled and nodded, he turned on Venzel. "You let her walk up all those stairs? And then expect her to walk back down again by herself? What are you thinking?"

Venzel regarded Zsiga's panicked face. He had felt that fear in his own heart recently, heard that anxiety in his own voice, and suddenly understood that Zsiga's concern for Senkali went well beyond what she meant to the colony. Realizing they needed to discuss these matters, he smiled at Zsiga and said, "I think we need to talk."

Looking at Senkali, Venzel said, "Wife of my brother, would you excuse us for a moment?"

Zsiga looked at Senkali sitting on the bed holding Destani and moved to make her more comfortable.

"I'll do that."

As Venzel lifted Destani from Senkali's arms and placed her gently on the bed, Zsiga picked up Senkali and sat her in the chair, covering her with a blanket.

Venzel opened the door to the balcony, and Zsiga followed him, closing it softly. Taking Zsiga's arm, Venzel pulled him into their mother's room.

"Forgive me, my brother, for endangering your wife's health. It was never my intention to put any of the colony's wives in danger. However, now that you have brought my thoughtlessness to my attention, I will make other arrangements. On the other hand, Zsiga, you could have told me."

"Told you what?"

"That you cared so much for Senkali."

"I don't think I realized it myself until just recently."

"As recently as ten minutes ago?"

"Possibly."

"Um-hmm."

Zsiga looked around his mother's room and smiled. It still smelled like her, and the thought of her presence calmed him and made him feel safe. Venzel followed his eyes and, recognizing that smile, felt the same way. A moment later, Zsiga tilted his head, and his smile faded.

"What is it?" asked Venzel.

"They get my wives tonight."

"Who gets your wives?"

"The visiting doctors." A fleeting expression of anger passed over Zsiga's face. He quickly shook it off and, with a look of resignation, sighed.

"Can I bunk in your old room?"

"No."

"No? I cannot bunk in your room?"

"No, they may not have your wives."

"I have no choice. They are guests of the colony, and we are taking turns sharing our wives with them."

"Yes, but your wives are occupied this evening and every evening for the next two weeks, helping my wife feed her son and staying in here, I think, to avoid climbing up and down the stairs."

"Really, Venzel?"

"Yes. The doctors will have to find someone else's wives to, um, entertain them this evening."

Zsiga tilted his head and smiled. "Thank you, my brother. Perhaps you will lend us Ezri to help move a few of their things in here?"

"Yes... and a few of your things, too, Zsiga. I do not intend to deprive you of the comfort of your wives for the sake of mine."

Zsiga's face grew serious. "Lalei?"

"You need not fear for that. I love you far more than I hate her. It is immaterial to me whether she helps or not, but it would be unfair to ask Senkali to do everything."

"Thank you for that, my brother."

Venzel turned to go, but Zsiga touched his arm.

"Venzi, there is one other thing to discuss."

"Yes."

"A name, your son needs a name."

"Didn't the collective dictate a list?"

"Well, yes, but we thought you might like to choose."

"Is that my consolation prize, Zsiga?"

"I… I didn't think of it like that."

Venzel looked in the direction of his young wife.

"What is the eighteenth name on the list?"

"Timaeus."

"Tell them that is his name, and this discussion, my brother, is over."

It was an uneasy ten days. Lalei left the room every time Venzel entered it and spent her days on the balcony looking westward for a rider who would never come, her blue eyes growing a little more desperate with every sunset. In the other room, Senkali, Ezri, and Venzel took care of Destani, who was slowly healing.

Toward the end of the second week, Lalei began having pain. Zsiga called the orderlies for a stretcher, and Zsiga had his first son, Taliph. Exactly fourteen days from the day she arrived on the balcony floor, Senkali was taken into the white room, and Zsiga had his second son, Taran. Both mothers survived.

Rauf came upstairs to give Venzel the news and examine Destani. He was gratified to see her incision had healed. When Ezri brought the baby, Venzel held Destani and fed the child as he had watched Senkali do, calling for Ezri when the boy was finished.

Alone for the first time in ten days, Venzel turned off the IV and disconnected it from her hand. Climbing into bed with her, he gently enfolded Destani in his cloak and, resting his head against hers, whispered, "Oh my beloved, it has been so long."

For the rest of the night, Venzel held Destani in his arms, singing to her and rocking her as though she was his child.

Sacrifice

Venzel awoke to light filtering into their room. He wanted to watch her eyes as they opened, to see if she remembered him—if she still loved him. Living through the past two weeks was the hardest thing he had ever done, but, as Senkali predicted, he felt confident he could cope with whatever came next.

Her eyelids fluttered, and Venzel held his breath. She opened them and seeing him, smiled. Then her smile faded, and tears gathered in her eyes.

"What is it, latif? Are you in pain?"

"Yes, for the rest of my life. My son is dead." Her eyes were so full of despair he could not bear to look at them.

"No, he lives. He's been waiting for you to get well. You have been ill, Destani. Very ill." She blinked back her tears, and he was encouraged. "I will get him for you. Just rest, my love. I'll bring him to you."

Leaving Ezri to stand guard outside the door, Venzel went to find his son.

It was Venzel's first visit to the colony's nursery. In the midst of fourteen identical neo-natal cribs, Venzel knew him immediately. Near the center of the group, smaller than the others and with eyes the color of the Aegean Sea, lay Destani's son. Unafraid, the child regarded him solemnly as Venzel lifted him from the crib.

Taking one of the blankets, Venzel folded it as he had seen Rauf do around the baby's face, head, and body, leaving only his mouth visible. He knew that she would not be satisfied with that, but he didn't want Ezri to see the baby without coverings.

Hurrying back to their rooms, he panicked when he saw the door flung open and Ezri and his wife gone. Not taking the time to return his son to the nursery, he ran down the corridor and descended the stairs. At that moment, Ezri ran into the house.

"Master, I cannot find her! She is so quick. One moment, she was asking me a question; the next moment, she was out the door."

"What was the question, Ezri?"

"If you were Venzel."

"And you told her?"

"Yes. Of course, Master."

Venzel's face became a thundercloud. There was nothing he wanted to do more than to hurl the baby to the floor and strangle Ezri, but he had to find Destani. Nothing else mattered. She would die in the desert alone.

Handing the baby to Ezri, he said, "Take him to our rooms and wait for me there."

Stepping into the early sunrise shadows, Venzel stood still and listened, waiting for the wind to tell him where she was. Not sensing anything at first, he caught a whisper of smoke on the desert air.

Before he could turn in the direction of the smoke, the morning's silence was broken by the ear-splitting screams of terrified horses.

Breaking into a dead run, Venzel circled the house in the direction of the stables. Immeasurable anguish and fear filled his heart. Calling for help and sprinting toward the sounds of panic, Venzel felt he was caught in a nightmare from which he would never awaken.

Lifting the lock bar from the stable doors, Venzel was nearly knocked off his feet as horses rushed past him wild-eyed with fear. Running first to Alazar's stall, he saw it was empty and was relieved that the stallion had escaped into the paddock. The open doors allowed the smoke to clear but also fanned the flames inside the stables. Venzel and two of the early—arriving stable hands fought their way through the burning building to the rear stall where Venzel kept the foals. By the sudden silence and stench of burning horsehair, he knew they would not find any of them alive.

No one there that day ever forgot the cry from Venzel's throat as it cut through the smoke and death of the morning. On the floor of the stable, legs and hooves red with blood where he had attempted to tear down the stall to free the trapped colts, lay Alazar. Beyond the split and broken doors, four colts huddled against the back wall, their eyes forever frozen in terror, Alazar's sacrifice unrewarded.

Covered in soot and reeling from the tragedy surrounding him, Venzel emerged like a madman from the ruins of the stables. He knew she was there. Scanning the line of workers and servants staring open-mouthed at the destruction before them, he saw her. Sitting under an olive tree with her back against the garden wall and her knees tucked under her chin, Destani rocked slightly, humming a lullaby.

With every step, Venzel's heart shattered a little more. Reaching her, he fell on his knees in the sand.

"Why, latif Destani? Why?"

"You killed my son, Venzel, so I killed yours."

"But our son is alive, karisi, alive… I was bringing him to you."

"That *thing* is not my son. You took my son, Venzel, and killed him. I saw you. You. Were. There."

With a fury he did not believe she possessed, Destani sprung at him like a coiled cobra, raking the sides of his neck with her fingernails.

He did not attempt to reason with her hysteria but swept her into his arms. Walking past Zsiga without seeing him, he carried her back into the house.

Rauf was waiting inside the door with a syringe. A moment later, she lay like death on Venzel's shoulder as he returned to their room. After saying a few words to Rauf, Zsiga followed his brother upstairs.

Ezri had watched the events unfold from the balcony. Sighing, he laid the baby in the cradle and filled the large tub with water.

Venzel placed Destani carefully on their bed. Stripping off his burned and blackened clothes, he threw them into the fireplace. Barely acknowledging Ezri, he slowly eased himself into the tub and clenched his teeth as hot water met burned skin.

Sensing that the baby would be better off in the nursery, Zsiga handed him to Ezri and told him to find Rauf. Walking over to Destani's sleeping form, he began singing Anya's song of protection.

"Too late, Zsiga, there is nothing left to protect."

"Her life, Venzi. I pray for her life. She still has a son who needs her."

"And her husband, Zsiga? Are there prayers for a husband who needs her?"

"No, my brother. For such pain, there are no words."

"There are no words…." echoed Venzel softly, and for several minutes, the only sound was the rhythmic dipping of the cloth in the water.

"Where is he?"

"Rauf is returning him to the nursery. Senkali will feed him."

There was a soft rap on the door, and a few hastily murmured words.

"What is it?"

"Nothing. It is not important right now."

"Is it the horses?"

Zsiga reluctantly answered, "Yes, they are not sure what to do with them."

"Tell them to put the ones that are still alive in the smaller camel corral. They can do what they like with the dead—except for Alazar, I will bury him myself—and tell them, Zsiga, I know what he looks like, and he had better be in exactly the same condition when I return. As for what remains of the stables, tell them to tear it all down. I do not care what they do with the pieces."

Zsiga tilted his head. "They have already pulled Alazar from the wreckage on a section of the wall and covered him with the purple and blue canvas from your tent. He was revered by all who knew him—or knew about him—you do them ill to believe they would mutilate him."

"Perhaps. But then, it is such a day."

"Yes." Zsiga looked down at Destani. Black streaks covered her arms and face where Venzel carried her. He dampened the corner of a small cloth and began walking toward her.

"Zsiga, I love you, but if you touch her, I will have to kill you."

Zsiga looked at Venzel standing in the doorway. Setting the cloth on the table, he sighed, "Perhaps. But then, it is such a day."

"Yes."

Venzel started to pull on his cloak, but Zsiga stopped him.

"Wait a minute."

Zsiga picked up the bowl of peeled aloe Ezri had handed him through the door. He carefully treated the seeping wounds on Venzel's back and shoulders where embers had fallen from the burning roof of the stables.

Venzel gingerly slid the cloak over the charred and blistered skin.

"Thank you, brother," he said.

Pouring some water into a small basin, he picked up the cloth that Zsiga had left on the table. Dipping it in warm water and soap, Venzel talked softly to his wife as he bathed her arms and face.

Zsiga was quietly leaving when Venzel stopped him.

"Two things, please, Zsiga. Send Rauf to me when it is convenient, and although I am grateful to Senkali, I want to know what time the boy should be fed."

Zsiga tilted his head. "Rauf is on his way, and in about two hours." He looked at his brother for a moment. "Venzel, what are you going to do?"

"Please bring the child in two hours. We will have more to discuss then."

He heard Zsiga open the door.

"Zsiga," he said softly, "thank you for following me up here. Had you not, I am sure there would have been more than just Alazar to bury today."

"You are my brother, Venzel. I will never leave you alone."

Rauf passed Zsiga on the stairs. "How are they?"

"She is still unconscious. He is calm."

"Calm?"

"Yes, why?"

"Humans are at their most dangerous when calm."

"You think Venzel is dangerous?"

"Zsiga, Venzel has always been the most dangerous member of the colony. However, he feels he belongs here with you, and it is this sense of belonging and love that has encouraged him since the beginning to help us survive. It has also kept him reined in and working as part of our team. Woe be to anyone who gets in his way if that bit ever comes out."

"What can I do?"

"Stay close to him. We need to know if you feel he is becoming insecure about his place here. He is valued and important, and we would like him to remain for the rest of his life, but we cannot tolerate unpredictability. We have let him have his way and will continue to do so—but no one is allowed to endanger the colony."

"I understand."

"Do you?"

"Yes. We are one."

"We are one."

Zsiga left Rauf and went down into the underground tunnels to the darkest section of the nursery. Reclining on the divan in the corner, Senkali was feeding their son. Hearing his footsteps, she looked up.

"Who is there?"

"Zsiga, my sweet."

"Ah, husband," she said, her hand waving in the darkness. He caught it and brought it to his face as he sat next to her on the cushions. Pulling her into his embrace, he gently kissed the back of her neck.

"That tickles," she said, laughing.

"You always say that."

"It always does, but I like it," she added softly.

"I'm happy, Senkali, very happy you like it."

As the baby slept in her arms, she dozed slightly in his. He had been lucky. Senkali survived the pregnancy, and because the babies were wrapped to protect them from the chill of the underground rooms, she did not notice their delicate antennae or their fused hands and feet. Already nursing hers and Aylala's son and, when Lalei was resting, Taliph as well, Senkali did not seem to mind the addition of Venzel's son that morning.

The baby moved his head, and she was instantly awake.

"He is still asleep, love, you can rest, now."

"Zsiga...."

"Yes, Senkali."

"How long do I have to stay in this dark room? I can hardly see the baby's face, or yours."

"Forever I'm afraid, my dear," he said, kissing her cheek and brushing the hair back from her still beautiful, but sightless eyes.

The Stranger Upstairs

Rauf turned to Ezri as he entered the room. "You may go. I will call you if you are needed."

Ezri glanced quickly at Venzel. Nodding, he crossed his arms and did not move.

Rauf looked at the couple on the bed and sighed. Humans, while essentially simple creatures, were so completely ruled by their emotions that they complicated the most rudimentary tasks. That quality also made them very easy to manipulate. Most of them.

Rauf closed the door. "You asked to see me?"

"Thank you for coming up here, Rauf. I know you are busy. I just have a few questions."

"How can I help you?"

Rauf recoiled slightly at the harshness of Venzel's laughter.

"You cannot help me," he said, "I am trying to help you." Venzel held Destani's hand to his lips for a moment while he regained his composure. "First, how long before the child looks like a human baby?"

"In two weeks, more or less. It depends on the mother and the amount of honey she eats. The more consistent she is, the quicker the child will develop."

"Second, what is the danger of keeping Destani in this half-sleep during that time so she will nurse him? And third, do you think that during that time, she could subconsciously bond with the baby so she will accept him when he looks like a human child?"

"There is no danger, but we will have to allow her some lucid periods every few days to cleanse her mind. I do not advocate stopping like we did today. We will do it more gradually next time. However, the last question is harder to answer because we are unsure how the acid has affected her mind. Bonding may not be possible because we don't know if she can be left alone with the child when she is fully conscious, possibly resulting in taking him back to Senkali permanently."

"Is there any danger to the child if she is sedated for another two weeks?"

"No. The drugs we use only put her brain to sleep and cannot be passed to the infant."

Venzel nodded. "Rauf, she thinks I killed our baby because, in her illness, she cannot accept the Lyostian features and believes the child is not hers. If we can keep her sedated until he looks human, waking her up slowly to see she is feeding a human child, then perhaps she will accept him and stop hating me."

Rauf did not think Venzel's plan would succeed. Centuries of archived medical history revealed that women did not recover once formic acid entered their bloodstream. Adapting to their underground world required the integration of ant DNA, but while it contributed to their survival, just trace amounts could damage their human mothers' minds and kill them. Even as he looked at her, Raul knew an infinitesimal amount of acid accumulated in Destani's brain each time the tainted blood ran through it, causing memory loss and hallucinations at first, but inevitably an embolism and death. He was tempted to tell Venzel that his plan would work. The child would benefit greatly from being nursed by his own mother, especially this generation, but he would not lie to Venzel. They were brothers.

"Venzel, when this happens, the mothers do not recover, and most never improve. If you are hoping that your plan will make Destani the person she was three weeks ago, then, my brother, I am truly sorry. The wife you loved will never return to us."

Venzel leaned his head back against the wall. "I know that, Rauf. My beloved Destani has gone from me. She would have never hurt—"

He paused for a moment to clear his throat. "All I hope for is that she will stop blaming me and...," he touched the welts on the side of his neck, "stop hating me. I could forgive much, my brother, if we could somehow make that happen."

Rauf nodded. He understood Venzel perfectly. Even in his desperation, Venzel still trusted the colony to help her, as it would, but it was his first and only hope.

"Zsiga is bringing the baby in two hours. As his wives now have children of their own, I will assist Destani myself. Thank you, Rauf. I will see you then."

Venzel took the camel whip next to the bed and tapped it once on the floor. The door opened immediately.

"Ezri, Rauf will be back in two hours with Zsiga. Don't let anyone enter before then."

"Yes, Master," he said, standing back so Rauf could leave. Trying not to disturb the silence in the room, Ezri soundlessly closed the door.

For two hours, she was his again. Venzel held Destani in his arms, pretending that it was twenty-four hours ago; Alazar was alive; she was just sleeping, and he still had faith that she would recover. He breathed in the fragrance of her hair, ran his hands along her body, and pulled her inside his cloak, reliving happier moments. Rocking her slightly, he sang to her as he had done the night before, talked of their past, tried not to think of the future, and told her how beautiful her son was. He asked her questions and responded as if she answered him. Sometimes, he laughed softly when he imagined her saying something pert or teasing him, and for those few tender moments, he let himself believe Destani still loved him.

At the end of two hours, Ezri opened the door for Zsiga carrying the baby, with Rauf following closely behind them with an IV stand. Sitting behind her, Venzel held Destani against his shoulder with one arm and cradled the baby with the other.

Lifting his burning eyes to Zsiga, Venzel said, "Please tell Ezri to come get the baby in fifteen minutes. Rauf, if you will write out a schedule and tell me what we need to do, I will make this work for the next two weeks."

Nodding to Venzel, they both quietly left the room. Watching them go, he realized how badly he needed their help if she was ever going to smile at him again. Unable to blame or hate the brothers he loved, Venzel looked down at the tiny creature attached to the breast of his wife and directed all his hate to him.

Venzel's plan seemed to work. In twilight sleep, Destani rested in his arms as she nursed the baby. When he sang to them, she was calm and occasionally smiled, but those moments were rare. Most of the time, she leaned her head on his shoulder and slept.

There were days, however, when Destani was not calm.

During her lucid moments, Venzel had to leave the room. If she saw him, she would fly into a rage and accuse him of murdering her son. Searching for the baby she said he had taken from her, she would tear the room apart. Ezri stood helpless nearby until, exhausting herself, she would cry herself to sleep, and then he and Venzel would quietly put the room back together.

During those days, Venzel stayed out of her way. Sitting in the hall, he listened to her conversations with Ezri, hoping to hear her say his name. One afternoon, she asked Ezri to walk in the garden with her, and Venzel followed closely enough to hear her admire the flowers. She sounded so much like herself that Venzel began to hope, but when she pulled an apple from her pocket and asked Ezri to give it to Alazar the next time he went to the stables, Venzel walked away and returned to his room in the tunnels to sleep alone. Once again, the birds and animals carved into the walls and ceiling were his only company.

Closing his eyes, he tried to forget the stranger upstairs and dreamt instead of his young bride.

Every morning, Venzel removed the blanket from his son and watched for the changes that could not come quickly enough. As Rauf promised, it was less than a month before the covering could be removed from the baby's head. Fine, dark brown hair concealed the antenna scars. He now had a nose, smallish but human ears, and only a few bandages remained on his hands and feet. Although his eyes still needed protection from sunlight, he was able to endure candlelight. As long as no one looked too closely, Destani's son could have passed anywhere in the world as a newborn human child.

Relying on his earlier success, Venzel was confident he could convince her it was all a bad dream. Knowing the timing was critical, he arranged for Ezri to bring the baby from the nursery as she was gradually waking from the induced sleep. He would be there with her, and Ezri would hand her the infant to nurse as if she had just given birth. Venzel believed, planned, and prayed that he could convince her that every moment of the last four weeks had never happened.

Worried that he would not be ready on time, Ezri went down to the nursery and brought the baby into the hall several minutes early. Rauf, who did not share Venzel's optimism but knew how important this experiment was to other affected mothers, had arrived early as well.

Seeing the look of concern on the doctor's face, Ezri asked, "You do not think his plan will work?"

"Regrettably, Ezri, I have only my experience and the medical archives to rely on in such cases. I do not think she will accept the child *and* believe Venzel's story. She may very well reject both. I am here only to monitor the child's well-being. As much as he needs his own mother, we cannot risk her harming him in any way."

Looking down at Venzel's son sleeping in his arms, Ezri nodded.

Both men dreaded Venzel's signal. Rauf, because he had a fairly good idea what was going to happen; and Ezri, because he hoped she would make Venzel laugh again and take the fierce look from his face, but in the grim presence of the doctor, that hope seemed impossible.

The tension in the hall became almost unbearable. Ezri nearly jumped when he felt, rather than heard, Venzel's whip tap upon the wooden floor.

He looked at Rauf.

"I will remain here unless I am needed. Perhaps it will be as he desires, and I have wasted my time."

With the same hope in his heart, Ezri entered the room holding the baby.

Leaning against the headboard with Destani in his lap, Venzel said, "Latif, Ezri is here with the baby. I'm sure he's hungry. Wake up, love, and meet your new son."

Destani blinked her eyes, took the baby in her arms, and slipped him beneath her robe. She smiled down at him as he began to nurse. Leaning back into Venzel's arms, she said, "Oh, he is so beautiful."

The men in the room and the one in the hall, who had barely breathed since the tap on the floor, took a deep breath. Venzel closed his eyes and said a prayer of thanksgiving. Ezri, sitting on his cushion by the door, smiled as Venzel's face began to relax. Rauf tilted his head and gave Zsiga the news. Sighing in relief, he turned toward the tunnel stairs.

Destani's happiness only lasted a few precious moments.

Pulling away from Venzel's embrace, she asked, "Who are you?"

Concerned but determined not to make too much of her abrupt change of mood, Venzel answered, "Your husband, karisi, and the father of your son."

"No," she said sadly, "this is not my son. My son is dead. Venzel killed my—" Looking at him closely, she recognized who he was.

"You!" she hissed. "You murdered my son!"

With those words, she leaped from the bed and stood in the middle of the room with the baby still in her arms.

Hearing the tone of her voice, Rauf raced back toward the room. Not wanting to interfere unless it was necessary, he remained in the hallway. The child did not seem to be in any danger, and he wanted to give Venzel every chance to calm her. Praying he would not need it, Rauf slowly removed the syringe from his bag.

"Destani, please love, I didn't kill anyone. You are holding your baby in your arms… It was a dream, latif, a dream."

Cautiously getting out of the bed, he pointed toward the baby and desperately tried to make her believe him.

"Look at him. There is your baby; he even looks like you… please, Destani," he begged.

Rauf stood in the doorway. Every pair of eyes in the room watched as Destani pulled the baby away from her and moved nearer to the window.

Pushing the blanket aside, Destani bent over the baby to examine his face. The moonlight streaming through the shuttered windows roused the sleeping infant. Still hungry and sensing her warmth close to him, his eyes looked into hers as the haustellum came up out of his mouth and found her breast again.

Horrified, Destani pushed the child away from her as her bloodcurdling scream echoed throughout the compound.

Oblivious to the source of her panic, Ezri only saw the baby falling and rushed over in time to save him from hitting the floor. Seeing her collapse from a dead faint, Venzel caught Destani, but not before the windowsill grazed the side of her head as she fell.

Sitting on the floor holding his wife's bleeding head in his hands, Venzel surveyed the wreckage of his life with tormented eyes: Rauf, poised over Destani's inert body, slipping a needle into her arm; Ezri cradling his son, whose scarred hands waved in the air reaching in vain for his mother; and, finally, the expression of disgust on Destani's face. Without waiting for Rauf to bandage her injuries, he tenderly lifted her, laid her on their bed, and turned her slightly on her side. Taking the baby from Ezri, he nestled him inside her robe and started for the door.

"Let the baby finish, Ezri, then Rauf will take him back to the nursery."

"Master—" began Ezri.

"Not now."

Rauf held out his arm toward Venzel.

"No, Rauf. I am going to talk to Zsiga. Please do what you can for her."

Zsiga, advised by Rauf that Venzel was on his way, met him on the stairs.

"Brother, I am so sorry. Everyone in the colony prayed that you would be successful."

"Thank you, and please extend my gratitude to everyone for their concern and prayers."

Venzel looked at his brother with resignation. "Neither my mind nor my love can heal her, Zsiga. Ezri can help with the baby, and maybe if I'm not here, it will be easier for her to accept him. Regardless, I need some time to think about how I am going to live the rest of my life. I have no pressing duties here right now. I have arranged for the surviving Arabian mares to be sold, the colony's stock of provisions is high, and the next caravan is not due to begin for several months. So, my brother, I am taking two pack horses, some supplies, and leaving."

Panic lit Zsiga's eyes. "But you can't, Venzel! You will be alone. Do you know what that means? No one to help you, no one to talk to. You will be in a soundless jar all by yourself." He reached out and grabbed Venzel's arm. "My brother, you could die."

Venzel laughed hoarsely. "Anya willing," he said, turning his back and walking toward the barn.

A moment later, Rauf joined Zsiga. "What are we going to do? We must stop him!"

"We cannot stop him, Zsiga. The only way to keep him from leaving is to kill him, and the collective will not allow that—he is still too valuable."

"He won't be valuable if he doesn't come back!"

Rauf looked calmly at his distraught brother. "Zsiga, he will come back… this is his home. Everything he loves in the world is right here. We will alert the other colonies in the area, as we always do, and keep an eye on him. And I promise you, even if he has his heart set on it, we will not let him die."

No one stood at the gate and watched him go, but every member of the colony knew when Venzel left the compound that evening. They could feel Zsiga's heart breaking.

Sanctuary

Setting off without a destination in mind, Venzel realized when the sun came up behind the palm trees that he was heading toward the oasis. He knew it was a mistake, but he could not make himself turn the horses in another direction. Perhaps somewhere lost in the shade or hiding beneath the water's edge, he would find her again. Or, at the very least, the desert wind would bring back the echoes of her laughter, her sighs. He had no hope of finding her but thought perhaps his beloved karisi would return to him in his dreams.

When Zsiga received word Venzel was at the oasis, he began to breathe normally. He knew Venzel would be safe there, and if that was as far as he planned to go, he would return.

As Venzel predicted, Destani was quieter in his absence, and a minor miracle occurred. During one of her lucid moments shortly after Venzel's departure, she asked Ezri about his baby. At a loss for words, Ezri got Rauf, who explained that it was not Ezri's baby she remembered but the son of one of the other wives who was ill. Destani made a sad face and asked if she could see the baby.

Afraid of the same scene they had witnessed before, Rauf told the child not to use his haustellum because it scared his mother. When placed in her arms, he nuzzled her gently with his newly formed nose, and she quietly allowed him to nurse.

She looked up at Rauf and asked, "Do you think his mother will mind?"

"No, I think she will be happy if you could help her."

Destani nodded and rocked the baby gently. For the first few days, either Rauf or Ezri was in the room when she was awake with the baby. After a week without incident, Rauf referred to the child as hers.

"Here, Destani," he said, "let me help you with your baby."

She did not object and asked his name.

When Rauf told her, she looked down and touched his cheek.

"Yes, Timaeus, I do believe you will be a great man someday."

At her touch, Timaeus sent her all the love in his heart. She blushed and smiled. It was not her old smile—the cut above her temple had damaged a facial nerve, resulting in a slightly crooked smile—but he felt her reflect his affection back to him, sparking a small white flame that warmed Timaeus's heart.

Venzel returned several days later as quietly as he'd gone. Rauf met him on the porch and told him what had happened.

"I want to see it," said Venzel skeptically.

Entering the room through the balcony, Venzel stood behind a screen as Ezri brought the baby to Destani. In front of Venzel's amazed eyes, she took the baby and fed him, cooing and smiling at him. After a little while, she handed the baby back to Ezri, who placed him in the cradle in the corner and, glancing toward the screen, quietly left the room.

As Venzel watched, Destani's eyes began to flutter. When she slept, he stepped into the room. Still looking at her face, he did not see the small footstool next to the bed and tripped.

Destani sat upright and demanded, "Who are you?"

Venzel quickly picked up a discarded towel from the floor and held it for her to see.

"No one important, Mistress, I'm just here to help Ezri clean."

"All right, but you must knock before you enter. My husband is very strict about that. I don't want you to be punished." Smiling a tentative crooked smile, she closed her eyes again.

As his hand reached for the door, he looked down at the sleeping infant. That she would hold *him*, love *him*, without understanding that he was the source of all their pain, was almost more than Venzel could endure, and another band of hate encircled his heart. It seemed to be the only thing holding it together anymore. Remembering her crooked smile and the nights in the desert without her, Venzel decided to be patient. Perhaps one day, she would accept him, too.

Venzel found Rauf in the nursery.

"Venzel, what happened? Did she see you?"

"Yes. She didn't know who I was. I pretended to be a servant. Rauf, if she will accept me as her servant, then that is what I will be—at least until such time as she recognizes me again."

Unwilling to say words that might drive him back into the desert, yet still refusing to lie, Rauf said, "Venzel, I want you to think this through for a moment. Who benefits from that arrangement? Although she seems relatively happy now, you have not been home long enough to know that she still has very bad moments. She does not benefit because today's acceptance could all come crashing down tomorrow if she recognizes you and rejects her son again. You do not benefit from it because I can see the pain in your eyes even as you suggest it, and your son does not benefit because he immediately feels anything that disturbs his mother. I will not stop you, Venzel. I can only suggest that you remain on the perimeter of her life and not in the day-to-day workings of it."

"Tell me, Rauf, will this get easier? Will this get better? Because although I thought I had accepted everything, I find upon my return that I have not. I am as much at a loss today as when I left in knowing how to proceed with my life. Do you have...?" he caught himself, "Wait, what do you mean *very* bad moments?"

Rauf sighed. If she had been anyone else, he would have already given her child to Senkali and killed her. It was his opinion that her death would have been merciful for all concerned, and the elders discussed it during Venzel's absence. However, the Lyostians were afraid if Destani was dead when he returned, Venzel would leave, the collective would take their wives and children, and their colony would become another outpost again. As before, they made every effort to conceal their deliberations from Zsiga; he was just not rational when it came to discussing matters involving Venzel.

"She runs away, Venzel. We do not know, and she probably does not know where she is going, but somehow, she gets by Ezri and runs into the desert. We try to keep sentries posted in the house to watch the gate, but the collective reassigned many of our brothers since the children were born. We should have more in a few months, but right now, we cannot watch her twenty-four hours a day, and although Ezri tries, he cannot be everywhere at once."

"The perimeter of her life, Rauf? All right then, I'll be in the background. Ezri and I will work out a schedule, and I will stay in my mother's room next to hers. Listening, watching, waiting. It's not like she could hate me any more than she already does." Rauf looked doubtful. "Well, let's use your argument. Who benefits from this? She does because I will not let her escape or harm herself trying. The baby benefits because the longer she is with him, the better his chances of getting the nourishment he needs, and me, well, I get to feel somewhat useful in her life, if only as her jailer."

"That is a harsh way of telling me how much you love her, Venzel."

"Perhaps, Rauf, but it is the only way I am allowed to love her, and it will, apparently, be my final role in her life."

"Venzel—"

"Do not tell me you are sorry, Rauf. The colony got what it wanted from her—and from me. The only sincere regrets in this situation are my own."

Rauf's words, "That's not true" died in the air as Venzel turned away to find Zsiga.

New Arrangements

Seeing the resolute expression on his face, Rauf tilted his head to let Zsiga know Venzel was in the tunnels looking for him. Zsiga found him first, and they walked into Venzel's room.

"A small light, Zsiga? It has been some time since I have lived in darkness."

"Certainly."

Shielding the match with his body, Venzel lit the candle and moved it to the uppermost shelf to keep the light from shining in Zsiga's eyes.

"Venzi...."

"No. Not yet, Zsiga. Please, let's talk about you. I have been... occupied with other matters, and we have not spoken privately in several weeks. How are your wives and children?"

"I think Lalei is dying. She will not eat and weeps soundlessly as each day takes away another piece of her life. She barely acknowledges her son and only holds him sporadically. I would send her home, but I do not think she would survive the journey even if it were possible for me to let her go."

"Senkali?"

"Well, she is quite wonderful, nursing the colony's infants, including yours, when necessary, of course...." Zsiga's voice trailed off at the end, and Venzel sensed hurt behind his brother's words.

"What is wrong, Zsiga? Is it Senkali?"

Although the light did not bother him, Zsiga brought his hands up and covered his eyes. "There were problems toward the end. She is so young her blood pressure was not monitored closely enough. The doctors said at first it was temporary, so I didn't mention it, but now it is apparent that her blindness is permanent."

"Senkali is blind?" Venzel thought back to the night of the engagement banquet and remembered her flashing eyes as they looked adoringly at Zsiga.

"Yes. It was so unexpected."

"I am sorry, my brother, sorrier than I can say."

"No, don't be. It's not… it's not because of who we are. Rauf said it happens in some births, even fully human ones, but it has made her a good mother, and well, she has become quite dear to me."

"I see." Venzel could not keep the smile out of his voice. "And tell me, Zsiga, have you become quite dear to her?"

"I think so. It feels that way. She smiles when she knows I am there and lets me, um, touch her, even when she is awake."

"And your sons?"

"Growing, much like yours. This new mutation, I cannot tell you the hopes the collective has for it—"

Suddenly, the teasing was gone from Venzel's voice. "But I want you to. And when you have finished telling me of the collective's hopes and dreams, then I want you to tell it of my nightmares. A wife, a real wife, who does not know me, and a son who should have been mine but who is now no more mine than yours or any of the other children born here. And when you have told them that, then ask them what I am supposed to do now… when a broken life and you are all I have left."

"It can be as it was before."

"Nothing can be as it was before. I didn't understand Zsiga, not really, why I was bringing these women here. I love you, I love all my brothers, and if you needed wives, then I was happy to find them for you—and if you wanted children, then I was willing to assist you with that honor—but

Kadri made it clear to me that the welfare of your wives and children were not my concern. I became so wrapped up in expanding the colony's base, raising horses, and planning the next caravan that I left them in your care. I cannot say I am innocent of some of their deaths. Obviously, they could not be allowed to leave, but I did not understand until now, Zsiga, that you fully expect to sacrifice these women for your children."

"We have no choice. Until such a time as we are able to produce our own females, we must either do this or die. Our predominant instinct is to survive at any cost—even if that cost must be paid by the women we cannot live without. And though we appreciate that your participation in any tragedy has been incidental and for our benefit, you must admit that since the very first caravan, you have been willingly and intimately involved in the process."

"Tell me, Zsiga, since I am 'intimately' involved, what happens next to these children the collective is so hopeful about?"

"Well, the good news is that we have enough mothers here to feed and nurture them to full development. In the past, we have had to send them away to nurturing colonies if we did not have any surviving or loving mothers, but that is not the case this year."

"Good. And then?"

"Training and education. As you know, our children are born knowing who they are and what our mandate is, but one of the expectations for this Tuzurias generation is to forge new paths and make new connections. They will receive specialized training in behavioral psychology as well as extensive leadership skills so they can operate within human groups as well as Lyostian colonies. Our mandate is to protect the earth, something we cannot accomplish alone, and if everything progresses as the collective projects, this generation will be the catalyst toward combining our culture with that of humans, a kind of synergetic connection to establish common goals and work together to achieve them."

"Work together? While we kill their women, their sisters, their daughters?"

"Venzi, as medical technology improves, so will the survival of our mothers. Many colonies have higher survival rates than we do because of our location and limited energy resources."

"Are any of those colonies, the ones with higher survival rates, located near here?"

"No, or we would use their facilities. The nearest one is at least a day's journey from here, and that is traveling above ground. Underground, it would take a lot longer."

Venzel stood motionless in the candlelight as a look of dread crossed Zsiga's face.

"Why do you ask?" he said slowly.

"I wish to suggest a change in our arrangement."

Expecting the worst, Zsiga sat down.

"Although I forbid anyone to speak to him of our relationship, I do not want my son—and do not quibble with me, Zsiga, about who is and is not my son—sent away to another colony. His mother, one way or another, will nurse him as much as possible; although it may be up to others to assist in nurturing him, I am not sure she will be capable of that. Further, I think that due to its *limitations*, this colony should cease operations as a breeding colony. As you say, there are other colonies better suited to caring for our mothers. This colony should be restructured as a training and education center for as many of the Tuzurias generation as it can support."

"But Venzi, your alliance and contributions to our colony are the main reasons we have been so successful. The collective will not want to waste such an integral member of the colony merely to raise our offspring, even those it regards as highly as the Tuzurias."

Venzel closed his eyes. There was only one way to prevent any other woman from dying here and still protect the people he loved; he had to maintain his value to the collective.

The strain of the last few months was evident on his face and in his voice.

"In return for this change of mission within my home colony, it will be my continued honor to visit nearby breeding colonies as needed and contribute in any way I can to their success. And, if my suggestions are approved, I have one last request. I know this realignment may result in changes to the colony structure, but Zsiga, if you wouldn't mind, and if the collective will allow it, I would be happy if you will stay and help facilitate these changes...."

Suddenly, Zsiga signed to him, *Senkali.*

"...as well as our mother, Senkali, who will represent the nurturing presence that all Lyostian children need."

Venzel blew out the candle.

"Thank you for your time, Zsiga. I must find Ezri and see to my wife and our son. Please let me know at once how the collective wishes to proceed."

Zsiga straightened his head. "When do you wish the changes to be operational?"

"When are the boys to be sent away?"

"In seven months."

"In seven months then, Zsiga. It is essential that their education and training is not delayed to accommodate us. They are too important to the future of the collective and our mandate. We must give them the best beginning possible. We will start renovations as soon as the collective makes its decision."

"I will proceed as you have requested, my brother," Zsiga said out loud, signing, *Thank you.*

But Venzel, turning to find Ezri, did not see him.

It became Ezri's responsibility to carry the baby back and forth from the nursery, and to make sure Destani ate properly. Venzel's only task was to stand at the door or on the balcony guarding her. Moving into his mother's room, he was always listening for the quick, light footsteps that indicated she had found a way out again. He didn't fight or chase her. He just followed her until she became tired. Holding her to him, Venzel sang softly while she cried as he carried her back to the room. More often than not, she would be asleep in his arms before he laid her on the bed.

Occasionally, he asked for the sleeping tea so he could spend the night with her. He embraced her as a husband, but it was like holding a doll. A beautiful doll he still loved as a wife but who, despite her sounds of pleasure, became blurred with all the other women who were unable to love him back.

During those dark days, Venzel watched as Timaeus went in and out of his wife's room. After several weeks, her initial enthusiasm for the child faded, and although she still accepted him, she held him only long enough to satisfy his hunger before returning him to Ezri without a smile or a word. Despite her lack of interest, Venzel was afraid of losing that link to her and would allow no one else to feed him, but every day, the sight of the child lying in Destani's arms that were forever closed to him increased the bitterness in his heart.

Zsiga could not misunderstand the look on Venzel's face as he stared at Destani's sleeping son.

"It was not your fault, my brother."

"Perhaps, but it will always be my sorrow. I should never have left her alone."

"Then why blame the child?"

"He has taken her and left me with nothing."

Destani

Since the morning the formic acid began leaking into her bloodstream, Destani's mind had constantly battled between love, hate, and anger. She knew who she was, but except for Ezri, everyone's identity shifted in her mind, and as the toxins accumulated in her brain, the distance between what was real and what she imagined slowly diminished.

She knew that Ezri was her beloved husband's servant who stayed with her while he was away on a caravan that would return any day. Try as she might, she could not remember either her husband's name or face, and no one, Venzel least of all, understood that somehow his name had become attached to her memory of Halil and that terrible afternoon they almost died. In her mind, Venzel/Halil had found her, taken and killed her son, then tried to make her believe that an animal was her son, an animal with no nose or ears and claws for hands. Every time she thought about her baby, her mind revisited those images and recoiled into a nightmare where her hatred and anger toward Venzel/Halil overshadowed the love she felt for a husband she could not identify.

Rauf faded from her memory until she only knew him as the doctor who gave her the baby, the endlessly hungry baby, the one who wasn't hers. In the beginning, she sometimes felt warm and happy inside as she fed him and pretended he was her son. Smiling, she talked to him of his father, tall, handsome, and strong, and her eyes glowed with love. When she remembered her husband was gone and her son dead, the light faded from her mind and her eyes. Handing what she believed to be another woman's baby to Ezri, Destani put her hands over her face and wept.

Some days, she arose early to prepare for her husband's arrival. To surprise him, she would, despite Ezri's constant vigil, cleverly slip away and run in the direction of the oasis to meet him. She rarely got far. A tall man, cloaked from head to foot, followed her until thirst made her tired or faint, and she wept piteously as he carried her to her room. He was kind, but he didn't understand how much she missed her husband, and for the rest of the day, she stood on the balcony looking southward, waiting.

Venzel waited on the balcony as well.

Without any idea that all she wanted was to see him again, he watched carefully for the moment her eyelids began to close. When she started to sway, he caught her and laid her gently on their bed, his face always carefully covered so if she looked, she would only see his eyes loving her.

One such morning, Destani remembered Alazar. Knowing he could take her to the oasis, she sent Ezri on an errand and slipped over the windowsill onto the balcony. Venzel, always watching from a distance, followed her down the balcony steps to the back porch. This was different. To Venzel's ever-hopeful heart, anything different could be a sign that she was recovering her memory.

Running to the back of the house where the stables once stood, she was surprised to find only a wooden platform without walls or horses. Venzel watched her pace back and forth, wringing her hands together and glancing at the platform as if she were trying to remember something.

He knew the moment she did.

"Alazar!" she cried.

Reaching out her hands as though to stop someone from striking her, Destani crumpled to the ground.

Venzel tenderly lifted her into his arms.

Witnessing it all from the porch, Ezri watched as Venzel carried her into the house, tears streaming from his eyes, saying gently, "Yes, my darling, shh, shh, I know it hurts, shh now, love."

Ezri sat down on the porch step, covered his face with his sleeve, and sobbed.

Destani never recovered from the events of that afternoon. Rauf became concerned because she wasn't eating, and although he could find no injury, he asked Venzel if she hit her head when she fell. Both he and Ezri said no.

She did not have the words to tell them that she was brokenhearted and grieving for Alazar. Although she did not clearly remember how he died, her mind only registered that he was dead, and she knew how much that was going to hurt her husband. There was little left for him to come home to, but she knew he would return. Regardless of her confusion, she never lost the assurance of her husband's love. Someday, when he came home, perhaps they would have another son—one they could keep.

Only the certainty of seeing her husband again kept Destani alive as she struggled to understand a world that was getting smaller and darker every day. No longer needing drugs to keep her calm, she seemed to have left all her resistance in the paddock yard and quietly did as she was asked. She ate the food and honey they put in front of her, would feed the baby when he was brought in, and bathed when Ezri's helper filled the tub. She stopped trying to run away, and as the months wore on, she became frail, her skin nearly translucent, and her turquoise eyes glittered like jewels in her beautiful face.

One day, Ezri stopped bringing the baby. When she asked why, Rauf came in and told her it was time the baby learned to eat other food.

She smiled when they left. Only the baby held her to the house. Since he didn't need her anymore, maybe the tall man would not follow her or bring her back. Finally free, Destani watched carefully for a chance to escape.

Venzel gradually assumed Ezri's duties in the room. She didn't object, and when he removed the scarf from his face, she didn't recognize him. Venzel felt Destani had ceased looking out from her luminous eyes but instead gazed inward; what she saw there, he was powerless to understand. All he knew was that she'd stopped running away and let him take care of her. Sometimes, when she slept, he picked her up and held her in the rocking chair all night. It wasn't much, but it was more than he thought he would ever have again.

Venzel and Ezri did not grow careless. They just didn't believe she had the physical strength to attempt another escape or enough mind to plan one. They were wrong. All Destani wanted was an opportunity. Her husband was constantly in her thoughts, and she believed he was waiting for her at the oasis. His tent was there, his beautiful horses were there, and more than anything else, she wanted to be there, too.

Except for the workers they hired—and therefore could control—the Lyostians avoided any outsider intrusion. Venzel, when he was home, or Ezri when he was not, drove to the village once a week for small supplies and the mail. Recently, due to the change in the colony's operations, the number of shipments made it easier for the mail wagon to stop at the compound before continuing to the village. Wanting these visits to be as brief as possible, everyone who could endure sunlight was outside emptying the wagon, and everyone who required shade was inside the house, moving the packages into the newly excavated classrooms and training areas.

Awakened by the noise of a particularly large delivery, Destani walked onto the balcony and saw Ezri and Venzel in the yard. Staying in the shadows, she quietly eased down the stairs.

Waiting in the garden until everyone was on the porch or inside, she ran to the horse nearest the gate. Quickly unhitching him from the wagon, she stepped on the running board and threw her leg over the horse's broad back. Leaning over his neck, she dug her heels into his sides.

The wind blew back her hair, and she was on her way. The tall man would never catch her now. At first, it was exhilarating, but in her haste to escape, she did not notice she was going in the wrong direction. Knowing where his stall was located, the horse raced toward the village. Destani, taught to ride on Venzel's horses that obeyed the slightest touch of a single rein on their necks, could not understand why the horse veered westward in response to her repeated attempts to guide him south.

Destani desperately struggled to gain control as the horse galloped over the uneven desert terrain. Frantically searching the horizon for a sign of the oasis, she did not see the dark chasm until it appeared in front of her. Using both hands and all her strength to avoid the ravine, she jerked the reins to the left. Unable to see where he was going, the horse tripped over his own feet, and together they tumbled over and over in the sand.

Suddenly weightless, she felt herself falling.

She was barely breathing when Venzel found her on the blood-stained rocks.

"Destani?"

She slowly turned her head toward the sound of his voice and smiled. In that single glance, Venzel knew she recognized him for who he was as love shone from her eyes. Kneeling beside her, he carefully lifted her in his arms.

She raised her hand to touch his face and smiled.

"You found me."

Trying to keep his voice steady, he said, "Yes, love, I was never going to stop looking for you."

Seeing the red stain spreading across the front of his cloak, he buried his face in her neck and cried, "Oh, my sweet wife, I'm so sorry!"

She put her hand on his head, "Shh, Venzel, shh, you'll wake the baby."

He stared at her. "The baby?"

"Yes, don't you see him? He is sleeping in his cradle by the door. Oh, Venzel," she sighed, "I love him so."

"And me, karisi?" he asked hoarsely. "Do you love me?"

"I've always loved you, Venzel, but I could not find you. There was something in the way, something dark and ugly." Pausing to catch her breath, she said simply, "It's gone now."

As he took her hand and brought it to his lips, his eyes hungrily sought her face.

It was heaven to look at her and see his wife in her eyes and to know that as they traveled over his face, she saw him and loved him still.

"Oh, my husband, I've missed you so much," she whispered.

Unwilling to accept that the very moment she'd returned to him, he was losing her forever; he pulled her closer.

"Don't leave me, Destani. You promised you would never leave me. Please try, love, please...."

Even as he said the words, he could feel her becoming lighter as she slowly slipped away from him. Trying desperately to accept the inevitable, he said, "What... oh my beloved, what will I do without you?"

"You will love our son."

Venzel's eyes grew hard. "No, latif, please do not say that. I cannot love him." Seeing the sorrow on her face, his voice softened, "Don't you understand, Destani? He has killed you."

Her eyes filled with tears. "No, Venzel, he loves me. You wouldn't believe how much he loves me."

She took a hiccupping breath and winced with pain. "So much like you. That's why I tried to love him back, but I couldn't... Everything was dark, and you were gone. Please, Venzel, please. You must promise to love him enough for both of us."

Unwilling to cause her one moment of grief, his resentment crumbled at the sight of her tears.

"Yes, my beautiful wife, I will love our son." Venzel bowed his head and whispered, "Oh, my love, I will do whatever you ask."

Destani smiled at him with all the love she had kept for this moment shining in her eyes. Her hand caressed the side of his face.

"Thank you, Venzel. Tell him, I love you… love you both… so much."

Before he had to endure the pain of watching love fade from her face, her lashes fluttered and closed as gently as a sigh.

Knowing she was beyond all suffering in this world, he pulled her into his lap and held her as he sang Anya's song of forgiveness and the lament. Unwilling to let her go, he talked to her about how they met, her beauty, and how much he loved her, and finally, Venzel talked to her about their son. However, it was not about Timaeus he spoke, but the son he imagined so clearly in the dappled sunlight of the oasis. The son that was promised to them… the one they could have kept if Venzel had been anyone else.

When the moon began to set, Venzel grew silent; it was time to take her home. Making a sling from her bloodied scarf, he carried Destani up the rocks.

At the top of the ravine, Zsiga grasped Venzel's arm to help him climb over the edge.

"Is there anything I can do?"

"No, Zsiga."

"Brother, I'm—"

"Sorry?"

"Yes, of course."

Venzel stepped over the kneeling camel's back. Bringing Destani's body into his lap, he clucked at the camel to stand. Seeing the redness of dawn in the east, Zsiga rewrapped the turban to cover his eyes and handed his camel's reins to Venzel. Slipping over his camel's back and clucking, the camel rose, and they began to move slowly toward the compound.

"Beyond everything, Venzel, I must ask you to forgive me."

"There is no forgiveness beyond everything, Zsiga. Did *you* do this to her?"

Zsiga answered his brother truthfully. "No, Venzi, I was not there. No one who knew her was there. But as it was done by one of us, however inadvertent, it was done by all."

"Yes." Venzel stopped the camels for a moment and looked at his younger brother. "So, you are not asking me to forgive you; you are asking me to forgive all of you."

Venzel watched as his brother signed to him. *I want you to forgive me for being part of something that has caused you so much pain. You are my brother, I love you. You may forgive the others in time, but I am asking you to forgive me now.*

Holding Destani's head against his shoulder, he whispered, "Yes, Zsiga, I forgive you. It is myself I will never forgive."

"Venzi—"

"No, my brother, there are no words, signals, or signs that can help me today."

A mile from the compound, Venzel broke the silence.

"Please ask them to dig a grave in the southeast corner of the garden and fill it with every flower in bloom. I do not want to see any color elsewhere. Have Ezri fill the basin in our room with warm water. I do not want anyone to speak to me, and the garden should be empty when I bring her down. I could not keep her to myself while she lived, but I will not share her with anyone else now that she is dead."

Zsiga tilted his head and sent the message as his brother requested. "It will be as you wish, Venzel."

"Thank you."

When they rode through the gate, Venzel did not see one flower in the garden. The corridors were quiet, and he met no one on the way to their room. He eased her out of the sling onto the carpet and bathed her. It took a while to get all the blood out of her hair, but he was patient; there was no reason to hurry. He dressed her in her bridal clothes and slipped the gold wedding bracelet on her arm. Before placing the beaded headdress over her face, he lifted the white and gold veil and kissed her for the last time.

Shortly after sunset, Venzel lifted Destani as though she were still the gentle girl he adored and pushed open the door. He did not expect to see Ezri standing in the hall holding Timaeus. Recognizing his mother's scent, the child's face was one of confusion as he tilted his head, searching for a sound he could not hear. Refusing to speak to Ezri or acknowledge the baby, Venzel shook his head once and walked away.

Venzel had ordered that no one could be in the garden, and Ezri had to obey, but Ezri loved Destani. Even after the baby, when everything became so difficult, she knew who he was and was kind to him. He remembered that Venzel did not say the balconies had to be vacant. Still carrying Timaeus, Ezri walked out on the covered balcony as Venzel lowered Destani onto the flowers.

Seeing her surrounded by a rainbow of flower petals, Timaeus tilted his head again to listen, but a forbidding silence had replaced her reassuring echo in his mind. Hearing the tall man begin singing Anya's lament as the soil was returned to the earth, he understood.

Ezri felt something warm on his arm and looked down. Wailing soundlessly into the black void for his mother, tears fell from Timaeus's turquoise eyes, and his scarred hands waved in the air, trying to recapture the graceful spirit that had gone from him forever.

Hoping the blind nurse would be able to offer some comfort to the grieving child, Ezri left the balcony to find Senkali as Venzel returned to the room. Seeing Timaeus so aptly expressing the feelings that he, himself, possessed, Venzel took his son from Ezri's arms and asked him to leave. As he closed the door, Ezri heard the key turn in the lock. Running into the next room to access the balcony, he arrived in time to watch the final shutter pulled closed and fastened. For months, Ezri had watched the way Venzel looked at the child. It was impossible to mistake his unremitting hatred for anything else. Alarmed, Ezri ran to get Zsiga.

Trying to respect Venzel's grief but unable to shake his fear for the child's safety, Ezri did not want all the brothers involved. Asking for Zsiga, he only said that Venzel wanted to see him. As they climbed the stairs, Ezri told him what happened.

Zsiga listened and tried not to panic. "Go to your quarters, Ezri. I will talk with my brother. I am sure the child will not come to any harm. Bring food in the morning before sunrise, and if I am not there, please find me and report what you see."

Although he did not share Zsiga's confidence, Ezri nodded. On his way downstairs, he prayed they would not be digging two more graves in the morning.

As Ezri's footsteps faded, Zsiga swiftly took the stairs two at a time. Quietly entering the adjoining balcony from his mother's room, Zsiga scanned the child's thoughts, detecting only heartbroken sorrow. *So, he knows and understands*. Most of their offspring did not notice when their mothers left them or died, and the ones who did usually accepted it and did not mourn or weep. However, the collective considered those who were aware *and* mourned the most intuitive and creative among the generations. Such children were allowed to choose their work and given the highest education available—a rare privilege in a society where education and work were based not on individual aptitude but on collective need.

Zsiga immediately transmitted Timaeus's reaction to the collective, and he was ordered to protect the wellbeing of the child. Timaeus was the third of the Tuzurias to exhibit this particular trait, and it was important to the collective to observe how it manifested itself within this advanced mutation.

Now Zsiga was alarmed. Being appointed the guardian of such a child was a dubious honor. If something the collective considered preventable happened, the repercussions would be severe.

Until he understood why Venzel locked the child in the room with him, he could not leave. Sitting on the balcony floor, Zsiga leaned his head back against the wall and listened. If he had to, he could tear the shutters out of the window, but he also knew that if Venzel wanted to harm the child, he would never be quick enough to stop him. Closing his eyes so he could concentrate, Zsiga heard movement on the other side of the wall, but he did not know Venzel was carrying the boy in his arms in a room that wasn't as dark as it should have been. It was just light enough so Venzel could see the color of Timaeus's tormented eyes gazing up at him.

After a few moments, Zsiga heard Venzel talking.

"Yes, yes, I know. It hurts, doesn't it?"

Zsiga recognized the tone of Venzel's voice. He remembered hearing it when their mother died. There was no anger in Venzel's words, and Zsiga knew the boy would be safe, at least for one night. Seeking the room he shared with Senkali, Zsiga descended the stairs.

Exhausted from the events of the last two days, Zsiga slipped into bed. Falling asleep immediately, he was unaware that in the harem where the surviving wives lived in luxury and comfort, the beautiful mother of his second son had succeeded in starving herself to death.

Venzel intended to burn Destani's clothes when he returned to the room as the final rite of her burial. The smell of dust and death overpowered the fading fragrance of her perfume, and he longed to destroy them, but mentally, emotionally, and physically shattered, Venzel could not make himself do it. Desiring the oblivion of sleep above all else, he set the grieving child in the cradle and went to bathe in the other room.

It wasn't long before he became aware that the apartment was quiet, too quiet. Venzel hurriedly wrapped himself in a towel, walked into the bedroom, and stopped. On the pile of his mother's blood-encrusted clothes, Timaeus was fast asleep—the edge of her silk scarf clasped in the curved fingers of his claw-shaped hand.

Staring at the creature with contempt, Venzel left Timaeus to sleep on the filthy clothes and crawled into bed; the promise made to his dying wife already forgotten.

Revenge

Venzel woke the next morning to the plaintive cries of sobbing women and the sound of a door key being tossed on the wooden table. He opened his eyes to see Zsiga pull a chair away from the table and sit down. Although he'd decided the night before not to concern himself further with the boy, the first words out of Venzel's mouth were, "Where is he?"

"I handed him to Ezri to be returned to the nursery," said Zsiga, glancing at the clothes on the floor. "He needed a bath."

Venzel ignored the underlying question in Zsiga's statement and asked one of his own. "Why are the women crying? I thought they knew about Destani yesterday."

"They did… but this," Zsiga passed his hand over his eyes, "this is because Lalei died in her sleep. Usually, I check on her to say goodnight, but it was late, and I… I was tired."

Venzel understood. Searching for Destani and bringing her home had been a long and arduous trek through the desert, and although he did not care about Lalei, dead or alive, she was still Zsiga's wife.

"I am sorry, my brother. I know you cherished her."

"In my way… yes, I did. Nevertheless, she never cherished me and was always miserable here. And, well, we both know why. I think I could have overlooked everything, forgiven her anything, but when she started calling our son—you know the name she called him—I took Taliph away

198

from her and gave him to Senkali. I monitored his thoughts; he barely noticed, and Senkali, well, I don't think there are enough babies in the world for her."

"She has been a blessing to us."

"Yes, she has, and I will forever be grateful to you for choosing her, and to her, for choosing me." Zsiga anxiously rubbed his face with his hands.

"But will you ever forgive me for bringing the other one?" asked Venzel. "And, and for not treating her with more kindness? You don't know how much I wish I could go back and... Well, maybe it would not have made any difference to me, but my brother, it might have made a difference to you. She was lucky to have married you, Zsiga. You were always the patient one."

"But not patient enough, Venzi. That's my point. It was my fault. I killed her."

"No. How could it ever be your fault? There was no heart, and very little truth, in her, and there were times when she wanted to die. You told me yourself Rauf was barely keeping her alive during her pregnancy and afterward."

"That was before the baby looked... human. Once Rauf removed the blankets, she practically fell in love with him. She stopped crying, and when Rauf said the baby would be healthier if she was, she ate everything we sent up to her. Taliph did not spend much time in the nursery because she was always holding him, playing with him, or nursing him. We thought she would do that with all the babies, but she only wanted Taliph. Then she started calling him," Zsiga's jaw clenched, and the word barely escaped his lips, "Halil, and I had the feeling she'd been calling him that all along, just not out loud. That was when I realized it wasn't *my* son she loved—but *his*."

"And...?"

"And when I asked her to call him by his real name, she refused. He is Tuzurias, Venzel. I could not risk him being confused as to who he is.

She said he was a baby, and it didn't matter what she called him. I tried to reason with her and gave her time to change, but she wouldn't stop. I, I began to believe she was testing me to see if I would take him away from her. So, I did. When I didn't give him back, she apparently stopped eating, and I… I never noticed."

"Oh, Zsiga."

"I'd like to think that she misjudged her strength and didn't mean to die on purpose. Then again, either way, it is still my fault for not being considerate enough, for not noticing how thin she was. My impatience and neglect killed her, Venzel. I, Anya forgive me, was a poor husband."

"Zsiga, you cannot blame yourself. As unfortunate as her death is, I know you never intended to hurt her, and you saved Taliph from the effects of her willful disobedience. Isn't his well-being just as important as hers?"

"Yes, but the collective takes a dim view of brothers who deliberately mistreat our mothers, especially a compliant, nursing mother."

Zsiga pressed his hands to his eyes. Venzel watched his lips move in prayer and tried to reason with him.

"I don't know how compliant she was when she would not do what you asked, and she has been unstable almost from the beginning, but we couldn't send her home after she willingly became a wife and mother."

Zsiga's only response was to continue praying. Venzel listened to the words and suddenly realized that Zsiga's comments were far more serious than husbandly sorrow at the loss of his wife; his brother was slowly falling apart because if the collective held him responsible for Lalei's death, its retaliation would be swift… and final.

"Wait, Zsiga, you cannot possibly be thinking they would…? NO!" Venzel got out of bed and started putting on his clothes. "I will not let this happen! Who do I have to talk to?"

Taking his hands from his eyes, Zsiga almost laughed. Venzel was so wonderfully human sometimes. One moment, he was thinking and talking like a Lyostian, and the next, he was brandishing an invisible sword and coming to his younger brother's rescue. Zsiga had loved Venzel all his life, but never more than in that moment when he stood in the middle of his room half-dressed and willing to fight the entire collective to save his brother's life.

"Rauf is doing the talking right now. He's basically telling them everything you've said but in more medical terms. And, it is not discounted, Venzel, that you are my brother—"

"And Senkali is your wife."

"Senkali belongs to the colony. She is only my responsibility because *she* believes she is my wife. Still, it may count for something."

"Zsiga, I'm not going to let anything or anyone hurt you. They will have to kill me first."

"Thank our blessed Anya, that won't be necessary," Rauf said, interrupting them and pulling out the other chair.

Zsiga tilted his head.

"No, Zsiga, I think we must discuss this matter between the three of us, so we won't have to do it twice."

Venzel sat on the edge of the bed.

"I was quite frank with my report to the collective. Several very pointed questions were asked and had to be answered fully. The truth is, Zsiga, they already knew she was ill from the surgeons' report indicating she was dangerously thin. After Taliph was born and she began eating again, I told them we rejoiced in her recovery and compliance, which, upon reflection, I now attribute to a hormonal rush. I pointed out that when those levels stabilized, she resumed acting erratically, deliberately endangering Taliph's wellbeing and undermining her own physical condition. As a last resort, you took the only course possible to preserve the mental health of Taliph by placing him with a loving, compliant, and *healthy* human mother. When they scanned his thoughts, they found no harm had been done by separating him from his natural mother."

"And Lalei's death?" Zsiga said slowly.

"Regretted, but not unexpected."

"Meaning what, exactly, Rauf?" asked Venzel.

Zsiga answered for him. "I will not be punished."

"You're damn right you're not going to be punished. It was my fault for not voicing my suspicions stronger, but I was distracted." Unbidden came thoughts of that night and how he hurried back to Destani, who was waiting for him, loving him. He brushed his hand over his face and pushed those thoughts away. "I will not let you be punished for something that was my responsibility."

Rauf looked at Venzel steadily. "You understand, Venzel, that if the collective chose to punish Zsiga—or any of us—it would not be something you could divert, prevent, or halt. Rules are made by the agreement of all for the benefit of all concerned. If Taliph was not Tuzurias, it could have gone much harder. It is one of our top priorities that the baby stays with his own mother as long as possible, and Zsiga disregarded one of our primary objectives. However, with this generation, we are not taking any chances with their mental state or their identity—it is imperative that they know who and what they are."

"Then why Timaeus, given Destani's...?"

"First, because at the time he was born, there was no alternative; she had to nurse him, or he would die. Second, by the time we had an alternative mother, he'd bonded with her, and it was more important that he stay with her, even if there was a delay in her bonding with him. And third, we monitored his thoughts, and while he accepted Senkali, it was nowhere near the feelings he had for Destani, and we felt he should stay with her—as did you—for as long as she could, and would, nurture him."

"Yes, you're right. It was something I wanted, too. I am grateful for your patience." He glanced in his brother's direction. "Zsiga, once again, I am sorry."

Zsiga shook his head. "You were not responsible for her behavior, Venzel."

Rauf stood up to leave. "I guess the remaining wives will be expecting a small service later." He sighed and tilted his head.

Zsiga straightened his head immediately. "No, not the garden," he said. "Put her with the others. Thank you, and my brothers, for asking."

Only two women were buried in the garden: his mother and Destani. Zsiga knew they would dig Senkali's grave there someday. He hoped he would not live to see it.

Zsiga did not move until Rauf closed the door. Crossing his arms on the table, he laid his head down and trembled so violently the table shook. Grief strangled in his throat behind his clenched jaw. Unsure what was tormenting Zsiga, Venzel sat next to him, put his hand on his brother's shoulder, and waited.

Eventually, the noises in Zsiga's throat ceased, and the waves that rippled through his body subsided. Venzel heard him take several deep breaths. He knew how difficult the last couple of days had been for Zsiga. Aware that traveling during the day, he was risking lightning headaches that would render him nearly useless, Zsiga refused to allow Venzel, panic-stricken and grieving, to search for Destani alone; and, although Venzel did not know Ezri had gotten Zsiga out of bed to monitor Timaeus, he could tell his brother had not slept much the night before. Waking to the sorrow of finding Lalei dead, followed by the anxiety that he could have been held responsible for the death of a surviving and compliant human mother, the one thing the collective—with all its accumulated wealth—could not buy.

Believing he had considered all the possible causes for Zsiga's anguish, Venzel was not prepared for Zsiga's face when he lifted his head from his arms. Venzel barely recognized him. The skin stretched tightly over his cheekbones, his eyes, flat and focused, were black bottomless pits, and his mouth was a thin white line. Venzel always believed he was the fiercer of Damla's two sons, but the expression on Zsiga's face shocked him. It was pure hatred.

"Zsiga, my brother, what is it?"

In a low steady voice that did not sound like Zsiga at all, he said, "Venzel, everything we've requested of you that you may have, perhaps, harbored human objections to doing, has come from the collective. You have never refused them."

"I never will, Zsiga. We are one."

"Are we?"

"Yes." Sensing the seriousness of Zsiga's question, Venzel asked in the same low voice, "What are my brothers asking me to do?"

"They are not asking. I am."

"What are you asking me to do, son of my mother?"

Kill him, he signed.

Staring at Zsiga, Venzel felt the tension of the last several days ease from his mind, and a smile that didn't make it to his lips shone in his eyes.

"Yes."

"We are one?"

"Always."

Zsiga leaned back in the chair, closed his eyes, and began to breathe normally. The detestable human, Halil, would die. The man who had tried to destroy Venzel's life, Destani's life, and, because Zsiga knew—despite what Rauf said—how close he came to being executed for Lalei's betrayal, his own life. No one, not even Venzel, could have saved him. His death would have left Senkali alone, his brother bereft, and the sons of his wives to be assimilated into the collective without any personal guidance. As tragic for all concerned as those outcomes would have been, they were not the only reasons for Halil's death—or the most important.

The human Halil was the impenetrable wall that had stood between him and the most delicious woman he had ever known. Zsiga would have been the happiest creature on earth if she had shown him one-tenth, or even one-twentieth, of Senkali's affection, but no. When she was awake, she trembled and cried when he came near her; when she was asleep, she dreamed he was Halil. During her pregnancy, he counted the hours until the evenings when he had her all to himself. Slowly, from one end of her to the other, he caressed her with his hands, his mouth, and tongue. As she became aroused, her temperature rose, and her skin became covered with a nectar so intoxicating it was impossible to leave her… until she woke up without her clothes and with whispers of Halil on her lips that smiled until she saw Zsiga lying next to her. Then she would cry, turn away, and say she hated him. Her rejection would have been less painful if she was aware of what he was, but it was who he was not that she detested.

He endured it until the day she called his son "Halil." Unlike Destani, embryonic toxins had not affected her brain. She knew what she was saying, and he would not allow it. She refused to stop, deliberately saying the name in his presence to taunt him. Lyostians, especially those at Zsiga's level, were rarely capable of independent action or thought. Such conduct did not contribute to the progress of the collective, and their genetically controlled evolution had filtered out such tendencies centuries ago, but whatever was unpredictably human in Zsiga could not tolerate it. As he'd threatened, without notice to or approval from the collective, he took his son from her. She did not protest but merely looked at him, her sky-blue eyes registering no emotion at all. With casual indifference, she waved to her son and said, "Bye-bye, Halil."

Little more than a week later, she was dead, and he may well have been responsible, but it was never Venzel's fault for bringing her to the compound. On the contrary, Zsiga would give almost anything for another night of her.

He blamed the owner of the name that had echoed in his ears for months, destroying any chance for happiness they might have shared. He would have preferred to kill Halil himself, but that was impossible, and perhaps taking care of this matter for him would give his brother a small measure of peace.

Venzel watched Zsiga's face and, although he could not read his thoughts, had, now that he knew what his brother wanted, understood most of it. There was no uncertainty in his mind that he would find Halil and grant his brother's request. At that moment, there were few things in life that would give him greater pleasure than planning Halil's murder.

Knowing their brothers would not be in the house this time of day, he leaned close to Zsiga.

"When?"

"As soon as you can without endangering yourself."

"How?"

"The most excruciating way possible without endangering yourself."

Showing no embarrassment, Venzel asked, "When will the colony be finished with her body?"

Zsiga hesitated. There was a reason Venzel had Destani buried where he could watch her grave.

"Um, why?"

"I want to take a certain person a… gift."

"Her heart?"

"No, my brother, her heart is too small. I want to give him something he will recognize. I want her long golden-brown hair."

"I will get that for you tonight… after the service. How much do you want?"

"All of it."

"You want me to cut off all of her hair?"

"Oh, no, Zsiga, I want you to scrape off all of her hair, and here…." He walked over and removed a long, thin ribbon from the pile of clothes on the floor. "Tie this around it."

Zsiga stared at the strip of silk, stained and stiff with blood. For a moment, he saw Destani's eyes when she looked at Venzel and realized how unworthy Lalei was for even this scrap of Destani's dress.

Misreading his brother's hesitation, Venzel said softly, "I will do it. Just let me know where she is when you have finished with her."

When Zsiga lifted his head, Venzel was not surprised to see his own expression reflected in his brother's face. Taking the ribbon, Zsiga pressed it to his lips.

"I loved her, too, you know."

"Yes, my brother, I know you did."

The next day, Zsiga handed Venzel a small cushion cover, and Venzel placed it on the mantel next to an exquisite ebony box he'd bought at a bazaar on his last trip to Constantinople.

Halil's gift was nearly complete.

Mustafa stared at the handwriting on the small parcel and walked into the first interior room of his tent. "Halil," he called, "someone has sent you a package."

With a questioning look on his face, Halil took the rectangular box from his father. He glanced at the address to make sure it was for him. For a moment, his heart stopped beating. It was a woman's handwriting. Instinctively, he shook the package and, not hearing anything, untied the string and tore at the brown paper. Nested in wood shavings was a beautiful ivory inlaid ebony box. Clearly expensive and rare, he turned it over and recognized the mark of a famous artisan. Momentarily stunned, he did not feel the wrappings fall from his hands or see a small envelope spill out of the carton as it tumbled to the floor.

"There's a letter," Mustafa said, handing it to him. "Do you know who sent this?"

"Maybe...."

Refusing to let go of the box, Halil opened the envelope. Immediately embraced by her unforgettable perfume, his hands trembled slightly as he removed the single sheet of folded paper. In the same feminine handwriting, he read the two words written there: *Remember me*. Halil's face grew pale, and he quickly sat down on the divan. The handwriting and the perfume drove every doubt from his mind that the package was from Lalei.

"Son, are you all right?"

"Yes, yes, I'm fine. Um, could you leave me for a few minutes, Father? I'd like to open this alone. It might be... I think it's a gift from *her*."

At those words, Mustafa's face reddened. He kicked the cardboard carton into a corner of the room and stormed out of the tent.

Mustafa was running out of patience. Halil had been half a man since the search party returned empty-handed. For two years, Lalei had teased Halil, first wanting him, then refusing him, then wanting him again. The last time she refused him, Halil called her bluff, and she hired herself out as a servant to spite him. Mustafa didn't know what the box contained, but it was never going to be enough for making Halil miserable for two years and useless for almost two more.

Lost in memories of Lalei, Halil was hardly aware his father had gone. Placing the box on his knees, he caressed the beautiful dark wood. His fingers traced the delicate ivory swirls, and he thought of her skin. Her perfume lingered in the air, and closing his eyes, Halil saw Lalei in his mind, her blue eyes shining and warm, and her pink lips smiling at him. Wanting to hold on to his vision of her as long as possible, he found the latch with his hands and gently lifted the lid. When he knew her gift was waiting before him, he slowly opened his eyes. Tied with a bloodied ribbon, Lalei's hair uncoiled into his lap with bits of dried scalp still clinging to the roots. Halil stared motionless for several moments. When he understood exactly what this "gift" meant, a low moan escaped his throat.

Standing behind the curtain, his mother heard his despair and ran to the entrance of the tent to call Mustafa.

Unable to move his eyes from the softly curling hair that still glinted gold in the sunlight, Halil did not see the small creatures emerge from beneath the silken strands. Nor did he feel them crawling onto his shaking hands and up his arms until they began stinging him. Within moments, his anguished sounds of grief became high-pitched screams of panic and burning agony as the venom raced through his bloodstream. Mustafa ran into the room in time to see one of the eight-legged arachnids crawl away from Halil's convulsing body and smashed it with his rifle butt. Leaving Halil to his mother's care, Mustafa ran out of the tent, determined to track down the devil that had brought this misfortune into their lives.

Filling his canteen at the village well, Venzel's courier dropped it at the sound of the first shriek. As the screams became more and more horrific, he turned his head in the direction of the outcry in time to see the bullet before it split his eye and shattered the back of his skull.

Venzel watched the scene unfold from the top of a dune. He knew his plan had succeeded when an older man rushed from the dusty orange tent, yelling, "Murderer!" as he aimed his rifle and shot the unlucky messenger.

Lalei's name echoed in agonizing shrieks throughout the encampment until—as sudden as the screams began—there was only silence. A woman, inconsolable and bent over with grief, emerged from the tent crying, "Mustafa!" and wailed that Halil was dead.

Recalling the expression on Zsiga's face, Venzel whispered, "For you, my brother."

Lowering the field glasses, he turned the camel eastward, careful to keep the dunes between him and the outlying tents and corrals. The sound of the woman's sorrow hung in the air. Venzel wished the venom's torment had lasted longer, but he wasn't taking any chances that Halil might survive. One black scorpion wouldn't have been enough... two would fight, but three... three was the perfect number, and if they found another victim or two as they crawled back into the desert, he could not be blamed.

It was who they were.

Compromise

Venzel kept his part of the bargain...

In the months immediately following Destani's death, Venzel traveled by car or helicopter to the breeding colonies requesting his attendance on their wives. When he thought about it at all, he felt his life had been reduced to that of the pistol in a game of Russian roulette. Sometimes, these nameless women lived; sometimes, they died, but either way, he was not responsible. Trapped like butterflies pinned to their silken pillows, Venzel made no effort to save them but treated them as lovingly as he could, apologizing in this way for whatever tragedy might follow. He had surrendered any hope of forgiveness. Regardless of how kind and gentle he was, Venzel knew full well the consequences of every kiss, each shudder of delight and soft sigh.

He did not begrudge the colony this use of his abilities, but to protect what remained of his humanity, Venzel built a wall of anger between his responsibilities to the colony and whatever sorrow resulted from those responsibilities. He still had one reason to live, and if existing within the shadow of that wall was the only way he could survive, so be it.

...and the collective kept its part as well.

Altering the former SCM outpost from a breeding to a nurturing colony required a change of staff, and Venzel met new brothers each time he returned to the compound. As he had requested, Zsiga and Senkali stayed, as well as the other surviving mothers. As the Tuzurias generation began arriving, some women came with their infants, and then infants arrived without mothers. By stabilizing their hormone levels with the honey they were served at every meal, the mothers continued to nurse Lyostian orphans long after their own children moved out of the nursery. These women were revered and lived in luxury with every wish granted—except the wish to leave.

The Fire Slayers

It was rare to find Venzel in the deeper tunnels. There were things he preferred not to see, so he kept to the higher, more public areas. But Zsiga knew when he was there—and why he was there. He did not wish to intrude on his brother's life and decided to ignore the occasions when he caught Venzel's scent in the nursery wing of the northeast tunnel.

It had been noticeably absent for several months as Venzel traveled for the colony, and Zsiga looked forward to his imminent return.

Zsiga.

Yes, Rauf.

Please go to the nursery immediately. Venzel is tearing it apart.

Venzel is back?

Obviously.

Do you know why he is so angry?

No. That is what we want you to find out… do you want us to join you?

No, I will take care of this.

As you wish, we will not interfere unless you call us, but hurry.

Hoping to find that Rauf had overstated the matter, Zsiga ran to the nursery and stopped in the doorway. Surveying the wreckage with dismay, he focused his eyes on Venzel.

"Venzi?"

Venzel turned on him, his eyes blazing with grief and confusion.

"Where are they?"

"They?"

"The children, Zsiga. Where are they? Did you wait until I was gone to send them away? His eyes narrowed as he walked slowly toward Zsiga. "I thought we had an agreement, or was I mistaken, my brother?"

Losing Venzel's trust was far more detrimental to Zsiga's well-being than any physical harm Venzel could inflict on him. Looking into Venzel's eyes, he said quietly, "I have not lied to you, Venzel, and I never will. The children are not here because we have moved them to a dormitory."

"They can barely walk, Zsiga. How can they be in a dormitory?"

A slow smile passed over Zsiga's face. "Come, Venzi, you have been gone for a while."

"Four months, Zsiga, is not 'a while.'"

"It's been nearly six… come with me."

Rauf.

Zsiga! Do you need any help?

No. Curiously enough, he was angry when he couldn't find the children in the nursery. I'm taking him to their dormitory now. He's settled down. Although he purports not to care, we must—casually—keep him informed of where the children are located.

The nursery?

As we have transitioned into a nurturing colony, we don't need it anymore. He just saved us the trouble of demolishing it ourselves.

You have a unique perspective of this outburst, Zsiga.

I have a loving brother's perspective… it is what I have for all my brothers. As do you.

Yes, well, thank you for handling this disruption so well. I think you will be a great colony leader, and I will miss you.

As we will miss you, Rauf.

Zsiga stopped in front of a room between the nursery and the rooms he shared with Senkali.

"Here is their dormitory, Venzi."

Venzel stayed in the hall as Zsiga walked into a large circular room surrounded by small cots placed end to end against the walls. In the center of this circle, twenty small boys played with balls of different sizes, bouncing the large plastic balls, and rolling smaller wooden balls. Except for the sound of the softer balls hitting the floor and harder ones knocking up against each other, the room was completely silent.

Venzel stood amazed as he watched something that more closely resembled a dance than child's play. Explicitly coordinated, the children would toss or roll the balls to each other, and then, with the tilt of a head and without a misstep, the pattern would completely change. Venzel looked at each small face until he found the eyes he sought and stared at his son. Several times, it was Timaeus who tilted his head, making the pattern more complex each time.

Instead of watching the children, Zsiga watched Venzel's face. As he calmed down, his expression changed from confusion to admiration. With regret in his heart, Zsiga saw the admiration in Venzel's eyes darken in pain as he turned and walked away. Zsiga looked at Timaeus. Although he was not missing his turn to toss, bounce, or roll the ball as it came to him, Timaeus's eyes were not on the game but stared curiously beyond the empty doorway.

Timaeus.

Zsiga.

A little simpler, please. Your brothers are getting tired.

Yes, thank you, Zsiga.

Timaeus tilted his head, and more than one child smiled in relief.

Leaving the room, Zsiga unexpectedly found Venzel waiting for him in the hall.

"Do you have some time, my brother? I have some questions about what I've just seen."

"Of course, and I want to hear about your travels. The conference room?"

"Yes." Venzel stood for a moment at the tunnel entrance, and Zsiga knew he was silently triangulating the exact position of the dormitory.

After first sharing the results of his recent excursions and hearing from Zsiga the news of the colony, Venzel took a deep breath and looked into his brother's face.

Nodding in the direction of the boys' dormitory, he said, "You did not do that when you were two years old."

Smiling, Zsiga shook his head, "No, I did not. But I was fairly good at catch—if you remember."

"You were very good at everything, but I have only seen coordination like that among trained acrobats or athletes. So, what I want to know is, these children, this new Tuzurias generation of leaders, what is their purpose?"

"Forgive me, Venzi, I sometimes forget that you do not have access to the archives. Yes, the Tuzurias force is a leadership level in our hierarchy, but their responsibilities go beyond colony leadership. Since the first Tuzurias generation, they have always been the vanguards of our society. This generation is the result of decades of research, and, well, their purpose is to lead our future generations out of their underground existence."

"How is that even possible? Zsiga, there is too much light—you would be in pain every minute. Wait, please tell it to me from the beginning. As much as you are allowed to, anyway."

Zsiga tried not to smile at the sudden interest on Venzel's face.

"Venzel, we live underground now not only because of our eyes but because we have always feared humans for their ability to turn anything into a weapon, their unrelenting aggression, and their reluctance to accept anyone... different. In fact, we have lived above ground several times in our past, but whenever we attempted a small settlement in a remote area of the world, our lack of aggression made us vulnerable to encroaching humans who had no patience for negotiation or talent for compromise. Even as we evolved to look as human-like as possible, we could not risk confrontation because of our limited and stratified population."

Zsiga moved his chair closer. "Because you understand how the loss of one brother can alter the entire colony structure, you have always respected and shared our keen instinct for survival. More than once, Venzel, you have kept disaster from our doors. Earlier generations, lacking a strong military tradition or colony defenders, had two choices—retreat or die. Many times, entire Lyostian colonies vanished underground in self-defense, leaving all they possessed behind because they could not effectively protect themselves.

"Our evolution had its costs. First, we gradually lost our capacity to produce our own females, then our physical ability to mate with human women. Due to these deficiencies, we have never been able to substantially increase our population. On the other hand, humans have reproduced prolifically all over the globe, constantly pushing us into underground colonies just to survive. Aware of the finite resources of the earth, our governing hierarchy realized we could not keep retreating if we were to fulfill our mandate to preserve the planet for future generations. They were determined to find a solution."

"And the Tuzurias was their solution?" asked Venzel.

"A major part of it, yes. The collective decided to isolate one segment of our social strata possessing the highest intelligence and fundamentally alter its genetic arthropod strand. By substituting the DNA of the myrmica strain, they deliberately designed a military level. They named these brothers the Tuzurias, or 'fire slayers' in your language. Carefully observing the effects of this genetic mutation within each subsequent generation, the reproduction serum was constantly revised until we created our own fighting force."

"So, Zsiga, if you've done this before, what makes these future soldiers so special?"

"For one thing, their training. Part of their education includes specialized instruction in psychological warfare and alienation techniques. They possess the ability to control their innate aversion to human men to get close enough to coordinate defensive tactics and lead their brothers in retaliatory operations. This inner strength is unique to the Tuzurias, making these members of Lyostian society very valuable and highly respected by all."

"Have I ever met a fire slayer? Before now, I mean?"

"No, we are quite safe here. In fact, one of the reasons you've never met one is because of you, Venzi. You have always protected our identity and have done much to keep us from harm. A few have passed through the village tunnels, but they have not stopped here because, as an elite fighting force, they are moved from one sector to another as needed for neutralization of any danger or threats against their assigned colony, including internal ones."

"Why internal ones?"

"Not all colonies are as cooperative as ours, Venzel. It is, of course, regrettable, which brings us to the reason for this particular generation."

"These children are different?"

"Oh, yes. At first, the collective believed it had the entire century to perfect this mutation, but we have lived in helpless dread as humans made a priority of improving their nuclear weapons technology. Despite witnessing the horrific results of this knowledge, they are becoming increasingly aggressive and destructive on a global scale. With their regard for the earth disappearing a little each day, it is suicide to wait much longer. The collective's plans to move above ground as quickly as possible have resulted in expecting more from every level of our society—especially the Tuzurias. In anticipation of this event, the serum has been refined for the last time. Marked with names beginning with *T*, the serum for this Tuzurias generation contains the highest concentration of myrmica acid."

"And that comes from…?"

"Fire ants."

Venzel hesitated for a moment.

"Zsiga, what has the collective made of my son… exactly?"

"Genetically created from flesh and fire, Timaeus will be one of the last Tuzurias leaders. The collective will not go forward with any future Tuzurias until this generation reaches its maturity in its twelfth year."

Zsiga paused, but Venzel did not respond.

"You have not specifically requested this information, Venzel, but I want to tell you that the governing hierarchy believes your son to be among the most intelligent and gifted Lyostians ever born."

Venzel was quiet for several moments as his mind raced back and forth over the knowledge Zsiga had shared with him. He pushed back his chair and stood up.

"Thank you, Zsiga, for your honesty. That was more information than I expected."

"I thought you should know… and Timaeus?"

"You said it yourself, 'among the most intelligent and gifted *Lyostians* ever born.' If he is not *hers*, then he can never be mine. Like the sting of a scorpion or a fatal disease, he is—as he has always been—the reason she died."

Zsiga stood up and faced his brother.

"Venzel, you must understand! He is so much more than that."

"Not to me."

The Broken Web

Nestled in the corner of the garden, nothing marked Destani's grave except a slightly raised area of grass with a small rectangle worn down to sand at its base where, if anyone noticed, Venzel stood or knelt, depending on whether he was leaving the compound or returning. Toward the end of the second year following her death, Venzel noticed a small woven arrangement of twigs pressed into the grass beside the grave containing a piece of broken blue tile and a cloudy piece of quartz. Believing a nest had fallen from one of the trees in the garden, he picked it up. Looking closely, he thought it resembled a shallow basket more than a nest and marveled at the ingenuity of the birds to construct something so uniquely interconnected without string or mud. Shaking the stones onto the ground, Venzel returned it to the nearest tree.

Months later, Venzel was preparing for his annual round of visits to the neighboring colonies. Never leaving without praying for her forgiveness, he walked into the garden and stopped. Staked to the head of Destani's grave was a spider web intricately constructed of reeds and braided lemongrass. Wedged into the center of the web, a small piece of broken glass cast a rainbow over the grave. Scowling, Venzel viciously ripped it out of the ground with one hand and, with his camel whip in the other, went to find Ezri.

Not seeing him in the tunnel bedroom Venzel had reclaimed after Halil's murder, he knew there was only one other place Ezri could be at that time of day and grew angrier with each stair step that ascended to the upper floor of the main house.

Thinking Venzel had already left the compound, Ezri was secretly cleaning the balcony rooms. He came up there as often as he could, trying to keep up with the dust that filtered in through the shuttered windows. He didn't have Venzel's permission, but he could not help it. He'd kept these rooms clean for her when she was alive and saw no reason to stop now.

Suddenly, the door slammed behind him, and the whip came down hard on the bed. Ezri hit the floor.

"Master! What is wrong?"

Without answering, Venzel threw the broken web on the carpet in front of him.

"How dare you!"

"Master, I humbly beg to understand. What has this to do with me?"

"You did not make this? Or put it on her grave?"

"No, Master, you have forbidden us to remember her. We... respect your wishes."

"If you 'respected my wishes,' why are you in here? I will not have it, Ezri! It is intolerable that you take such advantage."

Ezri closed his eyes. It would be so easy to provoke Venzel into killing him, but there were memories he was not yet willing to surrender, so he tried to reason with the madman holding the whip.

"I clean in here, Master," he said calmly. "It is dusty, and so I clean as I would clean any other room. But this," he said, pointing to the twisted reeds on the floor, "this I did not do."

"Do not lie to me! You are the only person who was there that day who would dare disobey me thinking, wrongly I might add, I would not punish you for that—or for this." Venzel waved his hands, taking in the scope of the room.

Ezri was silent for a moment. "Punish me for cleaning the room if it will ease your anger. But, Master, I am not the only one who was there that day." Sitting back on his heels, Ezri picked up the delicate memorial and looked up at Venzel. "It is a child's toy."

The briefest expression of surprise crossed Venzel's face before he crushed it back with the unrelenting hatred for the creature that killed his wife.

"Impossible. You should have seen it before... before I removed it. It was beautiful, special, and almost alive. No. A child that age would never have the patience or intelligence to fit the glass. Especially..."—he said through clenched teeth—"...that child."

Contradiction not being possible for a servant, Ezri said nothing and looked down at the pieces in his hands and, wishing he had seen it whole, sighed.

"I will not believe that!" Venzel said, spitting out the words.

Turning to leave, he saw the cradle still sitting in the corner of the room. Grabbing it up, he repeatedly crashed it against the doorframe until the cradle splintered into pieces. Fighting back the sobs in his throat, he tossed the broken fragments into the corner and stormed down the corridor.

Realizing the heartbreak that lived in that room would never end for Venzel, Ezri quietly finished cleaning. On his way out, he gently pulled the door closed as if she were still sleeping. Taking the key he wore on one of her ribbons around his neck, he locked the door for the last time.

Zsiga knew Venzel was still alive because of the positive reports he received regarding his brother's visits to the other colonies. Usually, Venzel came home between these trips, but not this time. He sent Zsiga books and packages from his travels but no letters.

Worried, Zsiga asked Ezri if Venzel had said anything before leaving. At a loss to explain their conversation, Ezri said only that he seemed angry about something. Zsiga was not surprised. Venzel had seemed angry for nearly three years and, keeping his pain buried deep in himself, would not let anyone reach where it hurt. Halil's death had given them both a sense of resolution, but Zsiga believed Venzel held onto his anger as a way of feeling alive.

It was several months before Venzel and the dark blue Mercedes returned to the compound. Every day near sunset, Ezri sat on the front porch watching the horizon for the pale smudges of silica dust signaling Venzel's return. For those two hours, he quaked inwardly as he thought of Destani's grave, and when Venzel did not arrive, he took a deep breath and slept that night. With the dawn of the new day, however, the dread grew greater because everything Ezri hinted at was true.

Each morning since Venzel left the compound, Ezri made a point of walking past the southeastern corner of the garden. For a while, the only evidence that anyone else remembered Destani was a small pair of footprints impressed in the sand. At first, there was only a simple oval outline made of twigs at the head of her grave. Gradually, the outline became the curved rim of a basket, with reeds going deep into the ground to stabilize the increasingly complex structure. One morning, there were triangular shards of broken glass suspended in the small oval opening in the center of the fragile monument. Chiming in the breeze and catching the sunlight, the iridescent fragments scattered music and flashes of color over the grass. In a small hollow beneath it were bits of blue tile and quartz sprinkled with crushed mica.

Ezri never caught the child working on it, but he knew no one else would dare.

Truth

When Venzel finally returned to the colony, he went immediately to Destani's grave. He stood there a long time. That evening, he found a shadow on the front porch and waited.

Timaeus did not turn around when he heard Venzel walk up behind him.

"I'm almost finished," he said, holding some small reeds in his right hand as he wove them into the structure with his left.

"You are finished now."

Venzel grabbed the boy's tunic and jerked him backward. Unable to control his rage, he raised his foot to crush the delicate memorial.

"Please do not do that. Mother was so happy there."

"Happy? Where?" Venzel asked, slowly lowering his foot.

"At the oasis," he said, pointing to the arrangement of rocks and mica.

Shining his small flashlight at the head of the grave, Venzel looked closer. It only took him a moment to recognize the oasis in miniature. He turned off the flashlight and put it in his pocket.

"Yes," he whispered, "she was very happy there."

Distracted by his grief for only a moment, he turned to Timaeus and asked harshly, "Why do you do this? It is forbidden."

"She is my mother and I love her... don't you?"

The simple question caught Venzel unprepared. "Why do you ask me that?"

"Because this," said Timaeus, patting the sand at the foot of the grave, "is where you are."

A stifled groan escaped Venzel's throat as he realized that, more than the boy could possibly understand, he *was* buried at Destani's feet. Venzel looked down at the small child and knew, even though he could not see them, that Timaeus was looking up at him with her eyes. The ache in his chest was more than he could bear. Knowing if he did not leave, he would hurl the boy headfirst into the garden wall, Venzel turned and walked to the back of the house. Sitting on the ground, he leaned against the porch steps and let his anguish seep out in hot tears that coursed down the sides of his face.

Timaeus followed Venzel and sat down with his back to the crescent moon. The tall man beside him was silent, and he could detect no thoughts in him, only a feeling of overwhelming sadness. He reached out his hand and softly patted the man's arm.

Crushed by his loneliness and so lost in the thoughts of the loving wife he missed more every day, Venzel was unaware of the small taps for several moments. When he finally opened his eyes, Timaeus saw all the pain in the world reflected there.

Timaeus only knew one human word for that kind of grief.

"Alazar," he whispered.

The expression in Venzel's eyes changed and narrowed as he looked down at the scarred fingers on his arm. No one had spoken that name in his presence for nearly four years. Where had this child heard it?

Fighting the urge to swat the small, curled hand away, Venzel asked, "Who has said that word to you, Timaeus? Was it Ezri or Zsiga?"

"No. Mother."

Venzel was scarcely able to form the words. "What did your mother say about Alazar?"

"It wasn't what she said. Whenever the word Alazar came into her mind, sadness would cloud everything, and she would cry inside. But not only for herself… there was someone else she cried for, someone else who was hurting, but I don't know who it was. I just knew Alazar was her word for sorrow."

It was impossible to explain his feelings to a child. To know that she understood his suffering, that she was sorry and shared his grief, shook loose some of the hate from his heart. Remembering the horrible nightmare of that morning when he lost the two things he loved most in the world in exchange for this, this…. Venzel looked down and, in the reflection of moonlight, saw Destani's beautiful eyes focused solemnly on his face. Recalling a promise he'd made years ago at the bottom of a ravine, he pulled Timaeus into his lap and told him the story of Alazar.

When Venzel finished, Timaeus nodded. "Yes," he said. "Mother was right. Alazar is sorrow."

Venzel touched the hand that still rested on his arm. "Yes, and bravery, too. It is essential to remember that there are things more important than your own safety. Some things, Timaeus, are worth dying for."

Timaeus pulled his hand away and hid it in his sleeve. Unsure of his safety in the presence of any human, Timaeus moved away and sat back down on the ground.

"My brothers," he said.

"Yes, our brothers are worth dying for."

Venzel was quiet for several moments. Fearing the worst but unable to stop himself from asking, he took a deep breath.

"How did your mother feel when she thought of me?"

"Who are you?"

"I am Venzel."

The boy began to back away. "You… are… Venzel?"

To Timaeus, it all made sense. He now knew why the man destroyed the gifts he'd left his mother, why he threw him to the ground and spoke angrily to him. This man did not love his mother. Venzel was the name that enraged her and darkened her mind so that Timaeus could not find her. Venzel was the name of the man who hated them.

Venzel had seen fear in the eyes of animals as well as in the faces of men and women, but it did not compare to the terror that completely possessed the small boy edging away from him. As he watched, Timaeus slowly began to tilt his head.

"You needn't call anyone, Timaeus. I will not hurt you. I would never have hurt you or your mother. She was ill and saw me differently than I am. I… I cared for her. Neither of you ever had any reason to fear me."

Timaeus did not sense any danger from the man sitting across from him, only sadness, and straightened his head.

Watching Venzel's face, he said in a steady voice, "Mother was not afraid… she was angry, but her anger made me afraid. When she thought your name, anger devoured her spirit, and she disappeared from me. When she came back, it was worse than when she was gone… each time changed her a little more." Looking down, his fingers raked a shallow trench in the sand and drew parallel lines above it.

Venzel closed his eyes and leaned his head back again. "I know, Timaeus, she disappeared from me, too, but she was very ill, and nothing could be done to help her. I…" — his voice broke — "…tried so hard."

When he could speak, he added, "She would have loved your sculptures. I'm sorry I ruined the other ones. They were beautiful, too."

Timaeus smiled inside. If this man knew that much about his mother and cared about her like he said, then perhaps he knew the answer to a question that Timaeus had asked several times that no one else seemed to know. The tall man was always leaving in the blue car. If he did not ask tonight, he might never have another chance.

"Venzel, do you know who my father is?"

"Why? You are Lyostian. What does it matter?"

"It was the only time Mother was happy." He looked wistfully in the direction of the garden. "She would say 'your father,' and her mind was all light. She would smile, touch my face… and for a few minutes, she loved me back." He looked down at the sand and added a few more lines. "It didn't happen often, and then one day it stopped."

Venzel closed his eyes. He'd had a mother for fourteen years, one who loved him and protected him—especially now that he knew much more about the colony's operations—beyond all reason. Although Timaeus had been in and out of Destani's room for nearly a year, he had so little knowledge of how a mother's love and protection felt that a piece of hate turned to compassion and melted from Venzel's heart.

"Were those the times she thought of the oasis?"

"Yes," Timaeus said, "how did you know?"

Venzel reached for his son, and although Timaeus still didn't trust him, he allowed himself to be brought back into his lap. Venzel's hand rested briefly on the boy's head, and he saw that his hair was honey brown and gold.

Breaking his own rule that Timaeus should never know, Venzel answered quietly, "Yes, child, I know who your father is." He sighed, remembering how quickly he had discarded Destani's last, and only, wish.

Venzel rubbed his hand over his heart as if to smooth its broken edges and looked at the boy. Seeing his whole face and not just the color of his eyes, he cried, "Oh, Timaeus, I am so tired of hating you."

Timaeus rubbed his hand over his heart, then placing it on Venzel's chest, said, "And I, Venzel, am tired of hating you."

Venzel nodded. Setting the boy on his feet, he stood and, taking the boy's hand, started to walk into the house but stopped when he noticed the lines in the sand.

"Timaeus, what have you drawn?"

"The new stables. I think we should put them over there," he said, "closer to the water."

Venzel gripped the little fingers tighter. "So do I, my son, so do I."

Timaeus stared at the long cylindrical package after Venzel left the room. Unsure when he would return, Timaeus climbed onto the table and shook out the building plans for the new stables. The blueprints unrolled across the table's surface like a wave, and he set cups along the edges to keep them flat. Looking at them closely, he traced the lines with his finger and picked up a pencil.

He was busily drawing when Venzel returned to the room.

"Stop!" Venzel roared.

Unafraid, Timaeus put the pencil down and looked up.

Expecting to see his flawless blueprints covered with a child's scrawl, Venzel rushed over to the table. "What have you done?"

"I added back doors," Timaeus said simply. "There were no back doors."

Their eyes met. Simultaneously, they said, "Alazar."

Recalling Timaeus's sketch in the sand and the exquisite memorials, Venzel looked closely at the alterations and saw that they were as finely drawn as the draftsmen who had prepared the plans. He pulled the other chair to the table.

"Let's look at these together. Perhaps there are other changes that should be made."

Turning his head toward Timaeus, Venzel saw something he thought he would never see again: love shining from Destani's eyes.

The Stables

Every evening after construction began on the new stables, Venzel took Timaeus out to inspect the work. Riding high on Venzel's shoulders, Timaeus pointed out where their changes had improved the original design. Twice during these inspections, Timaeus discovered measuring errors that could have delayed completion of the building, and he continually impressed Venzel with his ability to see three-dimensionally from drawings on paper.

For Timaeus's part, he didn't know such happiness was possible and excelled in his studies so he could be on the porch by sundown. He would not have missed the hour with Venzel for anything, and though neither would admit it, the hour after sunset was the best part of their day.

It didn't take long for Nesim, the colony's new doctor, to seek out Zsiga.

"Zsiga."

"Nesim."

"The other boys do not understand why they are not allowed to go out to the stables, and I, for one, do not understand it either."

"Is it making them ill, Nesim?"

"No, but it is singling out Timaeus, and if one must be technical about it, he is not Venzel's only son in the colony."

Venzel's words rang in Zsiga's mind: *do not quibble with me, Zsiga, about who is, and is not, my son.*

Zsiga decided to be diplomatic. "It is not fair to make Venzel responsible for each child's well-being on the premises. However, you make an interesting point. It would be educational for the boys to see the math and materials humans use to construct their buildings. I will not make the children who are uninterested attend, and I will not impose the interested children on the time Venzel spends with Timaeus alone. I will bring them to the stables myself and invite Venzel or Timaeus to supervise and explain."

"I do not know what you think Timaeus can explain."

"Then perhaps you should come, too."

It was an educational experience for everyone. Venzel understood much more than Zsiga how important it was that Timaeus not be thought of as different. On the evening the boys came to the stables, Venzel and Timaeus were prepared with a thorough presentation starting from lines in the sand to the altered blueprints and how those plans translated into an actual building. Several of the boys took turns riding on Venzel's shoulders as he pointed out the underlying foundation, the beams, and the struts of the roof.

Taran looked up at Zsiga, and he lifted Senkali's son on his shoulders. Taliph, Lalei's son, did not wish to join the expedition to the stables, preferring instead to review the periodic table in the chemistry lab. Riding almost as high as Timaeus, Taran watched Timaeus leap from Venzel's shoulders to a supporting beam and climb to the top of the joist. Thinking there could be nothing better, Taran quickly followed him up, and soon there were seven boys standing on the joist surveying their brothers and the stalls below.

Venzel smiled at Zsiga and asked, "How are we going to get them down?"

"Guess they will have to jump."

Most of the boys suddenly had very doubtful looks on their faces. Taran yelled down, "We can climb."

"No," said Zsiga. "You must jump. Nesim is here in case we miss catching you."

For a moment, the look in Venzel's eyes changed as he thought how easy it would be to miss catching Timaeus. He could die.

Reading the fleeting expression on Venzel's face, Timaeus immediately sang out, "Me first."

And jumped.

There was no hesitation as Venzel rushed under Timaeus and caught him.

"Thank you," Timaeus whispered, placing his hand on Venzel's cheek. Turning so none of the other boys could see, Venzel quickly clasped him against his chest and then set him down.

Zsiga, not missing any of this, suddenly looked up and said, "Taran, you're next."

Every face turned to look at Taran and did not see Venzel brush his hands across his eyes before he turned back around.

Zsiga caught Taran when he fell like a stone from the rafter. Afterward, the other boys took turns jumping, some making cheering sounds as they fell, others with their eyes closed. Only Aylala's son, Toros, remained standing on the joist. Climbing up because everyone else did, he had given no thought as to how he was going to get down. It wasn't that he was afraid—he was petrified. The boys all tilted their heads, and some called out for him to jump. Toros could not speak or even tilt his head to reply.

In less than a minute, Timaeus was on Venzel's shoulder. Climbing from the beam to the joist, he stood next to Toros and put his arm around the boy's shoulder. Signaling Venzel, they jumped together. Zsiga quickly joined hands with Venzel, and they caught the boys. When the men set them down, the other boys all gathered around Toros, touching him with their hands and foreheads. Timaeus went to stand with Venzel.

The experience was not wasted on Nesim. On the way back to the house, he saw Timaeus walking between Toros and Taran.

"Zsiga."

"Nesim."

"So, he is the one."

"Yes. His awareness of his mother's death—and the depth of his grief—was unlike any child I've ever known."

"How many exhibited that level of sensitivity in this generation?"

"Three throughout all our colonies: Timaeus, Tividar, and Tomi."

"He is the only one here?"

"Yes. The other two were born in different parts of Europe. I don't know anything else about them."

"Rauf was not his guardian?"

"No. I was appointed, but we are all his guardians."

"Is that the reason you let him spend so much time with the human?"

Zsiga stopped and looked at Nesim.

"Venzel is not 'the human.' He is my brother and, therefore, your brother as well. All you see here is because he turns over every lira he does not need for the upkeep of the stables to the colony for our benefit. It is with those funds and his contacts outside our perimeters that have enabled us to enlarge the compound, and construct the walled garden and outbuildings. His contributions have allowed us to excavate additional tunnels and reinforce many of the underground structures, as well as provide much of the comfort you enjoy in our living quarters. He may not share our mandate, but he shares everything else. We are one."

Nesim nodded and never interfered again.

In the evenings, as Timaeus waited on the porch, Venzel occasionally found him pressing his hands together. Venzel originally thought he was praying, but seeing his face red with exertion, he became concerned.

"Timaeus, what are you doing?"

Putting his hands in his sleeves, he said, "Nothing."

"Were you praying?"

"No."

"Then what, exactly, were you doing? And Timaeus, do not say 'nothing' to me again when I ask you a question."

Embarrassed, Timaeus looked down at his hands. "I was trying to flatten my fingers. Nearly everyone else's fingers are flat, but not mine. They still curve… like I was a baby."

Venzel knew why his hands were different from the other boys. "Has anyone ever said anything to you about them?" he asked quietly.

"No, but they stare, and sometimes I hear what they are thinking."

"I see."

Sitting down next to the boy, Venzel took one of Timaeus's hands and held it against his own much larger hand. It astonished him to see that, except for the scars and the slight curve to the smaller fingers touching his, their hands were shaped exactly alike.

"Tell me if this hurts."

Venzel pressed Timaeus's hand against the floor of the porch. There was a little resistance, but the fingers, with the steady pressure from Venzel's hand, flattened perfectly against the wooden boards. He looked up quickly to see the boy's face.

Timaeus's jaw was clenched, and there were beads of sweat around his temples, but the smile of surprise that his hands could look like everyone else's outweighed the pain.

"Well," said Venzel, "it seems possible, but we will have to do something soon; you are growing very fast."

"Do what?"

"I'm not sure yet, but we will think of something."

After their hour together, Venzel went to find Nesim.

"Yes, yes, I know," Nesim said, "but there is little to be done. Rauf should have taken care of that as soon as the bandages came off, but it is probably too late now. It would necessitate wearing a brace every night and, well, you know they all share a room, and—"

"And it would make him different."

"No, he is already different. It would just emphasize that difference and make him look, well, weak… as though it bothered him."

Venzel nodded. Born early, his fingers and toes were still fused and curved like claws when the other babies' fingers started separating. He knew why Rauf had not straightened his hands when he surgically separated Timaeus's fingers and toes; Destani was having enough difficulties accepting the baby, and they needed to make him appear as human as possible. Bracing his hands would not have been consistent with that image.

Venzel knew it was his fault, too. Constantly watching over his wife, he did not have the time or heart to care about his son's hands. When the collective agreed to repurpose the colony as a school, Rauf and Zsiga had to deal with babies arriving from all over the SCM region, and somewhere the issue of his son's hands got lost in the other priorities of the colony—and his own.

"They're just boys, Nesim. If they knew how painful it is going to be for him, wouldn't they see him as strong and respect him?"

"Yes and no. Yes, that is how they would see it, and no, they would not respect him because he would be winning a race they could not run. It would be a personal triumph, not a shared victory."

"How long would a brace be necessary? One month, six, a year?"

"If it is possible to do at all, it would take approximately four months. If his fingers do not straighten in four months, they will never be completely straight."

"Do you have such a brace on the premises?"

Nesim tilted his head. "I am requesting one to be shipped. It will not take long. But how will you—"

"Let me think about that."

A few days later as they walked back to the house, Timaeus said, "The roof is complete, and the stalls have gates now. When do the horses come?"

"They come when we go get them."

"We?" Timaeus looked at the house and then back to Venzel. "I can't leave. Everyone is here. If I go too far away, I will be alone."

Swinging the boy from his shoulder to the porch, Venzel looked at his son.

"Timaeus, if it can be arranged so that you will not be alone, would you like to go with me to find the horses? I will understand if you would prefer to wait until I return with them."

He did not hesitate. "Yes. I would like to go, but it is impossible."

"Timaeus," Venzel asked softly, "are you arguing with me?"

There was a certain tone in Venzel's voice that Timaeus had never heard before, yet it sounded faintly familiar, almost as though he had heard it in a dream, long ago.

"No, Venzel."

"Good."

Venzel spent the next morning combing through the papers that had sat in Zsiga's office for five years. On his next trip to the village, he made several phone calls and jotted notes on the receipts from Zsiga's files. Stopping at the post office on his way back to the compound, he found, among the letters, books, and newspapers, a small package addressed to Nesim. Venzel put it in his pocket.

An hour after sunset two days later, Timaeus came out for their usual inspection and saw the dark blue Mercedes parked next to the porch. His heart fell. The car only meant one thing: Venzel was leaving again. There would be no horses until he came back, and that could be months.

Zsiga and Taran stepped onto the porch. Seeing the look of dismay on Timaeus's face, Zsiga said, "It is not so bad as that, Timaeus. Venzel has arranged for us to look at some horses."

"All of us?"

"Yes. It will be quieter than you are used to, but between the three of us, we will be fine." Zsiga crouched down and looked into the boys' faces. "Don't be scared. Thanks to Venzel, our tunnels are extensive, and we have brothers visiting all the time from the village. We will not be alone."

Taran and Timaeus looked at each other. The village? To the children, it seemed as far away as the moon, and they edged closer together. A moment later, Venzel walked out of the newly completed stables with a horsewhip in his hands. Opening the car doors, he tossed the whip to Timaeus.

"Hold on to that for me."

The ride to the village did not take thirty minutes, but the boys thought it seemed much longer. They knelt on the backseat and gazed through the window, watching the compound grow smaller, and the voices they recognized fade away. When the compound was out of sight, they dropped to their seats and sat very close to each other, their heads almost touching. Although he let Taran feel it, Timaeus held onto the horsewhip as though it were a lifeline.

The tension lessened once they got to the village. Although the boys did not know where their brothers were, it was clear that the collective had a colony nearby, and Taran and Timaeus relaxed a little. Venzel stopped the car at the door of a large wooden building, and opening the glove compartment, he handed Zsiga three pairs of sunglasses.

"Wear these until we get inside. Streetlamps can be brighter than sunlight."

Taran tilted his head, and Venzel whispered into Zsiga's ear. Kneeling and bringing the boys close to him, Zsiga said, "Do not think to each other… talk out loud until we get back into the car."

Each taking their son's hand, Zsiga and Venzel walked into the stables. In the dim light, they removed the sunglasses and saw a groom standing next to each stall. Timaeus stared. Horses were a lot bigger than he thought. Still holding tightly to the whip, he edged nearer to Venzel and grasped the seam of his tunic.

"Now," said Venzel.

As instructed, the grooms opened all the stalls at once and held their horse's bridle by a single rein. Venzel gave a low whistle.

Of the eight horses, only three mares stepped forward at the sound of the whistle. When Venzel moved in front of them and made a subtle movement with his hand, all three bowed to the ground. Taking Timaeus to the first horse, Venzel settled him on top of her, then picked up Taran and put him on the third one. Zsiga mounted the horse in the middle, admonishing the boys to "Hold onto the mane with one hand and the reins with the other."

Backing away, Venzel turned his right palm upward, and all three horses stood. The boys rocked a little unsteadily but stayed on. Making a cupping motion, the horses walked forward until Venzel raised his hand, and they stopped. Turning it palm down, the horses knelt again, and Zsiga helped the boys dismount.

Timaeus could not resist running to Venzel as soon as his feet touched the straw.

"Did you see, did you see?"

"Yes, I saw," he said, setting Timaeus on his shoulder as he and Zsiga, with Taran on his shoulder, went to buy back three of Alazar's stablemates.

As Zsiga arranged the mares' delivery, Venzel turned to the five remaining horses. Knowing Alazar's conformation by heart, Venzel ran his hands over their legs, looked into their eyes and mouths, and felt carefully from withers to tail. Three he dismissed outright. One mare could have gone either way, but when he saw the three-year-old in the corner stall, he knew the young stallion's sire had to be Alazar. Venzel regarded the skittish grey horse steadily. After setting Timaeus carefully on the railing, he went into the stall alone.

Timaeus was entranced as Venzel, talking softly, moved his hands slowly over the horse's body. Comparing his memory of Alazar with this horse, he examined every muscle and tested the strength of every bone, nodding slightly as he mentally checked off a list of requirements.

"And this one. Not the mare." Lifting Timaeus from the rail, he said, "That is Alazar's son."

On their way back to the car, Timaeus asked, "Why did we bring the whip? We didn't use it."

"Because horses know what the whip represents. With a smart horse, that is all you need."

The boys didn't want to talk about anything else as they rode back to the compound.

Listening to their enthusiasm, Venzel said, "I think it would be good if a couple of the boys could help with the horses in the mornings and then another couple to help in the evening, at least in the beginning." Venzel glanced in the rearview mirror. "That is if you know of any who might like to help."

"Me, me," echoed from the backseat.

"Well," said Zsiga. "They will have to take turns with the other boys. I won't make them, but we will see how many are interested and set up a schedule."

"There's just one thing, Zsiga. If I go down and wake them every morning, I might end up waking everyone. What I think will work best for the morning crew is… oh, I don't know, if Timaeus slept in my room so he could call whoever was helping that morning without bothering everybody. In a few months, once the horses are settled in, we can hire some stable hands for the morning and let the boys who wish to help come in the evenings."

Timaeus and Zsiga stared at Venzel. Pretending not to notice the sudden silence, Venzel drove along like it was a normal part of the conversation to request removing one of the boys from the dormitory environment to put him with an adult human male for even one night, let alone months, regardless of their relationship. Zsiga tilted his head, and Timaeus answered in the same way.

"We will try it for a few days."

"Of course."

The horses arrived the next day. Venzel was up early, layering straw and sweet hay in each stall, and trying not to remember. He had purposely omitted putting a stall in the same position as the one he'd shared with Destani and built a tack room instead. He stabled the grey stallion in Alazar's stall near the front doors and put the other horses on the opposite side of the practice ring.

Telling Zsiga that he would care for the horses himself for the first day to help them adjust to their new home; he would not even allow Timaeus in the stables. The boys were small, and horses could be unpredictable in a new location. He'd promised Taran and Timaeus they could come and bring their brothers the following evening.

Breathing familiar scents and hearing the comforting sounds of the horses helped alleviate his loneliness, but it was hard work getting the horses settled in alone. When there was nothing more to be done, he went to his room and quickly fell asleep.

Venzel.

He awoke with a start.

"Destani?"

There was no response, and hoping to recapture the dream of her, he drifted back to sleep.

Venzel.

This time, he sat up. He knew it must have been a dream, but a sense of uneasiness came over him, and he immediately remembered the horses. Walking out to the back porch, Venzel saw one of the stable doors open. Dread filled his mind as he ran toward the stables, and although he could not smell any smoke, something was not right. He could feel it.

Rather than running into the building, Venzel walked slowly to the edge of the door. Looking in, he saw the grey in his stall. Catching a small movement from the corner of his eye, he turned to see Timaeus, horsewhip in hand, controlling the three mares exactly as he had seen Venzel do the evening before.

Venzel was spellbound. With his back to him, Timaeus looked like a miniature ringmaster as the horses knelt in front of him, stood up, came forward, and stopped. Directing them to kneel once more, he walked over to each of them, placed his head between their ears, and signaled them to stand up. Returning two to their stalls, he motioned the remaining horse once again to her knees. Climbing over her neck and settling on her back, Timaeus pulled up on the horse's mane. Obeying his command, the horse stood and began walking toward the open door.

Trying not to panic, Timaeus gripped her mane tighter, but she only walked faster. Without a bridle, he had no idea how to turn her around or stop her. His eyes darted in every direction, looking for a way to get off. Judging the ground too far away, and the limitless desert too close, he raised the whip thinking he could make her stop.

His arm poised in the air to strike her, Timaeus was immediately distracted by a flying apparition. Venzel, appearing seemingly out of nowhere, swept him from the horse's back and snatched the whip out of his hand. Setting him safely down, he broke the whip in half and threw the pieces at the boy's feet.

"Do not move."

Catching the mare, Venzel whispered and stroked her neck as he calmly led the horse to her stall.

Returning to the center of the practice ring, he found Timaeus staring down at the broken whip. Venzel put his hand under the boy's chin and lifted his face.

"Do you understand the sequence of cause and effect, Timaeus?"

"Yes."

"Then why did you not think this through?"

"I wanted to see if I could do what you did—if they would obey me. Then I remembered how nice it felt to ride, and, well, I just decided to get on the horse."

"Without any thought of how you were going to get down?"

"Yes."

"Timaeus, who sleeps in the back of the house?"

"No one."

"Who would have heard you if you yelled for help?"

"No one."

"And with our brothers asleep in the dormitory rooms, who would have been able to come out here in time if you thought for help."

"No one."

"Listen to me, Timaeus. If you had struck her with the whip, she would have bolted through the stable door, jumped over the paddock gate, and raced into the desert. Then, one of two things would have happened. Either you would have fallen off, possibly been trampled and killed, or, if you stayed on her, we would have found you days from now in the middle of the desert where you died of thirst. Alone."

Timaeus listened to every word Venzel said, but when he heard the last one, it blotted out everything else. Feeling suddenly lightheaded, he sat down.

"I do not want to scare you, Timaeus, but every action has consequences. You must think things through before moving forward. If you do not see a successful finish, then go over each option until you find one. This is true of all things, not just riding horses."

He pulled the boy to his feet, and together they walked back to the house.

As they descended the stairs to the lower levels, Timaeus looked up at Venzel.

"How did you know?"

"Your mother told me."

Timaeus nodded and held Venzel's hand the rest of the way.

An hour after sunset the next day, five small boys swarmed out of the back of the main house and into the stables. Timaeus and Taran had told them about the horses that could read hand signals, and they were all excited. However, before Venzel would let them ride the horses, they had to feed them and clean their stalls. Then, one at a time, he brought the three mares out and showed the boys how to brush and groom them.

"Taking care of a horse is hard work, but how they make you feel can be magical."

Once the horses were brushed and fed, Timaeus and Taran showed their brothers how to hold on, and each boy rode several times around the stables.

"Tomorrow evening, we will do everything we did tonight, and then we will learn a little more."

Nesim and Zsiga stood on the porch, watching the boys come out of the stables. Smiling from ear to ear, their heads tilted and laughing. Only Timaeus remained in the stables with Venzel.

"Why didn't we feed and brush this one?" he said, pointing to Alazar's stall.

"Because that is your horse… and you take care of your horse."

"All by myself?"

"I will help in the beginning, but it will be more showing you than doing it for you. If you do not want this, tell me now."

Timaeus thought for a moment. "He will be our horse, but my responsibility."

Venzel nodded. "And he will need a name, but for now, everything we did for the other horses, you must do for this one."

Venzel got a small stool out of the tack room for Timaeus to stand on, and together they groomed and fed the grey. When they came out of the stables, Nesim and Zsiga were still on the porch.

"Get cleaned up and come to my room when it is time to sleep."

"Yes."

After Timaeus went inside, Nesim caught Venzel's arm. "Why your room?"

"You know why."

"It arrived?"

"Yes."

"Do you want me to do it?"

"No, I looked at it. It's relatively simple if you've ever seen a straitjacket."

"And it will be painful. Are you prepared for that?"

"His pain or mine?"

"Both."

"If he can stand it, I can."

Zsiga, looking more frustrated by the moment, tilted his head and then said, "Oh, right…." Looking at Venzel, he asked, "Why didn't you just say so?"

"He doesn't want anyone to know it bothers him."

"I hope it works. It will be a lot of pain for nothing if it doesn't."

"It will work."

Zsiga motioned to Venzel to wait in the shadows of the porch until Nesim's footsteps faded.

"Why are you doing this, Venzi? I understand rebuilding the stables, but I don't understand why you are concerning yourself with such a minor inconvenience."

"He doesn't think it's minor."

"But it is," Zsiga said softly.

Venzel didn't respond, but Zsiga recognized the set of his jaw and signed, *Why?*

Venzel turned back toward the stables without looking at him.

"I have a promise to keep," he said.

That night, Venzel heard a small knock on the door. Opening it, he saw Timaeus in a night tunic standing next to Ezri. Smiling in welcome, Venzel let the boy in and closed the door.

Seeing his cot made up near the fireplace, Timaeus was grateful he would not have to sleep on the floor and started to get into it when Venzel stopped him.

"Come over here for a moment."

Timaeus saw the small box on the table in front of Venzel and hoped it had something to do with the horses. He was disappointed when he saw thin metal splints, straps, and a pair of small fingerless leather gloves.

"What are those?"

"They are for your hands."

Timaeus reverently picked up one of the steel splints. "Will they work?"

"We'll see. Timaeus, this is—"

"Going to hurt?"

"Yes."

Holding out his hands with the cupped fingers upward, everything that was a child in Timaeus disappeared.

"Do you think this doesn't? I know I killed her; I know it was my fault. Sometimes, I almost forget, but then I see these... ugly things, and I remember. I don't care how much it hurts. I killed my mother. Nothing you can do can ever hurt as much as that."

Realizing that the thoughts torturing Timaeus were the same thoughts that tormented him, Venzel stared at his son and whispered hoarsely, "It wasn't your fault, Timaeus; it was mine. I left her alone. I thought I had protected her, but I hadn't. And then, afterward, when she hated me, I tried to blame you, but I was wrong. My son, it was never your fault." He shook his head and cleared his throat. "Now, let's see if we can get these on—"

Without any warning at all, Timaeus threw himself against Venzel, and in those brief moments, they forgave each other for the guilt-ridden years of endless regret and despair.

Timaeus slowly pulled back and put his hands on the table.

"I'm ready, Father."

"As am I, Son."

The splints were more painful than either of them expected. It was Venzel's plan to tighten them incrementally, flattening the fingers a little more each day, but when he woke up the first morning to find teeth marks in the soft leather where Timaeus had pulled the straps as tight as he could,

Venzel did the same. However, it was not easy, and the boy's hands hurt almost as much coming out of the braces as they did being strapped into them. Venzel watched his son working in the stables, breathing through the pain of grasping anything from a dandy brush to bridle reins. When he thought no one was looking, Timaeus pressed his hands together to see if the straps were working.

The other problem was sleeping. Timaeus was used to the sounds of his dorm room with nineteen other boys dreaming and talking, as well as the sounds of the dreams from visiting brothers, the teachers, Nesim, and Zsiga drifting through his mind. Venzel's room was in the tunnels but higher than the dormitory level, and it was quieter here, but that wasn't the only reason he couldn't sleep. The lack of familiar sounds was nothing compared to the agony of his fingers strapped to the cold steel of the metal splints. They were also dangerous. Waking up after a particularly restless night, he couldn't see. His eyes were glued shut.

"Father!"

Venzel ran to the little cot to find Timaeus's face covered in blood from a cut above his eyes and ran to get a wet towel. "Stay still."

"What is it?"

"The corner of one of the metal splints scratched your forehead, and you have blood in your eyes. Relax for a moment so I can clean it out, and we will get Nesim to look at it."

"No."

"Why?"

"He will try to make me stop, and I am not going to stop."

As Venzel cleaned the wound, he found it was not as bad as he thought, but he knew something had to change. The next injury could be to one of his eyes, and there would be no help for that.

After Venzel and the boys mucked out the stables and fed the horses, the boys went to their lessons, and Venzel went back to his room to look at the braces. Then he went to find Nesim.

"Nesim."

"Venzel."

"I need some bandages, gauze, or something like that."

"Why? Who is hurt?"

"No one, much. Yet."

"Explain, please."

Taking one of the splints out of his pocket, Venzel demonstrated what happened to Timaeus. "If I wrap the edges of the splints, then this, or worse, won't happen again."

Nesim nodded and, using Venzel's hand, showed him the best way to wrap the bandage. Venzel nodded and was getting ready to leave the room.

"Should I look at the cut?"

"It isn't deep, but I think you should only look. Please, don't ask him how he got it."

"You are very good with them, you know."

"I had hoped for many sons," Venzel said with a sigh.

"And you have them."

"No, I have only one son, but he has many brothers."

There were no more cuts or scratches, thanks to Venzel's careful wrapping, but the pain wasn't getting any better, and sleep was becoming nearly impossible for both of them. Timaeus, because not only were his hands in pain from the splints, but they were also burning up because the leather and metal encasing his fingers were now insulated by layers of gauze; and Venzel, fearful of another accident, anxiously listened to every sound coming from the cot across the room.

After a few days, Timaeus was falling asleep during lessons, and Venzel was becoming short-tempered.

Zsiga tried to intervene.

Venzel argued with him. "No, give us a couple more weeks. It's got to get better."

"No. We said we would try it for a few days, and no one seems to be benefiting from this arrangement. He will learn to accept his hands the way they are."

"No, Zsiga. He may have to accept the scars, but he doesn't have to accept the way his fingers curve if we can help it. And now he knows what he needs to do. If he has to, he will make the splints himself, but they won't be the same, and he could do more harm than good. Give me until the end of the week. If he is not sleeping better by Monday, we will seek a different solution."

"Until Monday, Venzel. You must know I am only trying to do what is best for everyone. It's my job."

"Yes, my brother, and no one could do it better. Thank you for your patience."

Once more, Venzel went to see Nesim. Taking one look at Venzel's bloodshot eyes, he said, "For you or for him?"

"Him."

Nesim shook his head. "No."

"Why?"

"Human drugs are toxic, and we have never needed anything like that."

"What was used to sedate him when Rauf separated his fingers and toes?"

"Nothing."

"What?" Venzel was already tired, but the thought of Rauf taking a scalpel and slicing the webbing between his baby son's fingers and toes without any kind of anesthetic pushed him over the edge. His face murderous, Venzel took several long strides toward Nesim.

"Wait," Nesim said calmly, holding up his hand. "It's not what you think. The pain receptors in the epidermis are not the same as in humans. We did not hurt him."

"He is hurting now, and I want it to stop."

"Then all you have to do is remove the splints."

"Impossible," said Venzel, storming out of the door.

Nesim shook his head again. If the collective and the colony did not need the human so much, he would be the first in line to petition for

Venzel's extermination. As it was, Nesim was starting to believe that Venzel would outlive them all.

That evening, as Venzel was strapping his son's fingers onto the splints, he tried not to tighten them too much.

"No, Father, that will not do."

"But we have to get some rest, Timaeus; it's just for a few days."

"I will sleep elsewhere."

"And who will benefit from that?"

"You."

"No, I will be twice as concerned."

"It will get better, Father. We must be patient."

Venzel looked into his son's eyes and realized that he had not lied to Zsiga. Despite the pain or lack of sleep, Timaeus was not going to give up.

Remembering he had told Nesim that if Timaeus could stand the pain, he could, Venzel tightened the straps.

His hands wrapped, Timaeus began getting into his cot and hesitated.

"Father?"

"What's wrong?"

"Nothing. I was wondering if you would tell me a story about Alazar. I am still trying to think of a name for our horse, and perhaps I will dream one."

"All right, but you are going to have to come up here. I am too tired to sit in a chair and tell stories."

Taking the blanket from his cot, Timaeus climbed over the trunk and onto Venzel's bed. Sitting on top of the coverlet, he looked at him expectantly.

With his back against the wall, Venzel began a story of Alazar, who became more marvelous as the tale progressed. Listening to the sound of his father's voice, Timaeus fell asleep. Too tired to get up and put him in the cot, Venzel pulled the small blanket over his son and promptly fell asleep himself.

The next morning, Venzel awoke to a bandaged finger patting his cheek. "Alatan, Father."

"Yes, Timaeus, I know it's dawn."

"Yes, but no. Our horse, Alatan."

"I like it." Realizing he had slept all night, Venzel looked closely into his son's eyes and saw that they, too, were refreshed and awake.

Thus began an evening ritual that neither ever forgot; Venzel would wrap his son's fingers and tell him a story about Alazar's adventures or mythical tales of the animals carved in the walls and ceiling, but mostly Venzel talked about all the wonderful things Alatan would do once he finished his training. Afterward, they fell asleep—Venzel under the coverlets and Timaeus beneath his small blanket.

At the end of four months, two wonderful things happened. Timaeus handed the splints and gloves to Nesim with his beautifully shaped and perfectly straight fingers, and that night, instead of a story, Venzel and Timaeus astride Alatan, slipped out of the stables and flew across the desert in search of their own adventures.

At Komutani

Timaeus was everything Venzel had hoped for in a son. He was bright, intuitive, kind, and helpful. He wasn't sure if Timaeus understood *all* the reasons behind his occasional absences from the compound, but he was confident that if his son wanted to know, he could find out. Venzel was just grateful that Timaeus never asked for an explanation. He had no idea that Timaeus not only knew everything his father did for the Lyostians but revered him for his commitment and generosity.

And his trust.

For nearly two years, Timaeus spent every free minute in the stables with his father. At sunrise each day, Venzel met with the men he'd hired from the village who worked until mid-afternoon. After sunset, the boys came out to the stables. Under Venzel's supervision, they brushed and fed the horses, played with the foals, and went riding together, sometimes staying out all night when the moon was new.

When Venzel traveled for the colony, he released the men from the village until his return while Zsiga supervised the care of the stables and horses. This routine worked so well that Timaeus was not a little surprised when Venzel asked him to attend an early-morning meeting with the workmen on the day he was to leave the compound.

Entering the stables at dawn, Venzel introduced him to the men and advised them that his son would be in charge while he was away. Timaeus barely managed to keep the shock from his face.

"He will meet you here every morning with your assignments, attend classes during the day, and will return in the evening to see if you have done as he instructed. Do not disturb him while he is in the house. If you have a question, you can discuss it the following morning."

The men looked at the boy who barely reached his father's elbow and could not contain their smiles. Venzel's expression did not change as he looked at his son.

"You can go in the house now, Timaeus. We will review the work schedule later."

"Yes, Father," he said, turning toward the stable doors. Shading his dark glasses from the sun rising beyond the haze and dust, Timaeus walked to the house.

It was impossible, Timaeus thought. He'd seen the smiles of the workmen. These men were not going to listen to him. He glanced at the list of chores and additions to the corrals that Venzel expected to have completed when he returned. For the first time in his life, Timaeus faced the possibility of failure.

The men in the stables watched the boy leave. Turning his face quickly toward them, Venzel noticed that they did not even bother to conceal the snide laughter in their eyes, and once again, he felt the same contempt for his race that the Lyostians had felt for millennia.

He stared at them until one by one they met his eyes and quieted. Some of them had worked at the compound before the fire. Others had heard the stories of the tall man who raised horses, beautiful and fast, and disregarded the tales of his fearlessness and cruelty. That was nearly nine years ago, and their recent experience was one of a congenial employer. However, looking into his face that morning, each of them knew the stories were true, and Venzel had not changed. The smiles faded from their faces.

"You thought, perhaps, I was joking?" he said seriously.

"No, sir. No, Master," they said, their voices low. The men who could not find their voice merely shook their heads.

"Do you like working here?"

To a man, they knew working at the compound was far superior to any other work they could get at the village. It wasn't hard, the money was good—and in silver. They all nodded and one man, who had three daughters he treasured but no sons, actually knelt.

"I will say this only once. He is my son. He has all my confidence and trust. If you cannot respect him as you do me, then you need to leave and never return because I will not allow you to disparage him among yourselves or flout his authority. If you must, give him your respect now out of charity to me, but I assure you, he will earn it before I return."

No one moved.

"Thank you. Two more things, if I am present and he asks you to do something, do not, I repeat, do not look to me to see if I agree. And, if he reprimands or dismisses you, you will find no reprieve in me. You have this one opportunity to ask me a question concerning this matter." He crossed his arms over his chest and waited.

Most of the men had nothing to say, but the man who had knelt came to his feet and asked, "What would you like us to call him?"

Venzel thought for a moment and smiled. "Unless he requests otherwise, refer to him as At-Komutani—horse master."

Each nodded and understood, and not one of them smiled back.

At dawn the next morning the dark blue Mercedes was gone, and Timaeus, clutching the day's assignments, walked into the stables alone. He glanced down at his hands and thought, I did that, I can do this.

The men were waiting for him. In what he hoped was a strong voice, he gave them their assignments. He paused for a moment before adding, "Are there any questions before I return to the house?"

"No, At-Komutani, we understand."

He looked to see if they were mocking him, but he did not detect insolence in their faces. He looked down at the paper in his hand, so they could not see his face.

"Why do you call me that? My name is Timaeus."

"Your father said that is what we are to call you… unless you prefer something else."

If that was what Venzel believed, then that was who he was and before their eyes, Timaeus grew up. He seemed to get taller, his shoulders a little broader, and he lifted his head and looked into their faces. The cloak his father left him to wear, that a moment before was too large, suddenly fit him. Sensing the force of the father in the son, the men no longer wondered if they could obey him.

The men who had boys recognized his transformation and found themselves wishing Venzel had been there to witness the gift he had given his son.

"It will be as my father wishes," Timaeus said.

That day and every day afterward until and beyond Venzel's return, the men did exactly as Timaeus requested, and, although they never grew fond of him, they respected his authority.

Venzel was not unmindful of the change in Timaeus, nor were Zsiga or Nesim. Although they did not talk of it, gradually all three began to rely on Timaeus, subtly positioning him for a leadership role within a hierarchy of leaders.

The Mind Killers

For several weeks, Venzel could sense something was bothering Zsiga, but as his brother did not share it with him, Venzel assumed it was an issue with the collective rather than the colony and didn't ask any questions. Late one evening, while finishing up in the stables with Taran and Timaeus, he watched as they both tilted their heads and looked in his direction.

He looked back at them and smiled. The more they grew, the more they looked alike. Almost twelve, only the color of Timaeus's eyes set him apart from every other boy on the compound. A few were taller, some with lighter or darker skin, but they all looked like brothers. He knew they were not all his children, but many were and, loving Timaeus so much it ached, that love spilled over onto the other boys, and Venzel could not help but be proud of them all.

"Yes?"

"Zsiga would like to see you in twenty minutes if that is convenient."

"Certainly, we'll be finished here soon. Conference room?"

"Yes," they said in unison.

"Well, then, let's get this done. Taran, you feed the colts, Timaeus…."

"Alatan."

"I'll get the rest."

Venzel was surprised to see Nesim sitting at the table when he entered the room. He still missed Rauf. Shortly after the colony's transition, the collective had reassigned Rauf to one of the breeding colonies near Alexandria, and, to the sorrow of everyone who knew him, he fell out of the collective three years earlier. Venzel missed his calm wisdom and counsel. He had grown to like Nesim better over the years, but he knew Nesim would never accept him because he was human. As a result, Venzel did not trust him the way he'd trusted Rauf.

Seeing the serious expressions on their faces, Venzel's heart went to his throat as his thoughts immediately turned to Timaeus. Glad they could not read his mind, Venzel's eyes hardened slightly as he regarded the two Lyostians at the table.

"Zsiga, Nesim."

"Venzel," they said simultaneously.

Looking at Zsiga, Venzel said, "My brothers, I see there is a problem. What is it, and how can I help?"

"We have received disturbing information from the collective," Zsiga began. "As you know, this is a new generation, and their projected development arc is being observed very closely. They are now entering their adolescence, and, as expected, the aggression phase has begun. This phase usually levels off after a short burst, but we are seeing some who do not transition. Their aggression keeps escalating until they are unable to control it."

"Is this for my information, or may I ask some questions?"

"No, please, ask whatever you wish."

"Is this due to my involvement with this generation? Primarily, I'm asking if you are telling me this because I may have contributed a trait that has caused this problem. If so, it would be easy to isolate the boys who are at risk for developing this tendency."

"No," Nesim replied. "That is one of the first things we determined. If it were only one variable, then it would be easy to identify the boys who require constant monitoring or isolation, but no, Venzel, there are many variables. We wish it was our fault... a contaminated vial of serum, for example, or an environmental factor we overlooked, but regrettably, there is no one identifier."

"Then you cannot know or predict which boys will be affected?"

"No."

"But they are so young. How do you know they will not pass through this phase if given enough time? Perhaps you are not waiting long enough."

Nesim sighed. He wasn't even sure why they were involving the human with this problem, but he had learned two important things about Venzel over the last decade: one, that he could be relied upon; two, that he treated all the boys as he treated Timaeus. Nesim had also learned to trust Zsiga's intuition.

"We cannot give them more time. After a certain point, they become a danger to the colony. No one, no matter how valuable, is permitted to put the colony in danger. He, or they, must be neutralized before the structure is threatened."

"But they are just boys, even if they are training to be soldiers. We are men. Surely, we can restrain them for a little while to see if they can find a balance. I know what you are saying, Nesim, and what you are not saying, and I don't like it."

Nesim passed the conversation to Zsiga.

"Venzel, these boys are capable of great harm… to each other, as well as to their other brothers in the colony."

"But you said you are monitoring them. Won't you be able to tell before something tragic happens?"

"Yes and no. We can monitor the thoughts that they do not intentionally keep to themselves and could pick up an unconscious intention before it becomes action. Emotions are more difficult to hide, and we are monitoring those as well. However, we may not be able to prevent them from becoming dangerous to us."

"Why? Like I said, they may be strong, but we are men."

"I've explained that this is a powerful generation of vanguards, Venzel, and the collective has certain expectations. One of those expectations is to enforce discipline in their assigned colonies. To fulfill that responsibility, in addition to sending verbal or emotional messages, fire slayers can also send pain. Like a migraine—we call it a fulguration or lightning headache—of varying intensities. They are not allowed to do this without permission, but, quite frankly, we are unable to prevent them from doing it to any of us."

"When you say, 'varying intensities'…?"

"Yes, Venzel, from a burning ache between the eyes to excruciating death."

"Do they know this?"

Nesim nodded. "They know they can hurt each other with their minds, but they also know if one attacks another brother that way, his other brothers will force him back, simultaneously and cumulatively."

"If they can control each other, what is the problem?"

"There are two problems. One is that the Tuzurias are the only brothers who have this ability. Zsiga, I, and the other brothers here who are not of this hierarchy have no mental defense against this well, power of the fire slayers. Our age, size, and experience are no match for a child who can stop us with a single thought, and problem number two is…." Nesim looked at Zsiga.

"They are scheduled to begin small arms training next week."

"Why do they need guns if they can kill with a single…?" Venzel stared into Zsiga's eyes until he finally understood.

"Yes."

Venzel stood up so quickly his chair crashed to the floor. "No. Don't do that. Wait until you know who will and who won't be able to control it. Why would you start that training now? If they are capable of doing what you say they can do, just one with a semi-automatic pistol in his hands could, theoretically, wipe out the entire compound."

"Regrettably, Venzel, it is more than a theory. It is happening in colonies from Europe to North Africa."

Venzel regarded them with horrified eyes. If what they said was true, everyone he loved could die. Even Timaeus was as vulnerable of becoming a victim as an instigator. Either way, he had to protect him. He picked up his chair and slowly sat back down.

"How can I help?"

"We have requested and, given the ongoing circumstances, expect to receive a six-month moratorium on weapons training. However, the weapons are already here, and I would not be surprised if the boys know where we are keeping them. We've made no secret of their arrival or storage. We have posted a guard, but now you know how ineffective that would be against one or more," Zsiga shuddered at the thought, "if they really wanted to get in there."

He placed his hand on Venzel's arm. "However, brother, they cannot harm you that way, and we believe that Timaeus would warn you if you were in danger."

A fleeting smile crossed Venzel's face.

"After much discussion, we have resolved to separate the ammunition from the guns. Venzel, would you take the ammunition and hide it somewhere in the stables so only you know where it is? You could guard it during the day, and we could post one of our brothers in there at night."

"No."

"No?"

"I agree with your plan, Zsiga, but if anyone is paying attention, they will want to know why someone is staying in the stables at night. I propose we move the ammunition a little at a time over the next few days, and I will hide it. As we approach the critical phase, the mares will need watching for one reason or another, so I will sleep there until the danger has passed."

Nesim was impressed. "It is a lot to ask. These boys are no longer small. They can hurt you, or worse... if desperate. Especially if more than one or two are acting together."

Since Destani's death, there had been little Venzel cared enough about to bring to the fore the full force of his personality. Standing, he looked at Nesim with everything he was shining from his blue/black eyes.

"Nesim, everyone I love is here. Right here. I will protect them with my life, and I," he said, smiling slightly, "I am not easy to kill."

He turned to walk out of the room.

"Where are you going?" asked Zsiga.

"I have a munitions cache to build tonight. We will continue this discussion later, my brothers."

There was no mistaking the admiration in Nesim's eyes as he watched Venzel leave the room. "I had no idea."

"I told you."

"Yes, um, I am glad he's on our side."

Zsiga smiled briefly. "That's what Rauf said."

Building a false bottom in the blanket chest only took a few minutes and created the least amount of noise. The next morning, Venzel filled two saddlebags with the surplus blankets and brought them into the main house. Looking for Zsiga, he found him talking to Nesim and motioned them back into the conference room.

"The cache is prepared, and we can start moving the munitions whenever you are ready. I have dropped off some saddlebags in my room. Zsiga, if you fill them while the boys are studying, then I will take them to the stables at noon, empty them, and bring them back. Will that work?"

"Yes, I'll do that. If you carry them back and forth while they are in classes, no one will see you. That will work perfectly."

"Good." Venzel hesitated. He wanted to sign to Zsiga to meet with him alone, but Nesim would have noticed.

"Anything else?"

"Yes. When are you going to tell them?"

"The general pediatric consensus is to let it happen naturally, without forewarning them of the consequences. We don't want them to suppress any thoughts or emotions that might help us identify the ones who need help."

"No, Nesim, you must let them know they are entering a new stage of development so these rushes of adrenaline do not scare them or make them think something is wrong. Perhaps you have boys overreacting to these feelings because they are afraid of them."

Zsiga smiled. "What are you saying, Venzel, that we should have the 'birds and the bees' discussion? I think they already know; they've been helping you in the stables for nearly eight years."

Venzel started to return Zsiga's smile but stopped.

"Not all of them," he said grimly.

"No," Zsiga said sadly, "not all of them."

When the horses first arrived, Zsiga set up a schedule, posting one in the dormitory and giving one to Timaeus. As arranged, each morning, while Venzel removed the splints from his hands, Timaeus would summon the boys whose names were on that morning's list. Since Zsiga was interested in monitoring the boys' reactions to this new routine, he also met them there.

The first couple of days were magical. Venzel had never forgotten how wonderful it felt when riding horses was new, and it was a joy to share that wonder all over again through the boys' enthusiasm. Zsiga, seeing Venzel's patience with their thousands of questions, incessant pleas to ride, and trying to keep them out of the way of the horses' hooves, was at once happy and sad. Happy that his brother seemed to have found some peace and a feeling of being in the world again; sad because not only should Venzel have had a brood of his own boys to love and teach, Zsiga knew there was no way this was going to end well. The collective would eventually call Timaeus and the rest of the boys, and they would answer, leaving Venzel alone again. Each time that thought occurred to him, Zsiga prayed to Anya to let him live a little longer—not for his sake, but for Venzel.

The magic faded, temporarily, on the third day. Taliph signed up to come to the stables because everyone else had, and he wanted to do whatever they did.

Taliph listened as Venzel began by giving a brief overview of the stables, introducing the horses, and handing each boy a shovel. When he found out what the shovel was for, he complained. Venzel took it in stride. Taliph wasn't the first boy to object to stable chores, and as the other boys did as he asked, Venzel mucked out the stall as Taliph watched and wrinkled his nose.

The other boys paid attention as Venzel demonstrated how to put the bridle on a horse and handed each one the reins to lead their horse into the small corral. Taliph, wishing himself almost anywhere else, did not hear Venzel's warning to hold the reins in one hand and the bridle bit in the other. Leading their horses into the paddock, neither Venzel nor Zsiga noticed that Taliph was only holding onto the reins. As soon as the mare was free of the stables, she realized no one was controlling her head and butted Taliph, pushing him face first into the sand.

Before Zsiga or Venzel could stop him, Taliph got up and hit the mare on the side of her head with all his strength. Startled and in pain, she reared up on her back legs. Clipping Taliph under the chin with her front hoof, he fell backward onto the ground. The mare's hooves pawed the air above Taliph's chest. Frozen in fear, he stared into the maddened eyes of the horse and waited to die.

A flash came between him and the horse, and he was pulled up and away from the ground. Leaping over Taliph's body, Venzel had grabbed the bit and turned the horse to the side. Coming down on all four feet, the mare landed shaking on the sand. After lifting Taliph from the ground, Zsiga felt his legs, arms, and shoulders and looked for blood.

Stroking the mare in long even passes over her neck and back, Venzel spoke in a low voice as he turned her toward the stables. He stopped and pointed a finger at Taliph.

"I will talk to you in a minute."

Zsiga, panicking at what might have happened if the horse had landed on Taliph's chest, was relieved to find only a small cut on his chin. The only real injury, other than the sand in his eyes, was to Taliph's pride. The last thing he planned to do was to be there when the human came out of the stables. Zsiga, hearing his thoughts, held him until Venzel returned.

Venzel needed to calm down as much as the mare and lingered for a few moments in her stall. He glanced longingly at the horsewhip, but instead of the lashing he wanted to give Taliph, he decided to turn this near tragedy into a learning experience for everyone.

Ignoring the boy in Zsiga's grip, he addressed the boys who were dutifully holding their horses by the bit and the reins.

"What happened?"

The boys tilted their heads, and Toros answered, "Taliph did not hold onto the bit, and the horse pushed him."

"Was he hurt?"

Again, Venzel waited until Toros answered, "No, Venzel."

"Then why," he said, turning to Taliph, "strike a horse that was, by the way, just playing with you?"

Taliph was silent. Venzel looked back at Toros. "Why?"

The boys tilted their heads. They didn't want to answer, but the horses belonged to Venzel, and they wanted to ride. Taran looked at Zsiga, who closed his eyes and nodded.

Taran answered. "Because he was embarrassed and angry, but most of all," Taran took a deep breath, "he doesn't want to be here."

It made sense, then. All of it.

"Does everyone understand why we do not mistreat our horses?"

"Yes, Venzel."

"Please let your brothers who are not present today know that if they do not wish to ride, they can excuse themselves. I understand it is hard work and not something everyone can appreciate," Venzel said, turning back to Taliph.

Taliph glared wordlessly at him.

Thinking if Lalei had married Halil, the boy would have been riding before he could walk—whether he liked it or not—Venzel only smiled. "Taliph, since you no longer have a horse, you may leave."

Taliph broke away from Zsiga and ran toward the house. Turning around on the porch steps, he yelled, "Who needs stupid horses when cars are faster?"

Taliph never returned to the stables.

Venzel broke the silence.

"I still think you should tell them. If not right now, then wait until you sense the phase has begun."

Nesim stood up. "It's worth a try. I will contact the collective and see if anyone has approached it that way."

When Nesim turned to leave, Venzel signed to Zsiga, *please stay*. Zsiga nodded. He had seen that look of determination on Venzel's face before. As soon as the door closed, he said, "No."

"But Zsiga, why not a 'birds and the bees' talk? If we tell them it is what every young man should expect without giving them too many details, they won't think it is just them. That is where the fear lies. They believe it is happening only to them, and they overthink it. If they can become as unstable as you say, then isn't that dangerous enough without making them unstable and afraid?"

"Venzel."

"Zsiga, it doesn't have to be a big lecture. I'll work it in the next couple of conversations when they are in the stables. And I'll tell them if they have any questions, they should talk with you or Nesim because, well, I'm human, and their experience will probably be a little different."

Zsiga was silent.

"It's what a father does," said Venzel, "or a big brother. Remember?"

"Yes," said Zsiga softly, "I remember." Smiling, he asked, "Who told you? Kadri?"

"Well, he and Rauf certainly helped with the details, but no, it was our mother," he said, putting his hands together in reverence of her memory.

Zsiga did the same and then, tilting his head, smiled. "It appears the collective agrees with you, Venzi. Again."

Venzel looked at his brother with amusement.

"You were going to tell them anyway, weren't you?"

"You teach these boys that all knowledge is power. It would not have made any sense to keep from them knowledge that may save their lives. Naturally, I am grateful that I can do this with the collective's approval. We are one."

"We are one, Venzel."

Venzel regarded Zsiga seriously and grasped his shoulder. "It has always been my only fear, my brother, that I will inadvertently do something so incredibly human that would necessitate my death, but they had better send you to kill me because I will try to stop anyone else." He started to leave.

"Why wouldn't you try to stop me, Venzel?"

When he turned around, Zsiga was surprised to see tears in his eyes. "Destani is only a heartbeat away, Zsiga. Who better to send me to her than you?"

Zsiga would not utter the only response that came to his mind. He watched Venzel leave the room to return to the stables and went to get the saddlebags.

Taliph

Over the next few evenings, Venzel had the promised conversations with the boys and asked that they share the information with their brothers, who, for one reason or another, no longer came to the stables. It was important, he told them, that everyone understood that they should expect changes in the next several weeks that would affect not only their bodies but their minds, and because they would all be having the same feelings, to be patient with each other.

However, with Timaeus, he had a different conversation.

"The collective will not wait to see if the boys who exhibit the extremes of this adrenaline surge will recover. They are considered too dangerous. My son, I tell you this for two reasons. First, if you feel yourself losing control, find me and take whatever aggression you feel out on me. Your thoughts cannot hurt me, and I will keep you safe until it passes. Regardless of how you feel, do not threaten the colony. I will not be able to bear losing you that way."

"A question, Father, please. Isn't there somewhere safe for brothers who may be affected, for everyone's protection?"

"No, the collective believes there is no safe place. If any one of you poses a danger, you will be killed. It is the will of the collective."

Timaeus nodded.

"Second, you are with these boys day and night. If you become aware of any danger from them, please do not try to help. Let Zsiga and Nesim know immediately, call as many of your brothers as you can gather, and then find me. I probably won't be in my room, but here in the stables. I think the mares will need special attention in the next few weeks."

Timaeus walked from stall to stall, smelling the air. "No, Father, not for at least a month. Why are you really staying in here?"

"To do what I can to protect everything I love from harm."

"Like Alazar, Father?" he asked quietly.

"No, son, I do not think it will come to that. The colony has several solutions in place in case the worst happens. I am only a small part of one of them."

Timaeus put his hands out in front of him and closed his eyes for a moment. When he opened them, he looked at Venzel.

"The ammunition is here."

"You do not know that."

"No, Father," he said, smiling slightly, "I do not know that."

No one had to tell Venzel when the boys began to phase into adolescence. Their attitude toward each other became strained, and although no one could say how it started, he'd had to break up more than one fight. He never missed an opportunity to point out to them that their feelings were normal. They were no longer boys but young men and must always remember they were brothers. What hurt one, hurt them all.

Another sign was that not as many came out to help with the horses and the ones who did just wanted to ride them hard, trying to escape the feeling that they were exploding in a dozen different directions at once. Timaeus was unusually quiet. Every night, Venzel watched him come into the stables, saddle Alatan, and ride out, usually with Taran or Toros close on his heels. Venzel let them go. He would be there all night to cool down the lathered horses and let them rest until they were needed the following evening.

A month after their aggression levels began rising, Venzel noticed that the boys were quieter and more subdued. The frenzied riding marathons seemed to be over. They had changed, but it was to be expected, and although he could not help but feel admiration for these young men, his heart hurt at the thought that his boys were gone.

The morning of the day Venzel was to begin returning the ammunition to the armory, Zsiga rushed into the stables. His face distorted, and his hands in fists at his temples, he gasped for air.

"Help me, Venzel," he said before collapsing to his knees.

Venzel could barely get the word out, "Who?"

A loud voice came from the direction of double doors.

"Taliph."

Taliph closed the doors and slid the locking bar in place. Walking toward them, he held a 9mm pistol in one hand and brandished a bloodied combat knife in the other.

Ignoring Zsiga's moans of pain, Taliph looked at Venzel and said calmly, "I need a cartridge magazine for this, and you are going to get it for me."

"No."

At that moment, Zsiga's screams became deafening.

"Get the mag, Venzel, or I will kill him."

"Stop Taliph! Think what you are doing. Stop hurting Zsiga, or they will kill you."

Zsiga's screams stopped for a moment. "Not if I kill them first. I need the shells, Venzel. Now."

He tilted his head and, for a moment, looked slightly worried. Walking over to Zsiga, he poised the knife above his neck.

"Now, Venzel!"

"You will have to kill us both, Taliph. I will not help you."

Zsiga gave a final shriek and fell completely to the floor. Venzel jumped back as Taliph lunged at him. It became immediately apparent to Venzel that he had not been in a knife fight for nearly fifteen years and, despite roughhousing with his brothers, he had never fought a Lyostian intent on murder. Dodging the knife, he grabbed Taliph's hand and held the knife above his head, but he could not make Taliph release it. Amazed at the strength of the boy, he knew if two had come at him, he would not have had a chance. He didn't want to hurt Taliph, but still unable to dislodge the knife, he threw Taliph backward and grabbed a horse blanket, hoping to keep him at bay until someone came to help.

Taliph, having similar thoughts, looked back at the stable doors.

"Worried, Taliph?"

"Only that you will bleed to death before I have finished flaying you alive," he said, lunging again.

Twisting away to avoid the blade, Venzel saw Zsiga start to get up. Still holding his head, Zsiga looked around for a weapon but found only a hayfork. Taliph, following the direction of Venzel's eyes, turned to look back at Zsiga. At that moment, Venzel quickly grabbed Taliph from behind and pinned him against his body.

"Zsiga, call for help!"

"I can't!" He dropped the fork and fell to his knees, screaming, "Taliph, please!"

"Stop it, Taliph! Stop it," Venzel demanded.

"No."

Using all his strength, Taliph broke away from Venzel and lashed out, slicing through Venzel's tunic. Venzel felt blood drip down his chest and knew he had to stop Taliph, or both he and Zsiga would be dead, and then there would be no one to stop him. Seeing his size as his only advantage, he took a deep breath and hurled himself on top of Taliph.

Slammed to the floor, Taliph lost his mental hold on Zsiga. Knowing he would not be stunned for long, Venzel stood up and looked for the hayfork Zsiga dropped. Feeling suddenly dizzy, he fell against a support beam and saw blood oozing down his arm from the gash where Taliph had buried the blade of the combat knife in his shoulder.

Taliph opened his eyes and smiled up at Venzel from the stable floor as Zsiga writhed in pain only a few inches away. Unable to dislodge the knife, Venzel realized he could not stop Taliph alone. As seconds ticked away their lives, he saw Taliph gasp for breath as he struggled to get up.

"Halil," whispered Zsiga.

Taliph stopped moving and turned his head to look at Zsiga.

Seeing Taliph distracted and still, Venzel had only one hope left. Staggering to the mare's stall, he threw open the gate and, as he fell against Zsiga, made a single motion with his left hand.

A blur of turquoise eyes hovered above his. "Destani?" he whispered.

"No, Father, Timaeus."

"Zsiga?"

"In the bed next to yours. Alive, thanks to you."

"Taliph?"

"Fell out of the collective."

"The horses?"

"By the time everyone got there, they were all out of their stalls. It was hard to determine which one killed Taliph, so all were spared."

"Thank you, son."

"It was not me. Taran got there first."

"But you were there together, before everyone else?"

"Yes."

"But how did you get in? The doors were bolted."

"Our back doors, Father. Taliph didn't know they open from the outside."

"Yes, yes. Thank you, both."

"Are we not both your sons, Father?" he asked gently.

Venzel closed his eyes.

"Yes."

From the other bed came a hoarse whisper.

"And Taliph."

Venzel covered his eyes with his free arm, but not before Timaeus saw the tears falling from the corners of his eyes. "And Taliph," he whispered back.

Timaeus tilted his head. "I must go. Nesim is coming to check on you, and Ezri will be bringing soup in about an hour. Try to rest in the meantime."

When the door closed, Venzel looked at Zsiga, who was staring at the ceiling. "I am so sorry, Zsiga… I tried so hard to stop him, but I could not let him kill you."

"Kill me, *too*, Venzel."

"Too?" Despite the excruciating pain, Venzel pulled himself up and looked at Zsiga.

"Yes. Nandor, guarding the armory, was killed at once. When Taliph could not find any cartridges for the gun he had stolen, he grabbed a knife and killed two more brothers who tried to stop him before mentally torturing Lukas into telling him I knew where the ammunition was stored. He stabbed Lukas in the heart, which I am sure was an unintended mercy. Contacting me, Taliph said that Toros had stolen a gun. He watched as I left the house and followed me to the stables, then, well, you know the rest."

"He killed four, nearly five, brothers, and you had no idea of what was going on with him?"

"We could feel a tension developing over the last several days. When we could not pinpoint anyone's specific thoughts, we hoped it was an accumulation of emotions rather than a single source. We had planned to isolate the boys for individual scanning but did not do it because we mistakenly thought the most critical phase was over. For a while, we, um, thought it might be Timaeus."

"Why?"

"Because we cannot scan him. Either naturally or intentionally, there is a wall between his thoughts and everyone else. He can receive ours, and we can receive the ones he deliberately sends to us, but we cannot read his random thoughts or emotional state and, truthfully, have not been able to do so for years. He would be the only one, we thought, who could hide from us, and we were watching him. But we were so horribly wrong. Oh, Taliph!" The anguish in Zsiga's voice was heartbreaking to hear. "He was so much like her."

Zsiga took a shuddering breath and closed his eyes.

Venzel painfully lowered his body back down onto the bed. His mind reeled with new realizations. Zsiga had loved Lalei. It wasn't anything Venzel could comprehend. She was selfish, petulant, and, preferring Halil, she would never have shown any wifely affection for Zsiga. Still, inexplicably, he loved her. Venzel now knew the real reason Zsiga wanted Halil dead was not that she'd taunted Zsiga into nearly being banished; it was because she would not stop loving him.

Venzel knew Senkali had loved Zsiga practically from the moment she met him, but somehow, her affection was not enough to erase Lalei from his heart. Taliph was poor consolation, but Zsiga saw in him someone he could not possess in reality and was suffering, not only because he had lost Taliph but because he had lost Lalei forever.

"Oh, my brother…."

"No, Venzel, please, let us not talk of this."

"Will you ever forgive me?"

"Yes, my brother… as once, in your pain, you graciously forgave me."

It wasn't the same, but the debts had piled so high on each side that it was impossible to untangle them now. Venzel reached his hand toward his brother. Zsiga grasped it in his and pulled it hard against his chest. In the silence of the room, Venzel felt the beat of Zsiga's broken heart against the back of his hand.

Timaeus walked into the room later that afternoon as they were eating their soup. Going to the counter, he picked up the clipboards and reviewed them.

Initially amused, Venzel stopped smiling when he saw the intense look in his son's eyes. Standing between them and watching their faces carefully, he asked, "Um, Father, Zsiga... do you think the collective would let me be a doctor?"

Percentages

Venzel helped Zsiga return the last of the ammunition to the colony's armory. He could not help noticing how many times Zsiga tilted his head as if he were an integral part of an important discussion. When he stopped, Venzel signed to him.

What is it?

Zsiga said, "One out of twenty is too low."

"One what, out of twenty?"

"The average number of boys who were adversely affected is ten to twenty-five percent. We were the only colony with less than ten percent."

"Up to five of them could have been affected?"

"Yes."

"We would all be dead, Zsiga."

"Yes."

"I don't understand. What is the problem? Shouldn't we be happy there was only one?"

"Yes, Venzel. Only—"

"Are you saying you think someone could have been affected and hidden it? At that level of aggression?"

"After seeing what happened to Taliph, he might try."

"There are only a few boys here strong enough to do that—if it's possible to do at all. At any rate, it's over, isn't it?"

"Gratefully, yes. We believe that telling them made the difference; they didn't have to contend with both aggression and fear. Once again, Venzel, you stood between us and tragedy."

"It was tragic enough, Zsiga… tragic enough."

Venzel put his hand on his brother's shoulder. "I'm going to return these saddlebags to the stables," he said without looking at Zsiga's face.

Zsiga watched Venzel leave; his eyes blurred with tears. There were only two who could have hidden it—or would have tried—Taran and Timaeus. Unable to bear the thought of losing either of them, he put the collective's statistics out of his mind. As he had told Venzel, it was over now, and, if possible, he loved Venzel even more for keeping their sons alive.

Zsiga never knew that he was only half right.

Racing the Wind

The years went by as swiftly as Alatan's hooves racing the wind on the desert floor. More boys arrived, and many advanced to specialized training in the medical and technical fields the collective deemed critical. For those who stayed at the compound, their interest in the horses depended on whether they wanted to ride, train, or race. Venzel shared the enthusiasm Timaeus and the boys had for his horses, and as Alatan's colts grew up beautiful and intuitive, the boys matured into intelligent young men with their own kind of beauty.

Zsiga never fully recovered from that afternoon in the stables. Nesim could not determine whether it was a result of the damage done to his cerebral cortex by Taliph's debilitating lightning flashes of pain or his grief. Unable to endue even a flicker of light, Zsiga kept more and more to the rooms near the nursery as Senkali and Ezri looked after him.

Nesim took over the general management of the colony's interior structure, and Venzel, with a little residual stiffness in his shoulder, continued to maintain the compound and the stables as well as whatever business needed to be done in the village. He still made visits to the neighboring colonies, but not as often as before. He was getting older, and although he was as virile as ever, the collective found more modern methods of impregnating their prospective mothers and needed his particular area of expertise only when those methods failed.

The Fire Slayers

Venzel was surprised to find that he did not care.

Zsiga's Warning

Senkali sat in Zsiga's chair and tried not to weep. Kneeling beside his brother's bed, Venzel held Zsiga's hand tightly in his fist and pressed his forehead against his brother's pillow.

"Please, brother, do not leave us."

"It's time, Venzel. You know we do not live long on this planet; maybe someday we will find a way, but now, well, I'm thirty-two, which, as you know, is longer than most of us live. Blessed Anya has been extremely good to me."

"To us, Zsiga, to us."

"Yes, Venzi, to us but… there are some things I must say and one thing I must ask."

"I am here."

Zsiga's voice dropped to a whisper. "Leave. Take whatever money you have saved and go. I don't know what the collective's plans are for the colony when this generation is called. They do not intend to send more children here, and we will become little more than an outpost. An unprotected outpost with no assignment has no future. Someone will come to destroy it. Sell your horses, take the money. Don't tell anyone. Just get in the car and go. Please try to find some happiness in the world, Venzel. There has been little enough for you here."

"Timaeus will still be here for a while, Zsiga. He is happiness enough for me. And Taran is still here with the other children of this generation. I must teach them what I can."

"Remember, brother, Timaeus does not belong to you. He will learn from you, and he will love you, but he belongs… to the collective, and they have very specific plans. He will obey them, always and in all things."

"Yes, Zsiga, but he is young, yet. There is still time before the collective calls him. But I will heed your advice, save what money I can, and leave quietly when he does. I will not wait for someone to destroy my home."

"May you be well, my brother, all your life. May I ask one favor?"

"You do not have to ask, Zsiga. You know I will not leave Senkali alone. We will leave together, I promise you."

"Before then?"

"She will be under my care and protection for as long as she lives, Zsiga. Please put your mind at rest, my brother. It will all be as you wish."

"Blessed Anya, mother of us all, watch over you both." The final darkness was entering his mind, and Zsiga was barely able to whisper, "Senkali."

Stepping away from the bed, Venzel took Senkali's hand and placed it on Zsiga's face. Joining Taran and Timaeus in the hall, they began singing Anya's hymn of lament. The sad, sweet melody echoed throughout the tunnels, uniting every voice in the colony. Sounding like a choir of angels, their prayers carried Zsiga's soul to Anya, who would guide him to Atjaro, the gateway to infinite light.

Senkali

After Zsiga's death, Venzel fell into an easy relationship with Senkali. It was natural that he became protective of her; she was Zsiga's wife, his sister, and revered by everyone in the colony. Venzel tried to bring her up out of the deeper tunnels, but she would not hear of leaving the rooms she'd shared with Zsiga.

However, Zsiga wasn't the only reason Senkali refused to leave her rooms near the nursery. The boys' dormitory was not far away, and she could hear them talking and laughing. Occasionally, one would wander down and hold her hand, ask her questions about this or that, or bring her some flowers or a treat from the kitchen. No, she would not leave her boys. She was their mother.

Making his responsibility to Senkali part of his daily routine, Venzel came down each evening between dinner and sunset to see that she was well, but soon he began looking forward to his visit. It was not sexual. Although she was as lovely as the first time he saw her, Venzel did not touch her. He sat in Zsiga's chair, grateful that the hardship of living underground had not affected her pleasant and loving nature. After a few evenings, he understood why Zsiga had to be near her. Lalei was the moon, alluring but distant and cold; Senkali was the sun, golden, warm, and gracious.

Basking in her kindness, Venzel talked about the things that meant the most to him. His hopes for Timaeus, Taran, and the other boys, his horses and, one evening, he mentioned Destani. He kept his voice steady so she would not hear when tears came into his eyes. Senkali had loved Destani, so they talked together as if she was away for just a moment and not forever. Venzel listened while she talked of Zsiga, and then he shared stories of their childhood that he remembered that she said Zsiga never told her. Although she could not see, whenever he mentioned Zsiga's name, her eyes shone with a special light that Venzel recognized, with nearly overwhelming compassion, as untainted and complete love.

Venzel would never have learned that Timaeus listened to his conversations with Senkali if not for one evening as they were grooming Alatan, he repeated an anecdote involving Zsiga that he had recently related to Senkali. Laughing, Timaeus added the end of the story. Suddenly, Timaeus realized he was laughing alone.

Looking over Alatan's back into Venzel's blue/black eyes, Timaeus knew he had been caught eavesdropping. Blushing, he looked down at the brush in his hands and stammered, "I'm, I'm sorry, Father."

"For how long?"

"Close to the beginning, I think."

"Alone, or is it a party?"

Offended, Timaeus looked up at Venzel quickly. "Alone. I thought about asking Taran since… well, but no, it's just me."

"Tell me why."

"At first, I was just curious, and after a few days, decided it was boring, but then one evening you mentioned Mother and… I, I couldn't leave."

Venzel's expression did not change as he regarded his son. It was true. Although he had been discreet, he'd talked more about Destani these last couple of weeks with Senkali than he'd ever shared with his son. Timaeus would be leaving for Cairo soon to attend the university there, and as life in the desert was precarious, Venzel decided it would be better to answer his questions now. Timaeus was old enough to understand.

"Please tell Nesim we're taking the horses overnight and ask Taran and Toros to take care of the rest while we're gone."

"But—"

His eyes never left Timaeus's face as he asked softly, "Timaeus, are you arguing with me?"

"No, Father."

"Good. Saddle Alatan and Fahar. I will return in a few minutes."

Walking quickly into the house, Venzel found Ezri and told him that he would be away, and if he was not back by dinner tomorrow, not to worry and to take care of Senkali while he was gone. Keeping his curiosity to himself, Ezri followed Venzel to his room. Watching from the doorway, he saw Venzel take the key from the mantel and open the trunk at the foot of the bed that had remained closed for nearly fourteen years.

Unprepared for the onslaught of her perfume, Venzel immediately dropped the lid. Taking a small satchel from the closet, he held his breath and lifted the lid again. He quickly removed a turquoise scarf, an embroidered sheath, and a red envelope. Letting the lid fall, he took a shuddering breath and locked the trunk.

Holding out the key to Ezri, he said, "Never open that trunk while I am here, and no matter what happens, never give this back to me."

Ezri took the key and nodded. Venzel grabbed two cloaks from the closet, pressed them against his eyes, and left the room. Untying Destani's ribbon from around his neck, Ezri threaded an end through the trunk key. It slid along the silk and rattled gently against the balcony room key. Ezri retied the ribbon and headed for the kitchen.

Nesim met him in the hall. "Where are they going?"

"They?"

"Venzel and Timaeus. He said they were taking the horses and would be away all night. Do you know where they are going?"

Ezri did not know where they were going. The oasis was too far away for only one night unless….

"I regret that he did not tell me where they were going. Perhaps, as it is for only one night, they are going to the village."

"Then why wouldn't he take the car?"

"My master prefers to ride."

The Oasis

Venzel was not surprised to find Ezri waiting for him on the porch with a large pouch of food, more food than any two men would need for one night.

"Thank you, Ezri. This is more than I expected."

"Yes, Master."

"I don't suppose, if asked, you planned to share your, um, suspicions."

"Of course not, Master. I could be mistaken."

Venzel looked at him for several moments. "Ezri, how long have you served me?"

"Twenty years, Master."

"Good years, Ezri?"

"Some better than others, Master."

"Yes, you're right."

"Um, Master?"

"Don't ask questions you don't want your eyes plucked out for the answers, Ezri."

"Yes, Master," he said, smiling slightly.

Venzel began walking toward the stables, stopped, and turned back. "It's Venzel, Ezri," he said softly.

Ezri paled and dropped to the floor. "No, Master, not once, not ever."

Venzel laughed. He must be losing his touch; even Ezri was arguing with him these days. Waving, he walked into the stables.

Standing, Ezri bowed slightly in Venzel's direction.

He could not bear to alter their relationship. Only a few years older than his master, he'd waited while Venzel's feelings toward him evolved from command to trust to companionship, and, in the last several years, Ezri had come to regard Venzel almost as a son or a brother he was responsible for, rather than a master he must serve and obey. There was nothing Ezri would not do for Venzel or Timaeus or, even though they were unaware of it, for the Lyostians, who Venzel once said had saved his life. To Ezri, Venzel's life was the only one that mattered. Whoever he loved, Ezri loved. Those who also found his life precious, Ezri cherished, and, although he was in no hurry to die, he would prefer Venzel kill him than set him free.

As his father requested, Timaeus saddled the horses and waited for him inside the paddock. He caught the cloak Venzel tossed in his direction.

"Where are we going?"

"Does it matter?"

"A little."

"If we get out of range of the collective and you start feeling uncomfortable, let me know, and we will turn back."

"I am no longer a child, Father. I can be out of hearing range for a day or so without fear."

"Then what is it?"

"Nesim wants to know why we are doing this."

"Because we should, and we must. You are leaving soon. The desert is not always a safe place to live, and you have questions that need answers. Answers you need to hear directly from me and not picked up on the other side of walls." He added quietly, "I would have told you whatever you wanted to know, son, you didn't have to do that."

"I did not know the questions to ask."

"Well, that is what we are going to find out."

They rode through the night. Timaeus talked of what he hoped to accomplish in school, what the other boys' plans were, and, inevitably, their horses. In fact, they talked about everything except where they were going and what they were going to do once they arrived.

Every hour or so, Venzel asked if he was all right. Timaeus always said he was, but as they traveled beyond the perimeter of his home colony, he gripped the reins tighter than necessary.

Venzel waited until Timaeus saw the trees on the horizon.

"The oasis," he breathed.

"Yes. Will you be at ease there?"

"Yes, I think so, for a little while."

"Good, we won't stay more than a couple of days."

Timaeus halted Alatan. "We told Nesim just overnight."

"I know we did."

"Why?"

"He might have tried to stop us, and I didn't want to put you in the awkward position of having to choose. That day will come soon enough."

"Father, I will—" he started to say loyally.

Venzel turned in the saddle and looked at his son. "Shh, Timaeus, don't finish that sentence." Adding softly, "I know what you will do."

Timaeus's face fell. His father was right. He was Lyostian—and Tuzurias—and now they *both* knew he would do as he was told.

"Race you to the water."

Venzel flicked the reins lightly on Fahar's flank, and she ran like the wind. Alatan, first at her heels, pulled up alongside. Racing neck and neck across the desert, father and son were laughing when they reached the lagoon. While the horses drank, Timaeus watched the lake and the lagoon glimmer in the moonlight and breathed in the fragrance of the palm trees.

"Oh yes… this is the place I saw—"

"In her mind?"

"In her heart."

Venzel nodded, looking away.

"Uh-oh, Father, it looks like we aren't the only ones here." Timaeus pointed in the direction of a new dark blue tent with thin white stripes set in the shade of the trees.

It wasn't the same to Venzel's eyes, but desert people had long memories, and blue and purple tents were still too dangerous.

"Well," he said, "let's go meet the neighbors."

As Timaeus stared, Venzel walked boldly to the tent flap, pushed it aside, and entered the cool darkness. A moment later, Venzel yelled his name. Grabbing his rifle, Timaeus rushed in after his father and stopped. Laughing in relief, he was delighted to find Venzel sitting like a rajah on cushions set upon a tapestry rug. Next to him was another pile of cushions. Timaeus ran and landed in the center of them and looked at his father in surprise.

"You did this?"

"I arranged for it to be done. For many reasons, Timaeus, your eyes are precious to me. It will be dark enough for you in here during the day." Remembering his son's other limitations, he looked up. "Are you all right? Can you hear them?"

"Yes, I can hear a general buzzing. No one is looking for me. Yes, Father, I'm fine. There must be a colony within three or four klicks from here."

"Do they know where you are?"

"Only if I want them to know."

"That's right, I'd forgotten."

"Forgotten what?"

"That Zsiga told me they cannot hear you unless you want them to—that there is a shield or wall around your thoughts, so they can't be scanned."

Timaeus sat very still.

"Is that true?"

"What do you mean? It's what you just said."

"I meant if I needed to call them for any reason. I did not know they were unable to detect my presence, or hear me at all, unless I reached out to them." Considering the implications of this discovery, he asked, "Did Zsiga say it was a trait of all Tuzurias?

"He said it was only you, at least in our colony." Venzel could not mistake the look of concern on Timaeus's face. "I know it's unusual, but is it a problem?"

It depends on who you are, thought Timaeus. Aloud, he said, "No, of course not. I just don't understand why they never told me."

Venzel yawned. "They probably thought you knew."

"Perhaps… why don't you get some sleep? I'll tie the horses next to the tent and join you."

"No, I'll get the horses, it's almost daylight."

As Timaeus flattened the cushions for sleeping, his mind reeled. His brothers couldn't scan him, or some of them couldn't. That's why they thought Taliph was the only one.

He also knew why Zsiga didn't tell him. Monitoring unguarded thoughts was the collective's method of pinpointing possible insurrections. If he knew they could not scan him, it meant he could have secrets.

I wonder why I am still alive.

He smiled grimly as he recalled that the collective, like the individual colonies, wasted nothing. Timaeus felt a chill as he contemplated their reasons for letting him live.

Venzel came in a few minutes later carrying the pouch of food and two rifles and set them inside the tent. He smiled when he saw Timaeus had settled the cushions.

"Hungry?"

"No, Father, just very tired."

"Me, too. We'll eat and talk more later."

"Yes."

Timaeus began to tilt his head; he should tell Nesim where he was—and truthfully how long he would be gone—then reconsidered. If

Nesim ordered him back, he would have to return, and he wasn't ready to leave yet.

No, he decided. *I'll wait until they start looking for me.*

Closing his eyes, Timaeus wondered at his lack of apprehension at being alone for the first time. Away from the walls of sand and stone, he felt he had shaken loose of the chrysalis that had sheltered him all his life. It was unexpected, this freedom of flight, and he wondered if his temporary sense of mental independence was the way humans felt all the time.

Drifting to sleep, he dreamed his mother was stripping away the remaining silk casings and setting him free. His newly formed wings unfurled as blood flowed into the tiny veins. He expected them to be wondrous—and they were—but he did not anticipate the pain. Although appearing translucent and weightless, every time he tried to expand them, an intense burning reverberated through his body, but he could not stop. Using all his strength, he extended them completely. He had never felt so powerful. Despite the rippling torment tearing him in half, he forced them further out until a luminescent glow surrounded him.

"Timaeus."

Only one person in the world spoke his name with such love. Standing across from him with the silken shreds still in her hands, Destani smiled up at him.

"You are beautiful, my son, beautiful."

He had missed her so much, but when he tried to wrap her in his wings, they wouldn't bend around her. More than anything, he wanted to hold her, but something was wrong. Unable to retract them, it was becoming unbearable to keep them open. Looking up at the wings he could no longer control, Timaeus saw the finely arched edges blacken and become jagged. Thin shafts of light pierced the translucent scales that moments earlier had folded perfectly around his body.

Unable to save them, Timaeus watched in helpless agony as his once-magnificent wings dripped blood upon the sand. Heartbroken and growing weak, he knelt before her.

"Forgive me, Mother. It is who I am."

Smiling tenderly, she bent down and touched his face. The wings disappeared, and with them, the pain. Able to stand, he looked into the mirror of her eyes.

"It is not all you are, Timaeus. You must remember, you belonged to us first."

Her image began to shimmer and fade, and he tried to catch her hand.

"Don't go, Mother. Please. Don't go."

Timaeus sat up, blinking at the silhouette of his father standing at the door of the tent.

"So, you're awake."

"Yes, what time is it?"

"Mid-afternoon, I'm afraid you're stuck in here for a little while."

"That's all right with me. The horses?"

"Just fed them. I promised them a ride around the oasis later. I thought we might find something to shoot for dinner."

Timaeus looked at him.

Venzel laughed. "Well, something for *my* dinner."

Timaeus smiled. Unless the birds had spared a few berries, he doubted there was anything he could eat out there.

Venzel sat next to him. "So, do you want to tell me?"

"Tell you what?"

"What you were dreaming. You said, 'Don't go,' just before you woke up."

Timaeus nodded and said, "Mother."

"What did she say?" Venzel asked softly. "It has been a long time since your mother visited my dreams."

Since Destani was the reason they were there, Timaeus felt he should be completely honest. "Only a few words, but the last thing she said was to 'remember I belonged to you first.'"

"Yes. Do you recall anything else?"

"Only that I was in a lot of pain, and when she touched my face, it stopped."

"Yes, son, she did that once for me, too."

Venzel walked over to the food pouch and set out the juice, honey, mashed olives in oil, and bread, giving the tray to Timaeus. Picking up the small bucket by the door, he walked back outside. By the time he returned, Timaeus had finished his breakfast, and Venzel poured water into two basins, handing him one with a small cloth. Together, they bathed away the dust of the long ride.

Sitting on opposite sides of a small carpet, Venzel took the embroidered bag from his saddlebag and placed it between them.

"Before we begin, please contact Nesim and tell him that we will be back tomorrow night. I really don't want any interruptions."

"As you wish, Father," said Timaeus, tilting his head.

"Thank you." Venzel paused for a moment and took a deep breath. "I am not sure," he said, "if you are aware of my more delicate responsibilities to the colony."

"Yes, Father. I am."

Venzel looked at him sharply. "Please explain."

"They may not be able to hear all my thoughts, but I can hear theirs. Anyway, Nesim and Zsiga were not especially discreet. They, we, are grateful."

Venzel nodded, and without protecting himself or anyone else, he quickly sketched out the history of his life as a member of the colony. When the discussion progressed to his last caravan, he opened the small, embroidered bag, and Destani's perfume filled the tent. Timaeus inhaled deeply and leaned forward, his hands moving in the direction of the fragrance as if it were alive.

"I know how you feel, Son."

Needing a few minutes to accustom himself to the scent of his wife, Venzel made tea and returned with a tall, narrow glass for Timaeus.

"There are some things in here I want you to have."

Venzel removed the red envelope first. Opening it carefully, he took out the marriage certificate and showed Timaeus their names, the beautiful drawings, the signature of the priest, and the seal of the village magistrate. When Timaeus handed it back, Venzel gently refolded the paper. Knowing he would never see it again, he reluctantly returned it to the red envelope.

Before he could change his mind, Venzel drew out the turquoise scarf from the bag and handed it to his son. Taking it in both hands, Timaeus could not resist pressing the fragrant silk against his eyes and whispered, "Mother."

Venzel never envied the Lyostians' ability to pry into each other's minds. Watching his son, however, he wished he could see what Timaeus saw when he thought of his mother and wished he could share his own vision with him. The crippled spirit that Timaeus loved was only a pale shadow of the wife Venzel still adored.

Timaeus lowered the scarf from his face and draped it under his cloak, where he could feel the silk next to his skin and breathe in her perfume.

He looked expectantly at Venzel.

"It was the scarf she wore at Anya's wedding ceremony." The memories of that evening: her beauty and poise, Zsiga's teasing, how he stole her away to bring her to the oasis where they'd shared so much joy crowded in on him, and he could not continue.

After a few minutes, he said, "I will answer your questions, Timaeus, but I cannot describe it to you."

"I have no questions, Father. Zsiga... well, Zsiga thought about the wedding often, and I saw Mother and you in his memories. You kissed the palm of her hand, and she loved you with her eyes, and yes, she was wearing this,"—he reverently touched the edge of the silk—"around her face like a halo."

"Yes," Venzel said, reaching out his hand and grasping his son's arm. "Yes, it was exactly like that. She was the most beautiful woman I'd ever seen."

"Well," said Timaeus, "According to Zsiga's memories, Mother was the most beautiful woman any of them had ever seen."

"He truly thought that?"

"Oh, yes."

He smiled inwardly. *Thank you, Zsiga, my brother, for that.*

He contemplated the bag silently for several minutes before sliding the dagger from the scabbard.

Timaeus looked at the weapon, and his eyes were everywhere at once. He watched his father's hands, his face, and the dagger. Had Venzel brought him all this way to finally kill him? Timaeus knew his father had thought about it and struggled against it, but perhaps he had just been waiting....

Venzel looked from the weapon to his son and read his face as easily as if he could hear his thoughts. He shook his head.

"No, son. Not now, not ever."

"But you thought about it. I saw it in your eyes."

"I just wanted the pain to stop. I would never have hurt you, never let anything hurt you. I could not have endured losing you both. I love you too much."

Timaeus was silent. He remembered the destruction of the gifts he'd left for his mother and being pulled away from her, and although the memories were faint, he had seen hatred on this man's face and felt the heat from his eyes. There was no argument Timaeus could make. Venzel's hatred had always been justified—it was because of what he was that his mother died. Sorrow and regret filled his mind, and for a moment, the fire and the pain he'd felt in his dream were real.

"Why do you say that? I know what I am and how I killed her. I've *always* known. Please, Father, do not lie to me now. I prefer your friendly indifference to lies about loving me."

Venzel looked at his son steadily and told him, with some slight omissions, about the last day he and Destani spent at the oasis.

"I was being so careful with her. We knew Anya had blessed us with you. I wouldn't even carry her back from the lagoon, afraid if I tripped, I would fall on her. I thought I had loved her before, but from that moment on, she was the most precious thing in the world to me because you were with her, and we were a *family*. I think that is what she meant, Timaeus, to remember that you were ours, and we loved you, first.

"All the self-loathing and sorrow that came after I realized I had failed to protect her was because I thought I had lost you *both*. That the happiness I was promised had been taken from me, and in its place was a son who wasn't mine and a wife who would never, could never, love me again. Then, that night in the garden, when I saw that you loved her, I realized that we shared that grief, and then, later, I remembered what I promised her—and I tried to keep it.

"What was the promise?"

"I will tell you tomorrow."

Timaeus nodded and reached for the small satchel. "Was this hers, too?"

Venzel looked into his son's eyes. "From the moment I met her, everything I had was hers; everything I hoped for, and everything I was changed the moment she touched my face. I don't think I ever told her." He swallowed back the lump in his throat. "You see, I thought I was going to keep her with me forever."

"I'm sorry, Father," Timaeus said, looking down.

Venzel took one of Timaeus's hands and pressed it hard against his heart.

"No! Don't be sorry. I won't let you be sorry. I saw you, as you are now, before you were born, and loved you. She knew you before you were born, loved you, and told me that it was your power that gave her the strength to save our lives. *All* our lives, Timaeus. So never tell me again that you are sorry. You saved her that day." His voice caught, and he released his son's hand. "And if there had never been anything else between us, I would have still loved you for the rest of my life."

Looking into Venzel's face, Timaeus knew it was true. Venzel loved him, had always loved him. Timaeus recalled the splints, designing and building the stables together, sharing Alatan, and so many other things. He touched Venzel's gifts: his mother's scarf on his shoulder, her dagger in his hand, and a red envelope that said they were his parents, and once, for a few moments in time and for eternity, they were a family—and they loved him, first.

"Thank you, Father."

"Thank you, Son."

Venzel watched Timaeus gratefully caress the few items that were Destani's and hoped his son would never understand how difficult the afternoon had been for him. Glancing at the tent door, he saw that no light peeked around the edges and smiled in relief.

"You get the rifles; I'll saddle the horses."

Without waiting for a reply, he stood and left the tent.

Smiling, Timaeus picked up the rifles and hurried out after Venzel. The questions he had been struggling with were answered. Surrounded by his mother's perfume and the quiet sounds of the oasis she loved, he felt that even without wings, he could fly.

The Ravine

Exploring the oasis by moonlight was exercise for the horses and sport for the men. Timaeus killed a cobra with one shot, which they gutted for the birds, ants, and scorpions. Venzel shot a rabbit, then skinned and roasted it for his dinner. Sitting by the dark lagoon, they talked until dawn chased them into the tent. Father and son slept better than they had in many years, and although Destani did not visit them in their dreams, both woke up thinking of her.

To distract himself from his thoughts, Timaeus signed to Venzel, *Breakfast?*

Venzel laughed. "When did you learn to do that?"

"Years ago. I knew something was going on and started paying attention when you and Zsiga were together. It didn't take too long. After all, Father, it is not a hard code to break, and I could hear Zsiga's thoughts sometimes, and that helped."

"Do the other boys know we used it?"

"Only if they wanted to. I think Taran probably does, but it was never important to him to learn it. Why did you create it in the first place?"

"Because I was jealous that his other brothers knew what he was thinking, and I didn't. So, we made up the hand signals to talk privately, and no one would know. Apparently, however, they did."

"Only if they knew when to listen to Zsiga's thoughts. Besides, I wanted to learn it. There might be something private I want to tell you someday."

"Or I you?"

"Yes."

Drowsing through the afternoon, Timaeus asked questions about life at the colony when Venzel and Zsiga were young, about his grandmother, and the exotic places Venzel had visited. They talked about the horses and Venzel's plans after Timaeus left for Cairo.

"I will do what I have always done, my son, help the colony acquire whatever it needs. Nesim has asked me to stay and manage the compound, and I will continue Alazar's bloodline. I will also make sure Senkali has all she needs. I suspect it will be very quiet after all the boys receive their education assignments, but there are always things to do. The stables bring in a nice sum of money, so the colony won't be dependent on the collective if we go back to being an outpost. But that, my son," he said smiling, "is many years from now."

Feeling the cool breeze of twilight seeping into the tent, the smile faded from Venzel's face. "We'll be leaving soon. It will be a slightly longer trip back, so we will need extra water. I'll go feed the horses now."

Timaeus prepared to leave. He returned his mother's things to the small bag and tied it under his tunic. Tilting his head, he told Nesim they were returning to the colony.

During those few glorious minutes between sunset and darkness, Timaeus walked to the water's edge and closed his eyes. He wanted to always remember this time and place. Stretching his hands out in front of him with his palms down, he felt the air brush past his fingers and breathed in the scents surrounding him. He connected all that Venzel shared with him with his mother's memories of the oasis and, opening his eyes, understood her joy.

Venzel walked around the tent with the horses and saw his son standing by the lagoon. Unwilling to disturb him, he waited quietly in the shadows. Despite what he'd told Timaeus earlier, he was not entirely sure what the next few years would bring or where he would be, but this journey was not the time to discuss *his* future.

Timaeus turned away from the water toward Venzel.

I miss her, he signed.

Venzel answered, *I know. Me too*.

Venzel handed Alatan's reins to Timaeus. Taking a slightly broader arc back to the compound, Venzel turned the horses eastward.

Perhaps where the rocks still stood as mute witnesses to a promise and a prayer, they would recapture Destani's spirit.

Lost in his thoughts, Timaeus did not notice the wide swath of darkness until it loomed before them. Realizing it was a deep ravine, he stared as Venzel dismounted and began climbing down the cliff. Without a word, Timaeus followed his father to the boulders below.

The wind and sand had nearly erased Destani's blood from the rocks, but Venzel did not need the weak light of the crescent moon to trace the reddish-brown outline that marked where she had fallen. Many times, over the years, sometimes out of loneliness, sometimes in despair, but always without hope, Venzel returned to this place of reclamation and loss. Standing on the cliff, he would stare down at the stained rocks, seeking her permission to join his blood with hers. Each time, regardless of what brought him there, her response was the same. Hearing the echo of a promise, Venzel knew he had no choice but to return to the compound and try to keep it.

Gently brushing the sand away, Venzel placed his hand on the rock. "This is where she died. I don't know what she was running away from or where she was going. I didn't believe she had the strength to do such a thing, or I would not have left her alone, but I was always afraid it would end like this. Rauf said it was a mercy. Naturally, it did not feel like that at the time… or even now. My only consolation is that because of this," his hand trembled for a moment, "*violence*, she knew who I was before she died.

"Destani was, is, my *wife*. The only woman I have ever loved, and part of me." He raised his hand from the faded brown stains. With tears in his eyes, he rubbed his chest as though trying to make the pain go away.

My wife echoed in Timaeus's ears. Venzel said the words as though they were the dearest words he knew. It was only then that Timaeus realized the depth of his father's loss.

Yes, Timaeus thought, *I, too, would have hated anything, anyone, who had stolen something that precious from me.* He laid his hand on his father's arm.

Venzel took a deep breath. "I was going to keep her with me forever and thought I could keep her safe. I was wrong, twice, but she forgave me. She has never let go of us, Timaeus, and is now, as she has been for nearly fourteen years, only a dream and a heartbeat away."

"How do you know she forgave you?"

"She touched my face and told me she loved us."

"She loved… *us*," whispered Timaeus reverently.

Timaeus gently pulled Destani's scarf from under his cloak, breathed in its fragrance, and placed it over the fading streaks to guard them against the desert sun and caustic wind. Setting stones around the edge, he fashioned a small crown, and Venzel, who brought her a gift each time he came, removed a gold bracelet from his sleeve and set it in the center.

Together, they sang Anya's song of lament and then helped each other climb back up the cliff.

Gazing down at their memorial, Venzel said, "I don't know what your life is going to be like, but if you ever find a woman who cares for you, loves you like that…. My son, please don't push it away. Try to find a way to protect that love and hold her for as long as you can."

"Father, I do not think we—"

"Zsiga did."

"But he did not love—"

"Yes, he did."

"It is possible for us?"

"I have known Lyostians who cared for their human wives for who they were and not only what they were to the colony and had that feeling returned. Zsiga told me your generation, the Tuzurias, is special, but I will never believe that you cannot love, Timaeus. I've seen how you care for your mother's memory, your brothers, and, to some extent, me."

"But," he said, looking at the scars on his hands, "what woman would love me?"

"That, my son, is for Anya to decide."

They both fell to their knees in the sand at the edge of the ravine. Pressing their fists to their eyes, they prayed similar prayers. Timaeus prayed that somewhere, sometime, a woman would touch him with love like his mother had in his dream; Venzel prayed that his wife, the beautiful woman who loved him, would never leave him.

When they stood up, Timaeus said, "You were going to tell me about a promise. Was it to Mother?"

"Yes. Before she died, she asked me to love you enough for both of us."

He gripped Timaeus's shoulder and looked into his eyes. "Did I do that, my son?" he asked, unshed tears strangling his words. "Did I love you enough for both of us?"

Timaeus glanced at his perfectly straight fingers, thought of the wonder that was Alatan, and felt the dagger at his waist. He knew how easy it would have been for Venzel to have left him as he was, deformed and stumbling in the twisted darkness of his mother's mind until he died, bloodied and broken, beside Taliph. He covered Venzel's hand with his own.

"Yes, Father. A thousand times, yes."

A Man on Fire

Timaeus left the compound shortly after their return from the oasis. Successfully completing the entrance exams, he was one of the youngest students ever admitted to Cairo University. Excelling in his studies and moving into medicine with a specialization in genetics, he also took courses in classical design, architecture, and psychology. He soaked up everything, creating associations between the obscure and the relevant to make the coursework more challenging. Finishing the six-year program in less than five years, he looked forward to spending the summer months at home before receiving his first assignment.

Unsure where his assignment would take him, he spent his final week in Cairo making one last round of the museums and bazaars. Searching for a book on astronomy at the booksellers' marketplace one evening, a stranger approached him.

"Take this, Timaeus," he said in Lyostian. "You are going to need it."

The man shoved a small flat box at Timaeus and walked away.

"Wait."

Timaeus tilted his head, but the man did not look back or respond verbally or telepathically. Unwilling to open the box in a crowded bazaar, he placed it in his courier bag.

It wasn't the first time one of his brothers had approached him. There were many at the university. Due to their physical appearance being too strikingly similar to walk together in groups, the Lyostians had secret entries into all the university buildings and traveled beneath the campus on their own, less crowded walkways.

Wearing heavily tinted glasses with specialized curved lenses that focused their eyes into one pair, he and the other Lyostian students were able to attend classes without too much difficulty. Always taking the closest seats near the doors in the classrooms, the Lyostians were the last students to enter and the first students to leave. They rarely answered questions and were often mistaken for one another. Using such similarity to their advantage, often two or three would take the same class, substituting on alternative days so there would appear to be fewer of them—and there were as few as possible above ground on any given day. According to Cairo University's records, there were only six Lyostian students registered for classes, but there were nearly a hundred underground listening to every word spoken and completing every assignment. It wasn't ideal, but the collective was aware they needed the most current advances in medicine and technology, and the only way to stay ahead of humans was to learn what they knew.

Protected, disguised, and one of the few students who was as exacting in the course requirements as the strictest professor, Timaeus spent most of his day in class or meeting with his brothers in the tunnels after classes to share the course lecture—but that was the only time he spent in the tunnels. The rooms all looked the same, and since he knew what most of his brothers were going to say or think before they did, he found repeating a lecture less tedious than conversing with them. As much as he detested their proliferation and waste, he found humans more interesting than his brothers, and horses far more interesting than humans.

Keeping up with his classwork and assisting his brothers left him with little leisure time for recreational pursuits or riding. Because it took a long time to build a rapport with a horse, and every horse he saw made him miss Alatan more, he did not ride. He did, however, occasionally attend the stakes races in the late evenings. It felt like home to walk around the stable yard, smell the hay, and listen to the sounds and stamps of the horses tethered in their stalls. Sometimes, he talked to the grooms, especially if he saw something in a horse that reminded him of Alatan, but since most of the grooms worked for the racetrack and not the owners, they were usually unaware of a horse's ancestry. Still, Venzel's stables and Alazar's fame had reached legendary status, and Timaeus knew he could enjoy a level of celebrity if he told anyone who he was, but part of the mystery surrounding Alazar was that no one knew exactly where Venzel's stables were located, and he instinctively kept that information to himself. This discretion, however, did not prevent him from using his expertise to wager on the horses.

Never betting much and careful to lose as often as he won, Timaeus rarely left the track without doubling or tripling his money. He was too busy to attend the races regularly, but sometimes he wanted something he could not afford—or didn't want anyone to know he wanted—and he went to the track to make his own money. The drawing table, the small Egyptian falcon carved from obsidian with wings tipped in gold, a vintage Persian shawl for Senkali, and once, about two years earlier, he sent his father a horse.

The owner of a beautiful ebony Arabian filly had announced she was for sale after losing a race against slightly older and more experienced horses. When Timaeus went back to see her, one whiff told him why she lost. Disregarding his own rule, he bet everything he had on the last race and won the largest payout of the day. Acting surprised and declaring himself the luckiest man alive, he cashed in at the window and bought the horse he named Ayca in honor of the evening's new moon and arranged for her transportation to the village stables.

Later that day, he sent a message to his father that he was sending Alatan a gift. A week later, he received a letter from his father saying she was a beauty, and Alatan was grateful. Timaeus laughed for several minutes and went back to his studies but could not resist drawing Alatan and Ayca racing across the desert with black and dappled grey foals in their wake.

The pencil snapped in his hand.

He was dreaming. The collective would never allow him to spend his life at the compound. Geneticists needed the kind of laboratories found at universities and hospitals. The best he could hope for was that if he did his work as assigned—and did it well—the collective might allow him to visit the compound every couple of years.

Jostled by the movement of the crowd, Timaeus became conscious of the press of humans around him and quickly fastened the flap of the courier bag. Determining it would be best to appear uninterested and continue his search, he delayed returning to his room to investigate the mysterious box until he purchased the book he wanted.

For the benefit of the university's records, Timaeus occupied a single room in student housing. However, he actually ate and slept in the tunnels below with his brothers, who were also required to rent aboveground rooms they never used. Unlike his brothers, however, Timaeus often sought the privacy of his room to study, draw, or write to his father. He kept a pencil drawing of Venzel sitting on Alatan pinned to the wall and glanced at it often when he wrote his letters, which always included small sketches of desert landscapes, horses, architectural designs, or small portraits of colony members.

The encounter at the marketplace changed his agenda for the evening. He did not go to the room to sketch or write a letter but to examine the contents of the box.

It was something he needed.

Timaeus removed the box from the courier bag and opened the single latch. Cast in black aluminum with an ivory handle, the Colt semi-automatic pistol nestled in black silk. Removing the magazine, he racked the slide and caught the ejected chamber shell. He sighted down the barrel and noticed the lightly etched threads at the end of it. Opening a small compartment inside the box that he assumed held more shells, he found a silencer.

Timaeus wasn't surprised. Like most of the Lyostians and all of the Tuzurias in the Mediterranean colonies from Morocco to Turkey, he was an expert in munitions as well as combat techniques, including hand-to-hand, fencing, archery, and knife throwing. As part of their daily training—except for their volatile developmental phase—the Tuzurias learned to disassemble, reassemble, and fire every type of weapon, from Glocks to Kalashnikovs to missile launchers. As future colony defenders, they had to be prepared for human governments that turned to violence as their first rather than last defense, or when local aggression spilled over onto their territories.

Timaeus smiled and reloaded the gun. The pistol was light and compact. He could carry it in a shoulder holster or a reinforced pocket. It was also versatile. He knew the compound armory had 9mm shells that could stop a buffalo at full speed. Appreciating the gun's balance, he liked the feel of it in his hand and decided it was a very nice weapon.

But why, he thought, *do I need a gun now? Do they expect me to be attacked on the way home? Is there a threat at the compound*? He immediately thought of Venzel's safety but knew his father always carried a knife, kept a rifle in the stables, and had access to the underground armory.

Returning the pistol to the box, he saw a small dark red image etched into the ivory handle.

It was a man on fire.

Recognizing the fire slayer insignia of the Tuzurias, Timaeus stared at the weapon in his hands and sat down slowly. This wasn't just any weapon. It was *his* weapon.

The Call

Arriving at the train station and expecting Venzel, Timaeus was surprised to see a man wearing a pilot's uniform holding a sign with his name written on it. Curious, he tilted his head, and when the man responded, Timaeus followed him to a helipad. Stowing his two suitcases and portfolio behind his seat, Timaeus climbed in and held on.

Flying into the night, Timaeus tried to ask where they were going, but the pilot tapped the headphones with his finger and shook his head. Timaeus bent forward and looked up at the stars. It only took a moment before he settled back into his seat. He knew where they were heading. Nearly two hours later, the helicopter began losing altitude, and Timaeus looked down. The lake and lagoon were beautiful from the sky. Shadowed beneath the palms, he saw the banners of the blue and white tent. Two horses were tethered next to it, one grey and one black. So eager to see his father, Timaeus could hardly wait for the helicopter to touch down before jumping out.

Grabbing his luggage, he waved to the pilot.

Wait, Timaeus.

Yes?

I will meet you back here in a week.

A week?

That is what I was told to tell you. There will be further instructions at your colony.

Thank you, my brother.

We are one.

We are one.

Venzel caught up to him, and they watched the helicopter disappear in the darkness.

"Well, what did you think of that?" Venzel asked, smiling, and pointing to the helicopter.

"It was great! What a surprise. Did you do that?"

"Well, um, sometimes they use helicopters to transport me when I visit the other colonies, so I asked Lorand if one couldn't bring you here from the train station. Look at all the time we've saved." Venzel's smile dimmed slightly. "Lorand told me you couldn't stay long, and I wanted to make the most of every minute."

Though disappointed at the short visit, Timaeus was grateful his father already knew.

"Do you like Lorand? Though I'm sure everyone misses Nesim."

"Yes, everyone misses Nesim, and although I don't think he ever forgave me for being human, I think he grew to trust me, which is hard, I know. Lorand is a lot like Rauf. He accepts that I am useful to the colony and does not seem to care whether I am human or not—except when there is something to be done outside the compound. Since all my helpers have moved on to other things," he said, grinning at Timaeus, "I spend most of my days training the horses with some stable hands from the village two or three days a week."

"How is everybody? We've talked about many things in our letters, but you haven't mentioned Senkali or Ezri in months."

"Well, that's because they are fine, just two years older than the last time you were home. Since her boys have left, Senkali allowed me to move her up to the same level as my room. It makes it easier on Ezri. It was a challenge, though. We had to set up her new room exactly like the old one so she wouldn't trip over anything."

"It makes it easier on you, too," Timaeus said softly.

Venzel looked at him steadily. "No, Timaeus, it has never been that way. She is my sister—no more—and certainly no less. She has been a blessing to us."

"Yes."

Venzel picked up one of Timaeus's suitcases as they walked toward the tent.

"And Ezri, well, I swear sometimes he thinks I work for him. He has become quite obstinate in his old age."

Speaking of age, Timaeus couldn't help but notice that Venzel was breathing hard while carrying the lighter of his two suitcases.

"When do we leave for the compound?"

"Tomorrow night. It was the only way Lorand would help me arrange this—but I am happy, my son, to be allowed to spend some time with you alone, here."

"As am I, Father."

Timaeus knew the curse of being a new doctor was an acute awareness of everyone's health, but he could not attribute the changes he saw in his father to just being a little older. Desert living was hard, and nearing forty-five, Venzel *was* approaching middle age, but years alone didn't account for the blueness under his eyes, his shortness of breath, or the way he barely paused to set the luggage down before sitting on the divan.

Timaeus got him some water and surreptitiously tried to examine him.

"How are you feeling, Father?"

"Now, don't you start. You've only been a doctor for a few weeks and are already beginning to sound like Ezri. I am fine. I'm just not thirty or, well, forty anymore. Besides, it was hard work setting up this tent."

Timaeus looked at him aghast. "*You* set up the tent?"

"No, but supervising is hard work." Venzel began laughing, and Timaeus joined him. Remembering how his father supervised, he doubted the workers did much more than unload the truck and hold the tent stakes.

"Where are they?"

"I sent them back in the jeep. They will come get the tent and your bags after sundown tomorrow, and everything will be at the compound before we get there."

Timaeus reached over and covered his father's hand with his.

"Good plan," he said.

Sitting at his father's feet, he looked up at him.

"What shall we do first?"

Venzel walked to the side of the tent where Timaeus left his luggage and picked up the portfolio. Sitting cross-legged on the carpet next to his son, he placed it between them.

"I would like to see your drawings."

As Timaeus narrated, Venzel turned page after page of cityscapes and desert landscapes filled with imaginative glass buildings that were structurally brilliant but impractical. After a few more pages of complex architectural sketches, there was a watercolor of the oasis and the blue and white tent. Venzel saw himself standing under the awning and the horses, Alatan and Fahar, drinking from the lagoon. Following these drawings were sketches of the compound, Taran, Toros, and the other boys. A sob caught in Venzel's throat when he saw a portrait of Zsiga so lifelike he expected it to speak to him.

Venzel thought he had seen them all when he noticed the top edge of a piece of paper protruding slightly above the back pocket of the portfolio.

"Father," Timaeus reached for it.

Venzel waved his hand away and removed the small drawing. It was Destani. However, it was not a picture of his mother that Timaeus drew, but a scene that had never existed anywhere except in Venzel's dreams. Destani looked at him as she had on their wedding night, her eyes shining with love. In her arms was Timaeus, but it was not a Lyostian infant she held so tenderly, but a human son. As he stared at the sketch, Venzel's hand began to shake, and it was with some difficulty that he returned the paper to the pocket of the portfolio.

He was silent for a few moments. "Some things are not meant to be, Son, but that doesn't mean that we cannot embrace the reality with joy."

He gently closed the portfolio, lingering another moment to gaze at the portrait of Zsiga. "Your mother would have loved these, Timaeus, *your* mother."

Venzel was tired. Although he was sure Timaeus did not intend to—and had tried to stop him—Destani's smile only brought back how much his carelessness had cost him. He rubbed his hand across his chest.

"It's been a long day for me. There's plenty of food and water in the coolers." He motioned to the right side of the tent. "I think I am going to rest for a while. It's quite wonderful, you know, to see you."

"Thank you, Father. It is quite wonderful to see you."

Venzel smiled and nodded. Spreading a coverlet over the flattened cushions, he laid down with his face toward the side of the tent.

Timaeus had forgotten the sketch was in the portfolio. He thought he had placed the drawings of his mother in the envelope at the bottom of his suitcase. He didn't know how to explain to Venzel that these sketches not only represented his father's loss, but his as well.

Stretching out on the cushions next to his father, he pulled the hood of his cloak over his face and slept.

"Timaeus."

His mother stood in a shaft of light calling him. Oblivious to everything else, he ran toward her. Suddenly, she put out her hand.

"Stop."

Looking down, Timaeus saw a chasm of darkness he could not cross.

Unable to leave her circle of light, she reached out to help him, but she was too far away. Her light began to fade until he stood alone in the infinite darkness of space.

"Please, don't go," he whispered.

The first thing Timaeus saw when he opened his eyes was his father's face.

"You dreamed of your mother again?"

"Yes."

"Tell me."

Realizing he sounded harsh, he added, "Please. She... she hasn't visited me in a long time. I am always afraid she'll never return. So, if she comes to you, then perhaps she is still here... somewhere."

He paused and rephrased his request. "Can you tell me?"

Timaeus tried to gather his thoughts. "Yes, but it wasn't a dream, Father. It was more like a nightmare. Mother was standing in a pool of light, and I was running to her, but she held up her hand like this." Timaeus lifted his hand in the halt signal they used with the horses. "When I did, I realized that if she had not stopped me, I would have fallen into—Wait! It was the ravine. She stopped me from falling into the ravine, and then she put her hand out to help me, but the ravine was between us, and I could not reach her. When the light disappeared, she was gone, and I... I was alone."

"In the dark?"

"Yes, but it was more like the darkness of space than total blackness."

Venzel thought for a moment. "Like being in the middle of space, surrounded by the night sky from every direction?"

"Yes. How did you know?"

"It's the way Zsiga described the Sidereal Chamber."

As though reading from a book, Timaeus tilted his head and recited, "The Sidereal Chamber is a four-dimensional section of space and time used by the governing hierarchy of the collective to communicate with the leaders of individual colonies."

"Is that how it is described in the archives?"

"Yes, why? Did Zsiga describe it differently?"

"Yes and no. He told me what it looked like, but he never used the word 'communicate.' He said it was like having his soul dissected and reassembled."

"But I'm not a colony leader. Why would Mother warn me?"

Venzel traced the pattern in the carpet with his finger. After a moment, he looked up.

"Are you in some kind of danger, Son?"

Timaeus remembered the pistol hidden in the lining of the larger suitcase. He hadn't decided if he should show it to Venzel, but his father's question made him think that if he was in danger, then showing the gun to Venzel might make him a part of it. Deciding to be discreet, he answered honestly, "Not that I know of, Father."

Venzel smiled in relief. "Well, then, keep your eyes open. All of them."

Timaeus smiled back. "I will." Then his face became serious. "What are your plans when I leave, Father? Are you going to continue raising horses at the compound?"

Venzel's face became troubled. He didn't want to lie to Timaeus and thought it was too soon to tell him of his plans, but they only had a short time.

"I am considering retirement."

Without thinking, Timaeus blurted out, "Are they going to let you do that?"

"Lorand seems to think it will be allowed. I am not going far; I've found a small house near the village stables. If you won't need them, I'll just take Alatan, Ayca, and Fahar, and train one or two colts a year—equestrian only, no more racing. I think the compound needs a younger, stronger man to run it."

"Senkali?"

"I have requested that she be allowed to leave as well. Ezri will look after us. It is my hope the collective sees this as an opportunity to broaden their base here." Venzel smiled and teased his son. "Maybe adding a laboratory or two. Wouldn't that be wonderful?"

"Yes, but I am sure they intend to send me to another university or teaching hospital. I don't think they will change their plans for me."

They did once before, Venzel thought.

"Well, perhaps we will come to you. It has been too long since I have traveled farther than where we are now. We will see where you are assigned and make whatever arrangements we can to visit you."

Timaeus nodded. Any plan that would ease the burden his father had carried for thirty years sounded good to him. "Father, may I have one thing before I leave?"

"Anything, my son."

"May I have one of Mother's scarves to take with me?"

Venzel smiled softly. He had not opened that trunk since their first visit to the oasis and never intended to open it again. "Yes, but you will have to ask Ezri to get it for you. He has the key. I… I don't open that trunk anymore."

He looked at the closed portfolio. "Ask him for the ivory one with the gold trim and crystals."

He saw the question in Timaeus's eyes.

"It is the one she wore when she saved our lives."

"Thank you, Father, I will treasure it."

"I know, Son."

They rode to the compound in companionable silence broken only by a sentence or two, or a question asked and answered. Although neither of them planned it, they made the wide arc and stopped at the ravine. Venzel did not attempt to climb down to the boulder, and Timaeus, respecting his father's limitations, knelt on the cliff beside him and prayed.

Waiting since the first streak of light in the east, Ezri met Venzel and Timaeus on the porch. When they had stabled the horses, Lorand and the other brothers in residence joined them for breakfast to welcome Timaeus home. Venzel nodded to the newer members of the colony. He had grown unsure of his place within the colony structure now that the last of the

Tuzurias generation had received their assignments. Lorand had found ways to keep him busy, but Zsiga's warning had been coming back to him more often. Now that Timaeus was leaving, Venzel felt there was no reason to stay. As he promised Zsiga, he'd saved part of the money he earned from selling the horses and was in final negotiations for the village stables and a comfortable house. He would have everything settled in the next couple of weeks.

Venzel knew Timaeus needed to talk with Lorand alone, so he pretended to yawn and said he would see them later. Walking to his room, he realized that although it had originally been a pretense, he really was tired. Knocking softly on Senkali's door, he let her know they were back and promised Timaeus would see her as soon as he could. He walked into his room, counted to ten, and then heard Ezri's knock on the door.

"Yes, Ezri?"

"How are you, Master?"

"I am tired, Ezri. How are you?"

"Well, thank you, Master." He paused for a moment and said, "And the boy, how is he?"

"Ah, Ezri, you were not paying attention. That is no boy downstairs. That is a young man about my age when we first met. Did you think I was a boy at his age?"

"No, Master." Ezri's eyes glanced at the floor.

"What is it?"

"He is not you, Master."

"No, but his mother told me he was powerful, and I see it in him. Let us hope he uses it wisely."

"I will pray for that, Master."

"As will I, Ezri. Oh, and speaking of his mother, he wishes a scarf to take with him on his journey. The ivory one with the gold trim and crystals. Will you get it when I'm not here and give it to him?"

"Yes. Um, Master…?"

"Yes, Ezri, you may take one for yourself, but never let me see it or smell it. There is only so much I can bear."

No longer able to scramble up and down on his knees, Ezri bowed low from his waist. "Thank you, Master. The honor is undeserved, but I thank you."

Venzel's eyes were beginning to close. "You loved her, Ezri. I saw it in your face, even during her worst days. It is not undeserved."

"Thank you, Master," he said, gently closing the door.

Leave Venzel.

Destani?

Leave now. He won't be able to stop them—and you won't be able to stop him.

I will, my love, in a few weeks when I can take Senkali and Ezri. I can't go without them.

Yes, you can. It won't make any difference. You must leave now.

I will, soon.

After no reply for several minutes, he heard her whisper, "*As you wish,*" and felt the brush of her lips on his.

Venzel awoke with joy, knowing that she was still with him, still cared about him, and, touching his fingers to his lips, still loved him. Then he remembered her message. They needed to leave. Now. He went to the new telephone in the main house and made appointments for the next day to settle the village house and stables. They would only stay as long as Timaeus and leave as soon as he received his assignment.

Taking Timaeus aside after Venzel went to his room, Lorand said, "The collective would like to speak with you."

"Speak with me? Directly?"

"Yes."

"Did they do that when they gave my brothers their assignments?"

"No. They went through me."

"Now, or may I rest first?"

Lorand tilted his head for a moment. "The collective requests your presence in the Sidereal Chamber without delay, Timaeus."

Confused and slightly shaken, Timaeus had no idea where the Sidereal Chamber was located.

"Where is it?"

In that moment, Lorand believed everything he'd heard about Timaeus: that he existed in a half-world between the tunnels and the stables and was allowed to call a human "Father." Such an indulgence would have never been permitted under his leadership. He didn't care how brilliant Timaeus's reports had been; his lack of the basic understanding of colony operations was disgraceful.

Almost sneering at Timaeus's ignorance, Lorand answered, "Level five, corridor five, room…?"

"Five?" Timaeus responded.

Lorand nodded.

Timaeus turned toward the nearest staircase. He paused for a moment and looked back at Lorand.

"Is there a sixth room on the sixth corridor in the sixth tunnel?

Lorand paled.

"Not," he choked out, "not here. That's the center of the collective. Not even the elders know exactly which colony has that, um, honor."

"You mean no one knows the location of the heart of the collective?"

Regaining his dignity, Lorand said, "I think, Timaeus, you will find very little heart in that room."

Intending to follow him surreptitiously, Lorand waited a few minutes so Timaeus would not hear his footsteps. The Sidereal Chamber was not a place for ambivalence, and the first visit was always the most unpleasant. As colony leader, he felt it was important to be available if Timaeus had any other questions when he came out.

If he came out.

Timaeus was immediately intrigued as he entered the collective's telepathic communication chamber. The table and chair in the room seemed solid, but the walls kept changing. One moment, he was standing within a cube of solid sandstone, and the next, a sphere-shaped microcosm of the universe with pinpoints of light surrounding him. Timaeus didn't know if he was walking on a solid surface or if he, and the table and chair, were suspended in an endless glass globe. The information in the archives did not begin to describe the wonder around him. He wasn't sure in which dimension the room existed, but he was relatively certain he was no longer forty feet beneath the desert floor.

When he moved into the center of the room, the walls dissolved completely. The familiarity of the starscape unsettled him, and once again, he was living the nightmare of standing alone in the darkness of an infinite number of flickering stars. The fear of abandonment chilled him, and he remembered the concern in Venzel's voice, "Are you in some kind of danger, son?"

Was he? He felt the dagger at his side, but the only person he could use it on was himself.

Unsure of the protocol, he pressed his fists to his eyes.

"I am here."

A voice seemed to emanate from the stars.

Timaeus.

Yes.

You may sit down.

Thank you. Where am I?

You are with us.

Where are you?

In you, around you, part of you, as you are part of the collective. By way of a more formal introduction, we would like to begin with a question.

Yes.

Who is "they," Timaeus? In his mind, Timaeus heard the words he'd said to his father the night before, "are *they* going to let you do that?"

Timaeus was silent.

There is no "they," Timaeus. We are one.

Yes, he responded, *we are one.*

Images of Senkali, Ezri, and Venzel flashed through his mind. *And these are....*

Humans.

Yes.

But my father....

You are a Lyostian drone, Timaeus. You have no father.

Venzel is Zsiga's brother, and he is our brother; we are one.

Not all brothers are... equal... are you unaware of this?

No. I understand why we established hierarchies.

Perhaps. Did you receive your weapon?

Yes.

Do you know how to use it?

You know I do.

Yes, Timaeus Tuzurias, we know you do.

The echo of his name within the collective and throughout the colonies on five continents resonated back to him with a million voices. At first, the sound filled him with a sense of belonging and pride, but the increasing volume became overwhelming. He fell out of the chair onto his knees and put his hands over his ears, but the sound was not outside his head but within. Just when he thought he would go mad if he could not escape, the voices disappeared as though someone had thrown a switch. In the sudden silence, the only sound he could hear was the blood pulsing through his heart, but there was no safety in the muffled echo of a single heartbeat. When his tentative attempts to reach into the collective memory failed, he tried to calm himself. He knew that he should be able to survive one day, maybe two, without direct contact, but he didn't see how that was possible. Everything he was sure of had vanished, and without a connection to the collective, he didn't even know who he was.

Please, don't....

...go? A single voice answered him.

Yes.

With that word, the fragile shell of humanity Timaeus had worn since he was four years old began to crack and split. In a demonstration of loyalty, he struck his chest with his fist. *We are one.*

Are we?

Yes. Please.

Are we "they," Timaeus?

There is no "they." We are one.

Yes. Now that you know who we are, we have questions regarding the disposition of your home colony. We hope you will help us with the answers.

Yes?

The human guests of your colony have requested permission to relocate away from us. Is it in our best interest to grant their request? Knowing what we do about human unpredictability, can we trust them not to expose us?

Yes. Venzel would never put us in danger. He has killed to protect our brothers and this colony. He would not betray us. Senkali is our mother, and she is blind; she could not hurt us. Ezri's loyalty to Venzel is unquestionable. We can trust them.

Timaeus, do you value these humans over your brothers' lives?

No, but Venzel would never betray us. He has spent a lifetime keeping our colony safe.

Perhaps, but he wants to leave us. Are you certain that in his disillusionment or loneliness at the chaos inherent in a human existence, he would not want to return to the colony—something that we could never, would never allow?

The thought of Venzel not being able to return to the colony rocked Timaeus to his Lyostian core. Like Zsiga, Timaeus's biggest fear for Venzel, for himself, or any brother, was that of being alone.

Timaeus, the voice said softly, *can we take the risk that he will not try to return?*

Timaeus hesitated. Venzel might try. The colony had been his home for almost forty years. Timaeus did not want to answer the question, but he knew the collective was in his mind; he could not lie.

No, he said.

Now that they have expressed a desire to leave us, can we make them stay? Can we take the risk that in their assured attempts to escape, they will not injure our brothers?

There was no one on the compound Venzel trusted more than his son, and Timaeus knew that even he could not make Venzel remain at the colony if he was treated as a prisoner. He also knew Venzel would not leave Senkali and Ezri behind. The three of them would have to fight their way out. Brothers could die.

No... no.

If we cannot allow the humans to leave, and we cannot make them stay, what must we do to protect ourselves, Timaeus?

The collective's line of questioning had left him with only one alternative. He could not say it. He could not even form the words in his mind.

In his anguish, a new voice, almost feminine, spoke to him. *Are you more important than your brothers, Timaeus?*

No.

Your brothers yet unborn—is your life more important than their future existence?

No.

The life and structure of our species—are you more important than any one of the many brothers upon whom it depends?

No.

Once again, the silence of deep space surrounded him, but this time, it was different; he wasn't alone. He could feel their presence. Millions of invisible hands were holding him up, keeping him from falling through the endless void. Their bodies pressed against his and when he raised his hand, he could feel the warmth of those above him. He was not merely another brick in a wall but part of a living, breathing brotherhood with one purpose: to protect their mother—the planet the humans called Earth—for all their future generations.

Timaeus did not know how long he was immersed in the collective consciousness, but when the feeling of solidarity passed, it shook loose the remaining shreds of humanity so gently that he barely felt them falling away.

Without warning, the stars in the great sphere of the universe melted together into a mirror that reflected his image a thousand times in a hundred fractured directions. Timaeus did not see the reflection of his face or his body, but only the camouflage he wore for the human world. Removing his clothes, he placed them on the table with his mother's dagger hidden within their folds. Returning to the center of the room, he crossed his wrists above his head in a position of submission. One after another, the angle of the mirrors shifted. Instead of Timaeus's body being visually echoed into infinity, the mirrors displayed rows of the generations before him. Each preceding generation was incrementally different; shorter, paler, their muscular torsos and necks long and slender, their faces thin, then becoming less defined, broader, and heavily boned, before narrowing and becoming increasingly delicate until a pair of silvery creatures remained. Their bodies, willowy and graceful, were nearly translucent. Antennae curved upward from the sides of their heads, and their hands and feet were without fingers or toes and curved under like soft hooks. Their angular faces were featureless except for a mouth and one pair of large eyes on which several irises floated independently. Although he saw their beauty, he was also aware of their vulnerability and marveled at the tenaciousness of his ancestors, who began with so little yet managed to survive and evolve.

His ancestors.

Timaeus continued to stare at the line of Lyostian evolution until the mirrors shifted, closed, and merged into one polished surface. Looking into the mirror with new eyes, he no longer saw his body's symmetry, strength, and perfection but a genetically created bioluminescent lifeform carefully crafted into a life-sustaining disguise. In grateful acquiescence to all that had been sacrificed before him, Timaeus knelt before the mirror. Crossing his arms over his chest, he bowed until his forehead was level with his knees. He began singing Anya's prayer of thanksgiving, and a thousand voices sang with him, rising and falling together as though from a single breath.

When the prayer was over and the choir of voices in his mind faded away, he stood and returned to the chair.

I am here, he said.

Yes. We have one final question before we give you our first assignment. Now that you know who you are, what must you do to the humans whose existence threatens the continuance of our society?

I must kill them.

All of them?

Timaeus looked down at his hands. *Yes.*

Because?

Our continued survival is paramount. They are human; by choosing to leave the colony, they have proven they cannot be trusted and are, therefore, a threat. No one is allowed to endanger the colony. Human threat neutralization is possible only through extermination.

Some brothers may object to our decision regarding the humans or discontinuing support of this outpost. What must we do to protect ourselves from dissenting brothers?

I must persuade them.

If you cannot persuade them, what must you do?

Timaeus hesitated. *Am I to kill them, too?*

Yes.

But we need every brother.

We will all die here unless we leave our underground colonies and confront the humans who are destroying our only planet. We cannot go forward into that future if we do not go as one. How do we prevent disobedient brothers from disrupting our plans, Timaeus?

I must kill them.

All of them?

Yes.

Because?

Our survival depends on moving forward together. Those who impede our progress or react with aggression when confronted with the collective's decision must be eliminated.

Yes.

This is my assignment?

Part of it.

When?

Tomorrow.

The helicopter pilot said next week.

Plans change.

You do not trust me.

You have not given us reason to trust you. Yet.

It was only then that Timaeus realized this interview was a test. If he failed, the collective would keep him suspended in the silent hell of endless space until he begged for death. Head bowed, he listened as the collective explained the magnitude of his assignment. He would not continue his research or use his medical degree, but under an alias and alone, he was assigned to infiltrate and destroy specific Mediterranean colonies without negotiation, mercy, or reprieve, including any brother who had thoughts of insurrection or disobedience—beginning with his home colony.

In revulsion and desperation, he gripped the edges of the table to keep from ripping his mother's dagger from its silken sheath and shoving it into his throat.

Finding the strength to save his life but not the courage to defy the collective, Timaeus abandoned any hope he had of protecting the people he loved.

Do you have any questions?

No. You have been quite clear.

Who are "they," Timaeus? The voice asked again.

Our enemies, both human and Lyostian, who threaten the progress of the collective.

Who are you?

I am Timaeus, fire slayer of the Tuzurias hierarchy. My existence is at the will and in the service of the Lyostian collective.

Yes. You may go. May Anya, blessed mother of us all, keep you well.

We are one.

Yes, Timaeus. We… are one.

The starscape rippled and once again became a cube carved from solid sandstone. The collective was letting him live. In gratitude, he pressed his fists against his eyes and promised to exceed the collective's expectations or die trying. His path chosen for him, Timaeus stood, picked up his clothes, and walked slowly to the door. As his fingers touched the handle, he took a deep breath before returning to the fifth corridor on the fifth level and did not look back.

Timaeus did not know how much his time in the Sidereal Chamber had changed him. Waiting in the corridor, Lorand heard the door open and stepped forward, but when he saw Timaeus naked and his face drawn back into a skeletal mask of pain, he withdrew into the shadows before those burning eyes fell on him.

As Ezri fondly observed, Timaeus may have still been a boy when he arrived home that morning, but little remained of the child he loved in the assassin who emerged from the chrysalis of the Sidereal Chamber as the collective's most formidable weapon.

Hearing his voluntary acquiescence and total submission to their demands, the governing hierarchy breathed a simultaneous sigh of relief. Had he shown even the slightest sign of rebellion, they would have killed him, but they did not want him dead. The governing hierarchy believed their indoctrination had successfully destroyed Timaeus's independent rationality and any compassion he'd developed for his targets, but they could not be sure. No one, not even the highest-ranking Lyostians, could monitor all of Timaeus's thoughts. They wanted to inquire how he had developed such a unique ability, but it was imperative to their social structure that Timaeus remain unaware he possessed such control.

It was because of that ability that they did not know the same question was tearing at Timaeus's heart. Seeking the privacy of the dusty hallway outside his mother's room, he sat with his back against the door.

Why? Why was he different? And why, dear sweet Anya, was he being punished so cruelly for something he did not understand?

Even Anya could not tell him that from the moment he instinctively constructed mental barriers to protect his mind from his mother's insanity to twelve years later when, in desperation, he strengthened them to conceal the emotional instability arising from the effects of his Tuzurias adolescence, that he—Timaeus of the last Tuzurias hierarchy—had self-evolved into the most dangerous Lyostian ever created.

Who by Fire

Unable to sleep that night, Timaeus rested on his cot in the nearly empty dormitory and telepathically searched the archives. It was as he expected. Never in their recorded history had the collective assigned any Lyostian the task of killing his brothers, unprovoked and defenseless, alone.

Reliving his interview in the Sidereal Chamber several times, he understood his place within the collective. They wanted a spy, but his mission was more devious than mere espionage. Unable to read his thoughts, his brothers would not be able to detect his intentions for visiting their colony, the collective's plans for its destruction, or identify their destroyer. More a designation than an assignment, protecting the security of the collective was a position he could not refuse. He would be the governing hierarchy's eyes, ears, and executioner, or he would die.

But kill Venzel?

He could not, but he knew if the collective wanted Venzel, Senkali, and Ezri dead, then they would die whether or not he killed them. The collective would just send someone else to kill them all. Regardless of the path he chose, there was no escape for any of them.

Remembering Venzel's admonition of the importance of thinking things through, Timaeus knew he would never be able to convince his father to leave; he would want to know why. Following their conversation to its most logical conclusion, he saw in his mind the depth of his father's outrage and knew, absolutely, that Venzel would fight every Lyostian on the compound to protect *his son* from a life of blood and death.

Timaeus sat up quickly.

That was the reason the collective wanted Venzel dead. He was the only colony member who was *not* defenseless.

They were afraid of him.

Timaeus's reasoning against killing Venzel was sound, but if Venzel was allowed to leave peacefully, he knew that once he learned of the colony's destruction, nothing would stop him from returning with an army and tearing the compound apart—above and below ground—looking for his son and the brothers he loved.

Timaeus stared at the walls in disbelief. The Lyostian governing hierarchy had deliberately trapped, manipulated, and lied to him. Being human was just an excuse; the collective condemned Venzel to death because he would fight to protect the people and home he loved—the very characteristic they had always found so valuable.

Quietly leaving the dormitory, Timaeus walked into the night. Entering the paddock area, he lifted the bar and eased into the stables. Alatan immediately came to the front of his stall. Laying his head against the horse's neck, Timaeus thanked him for being so wonderful. Hearing his voice, all the horses stamped and whickered for attention, and he went from one to the other, saving Ayca for last. His hands pale against her darkness, he stroked her neck and whispered how beautiful she was. He moved to the center of the paddock and took it all in the horses, the smells, the sounds, the feelings of acceptance, respect, and, unexpectedly, love that surrounded him.

Yes, as my father's son, I could have happily spent the rest of my life here.

Twice betrayed, Timaeus felt the same sense of loss that had haunted Venzel for eighteen years. Touching his forehead between Alatan's eyes in farewell, he quietly closed the double doors and walked around the main house to the southeast corner of the garden.

The white woven nightshirt was neatly folded on the grass, and a dagger's sheath lay next to it, empty. Casting these remnants of a simpler life into darkness, the shadow of a young man knelt at the foot of his mother's grave. With eyes closed and his arms crossed over his bare chest, he whispered Anya's prayer of forgiveness. Locking his fingers together behind his head, he took a deep breath and opened his eyes.

A shimmering image was kneeling beside him.

Mother!

Stop, Timaeus, she said, pointing to the half-buried dagger in front of him. The exposed blade gleamed in the silver light of the crescent moon.

I will not kill him, Mother.

It is who you are.

He looked at his hands. *It is not all I am.*

Destani did not move her eyes from the dagger. *He would rather die than you.*

How can I be sure of that?

Let him choose.

Mother... I—

Let him choose, Timaeus.

Mother, I love—

I know.

Destani turned toward her son and touched his cheek.

Looking into his mother's lovely face, he only knew one way to protect her from the sorrow to come. Staring beyond her eyes into her soul, Timaeus captured all that remained of his mother and hid her away in the dark caverns of his heart.

Placing his hand on his chest, he whispered, "Only until it is over, Mother," he promised, "only until it is over."

His mother was safe, but the dagger's blade still beckoned.

He thought briefly of joining her and freeing both of their spirits. Then he remembered Venzel.

Not tonight, he thought, shaking the sand from the dagger's hilt and sliding it into the sheath. He pulled on his nightshirt and returned to the tunnels. Attaching his sketchbook to Zsiga's old wooden clipboard, he walked through the maze of sleeping brothers to the conference room.

There were plans to make.

The final day of operation at Outpost SCM, Sector 1/51, dawned early. Checking the projected sequence of events, Timaeus searched until he found Ezri in the hall outside Venzel's room.

"Ezri, Venzel has relented and will allow me to plant flowers on Mother's grave. Please have one of the workmen dig a space about two feet wide and two feet deep, including that sandy spot at the bottom."

"But, young master, that is almost too deep."

"Almost. However, it is necessary to mix topsoil with the sand for the small plants and seeds to take root. Please have it done this morning. I will be leaving soon."

"Yes, young master, the, um, marker?"

Each time the desert wind or heat from the sun deteriorated the intricate lacing of the loving memorials he created for his mother, Timaeus designed something a little more elaborate. The most recent was a delicate trellis interwoven with aquamarines and crystals that created music in the evening breezes and flashed rainbows around the garden with every morning sun.

"Ask them to move it against the wall. I will reset it when I am finished."

Almost as an afterthought, he added, "And have a layer of hay placed at the bottom for a good foundation."

"Yes, young master," Ezri said, starting to move past him.

When Timaeus didn't move aside, Ezri looked up at him expectantly.

"Anything else, young master?"

Then Ezri remembered. Taking a small paper-wrapped package from his vest, he handed it to Timaeus.

"Your father said to give this to you."

Timaeus's face did not change as he regarded the ivory scarf wrapped in the thin paper. Only the quickness of his hands gave away how much he wanted to touch it. Returning the wrapping to Ezri, Timaeus re-folded the scarf and draped it under his tunic.

"Thank you, Ezri. Before I leave, I want to thank you for everything you've done—for my mother, for my father, and for me. Sometimes, I think you saved us all. You are one of the best people I have ever known."

Ezri did not cry when Destani died or during those terrible years afterward when Venzel barely tolerated his presence, and he thought he had lost him as well, but seeing only his eyes reflected in the dark lenses of Timaeus's glasses, Ezri recognized for the first time the set of the young man's head and shoulders, the confidence of his manner, and the underlying authority in his voice. Sensing a subtle shift of power from father to son, he felt suddenly bereft, as though everything beautiful in his life was over. Not trusting his voice, he nodded, bowed, and walked away.

Overwhelmed by the changes he could not prevent, Ezri ducked into the first empty room and broke down, crying into his sleeve.

Timaeus walked swiftly through the underground corridors and up the stairs. There were several things he needed to do that morning without attracting anyone's attention. Knowing Venzel would be exercising and training horses most of the day, and the workers would either be in the stables or digging in the garden, he had at least an hour without any human interruptions. Staying deep in the shade, he walked around the porch.

"Timaeus?"

Turning, he saw Venzel.

"Good morning," he said.

"I'm glad I found you. Lorand just told me that the collective has approved our request to leave the compound. I'm taking the jeep to the village this afternoon to finalize the negotiations, but don't say anything to Senkali—I want to surprise her."

"She'll like that. I'm happy everything is settled. I don't know how we will get along without you."

"Lyostians lived in this colony for centuries before they brought my mother and me here, and, my son, I am sure they will be here for centuries after we've gone."

Venzel's last words hung in the air, and, for the first time, there was an awkward silence between them. Timaeus could sense something was bothering Venzel and wondered what else Lorand had told him.

Suspecting he was being monitored, Timaeus signed, *What is wrong?*

Lorand said you were called to the Sidereal Chamber.

Yes.

Are you all right?

What do you mean?

I didn't tell you everything Zsiga said about the Sidereal Chamber because I didn't think you would have to go in there. I've been worried.

It was intimidating at first, but not bad. I've been asked to… travel for the collective.

Venzel's face relaxed, and he smiled.

"Well, that's fine, just fine. Perhaps you will travel back here sooner than we expected."

Timaeus fought to keep his face neutral.

"Perhaps." Looking toward the stables, he asked, "How long will you be at the village?"

"Most of the afternoon. I'll leave right after lunch and try to be back at sunset. I was hoping there would be time for a ride this evening."

"Yes, there will be time for that."

With this new information, Timaeus scanned the location of the brothers who resided in the colony and, managing to evade them, went back into the tunnels to set the explosives. There would be no mercy. Once the order to evacuate was given, Lyostians who were slow to obey would be crushed when the explosives collapsed the tunnels. Any Lyostian refusing to leave would die in excruciating pain as Timaeus telepathically destroyed his cerebral cortex. All humans would be personally exterminated.

The governing hierarchy was explicit that the destruction of his home colony was just the beginning but had not given him any indication of when, or if, his assignment would end. The elders made no mention of his medical education or training, and Timaeus believed his dreams of researching the next genetic leap in Lyostian evolution in the laboratories and hospitals of the world would never be anything more than dreams.

The day ticked slowly by as Timaeus set the incendiary devices, accelerants, and detonators in place. He tried to concentrate on the math and physics of the assignment and not on the result, but every wire, timer, and fuse he connected brought him closer to the moment when he must destroy the family who loved him.

He was saving that part of his assignment until sunset, when everything was set, and his mind was clear. There were questions about his mother that he wanted answered. Ezri and Senkali had spent time with her, talked with her, and heard her laughter. Perhaps they would tell him something that Venzel forgot or didn't want him to know.

Focusing only on the logistics, relays, and timing kept his mind occupied, but they were not enough to make him forget, and when his hands trembled, he clenched his jaw and willed them to complete each of the tasks he had set down the night before. Such unrelenting discipline sustained him through the afternoon, but as the shadows lengthened in the garden, Timaeus became painfully aware that by killing the only people who remembered Destani, he was killing his mother all over again.

Just before sunset, the collective alerted the colony to evacuate.

Walking past brothers who were hurrying through the tunnels, Timaeus began the inescapable climb to the upper levels.

Timaeus hesitated outside the door. The whoosh-clank-whoosh-clank of the loom told him she was awake. He walked in without knocking.

"Senkali?"

"Oh, Timaeus, it's you. Your father told me you were home." Senkali's voice was as kind and loving as it had always been.

"Yes."

"Are you a doctor now?"

"I have a piece of paper that says I am."

"Is something wrong?"

"Only that I have to go away soon. Not the long visit I'd hoped for."

"Well, don't worry about us. We'll always be here to welcome you whenever you come home."

Timaeus moved in front of her so he could watch her face. "Senkali, I want to thank you for being such a good mother to us all. We love you very much. Do you know that?"

"Yes. Zsiga used to tell me how you all felt. It was wonderful… quite a wonderful life actually, but sadder these last few years. Not so many boys to care for, and, well, of course Zsiga has been gone almost ten years now."

"Yes," he said, "I miss him, too."

"Your father has been kind since then, but he has his own memories. Not at all like the man who terrified us nearly twenty years ago. You've worked a great change in him, Timaeus; you've been a blessing to him. Zsiga always said Venzel was the best of his brothers, but then, he may have been biased. I know he loved your father."

"Yes… Senkali?"

"Yes, dear."

"Would you tell me about my mother? The way she looked, the sound of her voice, did she laugh much?"

"I always knew one day you would ask me about her, and I've carefully kept Destani alive in my memory so that I would be able to tell you. But it's hard to think of her without recalling how much your father loved… loves her. I can still hear it in his voice. I didn't see them together often, but I remember seeing him kiss her once. I'm sure they didn't know I was there. Your father was so careful with her. He would never have allowed anyone to see her like that, not even another woman. I was jealous at the time because that was before Zsiga loved me, and no one had ever kissed me that way."

"Yes."

"She was shorter than I am, dainty, and so light that he lifted her from the floor and just crushed her to him."

"And she...."

"Wrapped one arm around his neck, her other hand lightly touched his face."

Putting her hand to her cheek, Senkali's voice became faint and far away.

"It was sundown, and they were standing behind an open door, but as the light edged around the door, they seemed to blend into the shadow. I could not tell them apart. It was like they were one person."

"And her hair was dark...." he said, leading her on.

"Yes, but not all of it. Black and copper it was, and she had long black lashes that set off her magnificent turquoise eyes. Zsiga told me how lucky you were to be blessed with her eyes."

Reminiscing, she laughed softly. "No one realized how beautiful she was until the wedding, and most of us felt like crows standing next to her. We were worried about our husbands, but she never cared for anyone but Venzel. Until you, that is."

"Until me?"

"Of course! As soon as she knew she was pregnant, you were all she would talk about. That you would look like your father, be handsome and brilliant, you know, the wonderful things you expect your son to be when you're imagining him. Oh, Timaeus, she loved you so much."

"For a little while, perhaps," Timaeus said, slowly pulling the pistol from the holster beneath his cloak.

Senkali went on as if she didn't hear him or didn't want to lose her place. "And then, when everything went dark for me, I came to live in the nursery. I never saw her or heard her voice after that. I knew she was ill, and then, one night, Zsiga came to our rooms and told me she had died. That was a sad, horrible day."

"Yes. Almost as sad and horrible as the day I was born."

"Perhaps, but despite the sorrow that followed, she would not have had it any other way. She would have rather died than you."

"It was already too late for her to make that choice."

Timaeus added the silencer as he walked behind her.

"We don't always get what we want. Sometimes, we have to find whatever happiness there is and take it, and never look back or regret what could — or should — have been."

"I will try to remember that. Did you find happiness here, Senkali?"

"Oh, yes. I found Zsiga here and more happiness than I thought possible."

Timaeus bent over and kissed her cheek. "Thank you, Senkali, for everything."

Knowing she would say words he could not bear to hear, Timaeus raised his pistol and fired the first bullet through Senkali's temple. The second bullet lodged in the base of her brain, and her head fell forward, nodding a little over her work, as though she were napping.

Without looking back, Timaeus slipped the gun into the holster and softly closed the door.

Ezri walked down the steps and turned into the corridor carrying a small tray. He was not surprised to see Timaeus coming out of Senkali's room and waited at the foot of the stairway. Timaeus took the tray and set it on the steps.

"She's resting, Ezri. Perhaps we should give her a few minutes."

Normally, Ezri would have left the tray in her room, but there was something in Timaeus's voice that made him do as he was asked. Bowing slightly, he backed against the wall so Timaeus could walk past him, but like earlier that day, Timaeus didn't move.

"Is the ground prepared?"

"It is as you requested, young master."

"Thank you. Ezri, you have known my father a long time?"

"Yes, nearly twenty-five years."

"Do you know why, when he could have been anyone, anywhere, he chose to stay here?"

"Yes. He told me once that when their mother died, he promised Zsiga he would never leave him, and, of course, he would not leave your mother… or you. He would not let them send you away. Instead, he had the other boys brought here. He would never have left you."

"Because of my mother."

"Perhaps in the beginning, but in her illness, she left him long before she died. Yet, he wouldn't give up. I can still see him standing on the balcony for hours that became days, and then months, just watching her sleep, waiting for the moment when she woke up and knew him again." Ezri sighed as he remembered the hope that never left Venzel's eyes.

"Ezri, did she love him?"

Recalling those few short months, Ezri's face reflected the thousand different ways Destani loved Venzel: the way she looked at him, her laughter, the sighs he pretended not to hear, her care and concern, and the way she accepted all that Venzel was and never wanted anything more.

"I regret my words are too poor to express how much your mother loved Venzel. I can only say that her love for him was a light inside her, a light that shone on all of us."

"Until I killed it."

"No, young master, no. You mustn't think that. She had never been so happy, making plans, imagining your future, trying different names, always telling me how smart, how wonderful you would be. Even before you were born, you were the darling of her life."

"The darling of her life."

"Yes."

"Thank you, Ezri," Timaeus said. "You can take the tray in now. I'm going to wait in the stables until Venzel returns."

"As you wish, young master."

As Ezri turned toward the tray, Timaeus reached into his cloak and fired two bullets into the back of Ezri's head. Moving in slow motion, Ezri took one step, stumbled, and then fell onto the carpet. Timaeus removed the napkin from the tray and gently placed it over Ezri's face.

The first phase of his plan complete, Timaeus checked his watch.

The colony's thirty minutes were up.

Making his way downstairs, he mentally located and killed every Lyostian remaining in the tunnels. Their screams echoed throughout the dark corridors and empty rooms.

Timaeus hadn't realized what he was born to be until that day, nor had he fully understood the violence of which he was capable or that he could do it so well. Despite the emotional price, he'd designed the demolition sequence, set the charges and gasoline bombs, and timed the fuses with less effort than a school assignment. Moving from one to the other, he'd killed the humans who loved his mother with minimal hesitation; then, because they rebelled, he imploded the brains of the brothers who defied the collective's directive or attempted to stop him.

As though anything could stop him.

After priming the detonators, Timaeus, the darling of Destani's life, walked through the main house to wait for his father. He had promised to meet Venzel for an evening ride and wanted to get him away from the compound before the charges ignited.

And, like Venzel, Timaeus kept his promises.

Lorand.

Forgive my impatience, but why have I been kept waiting in the Sidereal Chamber for half a day?

We have questions.

I am happy to answer them.

Events are happening in the human world that have caused us to reevaluate our colonies in your region. As you may know, neighboring state governments have mobilized five hundred thousand soldiers affecting our territories. We know you are well hidden, but this human rebellion has re-focused our attention on outpost colonies in your area.

We are hardly an outpost. We have revenue that we use to help our brothers in neighboring colonies and—

Yes. Some of our questions concern the source of such revenue and its distribution. We will discuss the distribution first. Tell us, Lorand, who authorized you to reallocate the assets located in your colony? Were you asked to do so?

Um, no. I just thought—

Yes. YOU just thought. We did not request it, and you did not ask for permission. There are always reasons for generosity toward our colonies—and our lack of it. YOU just thought you would usurp the authority of the governing hierarchy of the collective.

That isn't what I meant.

Do not prevaricate with us, Lorand. It is what you said and what you did. We have not misunderstood your actions… have we?

No. Forgive me, please.

Our next question concerns the human who is the sole source of the revenue your outpost has enjoyed for three decades. What would be your colony's position without him?

We would have less, but—

You read Nesim's report in the archives, did you not?

Yes, but I thought—

YOU thought it best to ignore his recommendations.

Killing the human did not seem viable at the time. We need him alive.

You were wrong, Lorand. A Lyostian colony dependent upon humans for survival ceases to exist as a Lyostian colony.

Timaeus needs him alive.

You were wrong, Lorand. Timaeus does not need Venzel. Timaeus needed to be reminded of who he is and why he was created. And YOU, Lorand, need to be reminded who WE are.

Please, forgive me.

Listen, Lorand, to what your independence and lack of judgment have brought to your colony.

Suspended in the Sidereal Chamber, Lorand recognized the screams of his brothers, many of them calling his name.

Please, forgive me, he repeated.

No.

His brothers' pain filled his mind. Wrapping his hands around his head, Lorand fell to the floor, and his screams joined theirs as the walls in the fifth room, on the fifth corridor, of the fifth level returned to sandstone for the last time.

Silica dust blurred the rays of the setting sun as the blue Mercedes raced toward the compound. A smile of bittersweet satisfaction played upon Venzel's lips as he pressed the car homeward.

Venzel shook his head. It wasn't his home anymore, and he tried to push back the memories of playing with Zsiga in the tunnels, seeing love rise up in Destani's eyes with the morning sunshine, and watching with pride as Timaeus put Alatan through his paces. Giving in to a moment's sigh of regret, he comforted himself with the knowledge that he was keeping his last promise to Zsiga.

Expecting to meet Timaeus in the stables, he was surprised to see him standing by the gate with only Alatan's reins in his hands.

Venzel stopped the car and rolled down the window.

Timaeus bent toward him, the hood of his cloak falling forward and shadowing his face.

"How did it go?" he asked.

"Better than I hoped, but longer than I expected. Let's go tell Senkali the news."

"Ezri just went down with her tray. Maybe we should give her a little while. Why not tell me? I'll even drive."

"You hate driving."

"Then we won't go far, will we?" he said, tying Alatan to the gate.

Venzel smiled and moved into the passenger seat. Timaeus got in, rolled up the window, and adjusted the air conditioning.

Turning in his seat toward Timaeus, Venzel told him of his progress that afternoon, outlined his plans for moving the horses, and described the house he'd purchased. So caught up in his enthusiasm, he did not notice that although Timaeus nodded and asked a few questions, he seemed to be driving randomly and changed direction several times.

Timaeus stopped the car.

"Where are we?" Venzel asked, looking around.

Seeing the ravine on his right, he turned to Timaeus.

"Why, Son?"

"I, I have to leave sooner than I expected, and I wanted to say goodbye."

"She is not here."

"She was."

Timaeus got out of the car and opened the door for his father.

Lost in their own thoughts and memories, they walked silently to the edge of the ravine.

"You are uncommonly quiet this evening, Son."

"Yes, Father."

"Are you anxious about being sent far away? I know it will be different, but don't be afraid. Every city is unique in its own way, with beautiful architecture, art museums, and so many different schools of design. I think you will like what you see."

"Yes, but regardless of what is above them, the tunnels are all the same."

Venzel could not understand his son's reluctance. "But you won't have to stay in the tunnels, Timaeus. Lorand was just telling me they are developing new contact lenses to protect your eyes. With that technology, you can go anywhere. Research laboratories, hospitals… your generation has limitless resources for more education. There will be many opportunities for you to see how far your mind can take you."

"My mind… yes, I hope so."

Venzel sensed there was something Timaeus was keeping from him and smiled gently.

"You are going to have to tell me what is bothering you, my son. I am not Zsiga, I cannot read your thoughts."

"Can't you?" Timaeus pulled the hood back and looked at his father.

Venzel could not mistake the sadness and farewell written on the face he loved, and he knew the day he dreaded had finally arrived. The Lyostians had claimed his son.

"This is more than just goodbye, isn't it? Is that why we're here?"

Timaeus clenched his jaw and turned toward the ravine.

The silence of this single gesture was more than Venzel could bear. He took Timaeus by the arm and pulled him around.

"You're not 'traveling' for the collective, are you? What have they asked you to do that is causing you so much pain?"

Timaeus's tortured eyes looked into his.

"I have been assigned to infiltrate certain colonies, identify and kill insubordinate leaders, and destroy them."

"Destroy?"

Pivoting, Venzel saw fire and smoke reaching toward the sky. Dragging his eyes from the flames, he turned to see a pistol in Timaeus's hand. Zsiga's warning rang in his ears.

"They sent you to kill me?"

"Not just you."

"Who, then?"

"Everyone who couldn't or wouldn't leave."

"Everyone? Even Senkali?"

"Yes," Timaeus said quietly.

Venzel was barely able to whisper, "Ezri?"

Timaeus nodded.

Venzel set his jaw and looked deep into his son's face.

"Did our brothers get out?"

Timaeus did not flinch when he said, "Most of them."

Realizing with horror what the collective had made of his son, Venzel's heart shattered for the last time. Defeated, he thought briefly of all the chances he'd had to kill this inhuman creature with Destani's eyes but held back, not only because of his promise but because Timaeus was all that remained of their love.

Feeling the full impact of the betrayal of the family he'd accepted, loved, and sacrificed his life for, Venzel's eyes did not leave Timaeus's face as the pistol was leveled at his heart.

Motionless, they stared at each other over the barrel of the gun. With fearless resignation, Venzel searched for regret in the features of the young man standing before him but found only a mask of indifference.

Timaeus smiled briefly, and, for a moment, the mask fell. The pistol flicked slightly toward the Mercedes as his right hand moved away from his body.

Leave, he signed.

Venzel knew disobeying the collective was a death sentence.

Not without you, he answered.

The hand holding the gun lowered slightly.

Please.

Venzel made a brief horizontal gesture with the index finger of his left hand.

No.

Timaeus raised the pistol.

The earth trembled without warning and heaved violently as the explosives blew through the underground tunnels in every direction.

Timaeus lost his balance.

Seeing his chance, Venzel grabbed the gun.

"I will not let them do this to you!" he said, pushing Timaeus to the sand. With all the love in the world on his face, he looked down and said, "We—"

"—are one," answered Timaeus.

Holding the gun to his temple, Venzel said, "Remember Alazar, my son."

Timaeus, unable to breathe or stop him, whispered, "Yes, Father."

Looking into the eyes he treasured for the last time, Venzel smiled and pulled the trigger.

Timaeus watched his father's body fall to the ground in front of him. Placing one hand on Venzel's heart and the other on his own, he thanked his mother for her wisdom.

He gently loosened Venzel's fingers from the pistol and carried his body to the car. Singing Anya's song of lament, he returned to the edge of the ravine with a handful of the blood-soaked sand and let it fall from his fingers onto the rocks where Destani died.

Shielding his eyes from the brilliance of the flames, Timaeus drove past the gate and into the garden. His shadow moved over the open pit as he turned his father face down on the straw. Timaeus arranged Venzel's arms above his head and tucked the red envelope into his hand.

They loved him first.

His father's decision haunted him as he refilled his mother's grave. Lifting the shovel over and over, the sound of Venzel's heartache echoed in his mind, "You see, I thought I was going to keep her with me forever."

Unable to prevent his father's death, Timaeus gave Venzel the forever the Lyostians denied him—an eternity of protecting his beloved Destani and keeping her safe.

The fire crawled slowly across the front lawn toward the garden. Lifting the trellis from the wall, Timaeus positioned it over the grave and lit the soft wood. It caught quickly, and Timaeus looked at it with longing. To fight his overwhelming desire to be incinerated as well, he turned quickly toward the back of the house.

Circling the stables, he lit the strategically placed petroleum-soaked bales of hay. He entered the building, unlatched the stall doors, and whistled softly. At his command, the horses stood side by side in the practice ring, and he smiled at their perfect conformation. Smoke began to filter through the open doors, and the horses snorted and stamped, but not one of them moved forward. Timaeus acknowledged their obedience with a slight bow and, in the space of a single breath, pulled the gun from under his cloak and shot each one between the eyes.

It wasn't madness, he assured himself, closing the stable doors behind him, but a mercy. It wouldn't have been fair to make them live without Venzel.

Returning to the center of the firestorm that had once been his home, Timaeus brushed the hood from his head. Although his eyes were closed, he was nearly blinded by the light of the flames surrounding him. Stretching one hand toward the stables and the other toward the garden, he united the scorching anguish of loss and loneliness in his heart with the torment raging in his mind. As permanent as the scars on his hands, he considered the exchange of a loving heart for this relentless pulsation of pain as his second gift from the collective.

Loosening the reins from the gatepost, Timaeus turned Alatan toward the oasis. Eyes wide with terror at the encroaching fire, Alatan needed no encouragement to flee the inferno engulfing the compound. Once they were out of sight of the fire and smoke, Timaeus stripped the singed and blackened cloak from his shoulders and let the wind wash away the tragic reality of the day. Focusing on the sensation of successfully completing his first assignment, he no longer wondered why the collective let him live.

He did not stop until he reached the oasis. While Alatan had all he wanted to drink, Timaeus bathed and pulled clean clothes from the saddlebag. Signaling Alatan to kneel on the sand, Timaeus sat beside him on the saddle blanket, closed his eyes, and tried to pray.

There were no words.

It was near dawn when Timaeus heard the blades of a helicopter cutting through the air. As it grew nearer, a rope with a noose knotted at the end was lowered until it was within reach. Alatan stood in fear and confusion, but Timaeus held onto his mane with one hand and caught the rope with the other. Sliding his foot halfway into the noose, he was slowly hoisted into the helicopter. Letting go of Alatan, Timaeus looked deep into the horse's dark amber eyes. Seeing only love and trust shining there, he lifted his hand. In joyful obedience, Alatan reared splendidly on his back legs, his front hooves pawing the air and his magnificent head tossing regally against the sky.

Thank you, Alatan... Venzel, Senkali, Ezri... for loving me.

Timaeus raised his pistol and shot Alatan through the heart. He looked quickly toward the open hatch, but not before seeing his betrayal reflected in Alatan's eyes.

Lifted high over the lagoon, Timaeus resisted the urge to step out of the loop and instead pulled his mother's scarf from under his tunic. Breathing in her perfume once more, he dropped the fragrant silk into the shuddering darkness. The son of Destani and Venzel—accomplished equestrian, gifted architect, and aspiring doctor—was dead.

Rising above the flames devouring his past, the collective's most powerful fire slayer turned his face away from the oasis with its memories of love and joy and sought the horizon without hope.

Timaeus Tuzurias, Fire Slayer

A Caravan of Blood

Trying not to think about the trail of implosions, fire, and death behind him, Timaeus dragged the shovel through the sand. It was a nuisance, but he had learned not to expect too much from the colonies he was assigned to destroy or the condition of the seemingly endless tunnels where there was never enough water to drink or bathe.

Believing the deplorable condition of the first few colonies to be exceptions, he soon realized how mired in humanity he had been, and, in the tunnels and catacombs of the underworld, he became something else. His unwashed hair hung in carelessly braided clumps; burns and bruises covered his hands, arms, and shoulders, and his perfectly straight fingers were calloused with broken yellowed nails that curved over their tips like talons. Unable to identify much of what there was to eat, he tried living on the honey that was the same in all the colonies, darkening his eyes and skin. Some nights, he dreamed of clean water and delicious food and made himself eat the dregs of whatever unrecognizable refuse was offered the next day in retaliation and self-punishment. Suppressing all feelings except those needed to complete his assignment, Timaeus endured the smells and endless filth only by vowing that if he survived, he would never live like this again.

Able to conceal his real purpose from telepathic scans, he entered every colony ostensibly just as another visiting brother, but his actual role was to investigate its inner workings and determine each leader's culpability as well as the extent of the colony's disobedience to the collective. Sometimes, all that was necessary were a few reassignments before he imploded the tunnels, but increasingly, his mission became a caravan of blood as evidence of deliberate insubordination within the colonies was weeded out at the cost of one brother's life after another. It wasn't a matter of banishment; it was murder, and those found guilty of dissension burned with the colony.

As he destroyed the outposts one by one, suspicions in the remaining colonies grew with each horrific report from fleeing brothers. After Timaeus walked into a situation in which he had to fight his way out, the collective began casually moving brothers throughout the other outposts in the sector. Timaeus saw the result of this tactic as well. Accepted by one colony, he watched as the leaders turned on a new arrival two days later. Timaeus talked them into releasing the captive but found him the next day, killed during the night as he slept.

Timaeus knew it should have been him as he gently closed his brother's eyes. Listening carefully, he discovered the men who conspired to kill this innocent brother and made sure they were not included in the call to evacuate. They all died screaming.

Vigilante justice aside, he did not kill any brother who obeyed the collective's evacuation instructions, but many resisted. For nearly a year, he desensitized himself to the collateral damage of his assignment and ended his rebellious brothers' screams and pleas for mercy with quick deaths.

Unless *they* attacked *him*—those were the brothers he tortured slowly and cruelly.

Occasionally, he allowed them to cry out for help, smiling slightly as they sobbed hopelessly when no one responded. Worse than their fear of being abandoned and alone, they were alone with him, and Timaeus learned to take his pleasure where he could find it, and, like Venzel, he also learned to take his time.

The fire that began in the garden was fed fifty times over destroying nearly every human feeling Timaeus possessed except hatred. He hated the humans he had once loved because that love not only resulted in their deaths but also initiated this relentless punishment of blood, loneliness, and self-loathing. He wasn't worthy of being a Lyostian; he wasn't even worthy of being a human. His metamorphosis complete, in every broken mirror that hung on a dirt wall, Timaeus saw a monster.

The governing hierarchy, watching Timaeus gradually devolve into the fearless killing machine he was genetically engineered to be, saw perfection.

Concluding his assignment with his body, mind, and loyalty intact, they now regarded him as the most valuable weapon they possessed. That he was also the most feared and hated Lyostian on the planet just made him easier to control.

His initial role in their plans to reclaim the surface was done.

It was time to bring him home.

Standing upwind of the fires consuming the northernmost colony in the last SCM sector, Timaeus patted his filthy cloak, searching for his mother's dagger. Measuring his strength by the days, weeks, and months, he did not use it on himself, he thought, *Tonight or tomorrow*?

For the fifty-first time, he looked longingly at the shining blade and decided, *Tomorrow.*

At the *whip-whip-whip* of the helicopter, Timaeus put his hand up to catch the rope. This time, when he stepped into the cabin, he saw clean clothes and a variety of fresh food. He barely glanced at the pilot or asked where they were going. He didn't care anymore.

Unexpectedly, the pilot looked back at him and said courteously, "We will arrive in Cairo in about forty-five minutes."

Suspicious and cautious, Timaeus nodded. After removing his weapons, he tossed his blood-splattered cloak and shovel into the flames. Sitting in the empty seat next to the pilot, he raised a tall glass of chilled juice to his cracked and bleeding lips.

Cairo

The echo of his escort's footsteps fading, Timaeus regarded the door in the easternmost tunnel of Cairo's central colony with skepticism. Tilting his head, he scanned the area and listened. Unable to detect anyone on the other side, he opened the door and stared.

It was a room—a real room with solid walls, furniture, and a private bathing area. Fresh food, honey, and juice were waiting for him. Wanting nothing so much as to be clean, he ignored the food and scrubbed himself from head to toe again and again. Finding new clothes in the closet, he pulled them on and only then sat down.

It was the most food he had seen at one time since leaving the compound and was exactly what he would have requested. Despite being ravenous, he ate slowly because, he thought, if this meal was to be his last, he wanted to savor it. When he had finished, he leaned back into the chair. Pressing the empty glass against his forehead, he wondered who they were going to send to kill him.

Fully expecting banishment and death as soon as he completed his assignment, Timaeus's only decision was how much resistance he intended to make or if he wanted to save them the trouble. With his mind clear, and his gun and dagger at his fingertips, he could take quite a few with him, but perhaps that was what the collective anticipated. Moving the chair to the farthest wall from the door, he pulled a third weapon from his pocket.

It was Venzel's flashlight. It wouldn't kill anyone, but it was very effective in temporarily blinding an attacker and slowing him down long enough to be killed.

He did not have to wait long.

In the silence of the room, the knock on the door sounded like a hammer. Scanning the hall, Timaeus detected only one answering echo.

Come in.

In spite of his suspicions, Timaeus smiled when he saw Taran and eased the flashlight back into his pocket.

Nearly four years had passed since the collective had called Taran from the compound. Looking into his face, Timaeus remembered with a moment's regret that Taran had his mother, Senkali's, eyes.

"Taran."

"Timaeus."

"How are you?"

Taran smiled. "I'm fine—you look like hell."

"Yes."

"May I sit down?"

"Of course. Is this your colony?"

"For the moment, the collective won't leave us both here."

"Is this my new assignment?"

Taran's eyes widened, and Timaeus saw a flash of fear in them.

"I hope not."

"As do I, Taran."

To break what was becoming a nearly unbearable silence, Timaeus said sincerely, "I want to thank you for such a nice accommodation."

Taran glanced around the plain sandstone room. It was barely adequate for a Lyostian of the Tuzurias hierarchy. It was, however, the best room available at this end of the tunnel system. The Cairo colony was the largest in the EMR and always teeming with brothers on their way to their next assignment. He would have preferred to put Timaeus in a more populated section, but there were too many stories circulating about him to ensure his safety.

"You're welcome. Do you need anything?"

"Yes. A reason. Why am I here?"

"The collective requested a meeting with you in two days. Until then, you are here. We can bring you food, books, whatever would make you comfortable."

Timaeus's eyes narrowed as he leaned forward. "*Bring* me food, books... Taran, am I your prisoner?"

Taran, who was as powerful as Timaeus, felt his heart racing.

"No, of course not. But the helicopter pilot told someone who you are... who you *really* are, and, well, almost everyone knows by now." Taran looked around the room. "That's why you—"

"—have a room in a secured tunnel?"

"Yes," he admitted.

Timaeus leaned back into the chair. "How long have you been here?"

"I was assigned to assist in the management of this colony about ten months ago."

"Like Zsiga?"

"If Zsiga was Tuzurias, yes."

The two brothers looked at each other in awkward silence. It was not the reunion Taran had anticipated and, tilting his head, scanned the colony searching for any reason to leave. Hearing his name, he stood up.

"There is a matter that needs my attention. Can I stop by later?"

"Yes."

"Can I send you anything?"

"Yes, please... a pencil, some drawing paper, and a mag of 9mm cartridges."

Taran's smile froze. "Timaeus...."

"Yes?"

Taran looked down into his brother's face. With the wary expression of a caged animal in his eyes, Timaeus regarded him as he would a stranger.

It was only then that Taran fully realized that the brother he loved was gone, and if only half of the stories he'd been privy to in his capacity as the colony's disciplinarian were true, a skilled and ruthless executioner had taken his place. Mentally reviewing the list of items Timaeus requested, he paused when he recalled the cartridges—nine-millimeter—and wondered if they were for the gun that killed his mother.

Timaeus tilted his head and answered the unspoken question. *Yes… we are one.*

Taran thought of his beautiful, loving mother and knew he had to leave the room before *he* died. He was certain that Timaeus would kill him without mercy or regret if he sought revenge. Moreover, Timaeus was right; what was done by the will of the collective was done by all.

"We are one. I will send you the items you requested, Timaeus."

"Thank you, Taran."

Moments later, everything Timaeus asked for was delivered with a message that Taran would be busy with colony matters all evening and wouldn't be able to see him until the next day. After wedging the chair beneath the door handle, Timaeus set the ammunition on the table. He didn't need it. He just wanted to put Taran on his guard, and he wanted an evening in this clean, quiet room to himself.

Seeking the images in his mind, Timaeus rolled the pencil between his fingers and inhaled the scent of the paper. Out of practice, his hand moved slowly over the white surface. He no longer drew pictures of horses, fantastical glass houses, or desert landscapes. Instead, he sketched his brothers as he remembered them, contorted and sprawled in terrified anguish. Their hands cupped over their ears or pressed against their eyes; their mouths open in soundless screams.

Food, towels, and honey-scented candles arrived the next morning with more paper and a box of colored pencils. Taran included a note saying he hoped Timaeus would have dinner with him that evening, as well as to ask the courier if he needed anything else.

Timaeus looked at the brother in front of him and noticed his hands trembled as he held the tray. They were about the same age, but eons apart. Timaeus smiled and rescued the tray.

"Please tell my brother," he said in his softest voice, "that I will be delighted to join him for dinner."

"I will… um, do you require anything else?"

"Yes. I would like a hooded cloak, please. Thank you."

Practically sprinting out of the room, the young man was already tilting his head before he closed the door.

Timaeus smiled grimly. It was a little too soon for anyone to be broadcasting to his brothers that he'd just survived an encounter with the *visitor*.

Within minutes, the courier returned and handed the cloak to Timaeus through the door.

Focusing his attention on the younger man's face, Timaeus tilted his head and smiled slyly. *Would you like to come in?*

I uh, need to get back, many things to do.

Yes, I know, but what could be more important than entertaining a… visitor?

The courier's eyes widened in panic with the realization that Timaeus not only heard what he'd transmitted earlier but also obviously understood that "visitor" was code for outsider. His eyes were everywhere, darting at Timaeus's hands, his face, and the door. The courier had no idea from which direction the attack would come, but he knew how it would end. He had insulted the deadliest Lyostian in the collective.

Yes, yes, you have.

I'm sorry.

I'm sorry, what?

I'm sorry, my brother. I beg you to forgive my rudeness.

Say, please.

Please forgive my rudeness.

Before the courier could react, his wrist was captured in Timaeus's steely grip. Turning the hand palm up, Timaeus pressed the soft flesh with his finger. Sighing, he shook his head and dropped the hand.

I will forgive you this time. Next time, you will entertain me. Do you fully understand what I am saying?

The courier became so pale that Timaeus thought he was going to faint and only managed to stay upright by grasping the doorjamb.

Yes, I do. Thank you, my brother, for your generosity and pardon.

Yes.

Closing the door, Timaeus was not surprised to find it suddenly very quiet in the hall.

Timaeus?

Come in, Taran.

Taran tried to look stern but failed. Laughing softly, he said, "It's not polite to terrorize the troops."

Timaeus's smile did not reach his eyes.

"I am not a 'visitor.'"

"No, you are not. But considering everything you discerned about him today, can you honestly say that you are Darkar's equal?"

"Yes, in that I would protect his life with my own or, even as I punished him, we would still be, dead or alive, brothers. We *are* one."

"*We are one*," echoed Taran strongly.

To understand why his beautiful mother had to die, Taran had spent every spare moment of the last twenty-four hours searching the archives and saw everyone else Timaeus had to kill that day. In gratitude that the collective had not commanded him to destroy everyone he loved, Taran stopped trying to understand and forgave his brother.

"Let's get out of here for a while. I heard you asked for a cloak, why don't you get it and let me show you around the colony."

When Timaeus turned to the closet, Taran tilted his head to let the colony know they would be in the corridors and dining room that evening.

"Giving them fair warning, Taran?"

"Yes… in one sense. Then again, you might also say I'm giving them an opportunity to meet you."

Timaeus laughed.

The sound was so joyless and harsh that it was painful to Taran's ears, and he could not even smile in return. *It was*, he thought to himself, *how a dead man would laugh.*

Looking for some distraction, he saw the sheets of drawing paper on the small table and picked them up. Timaeus's laughter creased abruptly.

Taran was stunned, but not by the drawings. The collective had put many such scenes evidencing Timaeus's executions into the archives for all the Tuzurias to access. It was not the horror of the sketches that surprised Taran but that these brothers—twisted and terrified unto death—all had Timaeus's face.

Taran looked up slowly. "How, when you felt that way, were you able to do this… again and again?"

"It was my assignment, Taran, and although their deaths were not my decision, it is still my pain. Perhaps one day, if I am allowed to live long enough, it will stop."

Although he had never killed anyone, Taran had also seen that anguish reflected on the faces of the brothers he'd punished. Nodding understandingly, he watched Timaeus slide the gun holster over his arm and pull on his cloak.

"Well, I'm ready. Do you think we can go outside? I have not seen Cairo for a long time."

"Hardly that, Timaeus. It has not been a year. In fact, I think some of the brothers you went to school with are here. Shall I call them to join us?

"And what, exactly, do you think we would talk about?"

"You could, um, tell them of your travels."

Timaeus stared at him.

"My travels?" he said, spitting out the word. "Moving from one filthy colony to another through hundreds of miles of tunnels, always alone?

Sleeping in narrow slots in stone walls while I listened to disobedience and insurrection, knowing that each voice meant another death, each colony another infestation of dissent that must be destroyed?"

Timaeus looked around the immaculate room.

"Did you ever wonder why our colony was usually full? It was because it was clean—the food, linen, water. Yet the outposts I saw were filthy, the food I've eaten—you wouldn't even call it food. You said yesterday that I looked like hell. Well, Taran, hell is where I have been. And you know, after a short adjustment period, it, ah… suited me."

"You can't mean that. Look at these pictures,"—Taran pointed to a face contorted in agony—"that pain cannot 'suit' you, Timaeus."

"No, not at first, but I developed certain skills over time. And, occasionally, even an executioner can find a measure of personal validation, even pride, if he kills quickly and cleanly enough."

Taran held up another picture.

"This was not quick or clean."

"Ah, well. I wasn't always in a hurry, and torture is a kind of art, and an artist should enjoy his work."

"Art!"

"Yes. I have refined two fundamental methods of torture. First, you either withhold something the target desperately wants, such as, in many cases, for the pain to stop, or, second, you give the target what he wants in such small doses that it is worse than not giving it to him at all. Either way, the result is the same. The art lies in correctly estimating how long to torture the target before he begs to die with exactly how long you have to kill him."

Timaeus looked at the drawing, and a smile Taran had never seen on anyone—Lyostian or human—crossed Timaeus's face, and he knew even Venzel would have feared his son in that moment. Setting the rest of the drawings aside, Taran decided he did not want to be in the room any longer and started backing away.

Yes, Taran, it is who I am now.

Taran stopped just short of the door. *What will you do?*

Go where I am sent and obey. I've grown accustomed, you know, to obedience.

Taran did not believe that for a minute.

Stepping into the hallway, Taran reached out his hand to guide Timaeus toward the closest stairwell.

Timaeus instinctively moved back into the center of the room.

"Do not touch me, Taran."

"All right, brother, I understand."

"Do you?"

Before Taran could respond, Timaeus pressed him against the wall with one hand as he expertly patted him down with the other. Taran did not resist; he had no weapons on him.

"Where is your pistol?" Timaeus demanded.

"What pistol?"

"You don't have a gun?"

"No. I mean, there are weapons in the armory, but I don't carry one." Taran looked into Timaeus's eyes and saw only confusion. "I discipline our brothers with my thoughts. Why would I need a gun?"

"That's right," Timaeus said, releasing him. "You only punish one, maybe two brothers at a time."

Taran nodded.

With resignation in his voice, Timaeus added, "A bullet is faster and a lot quieter."

At a loss for words, Taran knew he would never, Anya willing, understand all that Timaeus had suffered in the last year and made no further attempts to touch him.

They did not meet anyone in the corridors or the dining room, and later, when they went out into the moonless night, the chairs and tables in the shadows of the veranda were empty.

Timaeus awakened early. Rested and alert, he bathed, trimmed his hair, and combed it away from his face. He put on clean clothes and pulled the new cloak over his weapons. Depending on the collective's evaluation of his assignment, he was ready to leave, kill, or die.

Taran could not find anyone among the colony's leadership willing to escort Timaeus to the Sidereal Chamber. Timaeus was his first brother, and although any hope of a relationship mirroring the easy camaraderie they had enjoyed as boys disappeared when Timaeus pinned him to the wall, it did not erase the bond forged beneath the watchful and loving eyes of their fathers. He would not leave Timaeus to find the way alone. The path was deliberately complex and the possibility of an ambush too great.

Regardless of what Timaeus had become, it was Taran's duty to protect any colony member who might be foolish enough to attack him, as well as the brother he once loved. Hoping it would not come down to a choice, he knocked on the door.

Timaeus?

Come in, Taran.

Taran entered the room and momentarily fell out of time. Standing in the half-light of the candle was Venzel. He knew it wasn't Venzel. The face was too thin, and the eyes, although darker, were too green. These were, however, minor differences. Venzel's fearless confidence and control, his cunning intelligence, and, beneath all of those attributes, the undeniable power that fused them into a single force now existed in his son.

"What is it?"

"You… look like your father."

"I am a Lyostian drone. I have no father."

There was nothing more Taran could say. Turning around, he left the room as Timaeus silently followed him to the fifth room in the fifth corridor on the fifth level of the Cairo colony.

Within moments of sitting at the table, the walls disappeared, and the voice of the governing hierarchy resounded in his mind.

Timaeus.

Yes.

You have done well.

Your expectations were met?

Yes.

And I have earned your trust?

There was a slight pause. *You have.*

Timaeus was silent. He would not ask.

There are some additional colonies we would like you to visit.

His heart sank. Fire and death were to be his life, after all.

Primarily those connected to hospitals where we would like you to consider assisting with the development of the hybrid serum. We hope you have not lost your interest in genetics.

Timaeus gripped the table. *I haven't.*

Excellent. Would you consider combining these assignments? Acting as colony disciplinarian as needed while continuing to research the hybrid serum?

Here?

No. We would like you to survey selected European colonies as well as synchronize our research and development teams. You leave this evening for Rome.

Thank you.

We appreciate the difficulty of your first assignment, Timaeus. May Anya, blessed mother of us all, continue to keep you safe. We are one.

We are one.

The room reappeared. Timaeus slipped from the chair to the floor as shudders rocked his body. When they subsided, and he could breathe again, he pressed his fists to his eyes and sang Anya's song of thanksgiving.

On the tarmac of the helipad, Taran handed Timaeus his airplane ticket.

"Thank you, Taran, for allowing me to rest at your colony. I hope my presence didn't make it too uncomfortable for anyone."

Taran smiled. "Well, it has been uncommonly quiet these last few days."

"Yes. This is for you," Timaeus said, handing him a tightly rolled sheet of drawing paper. "Goodbye, Taran."

"Goodbye, Timaeus."

Stepping into the helicopter, Timaeus smiled in recognition at the pilot who had flown him to Cairo.

Taran's heart only began beating normally after the helicopter lifted into the air. He tilted his head and felt the entire colony breathe a simultaneous sigh of relief. Walking down the gateway to the tunnels, he unrolled the sheet of paper. His mother's eyes, bright and seeing, smiled at him from the drawing. Beneath the sketch, Timaeus wrote, "She was a blessing to us." Taran re-rolled the paper and slipped it into his sleeve.

When informed that the helicopter crashed and burned during its return flight to the colony, Taran asked only one question. Upon learning the answer, he removed the paper from his sleeve and looked at the lovingly rendered portrait. Although grateful for the drawing, he realized he no longer understood or loved Timaeus and silently prayed he would never see him again.

Timaeus said the same prayer as he wiped the helicopter's fuel line residue from the blade of his dagger.

Research

Timaeus looked up from the microscope into the expectant faces above the blood-soaked gowns of the surrounding physicians.

"Success," he said, setting the fourth specimen slide into freezing solution for transport.

The doctors smiled broadly and tilted their heads. Several interns entered the operating room. Timaeus pointed to the bodies on the operating tables.

"You can take them back to the catacombs," he said.

Without waiting to hear their unasked questions, he added, "Yes, of course, I do not care what you do with them. Some are still warm." Indicating the still shape under the bloodied sheet closest to him, he said, "However, I am not finished with her."

She had been the last to die.

Without thought or word, the senior medical intern nodded to his assistants as they wheeled the last of the gurneys from the operating room. Timaeus followed them and locked the door.

It had been a long day, but he knew how it was going to end and came prepared. Stripping off his bloodied clothes, Timaeus opened the drawer under the table and took out his cloak. From the hidden pocket of the sleeve, he removed a small candle, a trench lighter, a newly sharpened scalpel, and several vials of bitter honey.

The scent of the candle masked the stench of the surgeries performed that day, but the single flame did not lighten the darkness of the operating room. Easing the heavy blanket from her body, he pressed the back of his fingers against her skin. She was still warm, about 86 degrees, he thought, and he quickly covered her up again. Raking her long dark hair to the side, he knotted it so it would not get in his way. With the honey in one hand and the scalpel in the other, he climbed onto the operating table. In the reflection of his bioluminescence, her face was pale and distorted. She was one of his patients who woke up too soon. Her eyes, open and wide, stared at the ceiling, and her lips, still red and soft, encircled a mouth frozen in mid-scream. Carefully breaking the seal of the first vial of honey, he let a few drops fall into each eye.

He didn't hurry. They were the only parts of her body that tasted better cold.

Transitions

For the next several years, it seemed the nightmare of blood and fire was over. Knowing no one could be in as much pain as he, Timaeus had little pity for brothers who disobeyed the rules of the colony and honed a new art of discipline, one without the sweet mercy of death.

In his role as a trained geneticist, he spent his time in the laboratories of the Lyostian colonies bordering the Mediterranean, analyzing the enzymes that added specific allele codes and switches during the gene-splicing process. The re-conception of the first hybrid generation was scheduled in five years. In thirty years, they would begin their reclamation of the earth.

Timaeus occasionally regretted he would not live to see the rise of a new Lyostian society, but it would mean war, and he had seen enough death for ten lifetimes.

The collective, never letting Timaeus—or any of the Tuzurias—out of its hearing range, received reports of his success and began paying even closer attention. Initially consulting him on small matters, their dialogue quickly moved to policy issues. With the Lyostians' greatest challenge looming on their dark horizon, the governing hierarchy decided to test him once again.

When not planning their new agenda for the retribution against mankind, the governing hierarchy was scrutinizing the fire slayers for two reasons: their innate instability and nearly unlimited power. Now fully mature, they were too dangerous to leave alive and with 240 scattered across three continents, much too close in proximity to one another. A united rebellion would overthrow the entire Lyostian social structure and jeopardize their survival as a species. Knowing there was only one way to prevent the power struggle they believed to be inevitable, the governing hierarchy decided to destroy the Tuzurias and their genetic formula for all time.

Inside the Sidereal Chamber

Shortly after his twenty-fifth year, the collective requested Timaeus's presence for his third direct interview. Entering the Moroccan colony's Sidereal Chamber, he was sure his report regarding the genetic mapping of the hybrid serum was exactly what the governing hierarchy wanted to hear, but within moments, his confidence faded. Two brothers he did not recognize were already sitting at the table. When their images wavered, Timaeus realized these brothers were not actually in the room with him but located in chambers at other colonies.

Knowing they could see him, he nodded and sat down. They returned his greeting.

Tomi, Tividar, Timaeus.

At the sound of Timaeus's name, Tividar and Tomi looked at each other and grew pale.

Yes, they responded simultaneously.

We would like you to join hands for a moment.

Knowing they could not disobey the collective and believing they were dead either way, Tividar and Tomi reluctantly stretched their hands toward Timaeus. Regardless of being hundreds of miles apart, a physical connection was made, and they could feel each other's power.

Listen and pray with us.

Piercing the silence of the room, two hundred and thirty-seven voices cried out in a single sound of anguished terror. Although they did not know who died, the small circle of brothers recognized the sound with sorrow and began singing Anya's song of lament.

Drifting beneath their prayer was a question, a question they would not ask.

When the lament ended, the collective responded to their silent inquiry.

The fire slayers of the Tuzurias hierarchy, having completed their assignment to bring order throughout our colonies, have ceased to exist within the collective consciousness.

Timaeus's expression did not change as he acknowledged that Toros, Taran, and all his boyhood brothers were now excruciatingly dead. The three surviving fire slayers at the table looked at each other and wondered why they had not died as well.

Once again, the collective responded to their unspoken thoughts.

Because the Tuzurias are still necessary to our progress. Tividar, we are sending you to our Nuremberg colony for any disciplinary actions necessary in all European and Mediterranean colonies, and Tomi, you will go to Kabul to monitor our Asian colonies. Timaeus, you are requested to remain in the chamber as our brothers are dismissed to begin their new assignments. We are one.

We are one, they echoed.

Timaeus watched the last of the Tuzurias brotherhood dissolve into limitless space.

Timaeus.

Yes.

We would like to discuss with you our plans for North America.

The discussion lasted all night and into the next day. Trusting the collective's promises for a future different from his past, Timaeus left his cloak—and the horrific memories of the Tuzurias legacy—at the Casablanca airport forever.

Farewell

Timaeus leaned against the seatback and assessed the well-being of the other Lyostians carefully placed throughout the airplane. With their heads slightly tilted, they pretended to sleep as they kept each other calm. Temporarily disconnected from the collective and having just each other's thoughts to distract them, they all counted the minutes until the plane landed. Timaeus, with his sketchpad on the tray table and pencil in hand, was the only one who counted the minutes in the first-class cabin.

Knowing it was the last time he would be outside the range of the governing hierarchy, Timaeus closed the privacy curtain and looked into the night. The moon had not yet risen, and he had a promise to keep. Kneeling in the darkness, he crossed his hands over his heart and pressed his forehead against the glass.

Venzel, my father, I know it is impossible for you who endured so much to call me son, but because you understood—more fully than I did—the promise and horror of my life, I ask forgiveness for these crimes against you and my brothers:

I visited the libraries and art museums of Europe and gazed with admiration at the architectural styles of a dozen different human cultures, then abandoned whatever humanity I found there with the partially autopsied women left scattered in catacombs along the Mediterranean coast.

I spent glorious hours of research into the genetics of the hybrid generation that filled me with personal validation and reverence for our species while deliberately causing agonizing pain to countless guilty, and some innocent, Lyostian brothers for the sin of independent thought.

Although I looked the other way when hearing my name spoken in hushed tones of dread to avoid seeing my brothers' faces as they discussed whatever savagery they'd heard of me, I cruelly punished others for believing I am a myth, an empty threat, or a cautionary tale.

In whatever good I have found in these last years, I have felt you at my side, but knew it was not to be. Allowed neither friends nor family, I am surrounded by brothers who do not love me and whom I cannot love because tomorrow they may be targets. In the midst of every colony, I am an unwelcome brother, a dreaded acquaintance, a visitor.

Unfailing obedience has earned me the governing hierarchy's assurances for a future different from my past, and I have every hope that my work in creating this new generation will be my greatest contribution to the collective. I share this hope with you, Father, because you were with me once, and after all this time, I believe my words will find you again.

In atonement for these crimes and with a son's undying gratitude, I return Mother to you. Forgive me for keeping her so long locked in my heart. Fearing unending solitude, I could not bear to lose you both.

Knowing my lips would stain her perfect skin, I only ask that you kiss her cheek for me with love and farewell.

Released from the dark caverns of her son's heart, Destani did not look back as she soared with the freedom of flight. Only the faintest shadow over rippling water tracked her spirit as it flew eastward, seeking the desert wind.

Destinations and Dreams

The plane circled the sky above Boston. Timaeus took a deep breath to calm his mind and looked at the airport below. In the dark vortex punctuated by flashing lights, he saw his life as a spiraling labyrinth of fire, each step flaring with enough light to impel him forward to this moment: suspended between a past he wanted to forget and a future determined by his final assignment as the leader of the matrix design team.

Awarded the most coveted role within the collective, his work would conclude with the final testing and implementation of the hybrid serum. It would be the only real honor of his life—that of being present when the first hybrid Lyostians were born. Created with just enough human DNA to allow their ascent and survival above ground, he smiled at the thought that in less than four years he would hold the newest evolution of infant brothers in his arms. There was much to do, much to look forward to, and he was ready.

In a moment of rare optimism, he heard Venzel's voice: *If you ever find a woman who cares for you, loves you… my son, please, don't push it away.*

He stared at his reflection in the mirrored darkness of the glass. Although nothing could change who he was, his new appearance concealed much of his real identity, and he thought perhaps Venzel was right. It *might* be possible that somewhere in this vast and unknown land, a woman with a soft voice and gentle touch was waiting for him, and he decided, if she was patient, he would find her. With a sense of finality, he turned his face from the window, pulled down the shade, and opened the curtain.

The white paper on the tray table glowed in the dim light.

Contemplating the possibilities of such a relationship and inspired by his earlier thoughts, he turned to a fresh page. Refusing to believe he was being too optimistic, he began drawing preliminary architectural plans for a nursery.

A shadow fell across his sketchbook.

"We'll be landing in a few minutes, Dr. Gates."

Although English words still felt strange and stilted in his mouth, he smiled up at the young woman.

"Thank you. And please, call me Grant."

Caverns of the Heart

The setting sun casts a tall shadow over the sheltered corner of a walled garden. The charred apple trees are twisted and bare, but the grave he has guarded for seven years is unchanged. Staring downward, Venzel's lips move in soundless prayer as he imagines his beautiful wife below the grass.

Darkness falls around him. The desert wind careening through the compound is not silent. This night, it carries the gift of reminiscence and a voice as sweet as cool water.

"I am not there, my love."

Praying her presence is not an illusion, he turns and takes her into his arms. Her perfume fills his senses, and her body presses close against his. Burying his face in the thick cascade of her hair, he cries, "My beautiful karisi, it has been so long."

When he releases her, she looks up at him with all the love she has saved for this moment shining from her luminous eyes. She gestures toward their balcony rooms.

"Shall we go home?"

Glancing at the blackened house, he whispers, "No, karisi, there is nothing left for us."

She places Alazar's reins into his hands.

"Oh, my dearest husband, we are together. We have everything."

Sitting astride Alazar, Venzel lifts Destani in front of him and wraps her in his cloak. Fulfilling a promise, he presses his lips against her cheek in grateful remembrance.

"The oasis, my love?"

Resting her head on his shoulder, she reaches up and touches his face. "As you wish, Venzel."

Turning Alazar southward, they wave to Ezri on the porch. At night, if the desert wind is kind, her soft laughter drifts back to him, echoing throughout the compound like wind chimes.

Every morning he waits until dawn and, holding the lantern high, stands by the paddock gate watching for two dark riders on a single grey horse.

Acknowledgments

Few books are written in a vacuum, and this book is not one of them. I must begin by expressing my gratitude to Terri and Richard Cohen for a lifetime of love, friendship, and encouragement. To my first readers, Lindsey Hoefert, Ricki Huff, and Emilee Valken, thank you for your equal amounts of enthusiasm and criticism. To the wonderful teachers I met along my writing journey: Christopher Burnside, Marybeth Carlson, Mark Ensalaco, John Heitmann, Mary Sikora, and Bro. Thomas Wendorf, I humbly thank you all. It would have been a longer and harder road without your guidance. I also want to thank Dustin Boyed for keeping my laptop running beyond all human expectations.

A special word of appreciation to Cherie Macenka, Deborah Alix, Liz Hurst, and Siân Hyleg, the editors and designers at Liminal Books and Between the Lines Publishing who took a leap of faith, and Erica Orloff, editor extraordinaire, for her diligence and kind words.

For my friends, Kim Gilley and Valeri Sweeney, and unforgettable students, Julie, Alpha Echo, Megan, Julia, Maggie, Erin, Grace, Abby, Preston, and Mark–I cannot thank all of you enough for your limitless powers of patient listening, and Steve and Nate because inspiration never dies.

And, lastly, I want to thank my family for their support every step, every word, of the way, and who never ceased to expect anything less than the beauty and wonder of this moment.

Copy editor turned fiction writer, PJ Braley loves to write "what-if" stories, but it wasn't until she started writing about Grant Gates, an alien assassin, that she had a real story to tell. *The Fire Slayers* was published in 2020, followed by *Finding Persephone* in 2022 by Between the Lines Publishing. *Persephone's Children* is forthcoming in 2024.

When PJ isn't writing about aliens learning to navigate the labyrinth of human love while trying to save the planet, you will find her sitting under the umbrella on the sundeck with her rescue corgi, Nymeria.

Learn more about PJ and the legacy of *The Fire Slayers* at pjbraley.com or follow her on Facebook at PJBraleyAuthor, and @pjbraley on Twitter.